Brant turned ~~she~~ ~~slowly to~~ ~~Samille.~~ As he'd done when she first entered the conference room, he studied her with eyes that gave nothing away while he noted every detail about her. She had a face that managed to be both exotic and wholesome, heart-shaped with high, slanted cheekb~~ones~~ ~~and~~ an alluring sultriness to her dark, thick-lash~~ed~~ ~~eyes.~~ ~~Luxuri~~ous ebony hair stemming from a wid~~ow's peak~~ ~~was~~ swept back into a severe knot~~, a no-nonsense~~ hairstyle that drew attenti~~on to her lovely features~~—although Bran~~t doubted it was in~~tentional. She had a slim, ~~straight nose that~~ hinted at defiance, and an inci~~ting set of lips~~ that begged to be kissed.

She wor~~e a simple, b~~ut tasteful black suit, the slim-fitting skirt endin~~g just~~ below her knees. The red-blooded male in him had responded to the sight of long, sleek legs sheathed in sheer black nylon. She'd shaken his hand, sat quickly, and crossed her legs. His groin had tightened almost painfully when he glimpsed the delicious curve of a shapely thigh. He thought about her earlier remark and wanted to laugh. There was no mistaking that Samille Broussard was a "big girl"—100 percent woman. If she were any more woman, Brant didn't think he'd be able to refrain from stretching her out across the conference table and making frantic love to her.

She watched him now, hostility simmering beneath the surface of her composed demeanor. He'd offended her. All her life she'd probably been told that she could do anything she set her mind to. In her youth she'd probably petitioned the school board to integrate the football team. He could easily envision her as president of a traditionally male-dominated intramural club, something like math or the debate team. She never backed down from a challenge and would resent anyone who stood in her way.

A HEARTBEAT AWAY

MAUREEN SMITH

ARABESQUE

BET☆ BOOKS

BET Publications, LLC
http://www.bet.com
http://www.arabesquebooks.com

ARABESQUE BOOKS are published by

BET Publications, LLC
c/o BET BOOKS
One BET Plaza
1900 W Place NE
Washington, DC 20018-1211

All Kensington Titles, Imprints, and Distributed Lines are available at special quantity discounts for bulk purchases for sales promotions, premiums, fund-raising, and educational or institutional use. Special book excerpts or customized printings can also be created to fit specific needs. For details, write or phone the office of the Kensington special sales manager: Kensington Publishing Corp., 850 Third Avenue, New York, NY 10022, attn: Special Sales Department, Phone: 1-800-221-2647.

1-58314-532-X

First Printing: September 2005
10 9 8 7 6 5 4 3 2 1

Printed in the United States of America

For my parents,
Dr. Anthony and Cecilia Morah

ACKNOWLEDGMENTS

With love and eternal gratitude to my husband Lorrent; my supportive family and friends; Demetria Lucas, editor extraordinaire; and the many readers who keep coming back for more.

PROLOGUE

Washington, D.C.
Thursday, November 6

Something is seriously off about this creep.

Jefferson Spangler shoved sweaty hands into his jeans pockets and cast a nervous glance around. He stood at the northeast end of the National Mall in Washington, D.C. He and his companion were partially obscured by one of the many elm trees that lined the endless stretch of manicured lawn. In the distance, the dome of the capitol was silhouetted against the clear night sky, a proud symbol of freedom and democracy. Tomorrow morning, crisply dressed senators would march down those hallowed corridors and into stately chambers to debate politics and partisan legislation. His father would be one of them.

Reluctantly Jefferson turned back to his companion and found a pair of dark, fathomless eyes already fixed on him. The stranger's face was shadowed beneath a hooded black parka, giving him an almost ghoulish appearance. Like the Grim Reaper.

The fine hairs at the nape of Jefferson's neck rose. He

told himself that his reaction had more to do with the brisk November air than the fact that he was scared.

"Relax, kid." The voice was a low drawl laced with cold humor. "If I didn't know better, I would think you were a narc on his first undercover assignment."

"Of course not," Jefferson mumbled quickly. "I just want to get this over with before someone sees us. The police patrol this area pretty often, you know."

"Yes, I know." But the stranger made no move to hasten the transaction. Those dark, penetrating eyes continued to watch Jefferson as if he were a foreign microorganism beneath a microscope.

Jefferson shifted impatiently from one foot to another. "I usually buy from Ace. Where did you say he is?"

"I didn't." A hint of a smile lifted one corner of the stranger's mouth. But the smile seemed more sinister than amused. "Don't worry, Jefferson. You're in good hands with me. I've got something that will make you more popular with your classmates than anything you've ever had before."

A sliver of apprehension wound its way down Jefferson's spine. He swallowed hard. "I—I'm not looking for the hard stuff, man. I just want some weed, that's all. Ace always hooks me up with a good stash."

"What I have is far better than marijuana, Jefferson. That's child's play. Don't you want to graduate to the majors? Aren't you bored with being a small-time pusher?"

Jefferson hesitated, intrigued in spite of himself. "Whatcha got?"

The stranger withdrew a small package from his parka and passed it to Jefferson, who stuffed it hastily inside his backpack without even glancing at the contents. His hand was shaking like that of an addict in withdrawal.

"How much do I owe you?" he asked, throwing another anxious look around the darkened park. Other than a shrunken old man walking an Irish terrier on a short leash, there was no one in sight.

"No charge, my friend."

Jefferson stared at the stranger in surprise. "You're giving me this stuff for *free*?"

"First time's on the house."

Jefferson snorted in disbelief. "Why? In case I'm not a satisfied customer?"

"Oh, you'll be satisfied, Jefferson," the stranger said, eerily soft. "You and your friends will be *very* satisfied. I guarantee it."

Jefferson suppressed an instinctive shudder. "What did you say this stuff is?"

"I didn't." Once again Jefferson thought he detected that sinister smile, but it was too dark outside to be sure.

"Is it Ecstasy?"

"Even better. Take my word for it, Jefferson. Once you and your friends get a taste of this stuff, you'll be the talk of the town."

Jefferson liked the sound of that. He liked being known for something other than who his father was.

He hitched his backpack securely onto one shoulder and started backing away. He was as eager to get home as he was to get away from the creepy dealer. "How do I get in touch with you if I want more?"

"I'll be around," came the vague promise.

Jefferson nodded and headed toward the sleek Mercedes Roadster parked at the curb. It occurred to him that he at least needed a *name* for the substance he would soon push off on his high school classmates. Everyone expected him to deliver good old-fashioned Mary Jane. If he had something better to offer, he could jack up his prices. But no one—not even the steroid-pumping jocks—would be stupid enough to fork over their parents' hard-earned dough for a drug with no name.

He turned, the question on the tip of his tongue.

But the stranger was nowhere in sight.

Jefferson's baffled gaze swept up and down the vast expanse of lawn. The old man with the mutt was receding in the distance. Two joggers had appeared on the path, their low laughter filling the air as they passed Jefferson.

There was no sign of the cloaked stranger. Just as suddenly as he had appeared to give Jefferson the mysterious drugs, he had disappeared. Vanished into thin air. Like a specter.

Jefferson shivered at the thought. Something like dread settled in the pit of his stomach.

He turned and hurried to his car as if the devil were on his heels.

CHAPTER 1

Potomac, Maryland
Tuesday, November 11

"DEA! Drop your weapon!"

A single bead of perspiration trickled down Howard Pinkert's face as he eyed the two DEA agents crouched in the spacious foyer of his Potomac, Maryland estate. Their nine-millimeter Glocks were trained on him with lethal precision. He had no doubt that one false move on his part would ensure his swift and violent death.

His hand trembled on the .45 he held at his side. He licked parched lips. "For God's sake, gentlemen. You're treating me like a Colombian drug lord! I am a well-respected physician in this community—"

"Drop your weapon!" the agents commanded a second time. The tallest of the pair had piercing blue eyes and dark blond hair cropped short in a crew cut. He appeared more than ready to pull the trigger.

Huddled in a corner behind Howard, his maid whimpered and crossed herself with the rosary beads she never left home without. For a fleeting moment, Howard considered grabbing her and using her as a hostage to gain his freedom. He'd never particularly cared for her anyway. He didn't like her suffocating lavender scent or the way she lingered over the silverware she was supposed to polish. He made it a practice to count every piece in the collection at least twice a week, despite his wife's protests.

His wife! She would be back from the charity auction any minute now. He couldn't risk her stumbling upon this disastrous scene. He had never meant for things to get so out of control. He'd been in the kitchen pouring himself a cup of coffee when the agents arrived on his doorstep, armed to the teeth and brandishing their arrest warrant. Naturally he'd panicked. While his maid kept the agents preoccupied with her hysterical shrieks, Howard had gone for the closest weapon he could find—a semiautomatic he kept hidden in the back of the pantry in a brown paper bag. He knew his wife would never accidentally stumble upon the gun. The only reason Grace Whitney Pinkert ever visited the gourmet kitchen was to bark orders to their cook, who was conveniently absent that afternoon and hadn't bothered to call with an explanation. Howard wondered if a member of his own household staff had turned him in to the authorities. If so, there would be hell to pay.

"Listen, gentlemen," he said, suppressing a quick surge of anger, "can't we sit down and discuss this like rational adults? Surely there's been some sort of misunderstanding—"

"For the last time, Dr. Pinkert," the blond agent said tersely, "we're ordering you to drop your weapon. Now!"

Howard hesitated, torn with indecision. The idea of being led from his own home in handcuffs was appalling. He was a pillar of the community, a successful private practitioner who served on several hospital boards and auxiliaries and was published in leading medical journals. He couldn't afford the scandal of an arrest. On the other hand, his chances of escape were looking more remote by the second.

"All right," he conceded reluctantly. "No point in allowing this to get any uglier than it already has."

"Lower your weapon slowly to the floor. *Slowly.*"

Howard complied, knowing he had no other choice. No sooner had his fingers left the semiautomatic than the agents were upon him. One retrieved his weapon from the floor while the other handcuffed him and re- cited the Miranda warning. Howard could barely deci- pher the words above the roar in his head.

"This isn't over," he blustered as he was escorted from the house. "You'll be hearing from my attorney, I can promise you that."

Samille Broussard watched as Howard Pinkert was low- ered into the backseat of an unmarked cruiser parked out- side his sprawling eight-bedroom estate. His homely appearance didn't match the enormity of his crimes. He was short and doughy in a rumpled shirt and pleated trousers. His round head was crowned with a thinning layer of gray hair that he normally concealed with a bad toupee. Although Samille had met the man on numerous occasions in the course of her investigation, his appear- ance always threw her for a loop. He looked more like a shoe salesman than the leader of a major drug operation.

Four other vehicles, including her own, lined the curb in front of the Pinkert house. The local authorities had arrived and blocked off the street with crime scene tape. Just in time, too. Someone had tipped off the media, and news vans bearing the emblems of local television stations were swooping in for the kill. Samille could al- ready see tomorrow's headlines: PROMINENT PHYSICIAN AR- RESTED ON PRESCRIPTION DRUG TRAFFICKING CHARGES.

Shaking her head, she started up the cobblestone

path to the front door. She entered the house and swept a glance around the luxurious interior, noting the original oil paintings and Baccarat crystal scattered liberally throughout the high-ceilinged parlor. The good doctor certainly believed in spending his money. Too bad he'd earned much of it illegally.

Her attention was drawn to a diminutive woman huddled in a chair in a corner of the foyer. The woman's dark head was bent as she sobbed and wrung her hands in consternation, barely coherent as she recited the Lord's Prayer in rapid Spanish.

Samille carefully approached the woman. "*Habla usted inglés?*"

The woman started violently. Dark, frightened eyes met Samille's in a round face creased with age and worry. "It is all a mistake! Señor Pinkert, he's a good man. He did no wrong!"

Samille knelt in front of the woman. "Are you his housekeeper?" she asked gently.

"*Sí, sí.* I answered the door, and those two men said they came to arrest Señor Pinkert. I don't understand. What did he do, señorita?"

Samille laid a soothing hand across the other woman's. "What's your name?"

"Isabel. Isabel Fuentes. I have worked for the Pinkerts for ten years, and nothing like this has ever happened before!" She burst into tears and lapsed into another round of rapid-fire Spanish.

Samille winced. "Is there somewhere you can go? *Hay en alguna parte usted puede ir?*" she repeated in fluid Spanish. She figured it might be easier to converse with the hysterical woman if she met her on her own terms.

Isabel Fuentes seemed gratified by the accommodation. She calmed down enough to tell Samille where she lived and how many children she had.

Special Agent Jackson Burdett strode into the house, took one look at Samille kneeling before the distraught housekeeper, and shook his head ruefully. "Christ, Broussard, what a bleeding heart you are."

Samille scowled at him over her shoulder. "Pinkert's office suite is on the lower level. Make sure you don't miss anything," she added unnecessarily. Jack Burdett was one of the DEA's best special agents. He was tough and sharp and executed his duties with a thoroughness that inspired the utmost confidence. It was little wonder that he had the highest caseload among the agents at the Washington, D.C. field office. Everyone wanted to work with Jack Burdett.

With a mock salute, Jack pivoted on his heel and headed for the rear stairwell. The agents who trailed him knew better than to utter a word to Samille about tending to the Pinkerts' maid. No one could match Samille's obstinacy in a battle of wills. Besides, what was she supposed to do? Ignore Isabel Fuentes while armed federal agents turned her employer's house upside down?

By the time Samille finished taking Isabel Fuentes's statement and assuring the woman that she was not under suspicion, Jack and the others had finished loading boxes of evidence into their trucks. Patient records, pharmacy receipts, falsified registration forms—all would be used to prosecute Howard Pinkert. After sixteen months of surveillance and investigation, Samille had finally nailed the affluent chiropractor who'd made a career out of creating fraudulent prescriptions to obtain the pain reliever OxyContin. Pinkert had supplied the drug to his associates for distribution on the underground market, a lucrative operation that went undetected for several years.

"We hit the jackpot this time," Jack said as he rejoined

Samille in the foyer. She'd arranged for a county police officer to take Isabel Fuentes home.

"Not only did Dr. Feelgood have a boatload of OCs in his possession," Jack said, "but we also found an arsenal of sawed-off shotguns—probably unregistered. Looks like he might have been dabbling in arms dealing on the side."

"Guess no one wants to earn an honest living anymore," Samille muttered.

"And miss out on all this?" Jack said, gesturing expansively around their opulent surroundings. Nordic blue eyes twinkled with mirth in a ruggedly handsome face.

Samille cast a dubious look around. "It's a bit pretentious, if you ask me."

Jack laughed. "Whatever you say, Broussard."

He followed her from the house and locked the door. Several curious spectators had gathered across the street. Some of their expressions were openly indignant, as if they couldn't believe that members of the outside world would dare encroach upon their exclusive sanctuary.

Samille sent Jack an amused sidelong glance. He wore faded jeans and a navy blue jacket with *DEA* printed across the back in bright yellow letters. "You'd better take that off before you're mobbed by an angry crowd," she teased. "You know these good folks don't expect drug busts to occur in their neighborhood."

"All in a day's work." Jack shaded his eyes with his hand against the late afternoon sunshine and looked down the street. He frowned at the procession of news vans lining the curb beyond the police tape. Several reporters had climbed out and were filming live footage for their respective stations. One ambitious reporter was already knocking on doors to interview neighbors.

Jack shook his head in disgust. "Bunch of vultures."

"All in a day's work," Samille quipped. She started for a Jeep Wrangler with a soft top parked at the curb.

"Where are you headed now?"

"Back to the office to finish my preliminary report. Graham will want it before the press conference."

Jack fell in step beside her. "What about this evening? Are you free for drinks? We could celebrate wrapping up this case and toast to Pinkert's future behind bars."

"As tempting as the offer sounds, I'll have to take a rain check. I promised my aunt and uncle I'd have dinner with them tonight. They've been nagging me to death about my long hours." Samille fished her keys out of the pocket of her wool blazer and made a face. "If I don't show up tonight, I'm afraid they'll send a search and rescue team after me."

Jack chuckled. "Nothing works better than an old-fashioned guilt trip. See you back at the office."

Samille climbed into her Jeep and started the engine. As she pulled away from the Pinkert property, she flipped down the visor to lessen the glare of the sunlight. When this didn't work, she slid on a pair of sunglasses. She thought of the mountain of paperwork that awaited her at the office and sighed.

Samille had joined the Drug Enforcement Administration six years ago after earning a master's degree in forensic science. The diversion of controlled pharmaceuticals and chemicals into the illicit drug market was fast becoming an international epidemic. As a diversion investigator, Samille had to conduct investigations of registered handlers of controlled substances—handlers like Howard Pinkert who abused their position to illegally obtain prescription medications.

Although Samille and her colleagues often felt that they were fighting an uphill battle, there were some days that gave her hope and strengthened her commitment to the DEA's diversion control mission.

Today was one of those days.

She smoothed a hand absently over her ponytail. She preferred the low-maintenance style for her shoulder-length black hair. Even if she'd had the time to fuss with her hair every day, the nature of her work didn't exactly encourage a glamorous appearance. When she wasn't in the field, she was buried beneath piles of regulatory policies and procedures and compliance forms. Even her wardrobe had been standardized. She owned more black pantsuits than Hilary Rodham Clinton.

Not that Samille minded the simplified wardrobe. She'd certainly never been accused of being a clotheshorse. In high school she had run track and served as president of the math and science club. She'd been voted "Most Likely to Succeed," not "Best Dressed."

Grinning at the thought, Samille turned on the stereo and surfed through stations before settling on WTOP news radio. She'd been immersed in the Pinkert investigation all day; it wouldn't hurt to find out what else was happening around the D.C. metropolitan area.

"In late-breaking news this afternoon, D.C. police are reporting that ten local teenagers were rushed to area hospitals over the weekend after falling suddenly and mysteriously ill. According to police sources, all of the teenagers attended a party on Friday night at a Georgetown residence and became severely ill early the next morning. Police are not confirming whether drugs were involved. We will update you as more details become available."

Samille frowned as the station segued to the traffic and weather report. Was it mere coincidence that ten people at the same party had gotten sick? Two or three, maybe. But *ten*? Of course, food poisoning was always a possibility. She recalled the rash of cruise ship illnesses last year that had caused many vacationers, including her aunt and uncle, to cancel their travel plans. Could these teenagers have fallen victim to another Norwalk-like stomach virus? Or had drugs been a factor? Samille's investigative instincts leaned toward the latter scenario. She had witnessed enough raids on nightclubs to know the kind of trouble unsupervised teens could get into. And she was more than familiar with the alarming statistics of illegal drug use among minors. Was it possible that all of these teenagers had overdosed after attending the same party?

Samille's frown deepened. Of course it was possible. If anything her job had taught her, it was that *anything* was possible where drugs were concerned.

CHAPTER 2

Samille shimmied into a straight-fitting black skirt and smoothed the material over her legs. She tucked her ivory silk blouse into the waistband, jammed her arms into the suit jacket, and thrust her feet into a pair of matching pumps. Halfway to the front door of her condo, she realized she'd forgotten to put on the sheer black panty hose she'd purposely laid across the bed before her shower. With a muffled curse, she strode back to the bedroom.

"*What* did you say, young lady?"

Samille cringed into the cordless phone cradled between her shoulder and ear. "Sorry, Aunt Noreen. I wasn't talking to you."

"I certainly hope not." On the other end of the phone, Noreen Broussard clucked her tongue in disapproval. "You've been working around men too long. You never used to swear."

"Of course I did. Just not around you. And for the record, I picked up the habit from Nate and Jared."

"I always knew those boys were a bad influence on you. Your uncle never believed me, but at least *I* could admit the mischief my sons were capable of."

Samille smiled as she carefully slid one leg into sheer nylon. There was no denying that Nathaniel and Jared Broussard had been bona fide hellions in their childhood, wreaking havoc on their mother's nerves and tormenting Samille as only boys could do. She still recalled the dirty pranks they'd played on her, remembered neighborhood brawls that had brought their father outside armed with his belt and an expression that caused the curious onlookers to scatter. Samille had loved Nate and Jared like the brothers she never had, and they had adored her. It was the Broussard brothers who taught her how to swim and ride a bike, how to pitch a fastball and deliver a mean left hook. The other things she'd learned under their tutelage—like how to make disgusting noises with her armpits—she'd sooner keep from her aunt. Besides, it made no difference how unruly her cousins had once been. Both had turned out exceptionally well, tamed by adulthood and the U.S. military. Nate was a high-ranking naval intelligence officer stationed in San Diego, and Jared was a decorated Air Force pilot who never stayed in one place very long.

"Speaking of the boys," Noreen Broussard continued, an unmistakable note of pride in her voice, "they're both on leave this weekend, and they're dying to see you. I thought we could all sit down to a big Sunday dinner like old times—except it'll have to be on Saturday."

"That sounds wonderful, Aunt Noreen."

"Think you can fit your family into your busy schedule?"

Samille groaned at her aunt's reproachful tone. "I'm sorry for canceling on you and Uncle Gabe last night. Like I told you, I had to finish a report and prepare some notes for a hearing I'm testifying at this afternoon."

"I know, I know. Believe me, Sammy, I understand how important your job is to you. You've always been very ambitious and there's nothing wrong with that." Noreen's wistful sigh filled the phone line. "It's just that I worry about you, sweetheart. Your old friends have stopped calling here looking for you because you never return their phone calls or e-mails. You're only twenty-nine years old, but at the rate you're going, I'm afraid you're headed for burnout. You've always made time for everything but yourself—whether it was grad school, those girls you mentor at the correctional center, or your job. You were at the office last night until ten p.m., and here it is barely seven o'clock and you're on your way out the door again!"

"You know my schedule fluctuates depending on my caseload. On most days I get home by six-thirty."

Noreen was dubious. "And do what? Eat a solitary takeout meal in front of the television until you drag your tired self to bed—alone, I might add."

Samille bristled. It didn't matter that her aunt's version of her life was as close to the truth as if she'd been a fly on the wall in Samille's apartment. She resented the lecture. She was a grown woman, no longer the helpless child who had needed to sleep with the lights on to keep the nightmares at bay. The same child who couldn't go to sleep without her parents' photograph clutched to her chest. A lot had changed since then. The nightmares, once so debilitating in their intensity, were less frequent. The eight-by-ten of her parents now held a place of honor atop the fireplace mantel in her bedroom. She was fully capable of managing her own life— she worked hard, paid her bills on time, maintained a decent stock portfolio, and exercised regularly. She could do a lot worse than being a workaholic.

"You're a beautiful young woman with so much to offer," Noreen Broussard continued plaintively. "You're strong, intelligent, cultured, and compassionate. And you even know how to cook—when you make time for it. Any man would be lucky to have you."

Samille groaned. "Please don't give me the marriage lecture, Aunt Noreen. Aren't you the one who always taught me about the proud legacy of African-American women who changed the world without the assistance of a man? Sisters like Harriet Tubman and Sojourner Truth, Angela Davis and Zora Neale Hurston. Besides, why is it acceptable for Nate and Jared to remain single and not me? They're both older than me!"

"How do you know I haven't said anything to them?"

"Because we talk every other week, and they're always teasing me about your matchmaking schemes. They even have a bet going about how soon you'll have me married off."

"*What*?" Noreen paused. "Which one of them gave me the better odds? I'll fix his favorite dish for Saturday's dinner."

"Aunt Noreen!"

"Oh, all right. I know that's not the point." But there was a hint of a smile in her voice. She heaved a resigned sigh. "I don't mean to pry into your life, Sammy. My mother was a perpetual nag and I swore I would never be like her. It's just that I want to see you happy."

"I *am* happy," Samille countered, ignoring the tiny inner voice that called her a liar. She changed the subject. "How's the book coming along?"

"Slowly. There's a lot of research involved." Noreen Broussard was a tenured English literature professor at Georgetown University. She'd taken a sabbatical that year to work on a nonfiction book that explored the early writings of various nineteenth-century African-American authors. The project was sponsored by the prestigious Ford Foundation Grant and would be released by a major New York publisher next fall. Samille

credited her aunt for introducing her to literature and
teaching her an appreciation for the classics. Some of
Samille's fondest childhood memories included sitting
at Noreen Broussard's feet and listening to the words of
Langston Hughes and Jane Austen come to life. As she
grew older, she'd cherished summer forays to the library
with her aunt to check out works by Charlotte Brontë,
Ralph Waldo Emerson, and Richard Wright. Her tastes
had eventually expanded to include mystery and science
fiction, but to this day, she couldn't open a literary classic without hearing her aunt's melodious voice.

A nostalgic smile touched her lips. "Just let me know
if you need any help with the research."

Noreen chuckled. "I remember how helpful you were
when I was studying for my Ph.D. You used to go to the
library and check out books for me. I called you my little
research assistant. Do you remember?"

"I remember." Reluctantly Samille glanced at her
wristwatch. "I'd better get going, Aunt Noreen. Give
Uncle Gabe my love."

"I will. Should we expect you on Saturday?"

"Absolutely. I'll come early and help you with dinner."

"I'd like that. See you then."

Samille disconnected. She grabbed her leather attaché
case and a cinnamon raisin bagel before leaving the apartment. It would be another half hour before traffic became
a commuter's nightmare, so she made it to the office in no
time at all. She parked in the underground parking
garage and took the elevator. The DEA's Washington field
division was obscurely located in a commercial building.
No sign announced the DEA's presence, and the building
directory did not include a listing.

Samille swiped her ID badge, entered her security
code, and stepped into a large suite with a maze of cubicles at the center. There were doors leading to offices

on both sides that were reserved for the diversion program manager, supervisory diversion investigator, and program analysts. Notes and bulletins were taped to walls and metal file cabinets. A poster reminded employees about Red Ribbon Week, the national anti-drug campaign that had been launched in memory of DEA Special Agent Enrique Camarena, who'd been murdered by drug traffickers in 1985.

As Samille walked toward the cluster of cubicles that housed the diversion investigators, she passed a group of agents discussing a surveillance assignment.

"Hey, Broussard, you showing a little leg today?"

"Lookin' good, baby. Lookin' *real* good!"

Samille didn't break stride. "You fellas really ought to get out more. You're probably starting to look good to each other."

Her remark was met with raucous male laughter. Jack Burdett, emerging from his supervisor's office, looked her up and down and grinned.

Samille skewered him with a look. "Don't even think about it."

Laughing, he held up his hands in surrender and moved out of her way. Samille reached her cubicle and dropped her attaché case onto the desk. She was sorely tempted to change into the pair of low-heeled pumps she kept in the bottom drawer for emergencies. As ridiculous as it was, she'd always felt like she was playing dress-up whenever she wore a skirt. The only reason she'd made the concession that day was that she had to appear in Judge Joseph Lambert's courtroom. He was a relic who believed women belonged at home, barefoot and pregnant. His extreme conservatism was legendary; it was rumored that he often ruled against defendants whose female attorneys wore pants inside his courtroom. Although Samille wanted nothing more than to tell the venerable judge where to stick his archaic beliefs, she understood the importance of playing by the rules. The last thing she wanted was for a criminal defendant to get off because the DI testifying against him had the audacity to wear pants to court.

"Oh, good. You're here. Got a minute?"

Samille looked up to find the diversion program manager standing in her cubicle. Alan Graham was a tall, imposing figure with a shock of silver-dusted brown hair. A pair of steel-rimmed glasses perched on his aristocratic nose gave him a decidedly studious look—a look Samille suspected he'd deliberately cultivated when he assumed the head honcho position eight years ago.

She was surprised by his sudden appearance. Alan Graham seldom interacted with diversion investigators. He was responsible for overseeing the operational activities of the diversion control program. He left the managerial functions of the office to the supervisory diversion investigator, who reported to him. His role was largely administrative and political. He spent a lot of time in meetings with administration officials discussing policy and government regulations that would have an impact on their duties.

Samille masked her curiosity with an easy smile. "Sure, Alan."

She followed him to the large office at the very end of the corridor. He closed the door and gestured her into one of the visitors' chairs opposite a large teak desk. Instead of reclaiming the chair behind his desk, he perched a hip on the corner and offered a congenial smile meant to put her at ease. Her hackles went up.

"Congratulations on wrapping up the Pinkert case," Graham said. "I know you poured a lot of time and energy into the investigation, and I commend you for it."

"Just doing my job," Samille countered. What was

going on here? Alan Graham hadn't called her into his office to praise her for doing what she was paid for.

"I appreciate your modesty, Broussard, but I must disagree. You weren't merely doing your job. Cheryl Norris has told me on numerous occasions what a consummate professional you are, how you go above and beyond the call of duty with every case you're assigned."

"That's very generous of her."

"I don't think 'generosity' has much to do with it. Your track record speaks for itself. You have the highest percentage of resolved cases in this office—heck, in this *region*. That's something to be proud of, Broussard. Especially given your tremendous caseload."

Samille crossed her legs neatly. "We're all pretty busy."

"True enough. And I know what a challenge it can be to conduct your various investigations without the full-time assistance of our agents. I want to assure you that we're addressing the issue and are once again reassessing the role of diversion investigators. Which leads me to the reason for calling you into my office this morning." Graham stood and went to sit behind his desk. Samille wondered if it was a strategic move on his part, placing distance between them at this juncture of the conversation. At any rate, he had her undivided attention.

"I'm sure you've heard about the recent overdosing of those teenagers in Georgetown?"

"Yes."

Graham nodded briskly. "Since hospital toxicology results proved inconclusive, our lab has taken over the responsibility of analyzing and identifying the second substance found in the victims' bodies."

"Second?"

"Traces of oxycodone were detected, but not enough to cause the kind of trauma that would lead to a coma.

Another substance was found that resembles Ecstasy—
only it isn't."

Samille arched an eyebrow. "We're looking at something entirely new?"

"So it appears." His mouth thinned to a grim line.
Both he and Samille understood the potential for disaster any time a foreign substance entered the market. Unusual compounds were constantly being created and
sold by illicit drug manufacturers. DEA forensic chemists
were faced with the challenge of quickly identifying such
drugs to prevent their availability on the underground
market. Sometimes it seemed a race against the clock.

"At any rate," Graham continued, "D.C. police is already
working with the Bureau—"

"The FBI is involved?"

"Yes. All of the victims are from prominent families
who weren't satisfied that the local boys could handle
the case. Not long after their kids were admitted to the
hospital, they started throwing their weight around, demanding a full-scale investigation into what 'evil' had be-
fallen their children." His lips twisted wryly. "These
people belong to the same country club and civic orga-
nizations, rub elbows at the same political fund-raisers
and social functions. You know how it is in those upper-
crust circles. Old money and good breeding. The parents are all singing the same tune, that their children
would *never* use drugs, not in a million years."

"Surprise, surprise," Samille drawled. No one wanted
to believe their own child was abusing drugs any more
than they wanted to believe their kid was a serial killer.

"They think something was slipped into drinks at the
party," Graham said. "The police questioned some students at the school yesterday to see if there were any witnesses at the party who saw drugs being sold. So far no

one's talking. A few kids admitted that there was alcohol at the party, but no drugs."

"Of course. If these kids *were* getting high, they're not about to come clean to the police and risk their own hides. Especially not if they think their comatose classmates are as good as goners anyway."

Graham nodded in agreement. "At any rate, in addition to providing our forensic resources, we've decided to lend our investigative support as well. That's where you come in."

Samille's eyebrows furrowed in confusion. She knew that the broad scope of certain investigations often required the coordination of federal, state, and local law enforcement agencies. But what did that have to do with her? Her role as a diversion investigator limited her to regulatory activities related to the diversion of controlled pharmaceuticals and chemicals. She went after the doctors and pharmacists who illegally distributed drugs. She *didn't* go after scumbag dealers who sold Ecstasy to a bunch of rich kids at a party—if indeed the unidentified substance was an illegal drug.

Graham steepled his hands on the desk and leaned forward intently. Aquamarine eyes held hers. "I've assigned you to work with the Bureau's representative on this case, Broussard. I can see that you're confused, so let me explain my reason for this decision. As I mentioned earlier, we're continually reassessing the role of DIs in the Office of Diversion Control. I share your belief that DIs *should* be given law enforcement authorities to combat the widespread diversion of controlled pharmaceuticals."

Samille blinked, nonplussed. "How did you know I felt this way?"

His smile was a touch sheepish. "I hope you don't mind. Cheryl shared with me some of your views on the subject. And she said that out of all her DIs, you'd be the best candidate for conversion to special agent status."

"I'm not sure that I want to become a special agent, per se. I just feel that it would make our jobs easier if we were at least granted the authority to carry firearms, make arrests, handle informants, and conduct surveillance in the event that an agent isn't available to assist us. It *is* frustrating to have an investigation delayed simply because an agent isn't available to substantiate evidence or make an undercover purchase."

"My sentiments exactly. Which is why I've pulled you into this particular investigation. Your successful collaboration with the FBI—in a criminal investigative capacity—will make a strong case for our argument."

No pressure. "And you don't feel that one of our agents would be better suited for this type of case?"

Graham shook his head. "I don't want to pull Jack or any of the other SAs off their pending cases—they're stretched pretty thin as it is, as we've both noted. Besides that, your vast knowledge of controlled pharmaceuticals may prove invaluable to the investigation. We already know that OxyContin is involved. Once the second substance is identified, you can access your ongoing case files to search for any red flags. Whoever distributed this new drug to those teenagers could very well be one of your registered handlers. Rather than giving the Bureau's investigators unlimited access to our case files, it seems more beneficial to work in conjunction with them."

Not to mention the fact that both agencies were highly territorial when it came to jurisdictional matters. Samille kept the thought to herself.

"You will be providing investigative support to the Bureau." Graham spoke as if he'd read her mind. "But technically their agent will be the primary in the investigation. But to demonstrate that there's no power struggle, the Bureau's sending him over this morning to meet with us. I checked your schedule. You're not due in court until this afternoon, correct?"

Samille nodded. "What about my ongoing cases?"

"We'll shift some of your caseload around to the other DIs. This investigation is going to require a great deal of your time and attention. At some point, depending on how the case unfolds, we may need to assemble a task force. But we have to exercise prudence in the allotment of our resources. As unfortunate as this incident is, there are many in the public who might accuse us of giving this investigation priority status simply because of who these kids are. We both know that the media would have a field day with that angle," Graham added with a pained grimace. "In a sense we're stuck between the proverbial rock and hard place. Because of the pressure from above, we have to make the case a priority. But we have to accomplish this without drawing too much attention to the fact. When, and *if*, we assemble a task force, it won't be publicized. Do you understand where I'm coming from, Broussard?"

"Perfectly." Samille had long ago stopped trying to rationalize all the politicking that went on between law enforcement and the media. She would never fully comprehend or accept how people's very lives could hinge on something as tenuous as public perception.

"Will that be all?"

Graham nodded. "For now."

She stood and crossed to the door. She paused with her hand on the doorknob. "Just out of curiosity, who's the Bureau sending over? Anyone we know?"

"You might have heard of him. His name's Kincaid. Special Agent Brant Kincaid. He's supposed to be one of their best."

Samille's pulse spiked several notches. Without another word, she turned and walked out of the office.

Samille had first encountered Brant Kincaid six months earlier at the DEA Training Academy in Quantico, Virginia. She'd been attending a one-week refresher training course that was offered to diversion investigators every two years. The course provided an intensive curriculum of legal updates, ethics and integrity, computer systems and headquarters issues. While there, diversion investigators were encouraged to take advantage of the training facilities, which were used for firearms training, physical fitness, vehicle and defensive tactics training. The training facilities were shared by the DEA and the FBI Academy, also located on the Marine Corps base in Quantico.

Samille and a fellow DI had joined a class of basic agent trainees grunting through a series of rigorous physical exercises. Samille was feeling a little cocky after completing fifty push-ups without breaking a sweat.

"Piece of cake."

Amanda Winters groaned as she got gingerly to her feet. Damp strands of wheat-blond hair had escaped her ponytail and were plastered to her reddened face. "Refresh my memory," she panted as they began jogging. "*Why* did I let you talk me into this again?"

"Because exercise is important, and we want to prove that diversion investigators are more than pencil pushers."

"No, *you* want to prove that we're more than pencil pushers. I'm perfectly content with the label as long as *I* know the truth."

"See, that's your problem, Winters. Sometimes you've gotta buck the system, demand more than the status quo." Samille grinned. "Think we can sneak into firearms training?"

Amanda snorted. "Go for it. I, on the other hand, will be back in our room soaking my corns and cursing you for talking me into this mess. Isn't it enough that we're subjected to information overload in our courses? Do we really have to punish our bodies as well? And just for the record, I have no desire whatsoever to learn how to blow someone's heart out of their chest. I'll leave that job to the special agents, thank you very much."

But Samille had stopped listening. Her eyes had fallen on a tall, dark stranger conversing with one of the training instructors on the sidelines. He wore denim blue jeans that hugged a trim, athletic waist and a black FBI Academy T-shirt that stretched across a wide chest and the broadest shoulders Samille had ever seen.

Arms folded, long legs braced slightly apart, he watched the procession of runners. Although his eyes were concealed behind a pair of mirrored aviator sunglasses, Samille sensed that he was staring straight at her. She stumbled and nearly collided with Amanda.

"Whoa, watch the toes! I can't take any more calluses!"

"Sorry," Samille mumbled, inexplicably flustered.

"What were you staring at?"

Samille chanced a look over her shoulder at the enigmatic stranger. She thought she detected the barest hint of a mocking smile on his handsome face. Her cheeks flamed.

Amanda followed her gaze and broke into a knowing grin. "Ohhh. Now I see."

"What?" Samille feigned innocence.

"His name's Brant Kincaid. He's an FBI agent. Scrumptious, isn't he? He's even yummier up close and personal."

"Do you know him?"

"Not personally, no. I have a friend at the Bureau who's an analyst, and he thinks Brant Kincaid is the coolest thing since sliced bread. They call him a bounty hunter in a double-breasted suit." She chuckled, her long ponytail swinging from side to side as she ran. "Once when I was meeting Corey for lunch at the D.C. field office—"

"Corey?"

"The analyst. Anyway, I had just walked into the building when Brant Kincaid appeared. I seriously considering propositioning him. Just marching right up to him and asking him if he dates white women."

"You didn't!"

"No, but I sure was tempted." Amanda slanted Samille a teasing look. "When we get back to the office, you should check out his dossier. It's pretty impressive."

Samille scoffed. "I'm not going to start digging into the background of a complete stranger. I'm not *that* desperate."

But she'd been intrigued. A few days later she used her security clearance to access the database of federal law enforcement personnel. "Impressive" didn't begin to describe Brant Kincaid's career profile. He'd double-majored in political science and psychology at Syracuse University and joined the Bureau after graduating at the top of his class from the FBI Academy. Over the course of his career, he'd successfully ensured the capture and prosecution of many violent offenders, including a few high-profile fugitives. He'd balanced a rigorous investigative caseload while earning a doctorate in criminal psychology, a degree guaranteed to put him on the fast track to becoming an FBI profiler. He was fluent in German, Russian, Italian, and Arabic. He boasted a genius IQ and was an expert marksman—an irresistible combination of brains *and* brawn.

Samille, who was never easily impressed, found herself utterly captivated by Brant Kincaid. And now as she faced the prospect of working with him, she couldn't decide whether to be excited or petrified. On one hand she looked forward to the new assignment; she was smart enough to know that she could learn a lot from a skilled criminal investigator like Brant Kincaid. On the other hand she was intimidated by his vast knowledge and experience. A man like Brant Kincaid would have little patience for errors. Samille knew her job and she did it darned well, but conducting criminal investigations was an entirely different animal. She didn't want to embarrass herself or her colleagues. God knew she'd already made a fool of herself by gawking at Brant Kincaid like an awestruck teenager and tripping over her own two feet.

Her cheeks heated with renewed humiliation at the memory.

"Earth to Samille. Is anyone there?"

Samille blinked as a manicured hand waved in front of her face. She looked up to find Amanda peering at her with a curious expression.

"Hey," Samille murmured.

"Hey yourself. Where were you just now? I called your name three times." Amanda inclined her head toward Samille's blank computer screen. "You forget your log-in ID or something?"

"Of course not. I was just thinking about something."

"Hmm, deep thoughts. Here, I brought you a caffeine fix." She handed Samille a cup of espresso from their favorite gourmet coffee shop across the street.

"God bless you." Samille wrapped her hands around the steaming cup and inhaled the rich, fragrant aroma. She took a sip and sighed contentedly. "What would I do without you?"

"Me or the espresso?" Amanda grinned and eyed Samille's Donna Karan skirt suit. "You look nice. Judge Lambert?"

"You know it."

"Ugh." Amanda rested a slender hip against Samille's desk. She wore gray cashmere slacks and a hunter-green turtleneck that accented her gold-flecked hazel eyes. Other than the Clinique blush she wore, her skin was the palest ivory. "I wonder if there's anything we can do to hasten that old windbag's retirement. I wonder if a sex scandal would do the trick."

Samille laughed and nearly choked on her coffee. Sputtering, she grabbed a napkin from her desk drawer and dabbed at her mouth. "Unless you're volunteering to be his Monica, I don't think it would work."

Amanda wrinkled her pert nose. "It's just as well. I don't think Judge Lambert would know what to do with a woman alone in his chambers, even if she sketched him a diagram. Although," she added speculatively, "I *have* often wondered if the real reason he makes us wear skirts in his courtroom is so that he can leer at our legs."

"You have an overactive imagination, Winters."

Amanda Winters had been with the DEA for eight years. Although she'd had her pick of many prestigious downtown firms when she earned her law degree, Amanda had chosen a career in public service. But unlike Samille, she had no interest in expanding the role of diversion investigators to include law enforcement capabilities. As the daughter of a retired Chicago police chief, Amanda was more interested in climbing the ranks of DEA leadership. She had her sights set on the head honcho position of administrator. No one had celebrated more than Amanda when the current DEA administrator, a woman, was named to the position two years ago. She took it as a sign that she was destined to assume the role one day.

"Speaking of my overactive imagination," Amanda murmured, staring above the cubicle toward the reception area, "guess who just walked into the office and is shaking hands with Graham?"

Samille's heart thudded. Her palms grew moist.

Before Amanda could utter another word, Samille's extension rang. Her hand trembled slightly as she reached for the phone. "Samille, your presence is requested in the conference room," the receptionist informed her.

"Thanks, Mary." She hung up and got slowly to her feet.

"What's going on? What's Brant Kincaid doing here? Not that I mind, but—"

"I have to go. I have a meeting."

"Are you all right?" Amanda's eyes narrowed suspiciously on Samille's face. "The last time you looked this flustered was at the academy six months ago when you saw . . . Wait a minute. Are you and Graham meeting with *Brant Kincaid*?"

"Yes. It's a long story. I'll fill you in later." Samille brushed past her colleague and headed down the corridor toward the conference room. Her racing pulse made her feel light-headed. *This is ridiculous*, she berated herself. *You've never reacted this way to any man before. Get yourself together before you make a complete idiot of yourself—again.*

She took a deep, fortifying breath before stepping into the narrow conference room adjoining the reception area. She immediately realized she should have inhaled *several* lungfuls of air, because the moment her gaze landed on Brant Kincaid, she felt as if she'd been leveled in the gut with a sledgehammer. Nothing could have prepared her for the piercing intensity of those incredible onyx eyes. He was even handsomer than she remembered, with hard cheekbones and a ruthlessly square jaw stretched taut across skin the deep color of mahogany. His inky black hair was cropped close to his scalp, matching the smooth texture of his thick eyebrows. His goatee was faint and trimmed with military precision, framing a firm, sculpted mouth. He looked tough, rugged, like a man who had seen too much to be surprised by anything ever again.

Alan Graham and Brant Kincaid stood in unison to greet her, but it was Brant's movement that held Samille's rapt attention. He unfolded his body from the chair and rounded the table with the fluid ease of a panther. Graham was tall at six-two, but Brant Kincaid seemed to tower over him, filling the room with the breadth of his wide shoulders and the sheer force of his commanding presence. She took in the clean lines of his dark suit and the crispness of his white shirt and silk tie. The cut of the suit accentuated his athletic build to mouthwatering perfection.

She swallowed and willed her heart rate to slow down. What on earth was wrong with her?

"Sammy, thank you for joining us," Graham said, oblivious of her predicament. "I'd like you to meet Special Agent Brant Kincaid."

Samille forced her legs forward as she extended a hand. "It's nice to meet you."

Her palm was enveloped in the warmth of a big, slightly callused hand. Frissons of heat licked through her body and made her breath hitch. Their gazes held.

"The pleasure's all mine," he said. His voice was as potent as the rest of the package. A warm baritone with pure masculine tones that quivered along her nerve endings. A voice like dark honey.

She quickly withdrew her hand and lowered herself into the nearest chair before her knees could buckle beneath her. Graham sat at the head of the conference table while Brant reclaimed his seat opposite Samille.

"As you're both aware," Graham began, "the DEA and FBI have decided to join forces in this investigation. We hope that by pooling our resources, we can crack this case wide open and possibly prevent another illicit drug from flooding the underground market. Agent Kincaid, you've no doubt been briefed on Sammy's role in the investigation?"

"I have," Brant said evenly. Samille thought she detected a note of displeasure in his deep voice. Did he have a problem working with her?

"Broussard is an outstanding diversion investigator," Graham continued. "I have every confidence that her vast knowledge of controlled chemicals and pharmaceuticals will prove invaluable to this investigation."

"I don't doubt Ms. Broussard's capabilities in her area of expertise," Brant countered, "and I certainly welcome any technical assistance she can provide. But as I've already expressed to my assistant director, I have serious reservations about her involvement in anything other than a peripheral capacity."

Samille's hackles rose at his remarks. It didn't matter that she'd already entertained the same misgivings about her role in the investigation. Brant Kincaid's implication that she couldn't handle the assignment rankled.

She lifted a proud chin. "You don't have to refer to me in the third person, Agent Kincaid. I'm a big girl. I think I can handle whatever you have to say."

His dark gaze settled on her face. That sensuous mouth twitched with wry humor. "Yes, I can certainly see that you're a big girl, Ms. Broussard. I apologize if it seemed otherwise." He clasped his large hands on the table and leaned forward. "I'm sure I don't have to tell you that conducting a criminal investigation requires a specific level of training and background. Based on my understanding of the work you perform here, you're not exactly qualified to assist in a criminal investigation of this nature."

"With all due respect, Agent Kincaid," Samille said coolly, "it's not your call to make."

"What Sammy means," Graham smoothly interjected, "is that while we certainly understand and appreciate your viewpoint, Agent Kincaid, the decision to involve her in this investigation was reached after much discussion and deliberation. The concerns you've just expressed were taken into careful consideration."

"Perhaps Agent Kincaid is worried that he'll have to do too much handholding. After all, I have two strikes against me: I'm a woman *and* a pencil pusher." Samille wanted to retract the caustic words the minute they left her mouth. She knew she was being defensive and emotional. She'd always prided herself on being the most levelheaded person she knew.

Brant turned his head slowly to look at her. As he'd done when she first entered the conference room, he studied her with eyes that gave nothing away while he noted every detail about her. She had a face that managed to be both exotic and wholesome, heart-shaped with high, slanted cheekbones and an alluring sultriness to her dark, thick-lashed eyes. Lustrous ebony hair stemming from a widow's peak had been swept back into a severe knot atop her head, a simple hairstyle that drew attention to the fineness of her features—although Brant doubted the effect had been intentional. She had a slim nose, a delicate chin that hinted at defiance, and an incredibly lush mouth that begged to be kissed. Her rich brown skin was flawless, hinting at undertones of warm sienna. He estimated her to be around five-eight and in her late twenties.

She wore a simple but tasteful black suit, the slim-fitting skirt ending just below her knees. The red-blooded male in him had responded to the sight of long, sleek legs sheathed in sheer black nylon. She'd shaken his hand, sat quickly, and crossed her legs. His groin had tightened almost painfully when he glimpsed the delicious curve of a shapely thigh. He thought about her earlier remark and wanted to laugh. There was no mistaking that Samille Broussard was a "big girl"—100 percent woman. If she were any more woman, Brant didn't think he'd be able to refrain from stretching her out across the conference table and making frantic love to her.

She watched him now, hostility simmering beneath the surface of her composed demeanor. He'd offended her. All her life she'd probably been told that she could do anything she set her mind to. In her youth she'd probably petitioned the school board to integrate the football team. He could easily envision her as president of a traditionally male-dominated intramural club, something like math or the debate team. She never backed down from a challenge and would resent anyone who stood in her way.

Brant bit back an impatient retort and kept his expression carefully impassive. When he spoke, his tone was low and succinct. "There are certain situations that may arise in the course of a criminal investigation, situations that require the use of firearms or defensive tactics. Have you received this type of training, Ms. Broussard?"

"Not formally, no."

Once again Graham intervened. "We're still hammering out the particulars of Sammy's role in the investigation. You may or may not be aware of the DEA's ongoing debate regarding the conversion of diversion investigators to special agents."

Brant inclined his head. "I'm familiar with it." His unyielding expression clearly conveyed where he stood on the issue.

Graham cleared his throat discreetly. "I think it would be beneficial if we used this time to bring each other up to speed on where the investigation stands.

Our lab is analyzing the specimens and will hopefully have their results back to us within forty-eight hours. This case has been given priority-one status. I understand that you've already met with D.C. police, Agent Kincaid?"

"That's correct. The detectives spoke to some students at the school, none of whom were very forthcoming with information. I've asked Matthew Blair, the student who hosted the party, to furnish a complete guest list by the end of the day. I plan to question those students tomorrow."

"Maybe I could go with you," Samille said, thinking aloud. "As part of the DEA's outreach program, Teens in Prevention, I periodically visit area schools to talk to the students about substance abuse and violence. The kids are pretty responsive to the presentations, and it might prompt one of our victims' classmates to come forward with vital information."

"That's a great suggestion," Graham said enthusiastically.

"It might work," Brant agreed more slowly. "How soon could you arrange the presentation?"

"Public Affairs can probably set up something for tomorrow. In light of what's happened, I'm sure the school officials will be more than happy to welcome us."

Graham nodded briskly. "Then it's settled. The two of you can visit the school together. Agent Kincaid, I understand that you have case files on all of the victims?"

"That's correct."

"Broussard, you may want to borrow the files from Agent Kincaid and review the victims' backgrounds. It might help bring you up to speed."

"Good idea, sir." Samille met Brant Kincaid's eyes with a veiled challenge in her own. "That is, if Agent Kincaid is willing to share."

Brant regarded her in silence for a moment, a hint of mockery in the curve of his mouth. "I think I can manage it," he drawled.

The three of them rose from the table as the meeting was adjourned. Brant and Graham followed Samille from the room.

Jack Burdett stood at the reception station retrieving his phone messages. He glanced up at their approach and grinned broadly when he saw Brant.

"Kincaid, what brings you here? Finally defecting from the Bureau?"

Brant chuckled, and Samille's belly quivered at the low, sexy rumble. She watched as the two men exchanged handshakes filled with warm, mutual regard.

"The Bureau got you doing covert ops again?" Jack ribbed. "Haven't seen you around for a while."

"I've been around," Brant said vaguely. He watched as Samille tried to edge past them without being detected. As if a woman like Samille Broussard could ever escape detection.

"Hey, Sammy, don't run off yet." Jack's arm snaked out to curve around her waist, detaining her. "I want to introduce you to Brant Kincaid."

"I've had the pleasure," Samille murmured, as if meeting Brant had been anything *but* pleasant. Brant noted the familiar ease with which Jack Burdett held her to his side. He wondered if the two were more than colleagues. Not that it made a bit of difference to him.

"Brant and I were in basic training during the same time at the academy," Jack explained to Samille. "Our firearms instructor tried to recruit Kincaid after he saw him in action on the firing range, but our friend here thought he was too good for the DEA. Ain't that right, Kincaid?"

Brant's expression was indulgent. "Whatever you say, Burdett."

Samille glanced at her wristwatch. "As much as I'd love to stay and play catch-up with you gentlemen, I'm due in court this afternoon and I need to finish preparing my testimony. Agent Kincaid, I'll be in touch."

He inclined his head in silent acknowledgment. He and Jack stood watching as she walked away, her hips rolling in an easy swagger that was purely feminine and unconsciously sexy.

Jack shook his head after her, a tiny smile playing at the corners of his lips. "She's really something. For a woman who hates wearing skirts, she sure knows how to wear the heck outta them."

"No argument there." Amused, Brant studied his companion's face. It was clear that Jack Burdett, who'd always struck Brant as such a tough guy, was completely taken with Samille Broussard. Brant wondered if she even knew, or if she returned Burdett's feelings.

Not that he cared, he reminded himself.

But an hour after he'd returned to the Washington, D.C. FBI field office, Samille Broussard was still on his mind.

CHAPTER 3

Samille crawled out of bed at six a.m. the next day and threw on a pair of black leggings and a gray sweatshirt. She drained a bottled water and did some stretching exercises before heading outdoors for her daily four-mile run.

Samille lived in Dupont Circle, the trendy Washington, D.C., neighborhood that was home to young urbanites and affluent empty-nesters who'd grown tired of commuting from Maryland suburbs. Many of Samille's neighbors worked on Capitol Hill or in downtown law firms and lobbyist offices. The community offered a vibrant blend of coffeehouses, bookstores, clubs, restaurants, and theaters—which had appealed to Samille immensely when she first started shopping for apartments two years ago. The neighborhood featured charming brownstones that were broken into apartments with tiny balconies and rear gardens. Samille's condo was located on the third floor of an end unit.

Daylight saving time had kicked in three weeks ago, so it was already light by the time she stepped outside. It was a balmy November morning, perfect for working up a nice lather. Fall had arrived in a brilliant profusion of orange, red, and gold leaves in the giant oaks lining the street. The rubber soles of her Nikes slapped the pavement lightly as she jogged past another early-morning runner and a young woman walking her dog.

As Samille ran, her thoughts drifted to the day ahead and, invariably, Brant Kincaid. She hadn't been able to get him off her mind since yesterday. In the middle of watching *Jeopardy!* last night, a pair of piercing dark eyes had penetrated her brain. And his face, oh, that face . . . Her pulse had skipped as if the man himself stood before her. Frustrated, she'd snatched a pillow and buried her face in it as if she could somehow erase Brant Kincaid's image. To no avail.

It was so unlike her to obsess over a man. She could count on one hand the number of serious relationships she'd had—and still have a few fingers to spare. It wasn't that she lacked opportunities to cultivate her love life, although the long hours she worked certainly didn't help. The truth was that she had no inclination to waste her time and energy on dead-end relationships. The men she'd dated in the past, while smart and successful enough, failed to interest her on any meaningful level. Very few of them understood her passion for her work; one or two had even suggested that she was too smart to toil away at "some government job." She'd had little in common with any of them, and the high-security nature of her position prevented her from sharing details about her various cases.

Over the years Samille had grown content with her single status and, like many of her female contemporaries, had focused on her career. She wanted to get a doctorate in forensic science and was interested in becoming a forensic chemist, either with the DEA or at the prestigious FBI Laboratory. Even a loyalist like Samille could concede that the Bureau's forensic technology capabilities were more advanced than the DEA's.

At the reminder of the FBI, she groaned audibly. Her attraction to Brant Kincaid presented a maddening dilemma. She'd been assigned the Georgetown case as a result of her professionalism and expertise, but neither would benefit her if she could scarcely concentrate on the investigation.

The men she worked with put her at ease and made her feel like "one of the boys." Against administration policy, they allowed her to accompany them on drug raids and stopped just short of letting her make arrests. She was as comfortable around them as she was around her cousins, Nate and Jared. But being around Brant Kincaid was an entirely different story. He made her feel desirable, incredibly feminine in a way she couldn't begin to comprehend. She was aware of her own sexuality as she'd never been before.

She didn't like it one bit.

As Samille neared her block, she noticed an unfamiliar black Ford Expedition with U.S. government tags parked across the street from her brownstone. As if conjured by her imagination, Brant Kincaid stepped from the truck and closed the door. He was impeccably tailored in another dark suit, his black wing tips polished to a high gleam. His eyes were concealed behind the mirrored aviator sunglasses he'd worn the first time she saw him at the academy.

Samille's throat went dry as he crossed the street with those relaxed, powerful strides. She slowed down as he approached. He stopped in front of her, towering over her, and she ran a hand self-consciously over her ponytail. She knew she must look a sweaty mess. She hoped to God she didn't smell, too.

Resentment stirred within her almost at once. This was exactly what she meant. If it had been Jack Burdett or any other man, she wouldn't have cared one iota what she looked *or* smelled like.

"You're early, aren't you? We're not due at the school until ten."

"I wanted to beat traffic." Brant extended a paper bag bearing the name of la Madeleine, an upscale French bakery and café known for its exotic pastries and baked goods. "I brought you breakfast."

Samille arched an eyebrow as she hesitantly accepted the bag. "A peace offering?"

His mouth twitched. "I didn't know we were at war. Just because I disagree with your role in the investigation doesn't mean I won't cooperate."

"How magnanimous of you."

Brant laid a hand upon her arm, halting her steps before she could walk away. She felt the warmth of his palm clear through her sweatshirt.

Slowly he removed his sunglasses, pinning her with those dark, fathomless eyes. Samille almost wished he'd put the shades back on. "Perhaps the more pressing question is: do *you* have a problem working with me?" he asked softly.

"Of course not. Who in their right mind would have a problem working with Special Agent Brant Kincaid? You're the best of the best! Not only do you have a proven track record of catching the bad guys, but you can also shoot a moving target from a thousand yards without breaking a sweat, giving you the enviable distinction of being one of the most skilled snipers at the FBI and DEA combined. You've garnered more commendations and merits of honor than agents *twice* your age. You have a genius IQ and a doctorate in one of the most challenging fields of study. I don't know whether to address you as Dr. Kincaid or Super Agent!"

For the first time since she'd met him, Brant Kincaid

seemed at a loss for words. He stared at her, dumb-founded, until heat stung her cheeks.

"I did some research," she grumbled sheepishly.

Humor tugged at the corners of his mouth. "I don't know whether to be impressed or alarmed."

"Be impressed. I need all the advantages I can get."

He chuckled and slid his hand forward. "Let's start over. Brant Kincaid, nice to meet you."

Samille hesitated, eyeing his proffered hand. Oh no. Not another handshake. Her nerve endings couldn't take any more electrical charges.

She clutched the la Madeleine bag in both hands, buying time. "Thanks for breakfast. Whatever it is, it smells great."

"You're welcome." He looked pointedly at his out-stretched hand. "Gonna leave me hanging?"

Samille huffed out a sigh to mask her nervousness as she accepted his hand. She forced herself to ignore the now-familiar tremors that rippled through her body at his touch. "Samille Broussard. Nice to meet you."

Brant held on a little longer than necessary. Samille gave her hand a discreet tug, and after another moment he released her. His expression was contemplative. "Why do you let them call you Sammy?"

She frowned. "What do you mean? It's a nickname. Everyone calls me that."

He shook his head slowly. "Not me. I'm going to call you Samille. It's a beautiful name; it shouldn't be wasted."

Her name rolled off his tongue beautifully. It was that smooth, dark voice of his. Like black magic.

She shrugged. "Suit yourself. Doesn't matter to me. We'd better go inside before this food gets cold." She started up the brick steps to her brownstone.

Brant followed her into the well-maintained old build-ing. He tried not to admire the outline of her bottom and shapely legs covered in black spandex, but it was next to impossible. She was in excellent physical shape, which invariably led him to speculate about the kind of stamina she would possess between the sheets. *Not* that he would ever find out. As a rule he didn't believe in mixing business with pleasure, and something warned him that getting involved with Samille Broussard spelled a recipe for disaster.

Not that she'd given him any reason to think he had a chance with her. On the contrary. Since their introduction, Samille had treated him with barely restrained hostility. He'd half expected her to send him packing for showing up two hours early with a lame excuse about beating traffic. *Traffic. Yeah, right.* The truth was that he'd awakened that morning still thinking about her, and it became imperative to see her as quickly as possible. In uncharacteristic fashion he didn't try to analyze or resist the overwhelming compulsion—he just went with it.

On the third landing, Samille unlocked the front door and gestured Brant inside. He brushed past her and walked into a small, neatly furnished living room. The walls were painted a rich color that reminded him of maple sugar. The furniture consisted of a camel chenille sofa loaded with multicolored throw pillows, a wing chair, a glass coffee table, and a large cherry-wood bookcase shoved against one wall and crammed with books. A couple of olive throw rugs littered the golden hardwood floors. A pair of French doors opened onto a little balcony overlooking a vibrant square of garden.

"Welcome to my humble abode," Samille announced.

Brant dipped his hands into his pants pockets as he looked around. "It's nice," he said sincerely.

"Thanks." Samille locked the door behind him and crossed the open space to the adjoining kitchen. It was a utilitarian room that offered a long breakfast counter to compensate for the lack of kitchen space. "Do you want some coffee? I can make a pot of instant if you like, although I must warn you that I almost *never* make my own coffee. I live near too many coffeehouses that do a much better job."

Brant chuckled. "I'll consider myself forewarned."

As Samille busied herself in the kitchen, he wandered over to the bookcase to examine the titles. Her reading collection encompassed everything from nineteenth-century literature to science fiction to tomes covering such topics as advanced drug analysis, criminal procedure, and forensic psychiatry. Not unlike his own library at home. He thought about the conversations he and Samille Broussard could have, and didn't know whether to be pleased or slightly mortified.

"How do you take your coffee?" Samille asked through the alcove.

"Black, one sugar." He lifted his head from thumbing through a volume that provided guidelines on giving expert testimony in forensic science. "So you graduated from Virginia Commonwealth?"

"Yes. How'd you know?" He inclined his head toward her sweatshirt, and she glanced down at herself with an embarrassed half laugh. The sound was incredibly appealing, soft and deep-throated like her voice. "I received my master's in forensic science from VCU. Got my undergrad in chemistry from Stanford."

"Very impressive." Brant reshelved the book and started across the room toward her. "What made you return to the East Coast?"

"Don't laugh."

"Scout's honor."

Those dark gypsy eyes narrowed suspiciously on his face. "Were you really a Boy Scout?"

"Yes." He paused. "Must have been in a past life

though. The first time I ever went camping, I instinctively knew how to build a campfire."

He could see her resisting the tug of a grin as she arranged their smoked ham croissant sandwiches on plastic plates. "The reason I moved back East is that I missed my family. They live in Maryland."

"What's funny about you missing them?"

"Well, you know . . . it just seems a bit childish. Like I couldn't handle being away for four measly years."

"I don't think it's childish at all." He smiled ruefully. "I don't know whether or not you uncovered this in your research into my background, but one of the reasons I attended Syracuse University was to remain as close as possible to my family. I'm originally from Brooklyn."

Samille looked sheepish. "Um, yeah, I did learn that you're from Brooklyn. Flatbush, specifically. And I could detect the accent in your voice." She carried their plates and steaming mugs of coffee to the breakfast counter. She glanced down at herself and wrinkled her nose prettily. "I should probably hop into the shower first. You can go ahead and eat without me."

"I don't want to eat alone."

"But I—"

"Samille. Join me."

The quiet authority in his voice halted her protests. She left the kitchen and rounded the corner to join him in the cozy breakfast nook. He waited until she claimed one of the cushioned bar stools before seating himself next to her. When their knees accidentally brushed, Brant was jarred by a lightning bolt of lust that shot through his groin. If Samille felt anything, she didn't show it. She ducked her head and became absorbed in her sandwich. Brant followed her lead, and they ate for a few minutes in companionable, if not a bit awkward, silence.

"What made you finally leave your parents in New York?" Samille asked.

"The Bureau. I got transferred from the New York field office after two years. How long have you been with the DEA?"

"Six years and counting. I got recruited through a criminal justice internship program at VCU while I was earning my master's."

"Have you always been interested in law enforcement?"

"I think I must have been, on some unconscious level. And not just because I always wanted to be the good guy when my cousins and I played cops and robbers. I've always been interested in criminal procedure, learning how the law works and the ways in which the system fails. There are so many intricacies—it's not always as black and white as people think."

"I agree." Brant studied her profile. Her cheeks were still flushed from her morning run. An errant strand of black hair had escaped from the ponytail to tease her earlobe. He resisted the sudden urge to reach out and wrap the silken strand around his finger.

"Why didn't you become a special agent for the DEA?" he asked, as much to distract himself as to learn more about her.

"I enjoy the investigative aspects of my job. Sure, there's a lot of regulatory work involved—evaluating record-keeping procedures for compliance, auditing, and implementing regulations. But the work can be challenging and rewarding. And the scientist in me enjoys learning about drug identification and chemical control." Her lips curved ruefully. "My family expected me to become a doctor."

"Expected or wanted?"

"A bit of both. They think working for the DEA is too

dangerous. They're worried that someone might recognize me from a drug bust and retaliate."

"And you don't share their concerns?"

"Not at all." She stopped and frowned, as if wondering why she had divulged so much to a complete stranger. She took a sip of coffee. "How many students were on the guest list?"

"Twenty. Blair's parents confirmed the count because the party was catered. It was his sixteenth birthday."

"Catered, huh? Whatever happened to chips and dip served with spiked punch?"

"Not for this crowd."

They exchanged ironic smiles. When Samille spoke again, her voice was almost shy. "You probably don't remember this, but I saw you at the academy six months ago. What were you doing there? I mean, you've been with the Bureau for eleven years. Surely *you* don't need additional training?"

"Sure I do. Agents are always encouraged to keep their skills sharp. But six months ago I was there instructing a firearms course."

Samille nodded. She didn't know whether to be relieved or disappointed that Brant didn't remember her. She'd been so affected by that encounter that she had dug into his background as voraciously as Alex Haley had researched his roots.

She stood and carried their empty plates into the kitchen. "Thanks again for breakfast. Those croissants were absolutely delicious. Sorry that the coffee was a bit on the watery side, but you can't say I didn't warn you." She realized she was rambling and promptly shut her mouth. She dumped the disposable plates into the trash bin beneath the sink and rinsed her hands. "I'm going to take a shower. I'll be ready in fifteen minutes."

"Samille."

She froze on her way out of the kitchen. Would she *ever* get used to the low, sexy timbre of the man's voice?

Reluctantly she turned around to face him. His dark eyes were hooded as he watched her intently. "You were wearing black shorts and a white DEA T-shirt—standard attire at the academy—but your shorts were a bit baggy because you had to borrow them from a classmate. Your hair was in a ponytail and you wore one of those scrunchies— a purple one."

Samille gaped at him in shocked silence. "You . . . you remember that? You noticed?"

His lips curved in a slow, lazy grin. "I'm an investigator. I make it my business to notice everything. Especially beautiful women who can do fifty push-ups in under a minute without breaking a sweat."

Samille grinned, undeniably pleased by his words and the fact that he'd remembered her. She lifted her arm and flexed a muscle, and Brant threw back his head and roared with deep male laughter as she sauntered to her bedroom.

St. Anthony's Preparatory School was an exclusive coed institution located in southwest D.C. The entire campus stretched the length of three city blocks, and the stately old buildings boasted architecture to rival any Ivy League university. The admission requirements were just as stringent. Only four hundred students were enrolled in the school, which ranged from ninth to twelfth grade.

Upon their arrival at the gate, Brant and Samille were directed to the main administration building and instructed to wait for the headmistress. The interior of the building was every bit as grand as the exterior, with antique furnishings, pristine walls, and vaulted ceilings that arched above gleaming parquet floors. Gilt-framed

canvas oil paintings paid homage to the school's found-
ing fathers, venerated Catholic saints with austere expressions and dark, reproving eyes that seemed to move
within their sockets.

Samille suppressed a mild shudder and glanced around
to find Brant watching her with an amused expression.
She shot him a dirty look and was rewarded with a soft
chuckle.

A door to their right opened and a tall, rail-thin woman
stepped from an office. Her brown hair was pulled back
from her face in a chignon so tight that her features appeared pinched. She wore a high-necked silk blouse and
a long black skirt over flat, sensible shoes. She moved with
a regal stiffness born of breeding and rigorous instruction.
Samille could just imagine the woman as a solemn schoolgirl, balancing textbooks on her head as she practiced
proper comportment.

"Special Agent Kincaid, Ms. Broussard, thank you for
coming," Headmistress Adelaide Hambleton greeted
them in clipped tones. "I apologize for keeping you waiting. I was on the phone with a concerned parent who
wanted to know if the police have made any progress in
the investigation of who drugged those poor students.
We've been receiving similar calls all week, from parents
and the media."

"I can only imagine," Samille murmured, falling in
step with the woman's brisk strides as they left the main
building and started across campus.

"Nothing like this has ever happened at St. Anthony's," Hambleton continued. "We pride ourselves on
the excellence of our academic curriculum as well as the
moral instruction we provide to our students. To think
that one of them may have . . ." She trailed off and gave
a delicate shudder.

She led them across a manicured lawn to the school's

chapel, a redbrick cathedral as magnificent as its surrounding buildings. "This is where we hold assemblies,"
Hambleton informed Brant and Samille as they followed
her through high arched double doors. "The students
have already been gathered."

The interior of the sanctuary didn't disappoint. The
stucco walls were elaborately gilded, covered with ornate
plaster statues and flowers. The vaulted ceiling was completely inset with paintings displaying crowned figures
and cherubs, biblical scenes captured in timeless reverence. A row of granite marble columns marched alongside the aisles. The morning sun sent flinty shafts of light
through the stained-glass windows.

The students were arranged in pews with uniform precision. All wore stark white shirts, the boys in pressed navy
trousers and the girls in plaid skirts. Some were whisper-
ing to one another, giggling and swapping notes. But the
moment they spied their headmistress, all activity ceased.
A hushed silence descended upon the sanctuary. Adelaide
Hambleton walked to the front of the altar, introduced
Samille, and briefly explained the purpose of her visit.

Samille stepped to the podium and found herself staring into a sea of inquisitive young faces. With the exception of a few minorities, St. Anthony's student body was
predominantly white. They were the sons and daughters
of politicians, diplomats and ambassadors, and prominent
businessmen. Some of them were driven to school in
chauffeured limousines. Many had trust funds worth more
than the average person earned in a lifetime.

And none of that mattered. They were as susceptible
to crime and the lure of illegal drugs as their inner-city
counterparts.

That was how she began her presentation. She didn't
merely recite the alarming statistics of teen substance
abusers. She didn't stop at discussing the dangers of

experimenting with drugs. She spoke to those teenagers about how substance use could affect *their* lives,
could destroy *their* futures.

From his inconspicuous position in the back of the
sanctuary, Brant watched Samille deliver her presentation. She appeared remarkably relaxed and confident
for a woman addressing a chapel full of rich kids. She
was knowledgeable and passionate about her subject.
Brant marveled that she managed to convey the dangerous consequences of illegal substance abuse without
seeming preachy. As he scanned faces in the audience,
it seemed that the majority of students were actually *listening* to her. It didn't hurt that Samille looked closer to
their age than most, if not all, of their instructors. Wearing little makeup and her hair pulled back into a ponytail, Samille could easily have passed for a college senior.
She wore a cream cashmere pullover, pleated khaki
trousers, and chocolate-brown leather boots with spiked
heels that looked downright lethal.

Samille was concluding her speech. "The bottom line
is that what happened to your classmates could happen
to any one of you if you're willing to experiment with
drugs. We want you to make smart, safe choices. I encourage you to come forward with anything you know
about what happened on Friday night. If you know of
someone who may have provided drugs at the party, talk
to an adult—whether it's a parent, a teacher, or the
police. We want to make sure this doesn't happen again,
but *you* have to help us."

Afterward, several students approached her. Some
wanted to know whether Hollywood's portrayals of drug
busts were realistic. Others had questions about career
opportunities with the DEA and whether Samille's job
required her to carry a weapon. A few older girls complimented her boots.

Just when Samille began to wonder whether she'd gotten through to them at all, a slim girl with dyed black hair walked over.

"Hello," Samille greeted her, bracing herself for another question about her shooting skills—or lack thereof. "What's your name?"

"Jillian Carrella," the girl mumbled. She glanced around nervously as if to make sure that none of her classmates were within earshot. Her short fingernails were polished black and a row of silver studs marched along one of her ears. Samille could only imagine how many demerits Jillian received for violating the school dress code.

"What can I do for you, Jillian?" Samille asked.

"I need to speak with you. In private."

"Of course." Samille looked up and made eye contact with Brant. They had agreed that he would remain out of sight until the end of her presentation. Even without the hefty FBI credentials, Brant Kincaid could be intimidating. His imposing physical presence had undoubtedly caused more than a few grown men to quake in their boots, let alone the effect he could have on a roomful of teenagers and adolescents.

When their eyes met, Samille gave a subtle nod. As Brant made his way up the aisle, she returned her attention to Jillian. "Would you like to step into one of the back offices? Ms. Hambleton gave us permission to use it if necessary."

Jillian hesitated, her dark eyes darting around the noisy sanctuary. Teachers were lining up the students and preparing to usher them back to their classrooms. Adelaide Hambleton was confiscating a Nintendo Gameboy from a sullen student.

Jillian turned back to Samille. "Okay."

Samille smiled at her as Brant approached. "You don't mind if Special Agent Kincaid joins us, do you?"

The girl eyed Brant warily. "Special Agent? As in FBI?"

"That's right, Jillian," Samille answered smoothly. "Don't worry. We just want to ask you a few questions, and then you can return to class."

Once again Jillian hesitated, silently assessing Brant through eyes heavy with mascara and black liner. She bore a striking resemblance to Ozzy Osbourne's misfit daughter, Kelly—albeit a slimmer, more tamed version.

Brant's mouth twitched. "I won't bite, Jillian. You have my word."

She shrugged, fighting a grin. "No rush. I don't mind missing religion class, anyway."

She led the way past the altar to a door leading to the rear offices, which were used by the school chaplain and his administrative staff. Halfway down the narrow corridor, they came upon a large unoccupied room filled with cardboard storage boxes. Positioned in the center of the room was an old wooden table flanked by four metal chairs. A small window overlooked the church courtyard where two students sat on a stone bench reading the Bible.

Brant pulled out a chair for Samille and Jillian before seating himself at the end of the table. Samille knew it was no accident that he positioned Jillian between them. Seated beside the girl, Samille could serve as the comforting confidante while Brant, at the head of the table, was the unmistakable authority figure.

"What would you like to share with us, Jillian?" Samille asked as gently as possible. The girl looked like a skittish mare ready to bolt at the least provocation.

"I'm not even sure I should be talking to you guys," Jillian mumbled. "I'm not trying to get anyone in trouble."

"Were you at the party on Friday night?" Brant asked.

"No." She made a face. "Matthew Blair only invites privvies to his parties."

"Privvies?"

"That's what we call the privileged kids."

Samille arched an eyebrow. At a prep school like St. Anthony's, wasn't *everyone* privileged?

As if reading her mind, Jillian explained, "If your family isn't related to any dead presidents or doesn't have blue blood running through the lineage, then you're not a privvie. You're nouveau riche. New money."

"I see." Samille and Brant exchanged faintly amused looks.

"I know. I think it's pretty stupid, too." Jillian gave a dismissive shrug. "But such is life in the hallowed halls of St. Anthony's."

"So you weren't invited to the big birthday bash." Brant folded his hands on the table and leaned forward. "Do you know who brought drugs to the party?"

Jillian swallowed nervously as she stared at him. "His name is Jefferson Spangler."

"Spangler?" The name struck Samille as familiar. Almost at once she knew why. "You mean Senator Ashton Spangler's son?"

"Yeah."

"How do you know Jefferson provided drugs at the party?" Brant asked.

Jillian stared down at her hands in her lap. "I just know."

"Jillian." Samille spoke gently but firmly. "Now is not the time to keep secrets. We need to know everything or we can't help."

"I don't want to get in trouble. My dad is pretty strict."

"I doubt that your father would have a problem with you helping us in our investigation."

"Not that," Jillian mumbled. She looked up at Brant worriedly. "My dad's a big-time criminal lawyer. I don't want to incriminate myself by telling you how I know it was Jefferson."

"Let me guess," Brant drawled. "Jefferson Spangler sold you drugs once or twice before. What was it? Marijuana?"

Jillian's eyes widened. "H-how'd you—"

"Educated guess. So Jefferson is the school supplier."

"Not really. He only sells marijuana to a small group of kids, mostly his friends. He knows they won't rat him out. The only reason he gave me any is that I caught him one afternoon after he'd just finished a sale in the parking lot. He told me that if I promised not to tell, he'd give me a freebie." Hot color suffused her cheeks. "I was curious. I wanted to know what the big deal was, why everyone was always talking about pot like it was the greatest thing since shopping malls."

"And was it?" Samille asked gently.

Jillian hesitated, then shook her head with a sheepish expression. "I got high while my dad wasn't home. It was pretty scary—I actually thought I was gonna die. After that I swore I'd never experiment with drugs again, and I haven't. Swear to God."

"I believe you, Jillian," Samille said mildly. "Do you know if Jefferson is in school today?"

"He's not. He's been out all week."

Brant and Samille exchanged glances. "Do you know if Jefferson ever sold anything other than marijuana?" Brant asked.

"I don't think so. He told me he didn't want to get into the hard stuff like coke and heroin. I think he was a little scared himself, although he'd never admit it. He likes to pretend he's so cool, but deep down inside he's nothing more than a geek."

"What do you mean?" Samille asked with an indulgent smile.

"Well, he's one of the smartest kids in school." Jillian ticked off his accomplishments on her fingers. "He's president of the math club and debate team. He wins every year at the national science fair and is a wiz at computers—he met Bill Gates once at a trade show and spent the next summer as an intern at Microsoft. I heard he's already been accepted into Harvard, Yale, *and* Princeton."

"Impressive." Samille marveled that such a bright, promising boy would be stupid enough to compromise his future by selling drugs. But then again, kids like Jefferson Spangler considered themselves untouchable. The thought of being arrested and sent to prison would never occur to him. He was above the law.

"You don't think he might have brought something stronger to the party?" Brant prodded. "To impress his friends?"

"It's possible," Jillian agreed, "but Jefferson doesn't need to impress anyone. He's Ashton Spangler's son. Everyone thinks his father is going to be the next president."

Brant looked vaguely amused. "So how do we know you're on the level with us, Jillian? How do we know you're not simply out to get one of the privvies?"

Jillian blushed furiously, and Samille sent Brant a sharp look. She didn't know a lot about interrogation procedure, but somehow she didn't think alienating a key witness ranked high on the list of do's.

But then Jillian spoke. "Maybe I am. Maybe I'm tired of watching kids like Jefferson Spangler get all the breaks just because their families have been rich a lot longer. Maybe I'm tired of being teased by Jefferson and his friends because I'm Italian American and they think my dad works for the Mafia. Just for the record," she added vehemently, "my dad has *never* defended any mobster. He is one hundred percent against organized crime. He earned his millions legitimately, every last red cent."

"Easy, kiddo." Chuckling, Brant held up his hands in

mock surrender. "I'm not accusing you—or your father—of any wrongdoing. I just wanted to check your motives."

"As much as I hate Jefferson and his friends, I have no reason to lie to you. God knows it's not because I feel sorry for those kids in the hospital. None of them ever did anything for me. I sit next to Caitlin Childress in trigonometry every day, and she's never spoken three words to me. Oh, wait—that's not true. There *was* the time she told me she liked my black nail polish, right before she turned to her friends and burst out laughing."

When Jillian's tirade was met with sympathetic silence, she sighed impatiently. "Look, I'm not trying to portray myself as the proverbial outcast, the loner rebel who dyes her hair black and wears goth makeup to mask her pain and loneliness. I'm actually pretty well adjusted. I have a ton of friends who go to other schools in the area. My biggest gripe in life is that my dad works too many long hours, and he and my mom hate each other's guts and haven't spoken in years. But I've even managed to use *that* to my advantage. Dad buys me a lot of 'guilt gifts' to make up for not being around, and my mom lets me travel around the world with her during the summer—she's a photojournalist for *National Geographic*. Technically she's not supposed to bring her kid on assignments, but Mom says it's the only chance we get to spend quality time together. I think she feels guilty for not fighting harder to keep custody of me.

"Anyway, the point is that I'm not trying to get back at anyone by coming forward about Jefferson." Jillian turned an earnest gaze on Samille. "What you said earlier made a lot of sense to me. What happened on Friday night could easily have happened to any one of us. It could have happened to me that time I smoked pot! Like I said, I thought I was going to die. That could have been *me* lying in a hospital bed because I was dumb enough to experiment with drugs. So if you're still wondering about my motive, Agent Kincaid, there it is. I may not like most of the dopes at this stuffy school, but I don't think anyone deserves to OD on drugs."

Brant nodded slowly. "I appreciate your honesty, Jillian."

"So do I," Samille concurred. "What you've done today takes a lot of courage. I commend you."

Jillian shook off the compliment, but Samille could tell she was pleased. "Just doing my civic duty."

"And speaking of duty," Samille drawled, "how do you get away with all the earrings and makeup?"

Jillian grinned. "My dad worked a provision into the school policy. Since the administration allows the foreign students to express *their* culture through makeup and jewelry, my dad argued that everyone should be allowed to express their individuality—within reason, of course. Somehow he convinced them that they would be violating my civil rights if they prohibited me from wearing the kind of makeup I like. So the school agreed to a compromise: two days a week the female students can wear makeup and earrings. It's not much, but I'll take it."

Brant shook his head in wry amusement. "Pays to have a lawyer for a father, doesn't it?"

"In more ways than one," Jillian agreed.

Samille glanced at her watch. "We don't want to keep you much longer. We'll be in touch if we need any more information. And you can call me if you think of anything else." She passed one of her cards to Jillian.

Jillian studied the simple white card as they rose from the table. "A diversion investigator, huh? Do you carry a gun?"

Samille rolled her eyes and pretended to miss the amused glint in Brant's dark eyes. His cell phone rang and he excused himself to take the call in the corridor.

The moment he was out of the room, Jillian grinned

at Samille. "He is *super* cute. You're so lucky to be working with him."

Samille grunted something unintelligible and sent Jillian Carrella on her way before returning to the empty sanctuary to wait for Brant. She sat in the front row of pews and looked up at the soaring arched ceiling of the chapel, to the intricate and towering glass mosaic window of Jesus with a lamb in his arms. She stared at the ornately carved crucifix, Christ gazing down at the high altar from his exalted place on the cross.

She remembered being a devastated nine-year-old staring at a similar statue in a different chapel, wondering how she would ever step foot in another church without reliving the anguish of seeing her parents lying in twin coffins at the altar. They had looked as if they could open their eyes and speak her name at any moment—except she knew that they never would.

"Samille."

Startled, she looked around to see Brant standing less than three feet from her. He said nothing, his hands shoved deep into his pants pockets as he watched her with a quiet, probing intensity. She wondered how long he'd been standing there, what conclusions he'd formed about her strange, distracted state.

She got swiftly to her feet. "I was waiting for you."

He took a step toward her. "Are you all right?"

She balked at the gentle concern in his voice. "Of course. Who was on the phone?"

"The lab." His expression turned grim. "They have more information about the second substance found in the students. I told them we'd be right over."

Something cold and ominous slithered down Samille's spine. She and Brant headed quickly out of the chapel.

CHAPTER 4

Largo, Maryland
DEA Laboratory

An hour later, they had the answer they needed. And it wasn't good.

According to the forensic chemist they met at the DEA laboratory, the second substance found in the victims' bodies was identified as a rare structural analog similar to methylenedioxymethamphetamine, or MDMA. It was so rare, in fact, that not one chemist in the DEA laboratory had ever seen the drug before. It had been manufactured in such a way as to make the oxycodone the only traceable compound in the bloodstream.

"It's a complex, highly sophisticated drug," explained the bespectacled forensic chemist. "Whoever manufactured it knew exactly what he or she was doing."

Samille and Brant exchanged wary glances. The fact that someone had deliberately gone out of their way to produce such an insidious chemical substance suggested premeditation and sinister intent. The perpetrator was not merely creating new drugs for distribution and profit on the underground market. It appeared that these victims had been specifically targeted, and the outcome of their gamble could very well cost them their lives.

The case had officially become a criminal investigation.

"This is so frustrating," Samille blurted as she and Brant waited for the elevator after leaving the lab. "The presence of oxycodone in this substance doesn't give us much to go on. Since OxyContin is a legal drug, it's supplied across the country for legitimate medical purposes. Nowadays just about *anyone* can get their hands on it. And given the increase in OxyContin abuse, it seems that everyone *is* getting their hands on it. Anyway, the Oxy isn't what put those kids in the hospital."

"You've never encountered anything like this in one of your cases?"

"Definitely not in one of my cases. Maybe it was something I once read or came across in my studies." She frowned and shook her head as if to dislodge a memory, a fragment of information that eluded her.

Brant waited, his gaze sharp on her face.

Finally she shook her head again. "The bottom line is that this compound could have originated anywhere. Trying to locate its manufacturer may prove to be like searching for a needle in a haystack. New drugs are created all the time, and not just from the underground market. Sometimes kids get their hands on their parents' prescriptions, and all it takes is a little imagination and a home chemistry kit and—*voila*! You're looking at New Drug XYZ. If we had a prescription bottle with a label, we could easily trace the drug's origin. If we had *one* measly tablet, which are uniquely marked in accordance with DEA regulations, we'd have something to work with. As it is now, we've got nada. Zilch. Zippo." She scowled up at the electronic panel above the elevator. "What's taking this darned thing so long?"

With a low chuckle, Brant reached out and pressed the button. "Guess it would help if we did this."

Samille grinned in spite of herself. They'd been so engrossed in their discussion, and she in her tirade, that they'd forgotten to summon the elevator. "What's our next move? Shouldn't we be questioning Jefferson Spangler?"

"I plan to. Alone."

Samille gaped at him. "*Excuse* me?"

The elevator arrived on their floor with a discreet chime. Samille was so distracted that she hardly noticed as Brant gently commandeered her inside. She was too incensed to acknowledge the warmth of his hand on her back or his clean, masculine scent—soap and the subtle spice of an expensive cologne.

Brant trained his eyes to the floor as the metal doors closed. His tone was flat. "You heard me. I'm questioning Spangler alone."

"Why?" Samille demanded with rising ire. "We interviewed Jillian Carrella together and it worked out well. Why can't we *both* talk to Jefferson Spangler?"

"There's a big difference between questioning a voluntary witness and interrogating a potential suspect. No offense, Samille, but we both know you lack the training for the latter. I saw the look you gave me when I asked Jillian about her motives, something that's entirely routine in the course of taking statements from witnesses."

"So I was a little surprised," she grudgingly conceded. "That doesn't mean I'm ill-prepared to assist you in an interrogation. And might I remind you that it was *my* idea to give the presentation at the school? If not for that, we may not have gotten any leads!"

"Point taken. But Senator Spangler isn't going to give anyone carte blanche to question his son. I'm betting that the kid has tighter security around him than Fort Knox. As soon as this case broke, the good senator from

Louisiana probably contacted his team of attorneys to be ready in the event that his heir apparent came under suspicion. Even if he's clueless about his son's illegal activities, he's smart enough to know that everyone who attended the party and *isn't* lying in a coma will be considered a potential suspect."

Samille knew he was probably right. Still, it didn't make it any easier to accept a backseat role in the investigation.

The elevator doors opened to admit an attractive brown-skinned man Samille had met on a few occasions, but whose name she always had difficulty remembering. He smiled at her as he stepped into the elevator.

"Hey, Samille. How's it going?"

"Can't complain," she said easily. "Heading out for a late lunch?"

"You know it. Got tied up as usual. You know how impatient people get when their computers crash—you'd think the governor had declared a state of emergency. I can't tell you how many times I've responded to a frantic call, only to discover that the solution was as simple as rebooting the machine."

Samille chuckled. "What would we do without you IT guys?"

He grinned. "I hope we'll never have to find out. Speaking of lunch, have you—" He broke off abruptly as Brant shifted slightly and folded his arms across his chest. Both men's eyes met above Samille's head as they took each other's measure.

Samille, rummaging in her purse for her tube of cherry-flavored Chap Stick, missed the entire exchange. "Hmm? What were you saying, Xavier?"

"Um, nothing." The elevator arrived on the first floor and Xavier stepped off quickly. "See you around, Samille."

"Have a good lunch."

Samille and Brant left the building and walked to the parking lot. Brant watched out of the corner of his eye as Samille rubbed Chap Stick onto her lips. He never thought he'd envy lip balm as much as he did in that moment.

"Do you make a habit of that?" he asked softly.

"What?"

"Being totally oblivious of men hitting on you."

She frowned. "What are you talking about?"

His mouth curved ironically. "My point exactly." He helped her into his Expedition and closed the door.

As he backed out of the parking space, he noted the moistness of Samille's lips and wanted to kiss her so bad it was a physical ache. Yet another reason he couldn't work with Samille Broussard. He wanted her too much, and the wanting increased every time he looked at her, every time she breathed. He couldn't inhale without filling his lungs with deep, greedy gulps of her scent— a light, clean fragrance that hinted at soap and citrus, not the heavy, cloying perfume so many women preferred. She sat with her hands folded in her lap as she stared out the window, and he couldn't help noticing how beautiful her hands were. Long, tapered fingers and short, unpolished, oval-shaped nails. He liked the feel of them in his own hands, appreciated the contrasts in size and the silken texture of her skin against his own callused flesh.

Brant scowled at the direction of his thoughts. He had no business indulging a physical attraction to Samille Broussard. Their investigation had just taken on a sinister cast. They were facing the very real possibility that those teenagers had been deliberately targeted and poisoned. Locating the drug's origin was absolutely critical in order to prevent further distribution. Brant hesitated to use the word *epidemic*, but he understood the severe ramifications of this dangerous chemical compound entering the illicit drug market.

He had a job to do, and he couldn't afford any distractions. Samille Broussard was a distraction. She measured an off-the-chart ten on the Richter scale of distractions.

"I'm going to talk to some of Jillian Carrella's instructors," she informed him. "Just to make sure our witness doesn't have any major credibility issues."

"Good idea." Brant's cell phone rang. He dug it out of his breast pocket and clipped, "Kincaid."

"This is Detective Lopez. We have a body you might be interested in."

"Where?" The detective provided a southeast D.C. address. "I'll be right there."

Samille sent Brant a curious look as he hung up. "Who was that?"

His expression was grim. "D.C. police. There's been a homicide. That's all I know," he added before she could ask for more details. He glanced at the digital clock on the dashboard and swore softly. "I need to take you home first."

"Why?"

"You're not accompanying me to a crime scene, Samille."

"Don't be ridiculous. If the police called you, there's obviously a connection to our case. We're out here in Maryland—don't waste valuable time driving me all the way home."

He slanted her a sardonic look. "You made other arrangements to get there?"

"You know that's not what I meant." She turned halfway in her seat to face him. "Sooner or later you're going to have to accept the fact that we're partners in this investigation. If you don't want me to go inside with you—"

"I don't."

"Fine. I'll wait in the truck. Now let's go."

Accepting the wisdom of her argument, Brant swung a hard right at the next intersection and headed for the beltway. Samille marveled that he didn't cause an accident as he maneuvered through afternoon traffic at breakneck speed, weaving in and out of lanes with the skilled ease of a NASCAR driver.

In no time at all they arrived at a public housing complex in southeast D.C. The squat apartments were dilapidated beyond repair, and the cracked cement sidewalks were littered with everything from empty liquor bottles to used condoms. A cluster of mismatched furniture sat at the curb as evidence of a recent eviction. The narrow street was already choked with police cruisers and two ambulances. A few tenants hovered in shadowy doorways watching the drama unfold.

Brant parked in front of the last apartment building on the street and turned to Samille. "Are you sure you're going to be all right?"

"Of course." She bristled when he looked unconvinced. "Look, this isn't my first time in the projects, Brant. You don't have to treat me like some prima donna from the burbs. I think I can manage without your protection for a while—been doing it for twenty-nine years, believe it or not."

A flicker of annoyance darkened his features. "Miss Independent," he muttered.

Samille flashed a mocking smile. When he made a sudden move toward her, she nearly jumped out of her skin. His mouth twitched as he reached into the glove compartment and withdrew the latest edition of the *FBI Law Enforcement Bulletin.* He dropped the publication into her lap.

"What's this for?" she mumbled. She felt incredibly foolish for overreacting to his sudden proximity.

"Reading material while you wait. Keep the doors locked and stay put." He climbed out of the Expedition and slammed the door. Samille watched sullenly as he strode toward the building and was met by two D.C. police officers.

"Victim's on the second floor," the first officer informed Brant, jerking a thumb behind him. Brant thought the young man looked a little green around the gills.

The odor hit him even before he climbed the last step. The stench of violent death and decay was thick and suffocating, a rancid scent that invaded the nostrils and crawled down the throat. Brant had visited countless murder scenes before, some that were tame and rather ordinary, others that were downright grisly. Judging from the smell this time, he estimated that the victim had met his end at least a week ago.

At his appearance, the conversation between the uniformed officers in the dim hallway subsided. Their grudging expressions registered recognition of a fed. Brant nodded curtly to their mumbled greetings. They stepped aside for him to enter the apartment.

"Christ," he muttered under his breath. The place was a mess. Dirty clothes were strewn across a disreputable-looking plaid sofa. Food had crusted over on plastic plates that littered a bare floor. The smudged walls were badly in need of a paint job—several coats.

Members of the Crime Scene Unit were already there, dusting for fingerprints and photographing evidence. A few plainclothes detectives were deep in discussion in one corner of the room. All held cloths to their noses. There was no sign of Detective Lopez.

Brant's gaze zeroed in on the victim. He walked over and crouched down to get a better look. White male, thinning dark hair, early thirties. He lay crumpled over a desk in the corner of the room, an empty husk drained of life. The cause of death was a single gunshot wound to the back of the head, fired at point-blank range, no exit wound.

Detective Marc Lopez entered the apartment and made a beeline for Brant. He was medium height and trim, with short dark hair that curled tight to his head and a pockmarked complexion that kept him from being conventionally handsome.

"Agent Kincaid. Didn't think you'd get here that fast."

"Tell me about the vic," Brant said without preamble.

"His name's Andrew 'Ace' Cason. Small-time dealer, a bunch of priors. No known relatives, no ex-wife or girl-friend. Neighbors called the landlord two days ago to report a putrid odor coming from this unit. The land-lord didn't come to investigate right away—he figured bad smells were commonplace in a joint like this. But the tenants persisted, so he finally showed his face. He said he knew what had happened even before he let himself into the apartment. He knew Cason was a pusher and he'd seriously considered tossing the guy out on his ear, but Cason always paid his rent on time and hey—money talks. Anyway, he called us as soon as he dis-covered the body."

"You think Cason supplied the drugs to our George-town kids?"

Lopez nodded as he slipped on a pair of latex gloves. He reached inside his trench coat pocket and withdrew a plastic bag containing what appeared to be a daily planner. He opened the bag, carefully removed the small leather book, and flipped it open. He held it up for Brant's inspection. "Check out last Thursday's entry."

Brant's eyes fastened on the name scribbled in ink at nine p.m.

Jefferson Spangler.

Andrew Cason had scheduled a meeting with Jefferson Spangler last Thursday evening.

Brant looked sharply at the detective. "Where'd you find this?"

Lopez nodded toward the desk. "Bottom left-hand drawer. There was nothing else worth mentioning. A drawer full of old receipts, some pencil sketches—apparently our friend here was an aspiring artist in his spare time. We're taking everything down to the precinct to log as evidence."

Brant nodded grimly. "It's time to talk to the Spangler kid. This is the second time today his name has come up. One of his classmates ID'd him as the one who brought drugs to the party." Briefly Brant told the detective about Jillian Carrella and the results of the lab analysis.

Lopez whistled softly through his teeth. "You think the Spangler kid offed Cason to cover his tracks?"

"Either that, or someone wanted to make it look like Spangler did the job." Brant nodded toward the desk. "Did you find any product manuals or warranties for a computer?"

"No." Lopez frowned. "There's no computer."

"Odd, don't you think? It's a computer desk."

"So? The guy was a pusher, and from the looks of this dump, not a very successful one. Owning a PC probably wasn't a priority."

"Maybe. But I'd like to see those receipts to check out Cason's purchases."

"I'll get them for you."

Brant nodded briskly. "And get some uniforms out there to canvass the block, see if the neighbors noticed anyone unusual coming or going from this apartment."

"You don't think Spangler's our man?"

"I'm not ruling it out. But if the kid is our perp, he did

a sloppy job of covering his tracks, leaving a vital piece of incriminating evidence in the victim's possession."

"The daily planner." Lopez looked a little deflated. "Makes you wonder if it even belongs to Cason. Doesn't seem likely that a small-time scumbag would be organized enough to schedule his drug transactions, know what I mean?"

"It takes all types. A handwriting analysis will let us know."

A movement at the door caught his eye. He looked up to find Samille frozen in the entrance, her stare fixed on Andrew Cason's lifeless form. Her expression was an alarming mixture of shock and horrified revulsion. Slowly her eyes lifted to his, and in the second before she turned and bolted, Brant knew that the revulsion had won.

He swore savagely under his breath and started after her. The officers who'd greeted him earlier were still clustered around the doorway. He shot them a disgusted look.

"Hey, it's not our fault!" one officer retorted defensively. "She came in waving her DEA creds and said she was with you!"

Brant didn't bother with a response. He galloped down the stairs and through the doors. Samille barely made it to the side of the building before the violent nausea overtook her. She was bent over, puking her guts out, and all Brant wanted to do was throttle her.

He fought to rein in his temper as she straightened slowly, wiping her mouth with the back of her hand. He pulled a handkerchief from his pocket and passed it to her.

"Thanks," she mumbled, accepting the handkerchief. She refused to meet his eyes as she dabbed at her damp cheeks and forehead.

"Are you all right?" he demanded.

"I'm fine."

"Good." Brant grasped her upper arm and steered her unceremoniously to the truck. He helped her inside and slammed the door.

Detective Lopez met him halfway to the building. His expression was curious as he eyed Samille inside the Expedition. "Everything okay?"

"Fine," Brant answered tersely. "I'm going to take her home, and then the two of us can go talk to the Spangler kid."

Lopez nodded wordlessly as Brant spun on his heel and strode back to the Expedition.

Samille dug inside her purse for a pack of mints to rid her mouth of the taste of bile. She shook several into her palm and crammed them into her mouth. She was mortified beyond belief, and so furious with herself she wanted to scream. She'd made a colossal fool of herself by getting sick. Her display of weakness had only affirmed Brant's conviction that she couldn't handle a criminal investigation. Tonight had been her first test and she'd failed miserably.

Brant opened the door and slid behind the wheel. He didn't start the ignition right away. Instead he sat for a moment without looking at her. His profile was hard as granite. A solitary muscle ticked ominously in his jaw. Controlled fury rolled off his body like heat waves.

Samille swallowed with difficulty. "Brant, I—"

The steely edge of his voice cut her explanation short. "What the *hell* did you think you were doing?"

"I thought . . ." She licked her lips nervously. "I wanted to know if there was a connection to our case."

"I thought I told you to stay in the truck." He turned to her and she nearly recoiled from the lethal glitter in his coal-black eyes. "I'm having you pulled from the case."

"What?" Panic clutched painfully in her chest. "You can't do that!"

"Like hell I can't," he growled. He started the truck and veered around a parked police cruiser.

"Look, I know I shouldn't have gone inside—believe me, I knew it was a mistake the minute I stepped into the building. But that doesn't mean I should be taken off the case. Besides," she hastened to add, "it's not your call to make, Brant. We've already established that."

"What we've *established*, Ms. Broussard," he said, his tone low and forbidding, "is that you can't follow simple instructions. In case you've forgotten, *I'm* the primary in this investigation; therefore *I* call the shots."

"You can't pull me off the case."

"Think again. If I raise enough of an objection, you'll be off this case faster than you can blink. You said it yourself this morning: I'm *Super Agent* Brant Kincaid. If they have to choose between you or me on this case, who do you think will be shown the door?"

Samille opened her mouth with a heated retort, then snapped it shut. Denial was pointless. She knew he was right. Her role in the investigation was on a trial basis. Brant had years of experience and a proven track record. One word from him, and Alan Graham would yank her off the case and chalk it up to a bad experiment.

She swallowed her pride and tried a different tack—humility. "I'm sorry for going inside the apartment. I thought I could handle whatever I would encounter, but I was wrong. Next time I'll think twice."

"There won't be a next time."

"Brant, please. I *need* this case. It's not just about my career. There are other diversion investigators who might benefit from my role in the investigation. Please think about that. *Please.*"

He said nothing. The hard line of his mouth didn't relax and the dangerous glint in his eyes didn't abate.

They rode the rest of the way in taut silence. Samille's nerves were stretched perilously thin. Remnants of bile burned at the base of her throat. All she wanted to do was go home and bury her head beneath the pillow and forget about this horrific night. She couldn't shake the image of the dead man lying in his own blood and excrement. And the odor of decomposing flesh had been unspeakable. Her nostrils still burned.

When they arrived at her apartment building, Brant double-parked in the front. He climbed out of the truck and came around to open her door. "Give me your keys."

Samille eyed him belligerently. "Why?"

Instead of answering, he held out his hand. His stony expression brooked no argument.

Samille grudgingly dug out her house keys and handed them over. Before she could react, Brant leaned down and scooped her effortlessly into his arms. She was too stunned to protest as he carried her into the brownstone and up the stairs to her apartment. Never in her life had she been so acutely aware of being physically outmatched by another. Brant's arms were bands of steel around her, his chest a solid wall of pure, male strength. He carried her as if she weighed next to nothing. Even as her feminist sensibilities railed against being overpowered in such a manner, she found it oddly . . . appealing.

Brant unlocked the front door and entered the apartment. The waning rays of daylight slanted through the French doors, casting the living room in shadows. He ignored Samille's muffled sound of protest and strode toward the bedroom. He flipped on the light and carried her over to a four-poster bed. She glared up at him mutinously as he laid her down on the bed.

He wasn't prepared for the sheer femininity of

Samille's bedroom. It was like stepping into the heart of a woman. White satin sheets that stirred a man's imagination. Pale gossamer curtains, rich bamboo furnishings that gave the large, airy room an exotic feel. Canvas oil paintings framed in gold leaf vividly portrayed distant landscapes and people; one particular portrait above the bed drew Brant's eye and made him pause. An older black couple embraced under a scorching Caribbean sun, their glistening brown limbs entwined in a way that made it impossible to tell where one ended and the other began. The artist had captured the couple's passion without cheapening the image; the result was the most aesthetically erotic work of art Brant had ever seen. He wondered what Samille thought of when she looked at the painting.

His gaze shifted back to her face. She was clearly perturbed. "You know," she said haughtily, "you didn't have to carry me inside my own apartment. I'm not an invalid."

Brant felt his own anger return. "You were ill. You looked like you needed some assistance."

Her eyes flashed with temper. "Oh, don't give me that! This was nothing more than your way of reminding me who's in charge, who's bigger and stronger. This was about putting me in my place, Brant Kincaid, and nothing else!"

"Whatever you say." He tossed her keys onto the bed, turned, and started from the room. Samille scrambled off the bed and hurried after him.

"Wait a minute!" she called, the barest thread of desperation in her voice. "We're not finished yet. I want to make sure you're not going to—"

Brant stopped and turned so abruptly that she ran into him. His arms came out to steady her as she stumbled and nearly lost her balance. Flustered, she mumbled a sheepish apology and cast her eyes downward.

Slowly, deliberately, Brant set her away from him. His nerve endings had gone haywire from the brief contact with her warm, supple body. The woman was driving him crazy, and in more ways than one. He had to get out of there before he succumbed to the fierce temptation to carry her back into the bedroom and devour her on those white satin sheets.

Her expression was imploring. She said softly, "I'm asking you not to have me removed from the case. Please reconsider, Brant."

He clenched his jaw in frustration. He knew how difficult it must be for a proud woman like Samille Broussard to make such a request. He knew she'd sooner crawl through fire than appear weak or suppliant before any man.

"If you ever pull a stunt like that again," he said in a low, controlled tone, "you'll be yanked so fast your head will spin. Do we understand each other?"

She nodded. "Perfectly." As he turned to leave, she asked almost defensively, "You didn't get sick at your first crime scene?"

Brant paused, his hand on the doorknob. His expression was indecipherable. "No."

Without another word, he walked out.

Samille locked the door behind him and sagged against it in relief. She'd dodged that bullet, thank God. From now on she'd have to toe the line, or she had no doubt that Brant would make good on his promise. She honestly didn't know what she feared more: being removed from the case or incurring his wrath. His icy, controlled rage had been more terrifying than if he'd ranted and raved at her.

Grimacing at the thought, Samille headed to the bathroom to take a hot shower. She wanted to rid her body of the pervasive stench of death that seemed to cling to her skin, even if there was no escaping the mental image. She peeled off her pullover sweater and reached for the waistband of her slacks. Suddenly she remembered the handkerchief Brant had given her earlier. She pulled it out of her pocket and straightened it carefully. It was monogrammed with Brant's initials in one corner—*B.K.* Samille hesitated, glancing guiltily around the room as if she weren't the only occupant. Unable to resist, she brought the handkerchief to her nose and deeply inhaled Brant's clean, masculine scent. God, the man smelled good. She'd always wondered how women could go bonkers over something as simple as a man's cologne. Now she understood.

Nonetheless she felt silly, standing in the middle of her bathroom with Brant's handkerchief pressed to her face. Hastily she folded it up and placed it on her vanity so she wouldn't forget to throw it in the washing machine. Even as she thought about returning the handkerchief to its owner, she was sorely tempted to keep it—at least until his scent wore off.

"Girl, you *really* need to get out more," she muttered to herself. Shaking her head in disgust, she finished undressing and stepped into the shower.

The phone was ringing as Brant entered his Arlington, Virginia town house that evening. He and Detective Lopez had gone to the Spanglers' Georgetown residence, only to be informed by an unsmiling maid that the family was out for the evening and was not expected to return until after midnight. Brant left his card with terse instructions for the senator to contact him immediately. But he had no intention of waiting for Ashton Spangler's phone call. He planned to show up on the senator's doorstep first thing in the morning—right as Spangler was kissing his lovely wife good-bye and preparing to be chauffeured to Capitol Hill.

The phone stopped ringing as Brant climbed a flight of stairs to the second level of the three-bedroom garage town house. His feet sank into thick Berber carpeting as he walked past the spacious living room and into the kitchen. A quick check of the caller ID display confirmed that the caller had not been Ashton Spangler, but a telemarketer.

Brant opened the double-sided refrigerator and grabbed a bottled water. As he drank, he sifted absently through his mail, discarding the junk and lingering over the financial statements long enough to ensure that the numbers added up. Although he implicitly trusted his broker to manage his diverse investments, Brant subscribed to the notion of being a vigilant, educated investor. He'd held this conviction long before stock trading scandals became national headlines. From the time he was old enough to identify currency, his father had taught him the value of earning and saving money. One of the first scripture lessons Brant had learned was the parable of the wise steward. It had been drilled into him so much that he'd mentally recited it every time he and his friends walked to the corner store for cream sodas, Nathan's hot dogs, and Bazooka Joe bubblegum.

A nostalgic smile lifted one corner of his mouth as he was flooded with memories of Brooklyn summers, street football games interspersed with trips to Coney Island. Old Mrs. Kowalski peering through her kitchen window and threatening bodily harm to any "upstart rascal" who came near her prized petunia garden. He remembered his own reverence in the face of such vitriolic threats, contrasted with Bryan's cocky insubordination . . .

Brant's heart clutched sharply in his chest. He'd almost made it through one day without remembering.

Almost.

He set aside the mail and left the kitchen, angrily jerking his tie loose. He removed his suit coat and shoulder holster with an economy of motion, laying the jacket across the back of a chair and setting his Glock on the dining room table. He walked into the living room, snatched the remote control, and punched on the television in an effort to drown out his own thoughts. He surfed through channels, wondering why he bothered paying for digital cable when he was never home. He finally settled on ESPN and glanced at his watch as a rebroadcast of *SportsCenter* began. Five, four, three, two—

The phone rang. Brant reached for the cordless with a wry smile. "Hey, Mom."

Audre Kincaid's soft laughter filled the line. "Am I *that* predictable?"

"Like clockwork."

"I took a chance that you might be home early tonight. Glad I did."

Brant sank into the buttery softness of a black leather sofa. "How are you?"

"Can't complain."

"You sound congested. Got a cold?"

"Just a little. It's more of a nuisance than anything else. Your father harangued me into closing the gallery early so that I could come home and get in bed. And wouldn't you know it? Minutes after he arrives home to pamper me, he's called back to the office for a meeting. Now I'm stuck here alone, bored out of my everlasting mind. Even your grandmother is out for the evening."

Brant chuckled at his mother's petulant tone. He visualized her prowling up and down their Brooklyn brownstone, too restless to stay in bed. It took a lot more than the common cold to contain Audre Kincaid. She was a veritable force of nature, the most energetic person Brant had ever known. As a child, he'd watched her organize canned food drives, bake cookies for school fund-raisers, serve on community revitalization committees, and participate in peace rallies—sometimes on the same day.

At fifty-eight, she showed no signs of slowing down. In addition to her volunteer work and lecturing at NYU, she owned and operated a fine arts gallery in SoHo, the art capital of the world. She'd been among the first to build an establishment based solely on the works of African-American and Caribbean artists. Her friends joked that she'd launched more black people's careers than Quincy Jones and Barry Gordy combined. Her clientele included world-renowned artists and sculptors. Her gallery drew collectors from around the world, and her cocktail receptions were attended by politicians, journalists, celebrities, and foreign diplomats. She'd been approached by more than a few corporations offering ridiculous sums of money to form a merger with her. Each had been turned down flat. Audre Kincaid wasn't remotely interested in expanding her business or selling out. Her reasons for operating the art gallery remained as simple as they'd been from the start: she was an art lover who wanted to give artists the opportunity to share their gift with others.

"Why'd you have to close the gallery early? Where's Alex?" Brant asked, referring to his mother's longtime assistant.

Audre sighed. "In Paris, attending the international art auction."

"Don't you usually attend the auction?"

"Not this year. Your father and I will already be in Paris for New Year's Eve. Besides, I thought Alexandra could use a change of scenery. She's been so down ever since she and her fiancé broke up."

Brant braced himself for his mother's next comment and was not disappointed. "You know, she's never been the same since you left home for D.C. I honestly believe she's been carrying a torch for you all these years, and that's why her relationships fail. She asks about you all the time."

"Mom, we've been over this a million times," Brant said patiently. "There's never been anything between me and Alex. She's always been Zora's best friend, nothing more."

"Just because she's your sister's friend doesn't mean she can't have feelings for you. And her being four years older doesn't make a bit of difference, either."

"I've never even looked at her that way. We practically grew up together—she used to babysit me, for chrissake."

"Don't you take the Lord's name in vain, Brant Kincaid," Audre warned. "We raised you better than that."

"Sorry," Brant muttered, rubbing his temples wearily. He wasn't in the mood for one of his mother's lectures on his nonexistent love life, which was where the conversation was leading. It had been a hellishly long day. All he wanted to do was take a hot shower and crawl beneath the covers—where sleep would likely evade him for several hours as his mind churned with theories and postulations regarding the investigation.

As if she sensed his fatigue, his mother's tone softened. "I'm the one who should be apologizing. I didn't call to harass you about Alexandra, although I *do* think she has a thing for you. Even Zora has the same suspicion. It's a wonder she's never come right out and asked Alexandra if it's true."

"How *is* Zora?" Brant asked, seizing the opportunity to change the subject.

Audre snorted humorlessly. "Driving everyone crazy, acting like she's the first woman on earth to be having her first child at thirty-eight. She's obsessing over everything, from childbirth classes to choosing the perfect border for the nursery. Over lunch the other day she even told me she's considering hiring one of those Zen masters to help her create the 'right aura' as she enters her second trimester. Have you ever heard of such nonsense? You're lucky to be there and not here, or she'd be driving *you* up the wall, too."

Brant grinned. "Poor Kenny," he lamented, thinking of his mild-mannered brother-in-law who'd patiently indulged Zora Kincaid's eccentricities for the last five years.

"God knew what He was doing when He paired those two. No other man could put up with your sister's quirks." Audre laughed and blew her nose delicately. "I heard about those teenagers overdosing in D.C. Is the Bureau getting involved?"

"Yes." Brant didn't offer more of an explanation, and his mother knew from experience not to probe. Everyone in his family had learned to accept that the sensitive nature of his job prevented him from sharing information about his cases, although each would be the first to admit that Brant had been a staunchly private person long before he joined the FBI.

"I guess you'll be preoccupied with the investigation for a while," his mother said, allowing a rare plaintive note to enter her voice. As a rule, Audre Kincaid eschewed emotional guilt trips. "Do you think you'll make it home for Thanksgiving this year? We all miss having you here in New York."

Brant pushed out a deep breath. "I can't promise anything, Mom. But I'll try."

"I know you will." She paused before adding gently, "He would want you to go on, Brant. You know that, don't you?"

He said nothing, staring at the floor between his legs until the dark flecks of fabric in the oatmeal-colored

Berber began to dance in his vision. He closed his eyes as the familiar tension roiled in his stomach, echoes from the past.

His mother continued in the same soft tone, reminiscent of one used to calm wild animals. "The sooner you learn to forgive yourself for surviving, the sooner you can begin to live again. Take it from me, darling. I know."

Brant got abruptly to his feet. "I should be getting to bed. I have an early morning."

"Of course, I understand. Do you want to talk to your father? He just walked through the door."

"No, just tell Dad I'll call him in a few days. And you take care of that cold—try to get some rest and don't overexert yourself."

"You do the same, baby. I love you."

"Love you too, Mom."

Brant disconnected and scrubbed a hand tiredly over his face. He hadn't intended to rush his mother off the phone. She meant well and God knew the last thing he wanted to do was hurt her, not after all she'd been through.

What they had been through together as a family.

Slowly, almost against his will, Brant walked toward the entertainment center, drawn to a photograph that rested on the top shelf. As he'd done countless times before, he stopped and stared at the framed image. The features were the same as his own, but where the camera lens had always captured Brant with a serious expression, Bryan Kincaid sported a mischievous glint in his dark eyes. As if he were up to no good—which had often been the case.

Brant gazed at his twin brother's smiling image. Bryan's face had not been allowed to mature beyond what was frozen in the high school graduation photo. He'd been robbed of life before they could celebrate their eighteenth birthday together.

The sorrow, the familiar sense of impote⌐ce and loss, settled on Brant's aching shoulders like a cloak. He tried to ignore it, but it was no use. It was as much a part of him as his DNA.

It had been sixteen years since Bryan Kincaid's death, and at times the grief could be as sharp and splintering as it had been during those first few months.

Samille Broussard's question whispered at the back of his mind like a veiled accusation: *You didn't get sick at your first crime scene?*

His numb response: *No.*

Brant's fist clenched. He laid the photo facedown on the shelf, spun away before he did something drastic, and headed upstairs to take a shower. He knew sleep would elude him that night.

What else was new?

She wore a dress the color of sunflowers. The hem was trimmed with white lace to match the socks and shoes on her dainty feet. She stood in the middle of a narrow country road flanked by dense woods. The moon hovered in the sky behind her, casting a silvery glow upon the wreckage before her. The pungent odor of exhaust and burned asphalt assailed her nostrils and made her eyes sting. The incessant blare of a car horn pierced the stillness of the night.

Moving with the shadows, she walked toward the twisted pile of metal that had once been a maroon Oldsmobile. The front end of the vehicle had crumpled from the collision with a telephone pole, shattering the windshield and instantly killing the man and woman inside.

The child's expression registered no emotion as she gazed upon the couple's silent, bloodied faces. She reached inside the passenger window and clasped the woman's slender palm, the flesh still warm to the touch. She dragged the woman's hand across the console to join her partner's hand, positioning them until she was satisfied that they would not slide apart.

As she pulled away from the window, she heard an engine roar to life. She looked up to see the other car reversing from the tree it had crashed into. She stared as twisted chrome and metal straightened and shards of broken glass flew back into place. It was as if the image were being rewound.

She winced against the bright glare of headlights as the restored vehicle faced her. She could barely make out the shadowy outline of a man behind the wheel. He revved the engine, and she watched in horror as the car gunned straight toward her—

Samille wakened with a scream trapped in her throat, her arms raised to shield her face from phantom headlights. As her eyes registered the darkness of her bedroom, the terror slowly receded. It was only a nightmare.

The satin sheets had twisted around her body as she thrashed in her sleep. She freed herself and climbed drunkenly from the bed, padding barefoot to the adjoining bathroom. She splashed her face with cold water and groaned softly at her reflection in the mirror. She looked downright frightful with bloodshot eyes and her hair a thick, tangled mess around her head.

She blotted her face with a hand towel and left the bathroom. Her cotton halter was drenched with sweat and plastered to her body like a second skin. She peeled it off in exchange for a clean one.

Knowing sleep would be impossible for a while, she shuffled down the hall to the kitchen. Although she craved a Mountain Dew, she knew caffeine was the last thing she needed if she hoped to get any more sleep that night.

She grabbed a bottled water from the refrigerator and

crossed the living room to the French doors. As she sipped her water and stared out onto the moonlit garden, she reflected on the nightmare. It had been months since she'd dreamed about the car accident that killed her parents twenty years ago. After all this time, the nightmare was still the same. She was nine years old, wearing the dress her parents had given her as a birthday gift the day before. She appeared at the scene of the crash and placed her parents' hands together. Just as she stepped away from the car, the other vehicle involved in the accident miraculously repaired itself and barreled toward her. She always awoke before the car struck her.

The family therapist who treated Samille after her parents' death had provided a rational explanation for the dream. Joining her parents' hands was symbolic of Samille's desire to preserve the love and affection they had shared in life, her attempt to ensure that they remained together for eternity. The regeneration of the other car represented her fervent wish to undo what had happened to her parents. Her fear that she would also be killed was reflected in the dream's ending, when the other driver came after her.

Everyone accepted the therapist's interpretation. No one, however, could explain Samille's accurate depiction of the accident scene. She had been at her aunt and uncle's house when the accident occurred. When police officers arrived to deliver the devastating news, Samille was instructed to wait in another room with her cousins. It had seemed an eternity before Noreen and Gabriel Broussard summoned her. She'd known something was terribly wrong the minute she looked at their faces and saw the tears glistening in Gabriel Broussard's eyes— Uncle Gabe *never* cried!

In gentle, halting tones they told Samille about the fatal accident. They didn't provide details; they simply explained that her parents' car had been struck by a drunk driver, killing them instantly. Shaking her head in denial, Samille had raced to the front door and flung it open. She fully expected to see her parents coming up the walk with smiles on their faces, as they had done countless times before. But she was met with nothing but empty darkness. An anguished wail erupted from her throat, and Uncle Gabe caught her as the ground tilted beneath her feet.

The nightmares began that very same night. It was weeks after the funeral before she learned the specific details of the accident and discovered how closely her dreams mirrored reality. Everyone was baffled, including the police investigators who handled the case.

Samille shifted from one bare foot to another. Did she believe that she possessed some sort of psychic link to her parents that enabled her to recreate the scene of the accident? The scientist in her rejected the notion and insisted that there was a perfectly logical explanation for the dream. After all, she had been a precocious child with a vivid imagination. Her accurate reconstruction of the events may have resulted from something she read or watched on television.

It seemed a cruel twist of irony that two people who had devoted their lives to saving others had died so tragically, so senselessly. Samuel and Camille Broussard, whom Samille had been named after, were top-notch surgeons at Johns Hopkins Hospital in Baltimore. They were on their way home from a late shift that fateful evening when a speeding drunk driver ran into them, forcing their car off the road and into a telephone pole. The driver, who sustained massive head injuries when his own car slammed into a tree, died three days later. His death brought little consolation to Samille and her family. Her parents were gone and there was nothing she or anyone else could do about it.

Now she wondered how long her sleep would be plagued by the nightmare. She wondered what would happen if, just once, she didn't wake up before the menacing driver plowed into her.

Samille rubbed her bare arms to ward off a sudden chill. She grimaced at her own morbid thoughts. It had been twenty years since her parents died. It was past time for her to move on with her life and finally find some closure. And what better way to honor her parents' humanitarian spirits than to help solve the mystery of who had poisoned the Georgetown teenagers?

She walked over to the bookcase and quickly scanned the titles before withdrawing two volumes of drug case studies. She switched on the floor lamp, drew a chenille throw over her shoulders, and settled into the wing chair. As she began reading, her thoughts strayed to Brant Kincaid.

She hoped he, at least, was getting a good night's rest.

CHAPTER 5

Senator Ashton Spangler emerged from his George-town residence at seven-thirty a.m. He adjusted the collar of his expensive overcoat and smoothed an elegant hand over the shock of silver hair that gave him a distinguished appearance. His skin was perpetually suntanned from hours spent outdoors engaged in his favorite pastimes: golf, sailing, and horseback riding. A gleaming black Cadillac awaited him at the curb. A tall, thin man in a dark suit and cap stood ramrod straight beside the car.

Brant climbed from his truck and started across the street. He had decided against ringing the senator's doorbell and announcing himself. He didn't want to be stonewalled by Spangler's maid or give the senator an opportunity to refuse his visit. Brant knew the element of surprise would give him the upper hand.

He removed his sunglasses as he approached the senator on the brick sidewalk. "Senator Spangler. A moment of your time, please."

Ashton Spangler looked up and didn't bother to mask the annoyance that crossed his aristocratic features. "Yes?" he said testily.

Brant flashed his identification with a practiced move. "Special Agent Brant Kincaid. I'd like to speak to your son about the party he attended last Friday night."

"Ah yes. You stopped by yesterday." Spangler's face relaxed into the easygoing expression that had earned him the trust of his constituents. "My wife and I were attending a performance at the Kennedy Center. I'm afraid we got home too late to return your call."

"We were told as much. Is Jefferson available?"

"No, Jefferson is out of town."

"When do you expect him back?"

"We haven't decided. He's been getting some much-needed R and R at the family estate in Baton Rouge."

Brant arched an eyebrow. "In the middle of the school year?"

Spangler offered his trademark congenial smile. "His instructors were generous enough to provide his coursework in advance so that he wouldn't fall behind in his studies. Not that this has ever been a concern. Jefferson is an exemplary student."

Brant didn't miss the relevance of the senator's last statement. Jefferson Spangler was a good kid, and good kids didn't commit crimes. "Senator Spangler, I'll cut right to the chase. Your son is wanted for questioning in connection with the overdosing of his classmates. It's imperative that I speak to him immediately."

The senator's face remained calm, implacable. "Surely you're not implying that Jefferson had anything to do with what happened to those students? He was absolutely traumatized when he received the news. Those were his friends, Agent Kincaid. He was so upset that we felt sending him home to Louisiana would do him some good. His older sister and her family have even joined him there to keep an eye on him."

"Be that as it may, Senator Spangler, I still have an investigation to conduct. I have ten comatose teenagers whose parents want answers. Your son may be able to provide those answers."

"I don't see how. Jefferson is as baffled about what happened as we all are."

"With all due respect, sir, I'd like to hear from him myself. Please make arrangements for Jefferson to return home today—or I will."

Spangler's composure slipped a fraction. His tone hardened. "Are you threatening me, Agent Kincaid?"

Brant gave him a cryptic smile. "You're an experienced attorney, Senator Spangler, so I'm sure I don't have to spell everything out for you. But just so that there's no misunderstanding, I will. Your son is wanted for questioning in a criminal investigation. Failure to comply with this request could be construed as obstruction of justice."

"My son is a model student at St. Anthony's Preparatory School," the senator snarled, dropping all pretenses in his indignation. "He would *never* sell drugs to his classmates. You're making a very big mistake, Kincaid."

"What would be a mistake," Brant said mildly, "is for your son to remain in Louisiana another day. This doesn't have to get ugly, Senator Spangler. All I'm asking for is your cooperation. You have my number. Please call me as soon as Jefferson arrives home, and I can meet you both at the precinct." He turned to leave.

"For the last time, Mr. Kincaid, my son had nothing to do with what happened. I strongly encourage you to think twice before proceeding down this road."

Brant turned slowly around. Ashton Spangler regarded him with the cold, eviscerating stare that had sent many of his political adversaries scurrying for cover.

Brant only smiled. A sharp, mirthless smile. "Let me give you some food for thought, Senator Spangler. If your son fails to come in for questioning, I'll be forced to issue an arrest warrant, which will undoubtedly be leaked to the press—you know how it works in this town. Just think what your loyal constituents would make of your son being arrested on suspected drug charges." He paused a beat, watching the senator's mouth tighten. "And then imagine how your political opponents would spin the news: Senator Ashton Spangler, biggest proponent of prescription drug legislation, can't even regulate the illegal drug use in his own household."

Spangler said nothing. His strained expression conveyed more than enough.

"I'll let you mull that over on your way to the Hill," Brant said softly. "Have a good day, Senator. We'll talk soon."

He turned and walked back to his truck. As he pulled away from the Spangler residence, his cell phone rang. He dug it out of his breast pocket and answered on the second ring. "Kincaid."

"Detective Lopez. I thought we could try the senator's place again this morning."

"Done. Jefferson Spangler will be on a plane home from Louisiana sometime today, and we can meet him and his father at the station as soon as they've rounded up their attorneys."

"Louisiana? What's the Spangler kid doing in Louisiana?"

"Long story. I'll fill you in later."

"I left you the box of receipts at Records and Evidence."

"Got them, thanks."

"I did some more digging around last night, and it turns out that Andrew Cason was a former DEA informant. But the records are sealed behind some sort of Justice Department top-security clearance. We could be looking at another motive—and perp—for Cason's untimely demise."

Brant frowned, unease settling in his gut. "Where are you headed now?"

"Back to southeast to check out a few leads and talk to more neighbors. We didn't have too much success last night; a lot of people were afraid to answer their doors. There's been a rash of gang violence lately, and folks don't wanna get caught in the cross fire or be seen co-operating with the police."

Brant nodded, making an illegal U-turn. "Keep me posted."

"You do the same."

Brant disconnected and headed for Dupont Circle. It was time to check in on his "partner" and get some answers.

Samille answered the door twenty minutes later. She looked sleepy and decidedly rumpled in a pink halter top, gray jogging pants with white stripes along the sides, and a pair of thick wool socks. Her hair was tousled as if she'd just rolled out of bed and hastily combed her fingers through the thick, silken strands.

She was less than pleased to find Brant on her doorstep. She eyed him up and down, taking in his pressed dark suit and the knife-blade crease of his trousers. The longer she assessed him, the more disgruntled she looked.

Finally she grunted something unintelligible and stepped aside to let him enter the apartment.

"Rough night?" Brant drawled.

"You could say that." She closed the door and brushed past him to head for the kitchen. His gaze was drawn to the way her halter outlined the jaunty swell of her breasts, and how lovingly her pants hugged the plump roundness of her bottom.

He swallowed hard and reached for his tie. "A bit

warm in here, don't you think?" It wasn't just his rising libido either. It felt like ninety degrees in the apartment.

"I got a little cold last night," Samille grumbled, slamming cabinet doors in search of her favorite ceramic mug. "It's fifty degrees outside. If it's too hot in here for you, there's the door."

Brant raised an eyebrow. "Touché."

Samille was instantly contrite. After spending half the night buried in old case studies, she'd found nothing resembling the chemical compound they were looking for. She was frustrated, exhausted, and beginning to wonder if she even knew what she was talking about. Brant's unexpected arrival at her apartment—and the fact that he looked as if he'd just stepped from the pages of *GQ* while *she* resembled a train wreck—didn't exactly improve her disposition.

Still, she had no right to take out her frustrations on him. "Sorry about that," she mumbled, settling for another mug. "I was about to make coffee. Would you like some?"

"No, thanks. Already had two cups this morning."

"That's your polite way of saying you'd rather drink mud than suffer through another cup of my watered-down version of coffee."

Brant chuckled, removing his suit jacket and draping it across the back of the wing-back chair. "Don't put words in my mouth."

Samille eyed the nine-millimeter Glock visible from his shoulder holster. He looked as comfortable wearing the weapon as he did in his clothing, as if it were part of him. Samille knew he probably had a backup piece strapped to his ankle. Special Agent Brant Kincaid: armed and dangerous.

"Have you talked to Jefferson Spangler yet?" she asked

as Brant struck a negligent pose in the arched entryway, propping one shoulder against the wall.

"Not yet." Briefly he told her about his conversation with the senator.

Samille frowned. "I don't suppose it would occur to Senator Spangler that another possible reason for his son's distress is that *he* supplied the drugs to his friends. Guilt can be quite a powerful emotion, and fleeing halfway across the country right after the fact doesn't exactly bolster his claims of innocence."

"No, not exactly."

"Think Senator Spangler will send for Jefferson?"

"I think so." Brant's mouth curved sardonically. "I made him an offer he couldn't refuse."

Samille smiled. She had no doubt that Brant Kincaid could be very persuasive when he wanted to be.

The coffee percolated and she turned to pour herself a cup.

"What do you know about a man named Andrew Cason?"

Samille's hand jerked, sloshing hot coffee over the side of the mug. She grabbed a checkered dish towel and mopped the spill from the counter. "Why do you ask?"

Brant straightened slowly from the wall and stepped into the kitchen. "Someone put a bullet in his head about a week ago, and I want to know who and why."

Samille whirled around, her eyes wide with shock. "Last night . . . that was *Andrew Cason?*"

Brant nodded. "We just found out this morning that he was a former DEA informant. Detective Lopez ran into a bureaucratic firewall when he tried to access more information."

"I see." Samille wrapped her hands around the steaming coffee mug and took a tentative sip, needing the infusion of warmth. "What do you want to know?"

"Whatever you can tell me. We're trying to see if there's any connection between Cason and Jefferson Spangler. According to a daily planner we found among Cason's possessions, he was scheduled to meet with Spangler last Thursday evening. Looks like he never made it."

Samille's temper flared. "Why is this the first time I'm hearing this information? I was there with you last night, and you never said a word!"

"I would have," Brant said laconically, "if you weren't so busy puking your guts out. Or have you conveniently forgotten that minor detail?"

Heat flooded Samille's cheeks. "Of course not," she mumbled, quickly averting her gaze. Would she ever live down that humiliating episode?

Brant's eyes narrowed on her face, sharp and discerning. Softly he said, "Why do I get the distinct impression that you're avoiding my question about Andrew Cason?"

"I'm not. Anyway, what would be the point? You're FBI—you could access the information with just a few keystrokes." Samille retreated to a far corner of the kitchen and brooded over her coffee.

"Samille."

She heaved a resigned sigh. "Andrew Cason *was* one of our informants. Over a period of five years, he received close to one million dollars for helping the DEA arrest several high-profile drug dealers. We considered him a valuable asset. He was smart and very thorough. Three years ago, he infiltrated a local drug ring and provided information that enabled us to successfully raid the group's warehouse and seize their cocaine supply—over a thousand kilos. It was a huge bust led by Jack Burdett."

She hesitated, her expression clouding over.

"Go on," Brant murmured coaxingly.

"Everyone thought the case was a slam dunk. And then

Andrew Cason took the witness stand." Her mouth curved scornfully. "It was like watching a train wreck in slow motion. He committed perjury and lied about everything from his own arrest record to how many degrees he had. The defense attorney ripped his testimony to shreds, and when it was all said and done, the only ones left standing were the drug dealers. It was even implied that Jack and Michael Parham, another agent involved in the case, knew about Cason's criminal record and continued using his services anyway."

"Did they?"

Samille was startled by the question. "Of course not! If Jack had known about Cason's priors, he never would have enlisted him as an informant."

"So how did he drop the ball on Cason?"

Samille bristled at the question and the cynical undertones in Brant's voice. "He made a mistake, all right? He didn't run a background check on Cason, an oversight he regrets to this day. He learned about Cason's arrests for the first time during the trial. You can imagine how furious he was, with Cason *and* himself. It was a colossal embarrassment for the DEA. No criminal action could be taken against Andrew Cason because of the immunity agreement he'd struck with the U.S. Attorney's office. Internal Affairs conducted their own investigation, and although Jack was cleared of any wrongdoing, I know that case still haunts him. It could have ruined his career."

Brant said nothing, watching her in that quiet, unnerving manner of his. Something in his silence felt accusatory. Her hackles rose.

She set down her coffee mug with a thud. "Look, I know what you're thinking, Brant. You think I'm this naïve paper pusher who's woefully oblivious of the rampant corruption that goes on around me. Believe me, I know that there's corruption within the DEA. I know that there are agents who kick in doors without warrants and perform illegal wiretaps on suspects, who rip off drug traffickers and pocket cash, jewelry, and drugs. I know that a lot of unethical criminal behavior goes unpunished on a regular basis. Before accepting a position with the DEA, I took into account their less than stellar reputation with the public. I asked myself countless times whether I wanted to be associated with an agency that was perceived by many as corrupt and mercenary—truth be told, there are occasions when I *still* ask myself that question. But the bottom line is that I truly believe in the war on drugs, no matter how much of an uphill battle it seems. I *want* to see dealers who sell crack to children punished to the full extent of the law. I *want* to help prosecute doctors and pharmacists who abuse their positions to distribute prescription drugs illegally. I *want* to eliminate the flow of drugs into this country, although there's enough evidence to suggest that our very own government may be largely responsible for the problem in the first place."

"Samille—"

"And while you stand there in judgment of the DEA, Agent Kincaid, don't forget to look in your own backyard. Last time I checked, it was the *FBI* who failed to identify a spy within their own ranks for over twenty years! It was the *FBI* who secretly wiretapped Dr. King's phones during the sixties because he was perceived as a threat to the Establishment. And don't even get me started on Waco and Ruby Ridge—the jury's still out on those two incidents!"

With a savage oath Brant descended upon her. He grasped her upper arm and gave her a firm shake. "Enough!"

The stark fury in his coal-black eyes gave her pause. She stared up at him, momentarily disarmed.

"Why do you always go off on these tangents?" he demanded. "I asked you *one* question, and the next thing I know you're launching into a tirade. I was not attacking you or the DEA, so get that out of your thick head right now."

She lifted her chin a defiant notch. "Sure sounded like it to me."

"Then you need to get your hearing checked, because I wasn't," Brant growled. "You think I'm going to stand here and defend the Bureau? Make excuses for some of their objectionable practices? Hell no. Like you, I believe in the work that I do, plain and simple. If I didn't, I wouldn't be here and we wouldn't be having this ridiculous conversation. God knows I can think of a million other things I'd rather do with my time than argue with you over whose employer is more corrupt. Hell, Samille, I can think of a million other things I'd rather be doing *to* you."

Samille's breath lodged in her throat at his unexpected declaration. The electrical currents between them changed from tense and hostile to something that was elemental, instinctive. Powerfully seductive. She was suddenly aware of how close he stood. Close enough that she could see the thick fringe of black eyelashes that rimmed those penetrating onyx eyes. Close enough that she could see the precise trim of his goatee. Close enough that some reckless part of her wanted to press her mouth to the firm, sensuous curve of his lips and see if he tasted as good as he looked.

As if he'd read her mind, Brant's dark eyes flickered and settled on her mouth. Her heart beat harder and faster.

The large hand that had gripped her arm moments before slid up to her bare shoulder, igniting frissons of heat along her nerve endings. His hand skimmed the nape of her neck before sinking deeply into her hair. Gently, but so that there was no mistaking his intent, he tilted her head backward. His smoldering gaze roamed across her upturned face in a slow, deliberate perusal that stole her breath.

"Brant—"

"You talk too much," he murmured huskily. "Do you know what you need?"

Before she could answer, he lowered his head and slanted his mouth urgently over hers. The heat of the kiss was searing. It was rough and wild, pure raw sex that sparked a hot, carnal response. He parted her lips and slid his tongue between them as if he had every right, plunging deep and retreating in a rhythm that was primal and blatantly erotic. Samille rose in his arms and into the kiss, answering with a hunger of her own. In that moment nothing else mattered. Not the case. Not their differences or her strict rule against getting involved with men she worked with. All that mattered was this incredibly virile man and the earth-shattering sensations he awakened in her. She trembled at the desire he had unleashed, consumed by the need to let go of her control and be swept away on this tidal wave of passion. She drowned in the taste of him, the warm masculine scent of him, the contrast in their size and strength.

His body was hot and hard, undeniably male. She was melting against him, on fire. She dug her fingertips into the corded muscles of his back and moaned as his tongue thrust against hers, possessing her. He banded his arms around her and lifted her against him like he couldn't get close enough. Samille responded by wrapping her legs tightly around his waist. Brant groaned, the sound both tortured and approving. He cupped her buttocks and ground his hips into hers, drawing a sharp gasp from her lips. He backed her against the refrigerator as the kiss grew wilder, more intense.

"I want you," he growled against her mouth. "I want to be inside you so bad it's killing me."

Samille shivered at the erotic images his words evoked, at the raw need in his voice. She could feel him against her belly, hard and ready to make good on his declaration. Fear and anticipation wound like a spring inside her. She wanted him just as much, had wanted him from the moment she first laid eyes on him six months ago. The experience of him holding her, crushing her against the solid warmth of his chest, was unbearably arousing. Her nipples hardened as his palms grazed the underside of her breasts. She arched her back and clung to his big shoulders as liquid fire spread between her thighs.

Brant was rapidly approaching the point of no return. Never in his wildest dreams could he have imagined what kissing Samille would be like, the exquisite havoc she would wreak on his senses. He couldn't get enough of her warm scent, the silken texture of her skin, the sublime curves of her body. He wanted to devour her. He dragged his mouth from hers to rain kisses across her cheekbone, then down her throat to the delicate hollow where her pulse beat madly. He flicked his tongue over the pulsing nerve and gently suckled, tasting her, savoring the nectar of her flesh. A soft cry escaped from Samille's mouth. She gripped the back of his head and brought his mouth back to hers for a greedy kiss. The rich, lush taste of her lips demanded that he lower her to the floor and make love to her right then and there, or take her standing. It didn't matter, as long as he was buried deep inside her.

But he couldn't. He ruled his life by a strict code, one that prohibited him from mixing business with pleasure. Once the lines were blurred, there would be no turning

back. And once would not be enough when it came to
having Samille Broussard. Once she got in his system, he
would be completely at her mercy. He knew that beyond
a shadow of a doubt. She was unlike any other woman he
had ever met. She utterly bewitched him. She was like a
drug, an elixir he couldn't get enough of. He was already
beginning to wonder if she'd cast a spell on him.

It took every ounce of his willpower to pull his mouth
from hers, and he almost reconsidered when Samille
moaned softly in protest. Need pounded through his
body and throbbed relentlessly in his groin. For several
minutes all he could do was rest his forehead against
hers as their ragged breaths mingled.

At length he raised his head. His heavy-lidded gaze
met hers. "Are you okay?"

Samille nodded, her tongue passing quickly over her
swollen lips. She didn't trust her voice. She unwrapped
her legs from Brant's waist as he eased her down and
stepped back. Her knees were so weak she feared they
wouldn't support her. She couldn't move from the spot.

Brant turned away to adjust his trousers. Samille wondered if he was as shaken by their kiss as she was. They
had known each other less than three days. Three days,
and they'd just come dangerously close to having sex on
her kitchen floor. He hadn't even removed his weapon
holster! She waited for shame and self-loathing to engulf
her, but all she felt was a hollow ache of regret. She refused to explore the regret, afraid of what it might reveal
about herself and her feelings for a man she barely
knew.

Brant walked slowly from the kitchen, and somehow
she forced her legs to follow. For the first time since his
arrival he noticed the pile of research books stacked on
the coffee table. He looked at her.

"Don't ask," she said before he could open his mouth.

"Trust me, you'll be the first to know if I find anything even remotely related to our investigation."

Brant nodded, his expression grim. "I know it's a lot of tedious work, but I've always believed in covering all my bases. I'm going through Cason's receipts to see if he ever purchased a computer." At Samille's inquisitive look, he elaborated. "You said Cason was a hacker. How many hackers do you know who don't own a computer?"

Samille frowned. "What are you getting at?"

"A computer was missing from his apartment. I'm wondering if he had some incriminating files stored on it, information that someone didn't want to get out."

"Is it possible that one of the drug dealers he betrayed killed him in retaliation?"

"It's possible. Definitely an angle worth exploring."

Samille folded her arms. "With all the money he earned from the DEA, I'm surprised he wound up living in a place like that."

"I'm guessing he wanted to keep a low profile. He couldn't risk anyone discovering that he was a DEA informant, especially not the dealers he'd double-crossed. Since the trial, he'd been flying beneath the radar by selling marijuana to high school kids."

"Like Jefferson Spangler."

"Exactly. I definitely believe there's a connection between those two."

"But do you think Spangler killed Cason?"

Brant grimaced. "I'm not ruling anything out. Someone sold Spangler the drugs he supplied to his classmates, and I doubt that his scheduled meeting with Cason was anything but a drug transaction."

"But doesn't it seem incongruous that Cason would have written down the appointment? If Cason *was* Jefferson's dealer, why would he take the time to record a meeting that probably occurred on a regular basis?"

"Maybe this particular meeting was different," Brant said speculatively. "What if Cason was blackmailing Jefferson? What if he purposely wrote down the appointment so that if something happened to him, the police would have a lead?"

Samille rubbed her bare arms as a fine chill passed through her. "And whoever went to Cason's apartment that night and killed him didn't bother to search through his belongings to make sure no evidence was left behind?"

"That's one theory. Another possibility is that the perp did find the daily planner and left it there to incriminate Spangler."

"Or planted it," Samille murmured.

Brant nodded. "We're having the handwriting analyzed to see if it matches Andrew Cason's. Something tells me that if we find Cason's killer, we'll find out where our mystery drug originated."

Samille watched him, seeing the wheels churning in his head and the sharply honed investigative instincts clicking into place. She was completely fascinated by the way his mind worked. "Do you have Cason's receipts with you?"

"In the truck."

"Why don't you bring them inside? I can help you go through them, and by the time you meet with Jefferson Spangler this evening, you might have a clearer picture."

Brant hesitated, his glance flicking past her into the kitchen.

"Don't worry," Samille drawled, interpreting his thoughts, "there won't be a repeat performance. What we did was a mistake. It won't happen again."

His mouth curved ruefully. Samille didn't know whether it was relief or regret that flickered in his eyes. "I'll get the receipts," he said.

When Brant returned to the apartment a few minutes later, she was in the kitchen. She glanced up from cracking eggs into a large stainless steel bowl. "I may be lousy at coffee, but I make a mean western omelet. Would you care to join me for breakfast?"

Brant smiled. "How could I refuse?"

For the second day in a row, they sat down to breakfast together. Brant was very complimentary of Samille's omelet and polished it off in short order, much to her immense pleasure. Her uncle and cousins were the only men she'd ever cooked for, and she was surprised by how good it felt to have her culinary skills appreciated by someone other than a relative.

Who are you kidding? Not just anyone. It feels good to be appreciated by Brant Kincaid, period.

She loaded the dishwasher while Brant sat on the sofa and cleared the coffee table in the living room to make space for the receipts. Samille turned on the television to CNN and settled Indian-style on the floor.

She wrinkled her nose at the pile of receipts. "Man, what a pack rat. Did he keep receipts for *everything* he ever bought?"

Brant chuckled. "Looks that way, doesn't it?"

"Too bad he wasn't organized enough to file them in chronological order."

Brant pushed a stack toward her. "Isolate the ones you come across frequently. Dry cleaners, clothing stores— whatever. It may be worth our time to visit some of those places and talk to store employees, find out if Cason was ever accompanied by a friend on one of his errands."

Samille nodded. "Good idea. But the main thing we're looking for is a computer receipt, right?"

"Right."

For the next two hours, they worked in companionable silence as CNN reporters droned on about the fluctuating economy, stock trading scandals, and a flooding disaster in Iowa.

Samille had always considered herself a consummate professional. She tackled every assignment with the utmost seriousness, whether she was testifying before a grand jury or poring through a dead man's purchasing history. But no matter how engrossed she was in her task that morning, memories of the explosive kiss she and Brant had shared still managed to penetrate her thoughts. The flashbacks were vivid, making her cheeks flame with renewed mortification at her own wanton behavior. She was haunted by one question: if Brant hadn't ended the kiss, would she have allowed him to make love to her?

A few surreptitious glances at his face told her she was the only one obsessing over the kiss. Brant was completely absorbed in his task, sifting and sorting receipts with methodical precision. But minutes later she glanced up to find him watching her, studying her. The heat he sent through his dark eyes surrounded her and left her with a liquid rush in unspeakable parts of her body. For a moment she sat paralyzed, unable to break eye contact. Brant saved her the trouble, sliding his gaze away. Samille almost sagged against the back of the chair, breathless from the assault on her senses. She didn't so much as look in his direction again.

An hour later, the deep timbre of his voice interrupted a CNN interview with China's prime minister. "Bingo."

Samille's head snapped up. "You find something?"

Brant stood and came over to her. She had to strain her neck to look up at him as he held out a wrinkled receipt to her. "Just as I thought. Cason bought a brand-new computer three years ago. Must have been top of the line, too. Check out the grand total."

Samille whistled softly. "Ka-ching. So, where was the computer last night?"

"Seems to be the question of the day."

"You think he hocked it to pay off some debt?"

Brant shook his head, his expression grim. "Not likely. The police found a stash of twenty grand in Cason's bedroom. He wasn't hurting for money."

Samille frowned as she climbed to her feet with Brant's assistance. She was getting a serious crook in her neck from staring up at him; he towered over her even when she was standing. "You think whoever killed Cason confiscated his computer?"

"So it appears. Cason was an informant. He may have had dirt on any number of people."

"But it's been three years since he worked for us. Why would anyone wait that long to come after him?"

Brant's smile was sardonic. "You'd be surprised, Samille. I've known of criminals who bided their time and waited forty years to get revenge against their enemies. What's three years?"

Samille chewed her bottom lip pensively. "Your blackmail theory is looking more and more plausible. Hey, where are you going?"

Brant was shrugging into his suit jacket. "To find Detective Lopez. He went to talk to Cason's neighbors this morning. I want to know what he learned."

"Such as whether someone saw the perp carting a computer from the apartment on the night Cason was killed."

"For starters." Brant paused at the front door and looked down at her. "Thanks for your help, Samille."

She waved off his gratitude. "That's what I'm here for. Anything else I can do?"

"I want everything you can give me on Cason."

"Done. What about the rest of the receipts? I found several places he regularly frequented."

"Start a list. We'll make our rounds tomorrow."

"*We?*"

"Yeah." His mouth quirked at the corners. "We're partners, aren't we?"

Samille smiled almost shyly. "Of course."

Brant winked at her before slipping out the door. She locked it behind him and stood there for a minute, contemplating the word he'd used.

Partners.

Yeah, she definitely liked the sound of that. Liked it more than she should have.

CHAPTER 6

Jefferson Spangler was everything Brant had expected. Trim and athletic, blond and aristocratically handsome. His pale blue eyes lacked the piercing depth of his father's, and he wasn't old enough to have cultivated the same commanding presence. Shoulders erect, he sat beside the senator in one of the downtown precinct's conference rooms. Detective Lopez, although eager to solve the case and make a name for himself, was under strict orders not to step on the wrong toes. Questioning Senator Ashton Spangler's son in an interrogation room was tantamount to treating him like a criminal, which was "unacceptable" at this stage of the investigation.

Ashton Spangler had decided not to bring legal counsel to the interview, and Brant recognized the strategy for what it was. Spangler wanted to show them that his son had nothing to hide and wasn't afraid to be questioned by the police. Besides, the senator knew his way around the legal system. Jefferson had probably been coached all the way from the airport. Brant scrutinized the boy's impassive expression, the calmness of his hands clasped on the table.

No doubt about it. He'd been coached, and coached well.

Ashton Spangler cleared his throat importantly. "Gentlemen, I hope this won't take long. My son has had a long flight, and I'm sure you can appreciate that he's eager to return home and get some rest."

"Of course," Lopez agreed, seated across the table from the Spanglers. "We just want to ask Jefferson a few questions in connection with the overdosing of his classmates."

"An unfortunate tragedy that Jefferson had nothing to do with," Spangler interjected. His eyes flicked meaningfully to Brant, who stood with his shoulder propped against the bulletin board in the conference room. His deadpan expression didn't change at the senator's words.

"Let's begin, shall we?" Lopez leaned across the table, clicked on a tape recorder, then stated their names, the date, and the time.

"Jefferson, a classmate has identified you as the person responsible for providing drugs at the party one week ago. Can you explain that?"

Ashton laughed scornfully. "That's preposterous! No student at that party would accuse Jefferson of something so outlandish. You're grasping at straws, Detective."

"With all due respect, sir, I think Jefferson should answer the question himself."

Jefferson looked at his father, whose subtle nod granted him permission to speak. "My father's right," he said in a clear, strong voice. "No one at the party would say I brought the drugs, because I didn't."

"Too bad we can't ask the kids in comas," Brant drawled.

Ashton shot him an annoyed look. Jefferson looked anywhere but at Brant.

"Am I to understand, Jefferson, that you've never

sold drugs to any of your classmates or friends?" Lopez
clarified.

"That's right."

"Where were you last Thursday night between the
hours of seven and ten p.m.?"

"At a study group."

"Where?"

"At a friend's house. There were six of us. Everyone
will vouch that I was there."

"Are these the same friends who would vouch that you
never sold drugs to them?" Brant asked.

Before Jefferson could respond, his father said in an
icy voice, "I resent the implication, Agent Kincaid, that
my son's friends would lie for him."

"It happens all the time."

"Not in this instance. We can provide you with a list of
the students. Call and ask them yourself. Talk to Bradley
Whitfield's parents—they were home that night and can
verify that Jefferson was there."

Lopez scribbled on his notepad. "What time did you
leave the study group, Jefferson?"

"A little after ten."

"Did you go straight home?"

"No. I stopped and bought gas at the Amoco station
ten minutes from my house."

"Did you use a credit card?"

"No, cash."

"Got a receipt?"

Jefferson shook his head. "I usually get one, but I
forgot that night."

"Too much cramming, huh?" Brant murmured.

Jefferson met his eyes briefly before glancing away. "I
just forgot."

"Where is this line of questioning going?" Ashton

demanded impatiently. "What does any of this have to do with Friday night's party?"

Brant walked over to the table, opened a file folder, and removed a black-and-white photograph of Andrew Cason. He slid the photo slowly to Jefferson. "Do you know this person?"

And he saw it. An unmistakable flash of recognition in Jefferson Spangler's eyes. Lopez saw it, too. His eyes met Brant's.

"He doesn't look familiar," Jefferson replied after pretending to linger over the photo in thoughtful scrutiny. He slid it across the table to Brant and met his shrewd gaze without blinking. "I don't know him."

"You sure?"

Ashton Spangler frowned. "If my son says he doesn't know this person, he doesn't."

"That's interesting," Brant reflected aloud, "because this person seems to have known you, Jefferson."

"You said 'have known' as in past tense." Ashton eyed Brant suspiciously. "What's going on? Who is that man?"

"His name was Andrew Cason. He was a drug dealer who was killed last Thursday."

The senator blanched. The skin around his mouth grew tight. "I hope you're not accusing my son of murder, Agent Kincaid."

Brant was watching Jefferson closely. The boy had grown as pale as his father. "I want to know why you were meeting with Andrew Cason at nine p.m. last Thursday," Brant said quietly.

"I wasn't—"

"Your name was written in his daily planner."

"This is absurd!" Enraged, Ashton sprang to his feet. "First you drag my son down here to interrogate him about selling drugs to his classmates, and now you have the unmitigated gall to accuse him of *murder*?"

"Please sit down, Senator Spangler," Lopez said wearily.

"I will not! This interview is over! My son and I have co-operated long enough with this nonsense. Come along, Jefferson." He assisted his son from the chair in a manner that brooked no argument from him or Detective Lopez.

"Make no mistake about it, Senator," Brant said in a low, precise tone that caused both father and son to pause and look at him. "We have enough evidence to pursue Jefferson as a primary suspect. He's been identi-fied by one of his classmates as a drug dealer, and his name has been linked to a dead man who also happened to sell drugs. Despite what you may think, Senator, I don't believe in coincidence. I suggest you advise your son to tell us everything he knows while he still has the opportunity to come forward voluntarily."

"My son has told you everything he knows," the senator spat, "but you refuse to listen. You and I both know that the so-called evidence you have is circumstantial. If one of Jefferson's classmates told you such a ridiculous lie, it's be-cause they're jealous of him and are trying to ruin him. As for your murdered drug dealer, I can't account for the turf wars that occur between those immoral people. I can assure you that my son had as much to do with that inci-dent as he did with the Watergate scandal."

He nudged Jefferson to the door. Before departing, he faced Brant and Detective Lopez once again. "If either of you so much as breathes my son's name to the media in connection with this case, you'll have not only an unsolved murder to contend with, but a staggering lawsuit as well. Don't test my patience."

"Patience is overrated," Brant countered coolly. "I'm about to lose what little I have left."

Spangler hesitated, his eyes narrowing on Brant's face. Deciding he didn't want to respond to the comeback, he herded his son from the room.

Lopez swiveled his chair around to look at Brant. "He's right, you know. The evidence against the kid is largely circumstantial. The girl you talked to at the school might have been lying for any number of reasons, and we don't know why Cason wrote Spangler's name in his daily planner—*if* in fact he did. We're still awaiting results from the handwriting analysis, and none of Cason's neighbors remembered seeing anyone coming or going from his apartment."

"The kid is lying about not knowing Cason. We both know that."

"But how can we prove it? Even if we prove that Cason *did* write Spangler's name, any defense attorney worth his salt could say that Cason was delusional, fixated on meeting the senator's kid or something. And we already know that Cason had serious credibility issues."

Frustration simmered in Brant's gut. He knew everything the detective said was true. Nothing about their case against Jefferson Spangler was airtight. All they could do was continue digging for leads and hope that Spangler would slip up somewhere along the way. Of course, with Ashton Spangler guarding his son like a rabid rottweiler, it would be an extra challenge to know *when* and *how* Jefferson slipped up.

Brant had never been one to back down from a challenge.

"I'll push the techs to get the handwriting results back to us tomorrow," Detective Lopez said, shoving Andrew Cason's photo inside the folder.

Brant nodded, heading for the door. "I'll be checking out some of Cason's hangouts tomorrow. In the meantime, put a tail on the Spangler kid—find out where he goes, who he hangs out with, whether he looks over his shoulder to see if he's being watched. I'll be in touch."

His cell phone rang as he left the building. He dug it out of his pocket and clipped, "Kincaid."

"Brant, this is Jack Burdett. Did I catch you at a bad time?"

Brant started for his Expedition in the busy parking lot. "What's going on?"

"Not much. Listen, I was wondering if we could meet for drinks. No special reason, just thought it would be good to catch up. You game?"

Brant hesitated, thinking of the hot shower he'd intended to take when he got home, the mound of paperwork he planned to pore through. He supposed both could wait a couple more hours.

"Same place as usual?" he asked.

Jack chuckled. "See you there."

Long ago, Brant and Jack Burdett had rejected D.C.'s trendy nightclubs and restaurants in favor of the lesser-known Blue-and-White Bar on K Street. Blue-and-White's regular clientele consisted largely of law enforcement officers and a sprinkling of Capitol Hill staffers who preferred the bar's low-key environment to the pretentious atmosphere common in other local nightspots. This crowd wasn't into name-dropping and vying for entrance to the VIP lounge—there *was* no VIP lounge. The bar was a semi-cave with midnight-blue walls and mahogany wood blackened with age. A pool table was set up in one corner, a television on the opposite side that dissipated some of the gloom. The bar at the rear of the restaurant was long and backed by a mirror that reflected its full length and doubled the light from above. Tier upon tier of liquor bottles with contents of amber, gold, and red liquids sparkled from behind proud old labels. Smoke hung in the air above the bar and surrounding tables.

Jack was already seated in a dim corner of the bar when Brant arrived. He was hunched over the small table and appeared to be on his second drink. Whiskey, Brant noted as he drew nearer. Something was definitely wrong. Jack Burdett never had anything stronger than beer.

He looked up as Brant pulled out a chair and sat. "Hey, Kincaid, you made it. Drinks are on me. What're you having?" He signaled for a waiter.

Brant ordered beer. When the waiter bustled away, he leaned back in his chair and regarded Jack lazily. "What's up, Burdett?"

Jack grinned. "Why does something have to be up? We haven't met for drinks in a while. I thought we were a bit overdue."

"Is that right?" The waiter materialized with his beer and a glass. Brant ignored the glass and took a long swig from the bottle. As he studied Jack's face, he was struck with a keen sense of recognition. After a moment he shrugged it off. He'd known Jack Burdett for eleven years. Of course Jack looked familiar to him.

"I heard about Andrew Cason," Jack said casually. "Can't say I was shocked. Chickens gotta come home to roost eventually."

Brant raised an eyebrow. "You think an old dealer took him out?"

"Wouldn't surprise me in the least. What do you make of it?"

The question was posed nonchalantly, but Brant sensed that his response meant more to Jack than he was letting on. "Cason was a pusher," Brant said dispassionately. "Anything's possible."

Jack's pale blue eyes regarded him another moment before he shrugged and took another gulp of whiskey. "I promised Sammy I'd put some feelers out there, tap into our underground prison pipeline."

Something inscrutable crossed his face, but Brant didn't know whether it was at the mention of Samille or the favor Jack had promised her.

"How's your mom?" Brant remembered a pale, thin slip of a woman with wispy blond hair and gray eyes that darted furtively about. He'd met her at the academy on the day he and Jack graduated from their respective programs. He'd had the vague impression that Jack's mother was a woman with many secrets, although he hadn't known the first thing about her.

"She's doing okay. I'm still trying to convince her to sell the house and move up here. She's digging in her heels though."

Brant nodded. "I'd have about as much luck convincing my folks to uproot from New York. Not that I ever would try."

Jack flashed a wry grin. "You don't think Councilman Kincaid will ever consider a run for Congress?"

"Nah. My dad enjoys local politics too much, being able to directly affect the community and keep a close eye on his beloved Brooklyn. And Mom would have a coronary if you suggested that she sell her gallery or limit her involvement in running the place."

"Set in their ways. Just like my mother." Jack drained his glass and signaled for another.

"What're you celebrating?" Brant drawled sardonically.

"Very funny. Does it look like I'm celebrating?"

"It looks like you're brooding. What's eating you alive, Burdett?"

Jack shook his head. "Can't get anything past you, can I?"

"You have to get up pretty early in the morning."

Jack laughed. He scrubbed a hand over his face and shifted restlessly in his chair. "Look, Kincaid, I didn't invite you here to cry on your shoulder."

Brant shrugged, glancing idly around the darkened barroom. "I'm not using it for anything else at the moment. Go for it."

Jack hesitated. "I need your advice. It's about a woman I'm interested in."

Almost at once Brant knew who the woman in question was. He suppressed an inward groan. He couldn't possibly give Jack Burdett advice about Samille, not when he wanted her as if his very next breath depended on it. Not when he couldn't have her.

"This is stupid," Jack said impatiently. "We're not in high school. I'm not going to sit here and make you guess the woman's identity. It's Samille, all right?"

Brant examined the label of his beer bottle. He waited for Jack to continue.

"You're not surprised?"

"Why would I be surprised?" Brant said neutrally. "You're not blind. She's a very beautiful woman."

Jack threw back his head and groaned. "And you know what makes her even more irresistible? The fact that she's totally unaware of how gorgeous she is. Man, that is *such* a turn-on."

Brant winced. He didn't want Jack Burdett—or *any* man, for that matter—getting turned on by Samille. Which was totally irrational. She didn't belong to him. He had no right to feel possessive over her.

"Have you told her how you feel?" he asked in a low, measured tone.

Jack shook his head helplessly. "I can't do it. Every time I think I'm ready to go for it, I punk out." His chuckle was full of self-recrimination. "You have no idea how difficult it was for me to admit that to you. Man, I *do* feel like I'm in high school all over again."

"How long have you felt this way about her?"

Jack snorted. "Long enough." He leaned across the

table in a confiding manner. "Don't take what I'm about to say the wrong way, Kincaid. But when I first met Samille, I'll admit that a lot of my fascination had to do with plain old-fashioned curiosity. I've never dated a black woman before."

"And you wondered what it would be like to experiment," Brant finished dryly.

"Well, yeah. But that didn't last long, because the more I got to know her, the more I saw how special she was. She's incredible. Smart, driven, tough as nails. But she's vulnerable, too—when she lets her guard down long enough for you to see it."

Brant concurred with the assessment. But he saw no point in letting Jack know that.

He took a long pull of beer. "So when do you plan to tell her how you feel?"

Jack laughed. "You don't know Samille. She'd sooner drop-kick you than allow you to open a door for her or pay her a compliment. I don't even *want* to think how she'd react if I came on to her. She's totally into her career and those juvies she mentors at the correctional center. I don't think she's interested in a relationship— with me or anyone else."

"Guess there's only one way to find out."

"You're telling me to go for it? Make my move?"

Brant's fingers tightened reflexively on the beer bottle. He liked Jack well enough, but the idea of him "making a move" on Samille made Brant want to put his fist through a wall—or through Jack's face.

"Look, Burdett, I'm no matchmaker. You have two options: tell Samille how you feel about her or spend the next six years pining after her like a lovesick puppy. Choice is yours."

"Thanks," Jack muttered. "I can always count on you to cut right to the chase. But it's not that black and white—no pun intended. Samille and I are the best of friends. She probably thinks of me as a brother."

Brant remembered the way Samille had fervently defended Jack earlier. She'd been ready to go to the mat for Burdett, which had led to their heated argument. Was it possible that Jack's feelings for her were mutual? Had their platonic friendship morphed into something deeper?

Brant felt sick at the thought.

"But I hear what you're saying," Jack continued. "There's only one way to find out how Samille feels about me. I'm gonna have to bite the bullet and go for it."

"Glad you decided." Brant drained his beer and fished some bills from his wallet. He threw them on the table and stood. "Hate to drink and run, but it's been a long day. You look like you could use an early night too."

Jack eyed him morosely. "Is that your polite way of telling me to get out of here before I drink myself into a stupor?"

Brant grinned. "Can't get anything past you, can I? Come on, Burdett. I'll follow you home."

"Why, Kincaid, I'm touched. I didn't know you cared."

"I'm more worried about other innocent drivers on the road than your pathetic behind."

"Blame Samille," Jack grumbled over his shoulder as he preceded Brant from the bar.

Brant thought about the mind-blowing kiss he and Samille had shared in her kitchen. Oh, he'd blame her all right. Blame her for another sleepless night, and for making him want her so bad he was starting to forget the reasons he couldn't have her.

CHAPTER 7

Samille slept in late on Saturday morning and awakened to the soothing patter of rain against the roof. She lay beneath the warm tangled sheets and satin quilt, unsure whether to feel relieved or annoyed that the soggy weather had ruined her daily running ritual. She yawned and snuggled deeper into the covers, deciding that she deserved the reprieve and would make up for it by doing double time tomorrow.

As she stared up at the ceiling, her mind wandered to forbidden territory. She remembered the taste of Brant Kincaid's kiss and the feel of his big hands on her body. Almost at once a lush, heavy pleasure filled her belly and brought a wanton smile to her lips. That kiss . . . Never before had she been kissed so thoroughly, so erotically. Guilt warred with a sense of gratification. She had no business fantasizing about Brant Kincaid. He was her partner in a criminal investigation, not her lover. She couldn't afford to compromise her role by getting involved with him. He was a man, and men were expected to cross the line as their libidos dictated. But, fair or not, women were held to a higher standard. Because women in law enforcement were still greatly outnumbered, Samille didn't have the luxury of making mistakes.

Getting involved with Brant Kincaid would be a colossal mistake.

"*That's* an understatement if I ever heard one," Samille muttered aloud. Still, she couldn't help but wonder if Brant thought about their kiss, if the sensations hung around him like a thick, sultry cloud as he lay in his bed that morning.

The phone rang and she groaned, willing the rest of the world away for a few more minutes while she basked in her forbidden fantasy. But the phone kept ringing.

Samille reached across the nightstand and snatched it up on the final ring. "Hello?" she grumbled.

"Good morning." Brant's deep voice poured into her ear like warm honey. Heat spread between her legs, and she closed her eyes against a fresh wave of longing.

She made her tone deliberately flat. "Oh, hi."

He chuckled. "Not much of a morning person, are you?"

"Actually, I woke up in a pretty good mood." *Daydreaming about you.* "What's up, Brant?"

"I just wanted to let you know that I'll be there to pick you up in a couple of hours."

"Okay. How'd everything go with Jefferson Spangler yesterday?"

"I'll tell you when I get there."

"All right." Samille glanced across the room as sheets of rain tumbled against the windowpane. "Is it pouring cats and dogs out there in Arlington?"

"Pretty much." He paused. "You like the rain, Samille?"

"Mmm, I love it. I'm just lying in bed wishing I didn't have to get up." *And wishing you were here beside me.* Her cheeks flamed at the unbidden thought. She cleared her throat abruptly. "I'd better get up now before I change my mind."

"See you soon," Brant murmured.

Samille hung up and fell back against the pillows with a muffled oath. Never mind competing in the male-dominated field of law enforcement. Keeping Brant Kincaid out of her system was going to be the toughest challenge she'd ever faced!

The phone rang again. Samille bit back an impatient sigh as she answered, "Hello?"

"Hey, baby."

Relief flooded her. "Hi, Aunt Noreen."

"You sound a little groggy. Did I wake you?"

"Nope, I'm already up."

"Just wanted to make sure you're still coming over for dinner. Nate and Jared will be arriving this afternoon."

Samille slapped a hand to her forehead. She'd been so preoccupied with the investigation that she'd completely forgotten about dinner at Aunt Noreen's. Mentally she kicked herself—once in the shin, twice on the butt.

"Don't tell me you forgot," Noreen said reprovingly.

"Of course not. It's just that I've been assigned a new case that's been taking up a lot of my time. I'm heading out in a few hours, as a matter of fact." She bit her bottom lip guiltily in the silence that followed.

Noreen Broussard's disappointment was palpable. "The boys were really looking forward to seeing you, Sammy."

"I know, and I really want to see them. I miss them so much."

"Then come to dinner. Surely you're not expected to work on this new case round the clock?"

"Well, no . . ." Samille thought about Brant. Would he think she was less committed to the investigation if she cut out early to have dinner with her family? Should she even care? This was her *family*, the people who had taken her in and nurtured her when she suddenly found herself an orphan. The people who had readjusted their lives to make room for her, and to make sure that she never felt less than wanted and loved.

"I'll be there, Aunt Noreen," she said decisively. Brant Kincaid could think whatever he wanted.

"Wonderful. You don't have to come early to help me out—get here as soon as you can."

"Thanks, Aunt Noreen." Samille swung her legs over the side of the bed.

"So, what's this new case you've been assigned?"

"You know I can't tell you that. But I am working with an FBI agent."

"A man?"

"Yes." Samille instantly realized her mistake.

"Invite him to dinner."

"*What?*"

"You heard me. Ask him to join us for dinner. It shows good manners."

"I—I don't really think he'd be interested."

"Nonsense. What man doesn't appreciate a good home-cooked meal?"

"Listen, Aunt Noreen, I really need to get going. I'll see all of you later."

"All right, baby. And don't forget to invite your friend to dinner."

Samille hung up the phone and shook her head in bemusement. Noreen Broussard's matchmaking schemes never failed to astonish her. She knew her aunt well enough to know that inviting Brant to dinner had little to do with mere hospitality. Noreen was relentless in her pursuit of a husband for her niece. She was hoping that Brant Kincaid would be a perfect match. It didn't matter that she knew absolutely nothing about the man. What he looked like probably didn't matter either. Aunt Noreen was that desperate.

Well, Samille *wasn't* desperate. She had no interest in getting involved with Brant Kincaid or any other man. She didn't need or want the distraction of a relationship. She had work to do, and a romantic entanglement would only slow her down.

The reminder propelled her from the bed and into the shower. As the hot water pelted her scalp and drove shampoo suds down her body, she mentally reviewed the Georgetown case. If Jefferson Spangler was responsible for selling the lethal drug to his classmates, had he known what the outcome would be? If so, what was his motive? He didn't fit the profile of troubled youth who went on school shooting sprees to get even with peers for perceived injustices. Jefferson Spangler wasn't an outcast; if anything he probably had more friends than he could handle. The mere fact that he was Senator Ashton Spangler's son earned him the respect and admiration of his classmates. He had no reason to poison them—unless he was just sadistic.

Samille had been in law enforcement long enough to know that anything was possible.

And then there was another niggling suspicion. Had Jefferson purchased the drug from someone else? What if someone had killed Andrew Cason in order to intercept Jefferson that Thursday night? If Jillian Carrella was right, Jefferson had never sold anything stronger than marijuana. Something had caused him to experiment. Something or *someone*. She was eager to find out from Brant what, if anything, yesterday's interrogation had revealed.

Samille stepped out of the shower and tugged on a terry cloth bathrobe. Her mind sorted tasks into a priority list as she blow-dried her hair and washed a load of laundry. She decided not to wash Brant's handkerchief right away, and ignored the tiny inner voice that called her all kinds of a fool. Keeping his hankie was one indulgence she would allow herself.

While Etta James's greatest hits poured from the CD player, Samille vacuumed and fixed herself a bowl of Cream of Wheat. As she ate, she finished the list of places she and Brant would visit that afternoon. Andrew Cason had frequented many establishments on a regular basis. Whether they would learn anything useful remained to be seen. But it was worth a shot.

After breakfast, Samille pulled on a pair of snug jeans and a black turtleneck. She parted her hair down the center and left it straight, knowing the humidity outdoors would do a number on any style she attempted anyway. She tugged on a pair of black ankle-length boots, applied lip gloss, and prepared to wait for Brant.

When he arrived fifteen minutes later, she met him outside. It had stopped raining, and just as she'd expected, the air was thick enough to slice with a knife.

Brant was on the phone when she climbed into the truck. He inclined his head in silent greeting, his gaze lingering on her hair. He wore dark blue jeans and a black long-sleeved shirt with a V neck. It occurred to Samille that they were dressed alike, except Brant had been smart enough not to wear a turtleneck. She tugged at her collar and hoped she didn't melt in all this humidity.

Brant got off the phone. "That was Detective Lopez. The handwriting analysis confirmed that the entry in the daily planner was Andrew Cason's."

"So we know he *did* have a meeting with Jefferson Spangler that evening."

Brant nodded. "He never made it though. The ME estimates that Cason was killed Thursday morning."

"Do you think the perp knew about his meeting with

Jefferson Spangler? What if Cason's killer wanted to get him out of the way so that *he* could meet with Jefferson, to sell him the drugs?"

"I've considered that possibility. Spangler, of course, denies knowing Andrew Cason. But he's lying—I know he recognized Cason when he saw the photograph. His father hustled him out of there before we could put the squeeze on him."

"I'm surprised the senator cooperated at all," Samille muttered. It angered her when public officials used their positions to receive special treatment. In her opinion, abuse of power was a crime punishable by death, or at least public flogging.

"He wasn't too pleased." Brant's mouth twisted sardonically. "I expect to be called into my assistant director's office first thing Monday morning in response to Spangler's complaint."

"You don't think you'll be removed from the case?" Samille's alarm was genuine.

"Nah. This isn't the first time someone like Spangler has taken issue with me, and it won't be the last." He gave her a lazy smile. "Sorry. You're not getting rid of me that easily, kiddo."

"I never said I wanted to get rid of you," Samille mumbled. *Just my crazy lust for you.*

Brant was watching her with such an odd expression that she wondered if she'd uttered the words aloud. Nervously she clutched the paper in her hand. "I have the list, so we can—"

"I'm sorry. May I?"

She frowned in confusion. "What?"

Brant reached over and gently touched her hair. Samille held her breath as he ran a hand down one side slowly, almost reverently. "God, you have beautiful hair," he murmured huskily. "You shouldn't be allowed to keep it in a ponytail. It ought to be a crime."

She swallowed hard, fighting the thrill of pleasure his words brought. "Thankfully it's not."

"It should be. And I'd enact the law myself if I could." With a look of patent regret, he pulled his hand away and started the truck. He steered out of the tight parking space with that smooth one-handed style of his. "Where's our first stop?"

Samille blinked at him, wondering how he always managed the seamless transition from personal to professional. Her nerve endings were still tingling from his touch.

He glanced at her out of the corner of his eye. "Where to?" he prompted.

"Um, dry cleaner's. On M Street."

Although Andrew Cason had lived in southeast D.C., he'd conducted most of his business on the northwest side of the city. Samille assumed he'd wanted to be near his Georgetown contacts—namely Jefferson Spangler. She couldn't imagine any other reason for him to travel all the way across town to get his clothes cleaned. Perhaps he'd even met with Jefferson while running his errands.

The petite Asian woman behind the counter lost her friendly smile the minute Brant flashed his badge. She glanced uneasily behind her, as if willing someone to emerge from the rows of plastic-covered garments to rescue her. She looked disappointed when no one appeared.

"Do you know this man?" Brant asked, showing her Andrew Cason's photograph.

She squinted at the picture. "Yes. He comes in here all the time. Nice man. Always polite."

"Have you ever seen him with someone else?"

"No, he always comes alone."

Brant withdrew Jefferson Spangler's photo from the envelope. "You've never seen him with this person?"

The woman frowned at Jefferson's image. "No, I've never seen him before."

"Is there someone else I can ask?"

"No. It's just me and my husband, and he doesn't deal with the customers. What is this about, sir?"

Brant retrieved the photographs and passed the woman his card. "Thanks for your time, ma'am. If you remember anything else, please give me a call."

Samille crossed the dry cleaner from her list when she and Brant returned to the truck. "You know what's ironic to me?" she murmured thoughtfully.

"What?"

"The fact that Andrew Cason kept his apartment like a pigsty yet cared enough to get his clothes dry-cleaned on a regular basis."

Brant's lips curved ruefully. "Guess he figured his personal appearance was more important than where he lived."

Their next two visits yielded the same results. Andrew Cason was recognized as a regular customer, but no one remembered seeing him with another person.

By the time they entered the empty bakery on Wisconsin Avenue, Samille was beginning to wonder if their efforts were nothing more than a wild-goose chase.

It didn't help that the gorgeous light-skinned woman behind the counter couldn't take her pretty green eyes off Brant. Samille might as well have been invisible beside him.

"I've seen him here before," the woman said, with barely a glance at Andrew Cason's photo. She propped her elbow on the counter and leaned closer to Brant. "He comes in twice a week and buys the same thing— half a pound of poppy seed bagels and half a pound of custard-filled lady fingers. We always tease him, asking him how he can eat so much and stay so thin. Not that *I* can't relate. I can pretty much eat whatever I want without gaining weight. I'm *very* good at burning off calories," she added with a suggestive wink at Brant.

Samille rolled her eyes. Surely Brant wasn't falling for this drivel. He was too smart, too savvy and self-assured to yield to such blatant flirtation. He was probably so used to women hitting on him that he'd heard every pickup line in the book.

He gave the woman a relaxed smile. "You think he was eating all those goodies by himself, or sharing with some friends?"

"Well, I never saw him with anyone. But he once mentioned giving the stuff to some homeless guys who did favors for him."

Brant arched an eyebrow. "Did he mention what kind of favors?"

She shook her head, and her long dark hair gleamed in the bakery's warm, recessed lighting. Samille took a little solace in the fact that Brant thought *she* had beautiful hair.

Brant produced Jefferson's photo. "You've never seen him with this person?"

Angel, as her name tag indicated, leaned even closer to inspect the picture. Any closer and she'd be sitting in Brant's lap, Samille thought peevishly. "Nope, the face doesn't look familiar. Now yours, on the other hand, does look familiar. Have we met before?"

Brant looked vaguely amused. "I don't think so."

"You're right. I would definitely remember meeting you, Agent Kincaid."

Samille pointedly cleared her throat. "Is there anyone else here who may have seen this person?"

Angel looked at her as if one of the chocolate éclairs had started talking. "Excuse me?"

"Your coworkers," Samille patiently clarified. "Or do you run this fine establishment by yourself?"

"Of course not. Not that I couldn't, though." She called to someone in the back. A minute later a short, balding man wearing a flour-stained apron emerged. He smiled at them.

"Yes, may I help you?"

"They're with the FBI, Les," Angel explained. "They want to know if our favorite customer was ever seen with the kid in that photo."

Les shuffled forward to get a better look at Jefferson's picture. He shook his head. "Not that I know of. Is Andrew in some kind of trouble?"

"I can't disclose that information," Brant replied. He passed Angel his card, which she eagerly accepted. "If either of you remembers anything else, don't hesitate to give me a call."

"Absolutely," Angel gushed.

Samille pressed her own card into the woman's palm. "Or you can call me. It doesn't matter."

Angel looked less than pleased as Brant followed Samille from the bakery with his hand at the small of her back. Inside the truck, she crossed the bakery off her list with vicious strokes of her pen.

Brant sent her an amused sidelong glance. "What was that all about?"

"Oh, please. Do you even have to ask? Did you not notice the way *Angel* was practically throwing herself at you? I half expected her to invite you into the kitchen for a lunchtime romp! 'Burning calories.' Give me a break!"

Brant chuckled. "She was a little obvious."

"A *little*?"

He grinned at her. "Jealous, Samille?"

"Of course not! Don't be ridiculous. I just think she was incredibly rude, coming on to you like that in front of me. I mean, what if you and I were involved?"

"We're not."

"But she doesn't know that! For all she knows, we could be one of those married couples who work together. We could have two-point-five kids, a chocolate Labrador, and a great big house in the suburbs. I could be *Mrs.* Brant Kincaid and—" Samille broke off, her cheeks heating with embarrassment. What was she doing? What on earth had gotten into her?

"That's a charming portrait you've painted," Brant drawled. "But don't you think we should get to know each other a little better before we buy a dog together?"

Samille gaped at him for a full thirty seconds. His lips quirked, and she burst out laughing. She didn't know what was more absurd, her irrational behavior or Brant's remark. And that was the beauty of it. She'd just made a complete fool of herself, and he'd put her at ease with a joke. She had to love him for it.

"Just for the record," he said softly, "I generally prefer a more subtle approach. I like having to wonder if a woman is interested in me. It keeps things interesting."

"Oh." Samille gulped hard and turned her head to stare out the window. "I'll keep that in mind."

"Believe me, Samille, you've kept things *mighty* interesting."

She didn't know how to respond to that, so she didn't. She changed the subject. "What kind of favors do you think the homeless guys were doing for Andrew Cason?"

"I can only imagine. Drug pickups, spying on Cason's contacts—you name it."

"Could one of them have killed Cason?"

"Bite the hand that fed them? Anything's possible, but

I still believe that whoever killed Cason also took his computer."

"Because he was blackmailing them?"

"Exactly. It's too much of a coincidence that Cason turns up murdered *and* his computer is missing. And I don't believe in coincidence."

Their next stop was an adult video store, a hole in the wall located in a run-down shopping center in southeast D.C. A few customers milled up and down the narrow aisles, browsing through porn videos. A bespectacled man behind the counter wore a T-shirt with a bright tongue protruding between a woman's pouty red lips. He regarded them suspiciously when Brant flashed his badge.

"Look, man, I don't want any trouble. I don't rent videos to minors. I *always* check IDs first."

"Relax," Brant said. "I'm not here for that. Have you seen either of these individuals before?"

Tongue Man examined both photographs. After a minute, he pointed a tobacco-stained finger at Andrew Cason's. "He comes in here all the time. Name's Ace, or something like that. I've never seen the kid before."

"What about others? Has Ace ever come here with anyone else? A buddy, a girlfriend?"

Tongue Man shook his head. "Nope." He frowned. "But there was that time . . ." He trailed off, wariness filling his expression again. "Is this guy in some kind of trouble? I'm not trying to get in the middle of anything shady."

"Tell me everything you know," Brant said sharply.

Tongue Man glanced at Samille, who nodded encouragingly. "Ace was here about a month ago," he began haltingly. "He'd just paid for his movies and stepped outside when this car pulled up out of nowhere—"

"Make? Color?"

"Jaguar. Black. Anyway, this guy jumped out of the car screaming at Ace."

"About what?"

"I couldn't catch everything because the store was busy that day. But I heard something about Ace having something that belonged to him. I think it was money. Ace told the guy to get lost." Tongue Man glanced uneasily around the store before continuing in a low voice, "And then the guy told Ace he was gonna kill him."

Brant and Samille exchanged looks. "Did you get a good look at this man?" Samille asked.

"Yeah. I ran to the door just as he was climbing back into his Jag, but I saw his face. And I remember that his hair was dark. Almost black."

"If you saw him again, could you identify him?" Brant asked.

"Probably. I'm pretty good at remembering faces."

"Good. I'd like to bring a sketch artist here so that you can describe this individual."

"A sketch artist? You mean from the police department?" Tongue Man looked stricken. "Look, man, I run a legit business here. I don't want cops crawling around the place—it might scare away my customers."

"I was trying to make it convenient for you," Brant drawled. "If you'd prefer, you can meet the sketch artist at the police station—makes no difference to me, as long as we get our composite sketch."

"Do I really have a choice in the matter?"

Brant smiled narrowly. "No."

"I can be there this evening after I close the shop," Tongue Man grudgingly acquiesced.

"Your cooperation is appreciated. What's your name?"

"Roy. Roy Clark."

Brant gave him his card. "I'll be in touch, Mr. Clark."

He dialed Detective Lopez as he and Samille left the

store and walked to the truck. When Lopez answered, he explained what the video store owner had witnessed. "We need to hook him up with one of your sketch artists today."

"That's going to be tough," Lopez said. "Milsner's out on vacation until Monday, and the freelancer we use is on other assignments until late tomorrow."

Brant frowned. Andrew Cason's murder investigation technically belonged to D.C. police. He'd have a hard time getting authorization to use the Bureau's sketch artists. Even if the request *were* approved, it would take too long.

"I recommend waiting for Milsner to get back on Monday," Lopez said. "He's the best we've got."

"Let me know the second he's available." Brant ended the call and unlocked the truck for Samille before returning to the video store to inform the owner what was happening. When Roy Clark seemed a little too relieved by the brief delay, Brant reiterated the importance of getting a sketch of the man who'd threatened Andrew Cason. Before leaving the store, he added a veiled threat about performing an audit of the store's rental records—just in case Clark changed his mind about cooperating.

"What do you make of it?" Samille asked when Brant returned to the truck. "Sounds to me like one of Cason's drug deals went sour. You think he owed this guy money?"

"Or something." Brant didn't start the engine right away. Eyes narrowed, he stared at the video store entrance. After a few minutes Roy Clark emerged, looking carefully to his left and right and scanning the parking lot. He couldn't see the Expedition parked beside a utility van—a deliberate maneuver on Brant's part. As he and Samille watched, Clark lit a cigarette and dug a cell phone out of his pocket. He spoke to someone briefly and hung up. He took a few drags on the cigarette before tossing it to the ground and crushing it beneath his foot. With one last glance around, he turned and disappeared inside the store.

Brant reached under his seat and removed a laptop computer. He entered Roy Clark's name and identifying data into the FBI's National Crime Information Center, a computerized database accessible to law enforcement agencies nationwide. Using the NCIC's technology, Brant ran a criminal background check on Roy Clark to find out if their witness had any credibility issues. He didn't like surprises.

Samille watched with wry amusement as he sent his query and logged off the computer. "All the information you need right at your fingertips. Nice, isn't it?"

"It has its advantages," Brant agreed. "By tomorrow I'll have everything I need to know about our friendly video store proprietor."

"Which reminds me." Samille reached inside her purse and pulled out a compact disc. She passed it to Brant. "I downloaded Andrew Cason's files last night. Everything you want should be there. Let me know if you need anything else."

"Thanks, Samille. I appreciate it."

"No problem." She reviewed her list as Brant started the truck and pulled out of the parking lot. "Looks like we've had a productive day. And it's not even four o'clock yet." Her cell phone rang and she dug it out of her purse. Her voice lowered to a soft murmur as she spoke.

Brant pointed the truck northwest toward Dupont Circle to drop Samille off. She was right. They'd had a productive day. He had to believe that they'd made some progress and uncovered a solid lead. If not, the frustration he'd been keeping at bay would eat away at him like an aggressive tumor. Although he'd only been working the case for five days, it felt like an eternity. He could only imagine what it felt like to the parents of the teenage victims. Their children had been comatose for a week now, and with each passing day, their chances for recovery grew more remote. Brant thought of the approaching holidays. He didn't want to imagine those ten families burying their teenagers as millions of other families settled around a festive Thanksgiving table.

Samille's low, brittle voice penetrated his gloomy musings. "I'd really rather not, Aunt Noreen. I don't think it's a good idea."

Brant glanced at her, but the heavy curtain of her raven hair had fallen forward to conceal her face. She was turned slightly away from him as if she didn't want him to overhear her conversation.

Brant reviewed the solitary evening ahead of him. He'd probably grab some takeout and head home to pore through Andrew Cason's files. It wasn't much of a Saturday night, but he'd never been one for an active social life anyway. His love life was practically nonexistent—not for the lack of opportunities, but because of his own unwillingness to put himself out there. He knew he wasn't capable of giving a woman the kind of emotional commitment she would demand. He'd accepted long ago that it just wasn't in him, and likely never would be.

Not that he'd lived like a monk. He had the requisite male urges that he indulged at the appropriate intervals with attractive, savvy women who understood that he wasn't seeking permanence.

Which was why Samille Broussard posed such a problem.

He wanted her, but he knew she deserved far more than he would ever be able to give. And yet he couldn't keep himself from desiring her, desiring her to the point of distraction.

"Fine. If you insist." Heaving a resigned sigh, Samille

held her cell phone out to him. "My aunt would like to speak to you."

"Your *aunt*?"

Samille nodded and rolled her eyes as if to say: *don't ask.*

Puzzled, Brant accepted the phone from her. "This is Brant Kincaid."

"Hello, Brant Kincaid," a woman's voice greeted him warmly. "This is Noreen Broussard, Samille's aunt. I don't know whether or not she told you, but we're having dinner together this evening. I wondered if you might like to join us."

The invitation caught him off guard. "That's very kind of you, Ms. Broussard, but—"

"I know it's short notice, and you may already have plans tonight. But if you're free, the family and I would love to have you. I've spent the whole day in the kitchen preparing a feast fit for kings. You won't be disappointed."

Brant met Samille's eyes. She looked utterly embarrassed, which amused him. He couldn't deny that a home-cooked meal sounded far more appealing than takeout. Not to mention the fact that he wasn't entirely ready to part company with his beautiful partner—which he knew was a mistake.

Before he knew what was happening, he'd opened his mouth and accepted Noreen Broussard's dinner invitation.

"Oh, good!" she exclaimed. "I'm so glad you can make it."

"Thanks for the invitation. I look forward to meeting you."

"The feeling is mutual, Brant."

He passed the phone back to Samille and grinned at her mortified expression.

She spoke into the phone. "We're not really dressed for dinner, Aunt Noreen, and I know how you are about jeans at your dinner table . . ." She paused, then nodded dutifully. "All right then. We'll be there in a little while."

She hung up with a loud groan and turned to Brant. "I'm really sorry about that. My aunt can be incredibly persistent when she wants to be—which is most of the time."

Brant chuckled, slowing for a red light. "Don't apologize. My mother's the same way."

"If you'd really rather not come, you can drop me off at home and I'll just tell Aunt Noreen that you got called away. You don't have to feel obligated just because she put you on the spot."

"I don't."

Samille blinked at him. "Don't what?"

"Feel obligated." He slanted her a knowing look. "If you'd rather I didn't come—"

"Don't be silly. You're more than welcome to join us for dinner. But only if you really want to, Brant. I'm serious."

He met her anxious expression. "I want to. Do we need to change first?"

"No. Aunt Noreen says everyone is dressed casually, so we can head straight there."

"Let's go."

CHAPTER 8

Samille's trepidation returned with a vengeance when Brant turned onto a winding country road flanked by trees blooming with riotous fall color. As the Broussards' sprawling brick house rolled into view, her fingers tightened reflexively on the door handle. She knew her anxiety bordered on absurd, but she couldn't help it. Apart from her prom date—who'd spent the entire evening ogling the head cheerleader in a backless gown—Samille had never brought a man home to meet her family. She hoped they didn't attach more significance to Brant's presence than was warranted.

More importantly, she prayed that Aunt Noreen didn't embarrass her.

"Nice house," Brant commented as they climbed from the truck.

"Thanks. We moved here when I was twelve."

Before they could reach the wide mahogany door, it was swung open by a slender, attractive woman whose smooth mocha skin defied her fifty-six years. Her soft black hair was worn in a short natural that accentuated the classic contours of her face. She beamed at them. "You're here!"

Samille laughed as her aunt swallowed her in a tight embrace. "It's good to see you again, Aunt Noreen. How long has it been—three weeks?"

Noreen Broussard drew back, her light brown eyes glinting with mild reproof. "Three weeks is too long, young lady. Especially when we live only forty minutes apart." Her gaze landed on Brant, and her smile widened with undisguised pleasure. "Why, hello. You must be Brant Kincaid. Welcome to our home. I'm Noreen Broussard."

"Nice to meet you," Brant said, shaking her hand.

"Come in, come in," Noreen urged, opening the door wider to usher them inside. "Oh, look! You're both dressed alike. Isn't that adorable?"

Samille and Brant exchanged glances. "It wasn't intentional," she mumbled to her aunt, ignoring Brant's amused expression.

The heavy thud of footsteps on hardwood floors announced the approach of the Broussard men. Before Samille could draw her next breath, she was enveloped in the solid warmth of Gabriel Broussard's arms.

Samille and Gabriel Broussard had always shared a special bond. Both had loved and adored Samuel Broussard. When he died, Gabe lost more than a brother, Samille more than a father. Both lost a vital piece of themselves, and their shared sense of abandonment bound them irrevocably together.

"Glad you could make it, Sammy," Gabe greeted her. His deep voice was a gravelly caress against her temple as he planted a kiss on her forehead. He drew back and tweaked her nose. "We were going to send out a search and rescue team if you didn't show up."

Samille grinned. "I know."

Jared Broussard grabbed her in a bear hug. Samille laughed as he hoisted her effortlessly into the air and spun her around, much as he'd done when she was a little girl.

"I can't believe it's you, baby girl!" he exclaimed, setting her down. He held her at arms' length as he gave her the once-over, his strong white teeth flashing in a grin. "I feel like I haven't seen you in ages."

"Me too." Nate Broussard stepped forward to hug her. "No more signs of Tidbit. She's all grown up."

Samille grinned at her cousins. "You guys act like it's been ten years since we saw one another. You both came home for Christmas last year, remember?"

Nate and Jared Broussard were identical in height at six-three. They had inherited their father's lean, handsome features and deep-set dark eyes. But where Nate had also inherited his father's mahogany skin, Jared's caramel complexion was a shade closer to his mother's. At thirty-five, Nate was two years older than Jared. Throughout their childhood he'd invoked his seniority at every opportunity—which meant he got to ride shotgun on trips to the grocery store, was allowed to stay up later during the summer, and got his driver's license first.

In unison the Broussard men turned their dark gazes on Brant. Samille quickly performed the introductions, and the four men exchanged handshakes and relaxed greetings.

"Too bad you guys didn't get here sooner," Jared said to Brant. "We just finished a game of football in the backyard, and we could've used another player to make the teams even."

Samille thrust her hands on her hips. "And what am I? Window dressing?"

Jared laughed. "Sorry, Sammy. Your tomboy days are long over." He looked to Brant for confirmation. "Aren't they?"

Amused, Brant gazed at Samille. "You would think."

She glared at him, which only increased his mirth.

Noreen Broussard watched the exchange with an intuitive smile. She rubbed her hands together and gaily announced, "The table's set and dinner's all ready. Samille, why don't you help me bring the food out while the fellas get settled?"

"Don't worry," Jared teased, "we won't tell Brant embarrassing stories about you. Well, maybe just one or two."

Samille shot Jared a murderous look before following her aunt into the large modern kitchen. Steam-covered dishes filled every available surface, including the center island.

"I can't believe you made all this food, Aunt Noreen!" exclaimed Samille. "Thanksgiving is less than three weeks away. Are you going to do all this cooking again?"

Noreen grinned. "You know how much I enjoy cooking, especially now that I'm on sabbatical. Cooking has gotten me through many periods of writer's block."

"I can imagine." Samille lifted one lid and drew a deep, appreciative breath of her aunt's signature chicken and sausage jambalaya. The recipe had been in Noreen's Creole family for generations, and she guarded the secret ingredients with the utmost vigilance. She'd promised to pass the recipe onto Samille once she got married, swearing that the jambalaya had placated her own husband on numerous occasions and kept arguments at bay. Samille balked at the notion that the way to a man's heart was through his stomach. If she had to appease a man's appetite in order to win his heart, she didn't want it.

Noreen appeared beside her. "Brant seems very nice," she casually remarked.

Samille braced herself. She knew what was coming next, and was not surprised when her aunt asked, "Is he married? I didn't see a ring."

Samille stopped just short of rolling her eyes. "No, Aunt Noreen. He isn't married."

"That's hard to believe. He's very handsome, you know."

"Yeah, I noticed."

"Of course. You'd have to be blind not to. How long have you been working together?"

"Since Wednesday. So we don't really know each other very well," she added pointedly.

"That doesn't matter." Noreen's light brown eyes twinkled with mischief. "I fell in love with your uncle in less time than that."

Samille groaned. "Aunt Noreen, *please.* Brant and I are colleagues. Nothing more, nothing less."

"Of course, *chère.*" Smiling, Noreen placed a steaming dish in Samille's hands. "Let's not keep our men waiting any longer."

Mealtime in the Broussard household had always been undertaken as a sacred occasion, a celebration of family, good health, and the blessing of food. No matter how busy schedules were—between the kids' extracurricular activities and Gabriel Broussard's long hours at the bank where he now served as president and board chairman—dinner was seldom missed. The family had often been joined by Nate and Jared's friends and teammates, and occasionally Gabe had invited his business associates.

Dinner that evening was nothing short of a lavish affair. In addition to jambalaya, Noreen had prepared succulent prime rib au jus and summer chicken with cream and tarragon sauce. The meal was consumed with collective enthusiasm, which pleased Noreen immensely as she urged everyone to take second and third helpings.

The conversation around the table was animated and sometimes chaotic, a colorful exchange of ideas and opinions. The topics ranged from the fluctuating economy and politics to sports and entertainment. But there was a cohesion in the cacophony of voices, a warm regard that encouraged the participation of all assembled.

Seated across the table from Brant, Samille couldn't help noticing the relaxed way he interacted with her family. He and Jared, in particular, seemed to have known each other for years instead of a couple of hours. As if sensing her appraisal, Brant glanced over and winked at her before resuming his conversation with Jared. The tiny acknowledgment warmed her immeasurably, and she blushed like a schoolgirl when she looked up and caught Noreen's discerning smile.

When her aunt addressed Brant, Samille found herself holding her breath in nervous anticipation of what Noreen would say. "So, Brant, where are you from?"

"Brooklyn."

"Is that right? You wouldn't happen to be related to Audre Kincaid, would you?"

"Actually, she's my mother."

Noreen's eyes widened in delight. "What a small world! I met your mother several years ago, back when she was a curator at the Museum of Modern Art. She gave a lecture on the Pollock exhibit, and I remember being thoroughly impressed with her knowledge and passion for his work. Afterward I had a lot of questions, so I waited and waited for the opportunity to introduce myself to her. Seems I wasn't the only fan she'd gained that day." Noreen smiled warmly. "I was struck by how incredibly gracious and down-to-earth she was. In the middle of answering my questions, she announced that she was hungry and asked me if I'd like to join her for lunch. We've kept in touch ever since. In fact, I was going to call her next week. My publisher has given me free rein to commission one of Audre's artists to design the cover for my upcoming book on nineteenth-century African-American writers."

"I'm sure my mother would like that," Brant said.

Noreen beamed at him. "You know, I wasn't at all surprised when I learned she'd opened her own art gallery. Like I said, she was very knowledgeable and enthusiastic about her subject matter." To Samille she explained, "Brant's mother is considered one of the leading authorities in African-American art. She was recently featured in *Smithsonian* magazine for a lecture series she did at NYU. You must be so proud, Brant. And how's your father doing?"

Brant took a sip of white wine. "He's fine, thanks for asking."

"Brant's father is City Councilman Maurice Kincaid," Noreen informed everyone at the table. "He was very active in the civil rights era, as was Audre. Both participated in Dr. King's historic March on Washington. In fact, that's how your parents met, isn't it, Brant? On their way to D.C.? They were barely out of high school, but both were very committed to our people's struggle for racial equality."

"Brant, you'll have to forgive my wife," Gabe Broussard said with an indulgent smile. "She's a professor. Lecturing comes as natural to her as breathing."

Nate and Jared chuckled. Brant smiled. "I'm flattered that you think so favorably of my parents, Mrs. Broussard."

"Please, call me Noreen. Did you inherit your mother's affinity for art, Brant?"

"Not quite to that extent." His eyes met Samille's across the table. "But I can definitely appreciate a work of art when I see one."

Samille's belly flip-flopped at the unmistakable meaning behind his words. Their gazes locked for only a few seconds, but if the exchange had lasted an eternity, it couldn't have been more charged. She forced herself to look away, only to encounter her family's knowing expressions. She took a hasty sip of wine and choked.

Seated beside her, Nate patted her gently on the back and grinned. "Easy there, slugger."

Samille wiped her mouth with a napkin and squelched the vicious urge to kick Brant under the table.

"Who's ready for dessert?" Noreen asked cheerfully.

For three hours every Sunday afternoon, Samille tutored juvenile inmates through a self-help literacy program, Read for Life. The program had been launched as a result of her encounter with one of the inmates, Portia Dawkins.

Portia was fifteen years old when she was arrested for drug possession, prostitution, and the attempted murder of her pimp—a man whom the DEA had been trying to take down for months. Tyrone "Sugar Bear" Langdon, a local street hood turned entrepreneur, had amassed a small fortune in the drug and prostitution trade.

Two years ago, Samille accompanied Jack Burdett and several agents on a raid to the Washington, D.C. residence that served as Langdon's base of operations and was known by neighbors as the "brothel." Inside the luxuriously furnished house, they discovered a cache of cocaine and loot—and an eerily calm Portia Dawkins standing over the body of Tyrone Langdon, a semiautomatic still clutched in her hand. Langdon survived the gunshot wound and was later tried and convicted for his crimes. But Portia Dawkins did not escape prosecution, either. The court system didn't share Samille's belief that the fifteen-year-old girl was a victim who had been forced into a life of drugs and prostitution due to an impoverished childhood, where neglect and sexual abuse were stark realities. She was depicted as a coldhearted mercenary who'd plotted to kill Tyrone Langdon and skip town with all his money. She was charged as an adult and sentenced to four years in a specialized medium-security institution in D.C.

Haunted by the case, Samille spent several months researching the prevalence of juveniles in adult correctional facilities. She was disturbed to learn about overcrowding conditions, the incidence of violence committed against incarcerated juveniles by adult inmates, alarming suicide rates, and the lack of vocational opportunities and substance abuse treatment and prevention programs. Although the law mandated that incarcerated youth should receive regular and special education services, there were far too many facilities that didn't adhere to the law, or offered the bare minimum.

Samille began to visit Portia Dawkins, and although she was satisfied to discover that the girl *was* receiving adequate GED preparation, Samille felt there was more she could do. She reached out to her contacts at the Federal Bureau of Prisons and Department of Corrections, spoke with her colleagues at the Department of Justice, and collaborated with policy analysts to draft a proposal for the self-help literacy program. With the additional support of high-ranking DEA officials, the Read for Life program was approved within a year.

The program was based on readings and essays from a list of federally approved materials. Upon completion of a reading assignment, the students were required to write an essay on the material's relevance to a chosen topic. The goal was to improve the participants' reading and writing skills, expose them to a broad range of literary works, and supplement their general education while they remained incarcerated.

Samille smiled as each girl bravely delivered her essay before the corrections officer indicated that their time was up. His presence served as a sober reminder of where they were, that instead of heading home to bedrooms done in hot pink and decorated with posters of pop idols, these girls were returning to drab cells and the regimented routine of prison life.

They stood and filed mechanically to the door, identical in their orange jumpers and white sneakers. Portia Dawkins hung back, her expression troubled.

"Just a few more minutes, Earl?" Samille said to the stoic-faced corrections officer.

He hesitated, and she gave him her most beguiling smile. He actually blushed. "I'll be back in a few," he consented before closing the door.

"Is everything all right, Portia?" It was a ridiculous question. The girl was facing two more years of incarceration. Of course everything was *not* all right.

Portia shrugged and toyed with one of her thick braids. "Some days are better than others," she mumbled dispiritedly.

"Want to talk about it?" Samille asked gently.

"What's the point? There's nothing you or anyone else can do about it. I got myself into this mess, and I have no choice but to live with it." She folded her arms across her small breasts and stared at the mottled linoleum floor, appearing almost as vulnerable as she'd looked the first time Samille met her, when the shock lifted and she realized she had just shot a man.

Samille's heart constricted once again. "Did something happen, Portia?"

Again the girl shrugged. "No, not really. I just miss being on the outside. I know that sounds crazy, considering the kind of life I had when you met me." She lifted dark, haunted eyes to Samille's face. "But there are some nights that I just lie awake staring at the ceiling, wishing I was anywhere but here. Sometimes I even think I'd rather be servicing some old pervert off the street than locked away in this place. That's how badly I miss my freedom, Samille."

Samille nodded wordlessly.

"You know, I called my cousin Jasmine this morning— the one I used to stay with when I needed to hide out from Tyrone. Did I tell you she started college this semester? She's going part-time and working two jobs to help pay tuition. I'm so proud of her. She's doing things the right way, unlike me."

"Don't beat yourself up, Portia. You can't dwell on the past."

"I'm trying not to, believe me. But it's hard." Portia sighed. "Anyway, Jasmine was talking about her classes and professors, and doing *normal* things I never had the opportunity to do. Last night she and her girlfriends went to a club and had a blast. When this guy approached Jasmine and tried to sell her drugs, she even had enough common sense to turn him down. Now if that had been *me*, who knows what I would have done? I probably would've taken the stupid drugs and wound up like those white kids in Georgetown."

Samille grew very still. "Did your cousin tell you what this guy looked like?"

Portia grinned. "She said he was wearing a mask and some sort of costume, even though Halloween was three weeks ago. Something with a hood. He told her he'd be back on Thursday night in case she changed her mind. She and her friends just thought he was high and laughed it off. You know people in clubs do weird stuff like that all the time, especially at *that* club."

"Which club?"

"Zydeco. You ever been there?"

"No," Samille murmured, the wheels churning in her mind, "I can't say I've had the pleasure."

Portia laughed. "You really need to get out more, Samille. I know you're DEA and all, but that doesn't mean you can't have a social life."

The corrections officer opened the door. "Time's up, Broussard. No exceptions this time."

When Portia looked crestfallen, Samille gave her a hug. "Try to cheer up," she said coaxingly. "You *will* have another chance to do the same things as your cousin Jasmine, and I know when the time comes, you're going to make the most of the opportunity."

"I know." Portia nodded resolutely as she backed toward the door. "See you next week?"

Samille's smile was gentle. "Wild horses couldn't keep me away, Portia."

Samille collected her belongings from the security entrance used by the corrections officers and spent a few minutes chatting with them before leaving. The correctional facility consisted of five separate multistory buildings that were adjacent to one another, presenting the appearance of one large structure.

Dusk had fallen, casting the compound in hulking shadows. Samille fished her keys out of her purse as she headed for the parking lot. Her cell phone rang and she picked it up. "Hello?"

There was nothing but heavy silence.

"Hello?" she repeated, fighting quick irritation.

Still no response. As she started to hang up, she heard it. Very faint, barely a hushed whisper. "*Nine lives.*"

"What?" Samille demanded, trying to ignore the twinge of unease that slithered down her spine. "Who is this?"

The line went dead. Her hand trembled as she slid the phone back inside her purse. She threw a quick glance over her shoulder, but there was no one in sight.

She immediately decided that the call had been a prank. Despite the fact that her cell phone number was unlisted and very few people knew it, she still received the occasional annoying calls from telemarketers. She supposed it was just as easy for a bunch of kids with nothing better to do on a Sunday night to begin dialing random numbers.

But the caller's cryptic missive whispered across her mind. *Nine lives*. What did it mean? Cats purportedly had nine lives. What was the person trying to convey? That Samille had nine lives? Was the message a veiled threat?

She shivered inside her wool jacket and hastened her steps to the parking lot.

Jefferson Spangler slowly hung up the phone. Beads of sweat clung to his upper lip, and he reached up and wiped away the moisture with a smile. Adrenaline was pumping hard through his veins, making him feel almost light-headed. Who needed drugs? Danger provided its own natural high.

He pulled a baseball cap low over his eyes and grabbed his varsity jacket as he left his bedroom. The house was silent as he descended the staircase. His parents were out for the evening attending a political fund-raiser, which meant he could escape without detection. None of the servants would dare question his movements. He'd have to evade the muscle-bound goon his father had recently hired to follow him around—"for his own safety," Ashton had explained—but that was no problem. If his father *did* become the next president, Jefferson looked forward to giving those Secret Service clones a run for their money. He was developing quite an appetite for cat-and-mouse games.

Jefferson had reached the front door when a voice

stopped him cold in his tracks. "Where do you think you're going?"

Heart in his throat, Jefferson whirled around to find his father's senior congressional aide standing there. "Jesus, Chad, do you have to sneak up on me like that?"

Chadwick Preston epitomized the kind of political staffers Ashton Spangler liked to surround himself with. He was clean-cut and polished, a Harvard Law graduate from a good southern Protestant family. With his carefully groomed dark hair, deep green eyes, and all-American good looks, he could easily have replaced Rob Lowe on *The West Wing*. Jefferson hated that show.

Chad crossed his arms and gave Jefferson an imperious look from behind his rimless eyeglasses. "I did not sneak up on you. And I asked you a question: where do you think you're going?"

Jefferson bristled. "Out. Not that it's any of your business. What're you still doing here anyway? Dad's not home."

"Not that it's any of *your* business," Chad said loftily, "but I'm drafting a speech for your father to deliver at a conference on Medicaid next week. Not that *you* take any interest in his activities."

"Give me a break, Chad. I'm seventeen years old. How many kids do you know who take an interest in what their parents do?"

"I guess if you're benefiting from the fruits of your father's labor, nothing else matters."

"You said it, not me." Jefferson reached for the doorknob.

Again Chad's reproachful tone halted him. "You're up to something, Jefferson. Your father may not know it, but I do. I can sense it."

A cold sweat broke out all over Jefferson's body. Panic ricocheted through him. Had Chad been in his bedroom?

Did he know about his secret stash of drugs? No, it wasn't possible. If Chad had known anything about Jefferson's illegal activities, he would have gone straight to Ashton Spangler. Chad was too straitlaced, too ethical, to keep silent about such matters. He would consider it his moral duty to inform the senator about his son's conduct, if for no other reason than to distance himself from it. Chadwick Preston was the epitome of a Goody Two-shoes. In his spare time he volunteered at local hospitals, participated in canned food drives, and contributed regularly to charities. He genuinely believed in the rhetoric that each person could make a difference in the world by giving back.

Jefferson forced a strangled laugh. "Get a life, Chadwick." He yanked open the front door and headed for his Roadster parked at the curb.

Brant leaned back against the leather chair in his home study and tiredly rubbed his eyes. Other than his routine ten-mile hike that morning, he'd spent the day indoors poring through paperwork and files on Andrew Cason. Samille had been right: everything he'd ever wanted to know about the dead man could be found in the files she'd given him.

Everything—except who had put a single bullet through his head.

Brant drained his fourth cup of coffee and grimaced. He'd really have to make a concerted effort to cut back on his daily intake. Sleep was hard enough to come by without all that caffeine sloshing around in his veins.

He got up and went to use the bathroom. As he washed his hands, he mentally reviewed Andrew Cason's history. A transplant from New Jersey, Cason came to D.C. to attend American University. His poor grades forced him to withdraw after three semesters. Around the same time, he began dealing heavily in drugs and became known as the supplier for campus parties. His frat brothers called him their "ace in the hole," but when the police came knocking on fraternity row and uncovered the stash of drugs, Andrew Cason was left holding the proverbial bag. He was expelled from the university and charged with felony drug distribution. Since it was his first offense, the judge went easy on him and gave him a light sentence. But Cason didn't learn his lesson. By the time he was twenty-five, he'd been busted so many times it was a miracle the courts didn't keep him permanently behind bars.

Brant frowned. How had Jack Burdett failed to perform a background check on Andrew Cason? It seemed incongruous that someone as thorough as Jack would have made such a monumental error, one that nearly cost him his job. Unless he *had* known about Cason's criminal history and used him as an informant anyway. But why? Why would Jack jeopardize his cases by employing the services of an informant with major credibility issues? Brant knew it happened all the time. He'd heard of unscrupulous agents who teamed up with crooks just to get a share of the profits, or who subscribed to the notion that real criminals made the best informants. But somehow he couldn't see Jack falling into either category. So what had caused him to skip protocol and look the other way where Andrew Cason was concerned?

Was it possible that Cason had been blackmailing Jack Burdett?

Brant paused. Even as he felt a stab of disloyalty at the thought, the investigator in him knew he had to explore all scenarios. Whether he liked it or not, Jack had a motive for killing Andrew Cason. The man's lies had cost Jack a major case and caused him to come under the scrutiny of Internal Affairs. One didn't forget such transgressions so easily. And if Cason *had* been blackmailing Jack—for reasons Brant couldn't begin to fathom—then murder was a very plausible conclusion.

But the pieces didn't quite fit. Brant was convinced that whoever killed Cason had also provided drugs to Jefferson Spangler. It wasn't a theory he could explain or support with solid evidence at this point; it was more of a premonition, a gut instinct. Which was why he was hell-bent on uncovering the identity of Cason's murderer. Even if he believed Jack capable of killing Andrew Cason, Brant couldn't imagine him selling drugs to a high school kid.

Resettling into his chair, Brant reviewed the NCIC report he'd received on Roy Clark. The video store owner was clean as a whistle. Brant looked forward to getting him in front of the police sketch artist. He hoped Clark's description of the man who had threatened Andrew Cason would begin to give them a clearer picture of what was going on.

His cell phone rang and he reached across the desk to answer it. "Kincaid."

"Kincaid, this is Lopez. I'm at GWU Hospital. You'd better come quick."

Brant frowned. "What is it?"

"One of our vics is dead." Lopez hesitated. "A note was left behind."

Brant swore softly. "I'm on my way."

CHAPTER 9

Detective Lopez met him at the entrance to the Intensive Care Unit. Deep lines of fatigue were etched into his forehead. His expression was grim. "Christ, what a mess. The media's going to be all over this place in no time."

"Have the victim's parents been notified?"

"I sent two uniforms to deliver the news in person. Chief Rucker says we'll need to hold a press conference first thing in the a.m. I'm not looking forward to facing any of those parents, least of all Bradley Whitfield's. What a mess."

Brant glanced around the busy hospital corridor. D.C. cops milled around, conversing with hospital staff and speaking into radios that crackled with static. One officer appeared to be consoling a distraught middle-aged woman in a white nurse's uniform. She swiped at her nose with a wad of tissue and wrung her hands in consternation.

Brant inclined his head toward the woman. "Is that our witness?"

Lopez nodded. "Her name's Clara Reynolds. She said she stepped away from the nurses' station for five minutes to check on another patient. When she came back, Bradley Whitfield was flat-lining."

"Was she the only nurse on duty?"

"No, there were two others. But they were downstairs in the cafeteria. Nurse Reynolds says visiting hours were over, so the floor was pretty quiet. She didn't see anyone coming or going."

Brant nodded briskly. "You said there was a note?"

Lopez reached inside his leather jacket and withdrew a clear glassine bag containing a single sheet of paper. He passed it to Brant. "Nurse Reynolds found this attached to the patient chart when she went into Bradley's room. She screamed so loud it brought an orderly from another floor."

Brant read the note quickly, his blood growing colder with each typed word. It was the first stanza of an old nursery rhyme, and the message was eerily haunting in its significance. TEN LITTLE INDIANS GOING OUT TO DINE. ONE WENT AND CHOKED HIS LITTLE SELF. AND THEN THERE WERE NINE.

Nine victims left.

He lifted his sharpened gaze to the detective's face. "She didn't see anyone in the corridor?"

"Not a soul. And she insists that she couldn't have been gone from her station more than five minutes."

Brant examined the note inside the bag. It was on plain white paper and had been generated from a standard laser printer. He reread the message, sifting through the text and isolating certain words. *Choked his little self* . . .

"Has the ME arrived?" he asked.

"He's in the room now. Nurse Reynolds says the victim's body was undisturbed. If not for the note, she probably wouldn't have been so stunned by Bradley Whitfield's death. She said she and the other nurses have been preparing themselves for this possibility."

"We need to talk to hospital security and get a look at the surveillance tapes, see if we recognize anyone."

"Already done. They said we can head over whenever we're ready. I was waiting for you to arrive. And I've alerted security at GU Hospital to keep guards posted outside each victim's room." Lopez inclined his head toward the note. "What do you make of it? Think it's our perp, or just someone with a twisted sense of humor?"

Brant frowned. He wished he could dismiss the note as someone's idea of a cruel joke, but training and instincts warned him otherwise.

Grimly he passed the bag back to Lopez. "We'll test it for fingerprints, but I doubt we'll lift anything. If our guy was smart enough to slip in and out of a hospital room without detection, he was smart enough to wear gloves."

Lopez grunted in agreement.

"We'll have to keep the note out of the press," Brant said in a tone that brooked no argument. "Under no circumstances do we want to open the floodgates for rampant speculation and copycats."

"*Ay dios!*" Lopez muttered in disgust. "Can you just imagine every crackpot in the city sneaking into hospitals to leave riddles at the bedside of dying patients?"

"Takes all kinds."

They looked up as the medical examiner and an assistant technician emerged from Bradley Whitfield's room. The body had been transferred to a gurney and was covered with a starched white sheet.

Clara Reynolds clapped a trembling hand to her mouth at the sight of the teenager's shrouded remains. The officer she'd been talking to draped an awkward arm around her shoulders.

Brant and Marc Lopez started toward the medical examiner. Henry Wilcox was a short, graying man with a sturdy frame and keen hazel eyes discernible behind a pair of wire-rimmed glasses. He wore a knit polo shirt and brown gabardine trousers.

He gave Brant a wan smile of recognition. "Agent Kincaid," he greeted him in a low, raspy drawl. "Long time no see, eh?"

Brant offered a half smile. "Not long enough, Henry. What's the verdict?"

"No sign of foul play," Wilcox said. "No strangulation marks, no evidence of suffocation. Kid looks like he just slipped away into never-never land, which is consistent with coma victims."

"How soon can we expect the autopsy report?"

"Let's see." Wilcox pursed thin, liver-spotted lips. "It's after seven on a Sunday evening, and I got called away from dinner with my wife and some guests we were entertaining—"

"Henry."

"Just for you, I'll make it a priority first thing in the morning. Don't have much of a choice anyway, considering the mayor and your boss are going to be breathing down my neck, too." He looked down at Bradley Whitfield's covered remains and shook his head mournfully. "Kid had his whole life ahead of him. What a waste."

After Wilcox and his assistant had wheeled Bradley Whitfield away, Brant walked over to Clara Reynolds and introduced himself.

"Detective Lopez says you were the only nurse on the floor when it happened."

She sniffled. "That's right. We were pretty short-staffed today—a lot of the nurses were out sick with the flu. Those of us here were just relieved that it was such a quiet night. Little did we know."

Brant nodded sympathetically. "You were right to call the police immediately, Ms. Reynolds. Now I need to ask another favor of you. Given the sensitive nature of our investigation, it's important that we limit the information made available to the public. I know this experience has been very traumatic for you, but I have to ask you not to discuss specific details with anyone."

"You don't want me to tell anyone about the note?" Clara Reynolds clarified.

"Especially not the note." Brant offered a conciliatory smile meant to gain her trust. "Do you think you could do that for me?"

A winsome smile trembled across the woman's lips. "I can do that."

"Good. I'm going to give you my card. If you think of anything else, absolutely anything, please call me."

She nodded meekly and accepted his card, sliding it into the front pocket of her floral-print lab coat.

Brant made eye contact with the officer who stood beside her. His name badge identified him as Corporal Fuller. "Why don't you take Ms. Reynolds downstairs for a cup of coffee? She could probably use a change of scenery."

Clara Reynolds sent Brant a grateful look as Fuller escorted her down the corridor.

"Smooth," Lopez complimented Brant, with a touch of genuine admiration. "I bet you could've talked the drawers off Sister Mary Agnes Spiro."

"Who's Mary Agnes Spiro?"

"A sourpuss nun at my old Catholic school. She was meaner than Lucifer himself, and her face always looked as if she'd been sucking on lemons." Lopez grinned lewdly. "Probably would've done her a lot of good to suck on something else, if you catch my drift."

Brant grimaced. "I do, unfortunately."

He walked into the vacated hospital room and looked around. Lopez stood at the door and watched as he opened drawers, inspected the interior of the closet and adjoining bathroom. Brant crossed to the window and peered through the darkness, hearing the rustle of dry leaves and a faint gust of November wind through brittle branches. People came and went from the hospital, visitors bearing get-well gifts, staff members heading home to sleep as shifts changed. All seemed normal enough, yet he couldn't shake the prescient sense of foreboding that crawled over his skin and seeped into his bones.

Lopez spoke from the doorway. "Are you ready to view the surveillance tapes?"

Brant stood at the window a moment longer, wondering if the perpetrator lingered in the shadows, waiting for the opportunity to strike again.

And then there were nine.

Slowly he turned to face the detective. "Let's go."

Samille's nerves were still frayed from the eerie phone call by the time she finished grocery shopping and went home. She was haunted by the cryptic message: *Nine lives.*

What did it mean? And what did it have to do with *her*?

Only after she'd checked every room in the apartment did she relax enough to boil a kettle of water for tea while she unpacked groceries. The temperature had plummeted overnight. It seemed hard to believe that only yesterday she'd regretted the decision to wear a turtleneck.

She fixed herself a cup of Earl Grey and decided to spend the evening doing research. When the doorbell rang, she jumped nearly five feet into the air. She walked cautiously to the door and checked the peephole. Brant stood on the other side, head bent, hands jammed into his jeans pockets. She told herself the relief she felt upon seeing him had more to do with her jangled nerves than the absurd possibility that she'd actually missed his company all day.

He looked up when she opened the door. "May I come in?"

Samille stepped aside to let him enter, then bolted the lock behind him and leaned against the door. She crossed one bare foot over another and arched an eyebrow at him. "A little late to be paying house calls, isn't it?"

His expression was grim. "I just came from the hospital."

Samille stiffened in alarm. "What is it?"

Brant hesitated. "One of our teenagers died tonight."

"Oh God," Samille whispered. It was the worst-case scenario, one she'd hoped would never occur. She pushed away from the door and walked toward Brant. "Which one?"

"Bradley Whitfield. The nurse on duty briefly stepped away from her station. When she returned, Whitfield had flat-lined. He couldn't be resuscitated."

"Dear God." Samille folded her arms across her chest as a fine chill swept through her body.

"A note was left in Bradley's room," Brant continued. "The nurse found it attached to the patient chart."

Samille frowned. "A note?"

"Yes. The first two lines of 'Ten Little Indians.'"

"Ten Little . . ." She trailed off as comprehension dawned with the force of a sledgehammer. *And then there were nine . . .*

Nine lives!

"Oh my God," she whispered. "That's what it meant."

Brant's gaze fastened, sharp as a scimitar, on her face. "What are you talking about?"

"This evening as I was leaving the correctional facility, I received a strange call on my cell phone. I couldn't identify the voice. The caller simply said 'Nine lives.' I didn't understand what it meant at the time. Now it makes sense."

"What time was this?" Brant demanded.

"A little after five-thirty. Every Sunday I work with juvenile inmates from two to five p.m. Today our session ran over a little, so I left later than usual. As I was walking to the parking lot, my cell phone rang."

"Did you see anyone? Hear anything?"

Samille shook her head. Another shiver rippled through her. "I—I thought it was just a prank, but now . . ."

"Do a lot of people have your cell phone number?"

"Not really. It's unlisted, so it's mostly just family, coworkers, the doctor's office—folks like that—who have the number." She stood and began pacing the floor. "Does this mean that the suspect knows who I am? And how is that possible? The DEA has deliberately kept a low profile in this investigation. I haven't been mentioned in any papers or news broadcasts. My own family doesn't even know I'm involved in the case. Unless . . ." She stopped pacing and looked at Brant. "Unless the person has been following me."

Brant swore savagely under his breath.

"Did the nurse at the hospital see anyone coming or going from Bradley's room?" Samille asked.

"No, and we couldn't identify anyone on the surveillance cameras. We viewed footage starting from four p.m., just in case the person arrived at the hospital earlier and waited around until visiting hours were over."

"Do you think Bradley was poisoned?"

"The ME doesn't think so. But we'll know for sure once he performs the autopsy."

"How could someone know in advance that Bradley Whitfield was going to die? He must have been poisoned."

Brant's mouth thinned to a grim line. "Or we're dealing with a phantom who, in addition to being clairvoyant, possesses the ability to slip in and out of hospital rooms undetected. And leaves a calling card."

Their eyes met and held as each contemplated the various possibilities, all of them ominous.

"I want you off this case," Brant said, his voice pitched low.

"Are we back to that again?"

"Whoever is responsible for putting those kids in the hospital knows who you are and went to the trouble of obtaining your unlisted cell phone number, to place what *I* consider a threatening call. If that doesn't concern you, I don't know what will."

Samille resumed her agitated pacing. "Yes, I will admit that the call freaked me out. But I don't think removing myself from the case is going to accomplish anything."

"Except remove you from harm's way," Brant countered through gritted teeth.

"You don't know that. And we can't jump to the conclusion that the phone call was intended as a threat. This person obviously enjoys taunting us, evidenced by the note left in Bradley Whitfield's room. For all we know, *you* might walk out of here and get the same phone call. That doesn't mean this person plans to harm you."

"In my experience," Brant said succinctly, "people who get off on taunting the authorities are sadistic and dangerous criminals who should never be taken lightly. It would be a grave miscalculation to underestimate this person's intent or frame of mind. Take my word for it, Samille: this case is going to get a lot worse before it gets better." He paused meaningfully. "*If* it gets better."

Samille stared at him, fighting the tremors that skittered along her spine. Resolutely she shook her head. "No. I can't walk away from the case. There's too much at stake."

"What's more important than your life?" Brant roared.

She flinched, but only for a moment. "I'm not removing myself from this case, Brant. Finding out what happened to those kids is just as important to me as it is to you." She planted her feet and stood her ground, daring him to contradict her.

"Go pack your suitcase."

Samille blinked. "Excuse me?"

"If you insist upon remaining on this case," Brant growled, "you're not staying here alone. You're coming home with me."

"*What?*"

"If this person has your cell phone number, he may already know where you live. I'm not taking any chances. Go pack your stuff."

"With all due respect, Brant, I don't think that's such a good idea."

"I don't care what you think."

"Obviously!" She flung her hands in the air in exasperation. "Look, Brant, I appreciate your concern for me, really I do. But we can barely remain in the same room together without jumping down each other's throats or, worse yet, jumping each other's bones! Do you really believe it's wise for us to become roommates?"

Brant's gaze was implacable. "I can think of a far worse alternative than us sleeping together, Samille." When she opened her mouth to protest, he held up a hand. "Please don't tell me you'd rather be killed than make love with me. I don't think my ego can take that."

Her cheeks flamed. "Don't be ridiculous. Of course I wouldn't choose death over—" She stopped abruptly and gave her head a vigorous shake, as if to dislodge the mental image of their naked, sweaty limbs tangled together in his bed.

There was a trace of humor in Brant's expression as he watched her. But when he spoke again, he was all business. "On Thursday you begged me not to have you removed from the case. If you don't agree to my terms, I'll make good on my promise to go to Graham."

"Y-you can't do that," Samille sputtered, indignant.

"I can," he said flatly, "and I will. Now for the last time, go pack your suitcase. Or I'll do it for you."

Samille stared at him, saw the uncompromising glint in his dark eyes and the hard set of his jaw. And suddenly she knew she had no choice in the matter.

Defeat was a bitter taste in her mouth. She glared up at him and said mutinously, "I'll pack light."

Brant said nothing as she pivoted on her heel and strode to her bedroom.

Samille insisted on driving her Jeep to Brant's place. "Just because you're forcing me to stay with you doesn't mean I have to be dependent on you for transportation."

Brant regarded her with a stony expression but didn't argue.

When they arrived at his town house, a three-story brick end unit, he parked at the curb and motioned for Samille to take the garage. As she climbed out, he retrieved her suitcase from the Jeep.

"Thanks for not losing me on the way here," she said wryly. "I've seen the way you drive, and I know it must have been killing you to keep below the speed limit."

The corner of his mouth lifted. "I figured it would defeat the purpose of dragging you here, only to lose you along the way."

They entered the house through the garage and stepped into a high-ceilinged foyer. Samille followed Brant up a winding flight of stairs to the second level, her feet sinking into a thick pile of Berber.

"Are you hungry?" Brant asked, setting down her suitcase and heading for the kitchen.

"I could eat." She glanced around the spacious living room, taking in the Italian leather furniture and mahogany entertainment center. The walls were painted a rich chocolate brown and trimmed with crown molding. A pair of canvas oil paintings captured wildly lush African safaris and golden horizons. Adjacent to the living room was a small dining area occupied by a gleaming mahogany table and four upholstered chairs. Samille found the contemporary masculine décor incredibly appealing.

"Nice place," she remarked. "Not bad for a bachelor pad."

"Thanks," Brant said from the kitchen. "Can't take credit for it, though. My mother and sister took the liberty of redecorating the house one weekend while I was out of town on assignment."

"À la *Trading Spaces?*" Samille teased, referring to the popular cable television show in which neighbors redesigned one another's homes—sometimes with disastrous results.

"Something like that." Brant reappeared in the entrance. "They figured the place needed sprucing up, and thought I would be pleasantly surprised when I got home."

Samille bit her lip to stifle a grin. "Were you?"

He grimaced. "Let's just say I was surprised. Don't know about the 'pleasantly' part."

"Oh, come on, Brant. They did a great job!"

"Of course you would think so."

She arched an eyebrow. "Meaning?"

"You're a woman," he said simply. He nodded toward the elegant crown molding. "Most women go for that sort of thing."

Samille planted her hands on her hips. "Of all the sexist, stereotypical—"

He grinned. "I did appreciate the spirit behind their efforts, and I told them so. And you'll be happy to know that the new design eventually grew on me, although it took some time." He held up two carryout menus. "Pizza or Chinese?"

"Chinese is fine." She crossed the room and plucked the menu from his hand, then settled into a dining room chair to review her choices. Brant poured two glasses of iced tea and joined her at the table. As he leaned close to get a better look at the menu, she caught a whiff of his clean, masculine scent and resisted the urge to draw voracious gulps of it into her lungs. How could one man's scent be so intoxicating that it was an aphrodisiac?

"I already know what I want," Brant murmured silkily. "Let me know when you're ready."

She swallowed hard, feeling disoriented. "Ready?"

He shifted a fraction closer, and Samille's knees went weak. Her pulse drummed in her ears. "To tell me what you want," he said.

"What I want?"

When she lifted her gaze to his face, his expression was one of pure innocence. He inclined his head toward the menu. "For dinner. Tell me what you want to eat."

"Oh." She chuckled self-consciously. "Dinner. Of course."

"What did you think I meant?"

"Nothing. Um, I'll have sesame chicken." Eager to put distance between them, she rose from the chair and walked into the living room, scorning her overactive imagination. How was she supposed to handle living under the same roof with the man if she couldn't even handle ordering takeout with him?

While Brant called the restaurant, she wandered over to the entertainment center. She studied framed photographs of people she assumed were his family members. A debonair, salt-and-pepper-haired gentleman who left no doubt where Brant had gotten his good looks. Maurice Kincaid posed with an exotically beautiful dark-skinned woman who had the regal bearing of Queen Nefertiti. Brant's mother, Samille surmised. Another photo was of a younger beauty with expressive dark eyes and long black hair worn in neat, attractive dreadlocks. Next she examined Brant's high school graduation picture. It was the same handsome face minus the trim goatee, and the features were not as hard or sculpted as they were now. But something else was different, something barely perceptible. The eyes?

She squinted, stepping closer to get a better look.

"Food will be here in twenty minutes."

Samille whirled toward the sound of Brant's voice. He leaned in the kitchen entrance, his shoulder propped against the wall as he watched her. Although his expression was inscrutable, she had the vague impression he was somehow displeased.

She was suddenly, inexplicably, nervous. "I was just looking at your family photos," she felt compelled to explain. "I hope you don't mind."

"No." His gaze flicked to the photographs, then back to her. "Are you cold?"

"Not at all. Why do you—" Belatedly she realized she'd started rubbing her arms. Abruptly she stopped. "Maybe a little."

Brant came off the wall and started toward her, and she marveled that such a big man could move so stealthily, so sinuously. She held her breath with every step that brought him nearer. At the last second he knelt at the brick fireplace and threw a couple of logs onto the iron grate. Samille walked back to the dining area where she'd left her iced tea. She raised the glass to her lips and took a long sip, wishing she had something stronger to calm her nerves.

She watched as Brant straightened, braced one arm on the mantel, and stood gazing into the roaring fire for several minutes. Something was up with him, but she didn't know what. He seemed a million miles away, lost in another dimension.

"What's your sister's name?" Samille ventured, hoping to break the odd silence between them. She walked back to the living room and sat on the sofa.

Slowly he lifted his head to meet her inquisitive gaze. "Zora."

"Zora. I've always thought that was such a beautiful name. Does she still live in New York?"

Brant nodded, and Samille sensed the tension slowly ebbing from his body. "She's public relations director for the Brooklyn Public Library. She and her husband are expecting their first child in April."

"That's wonderful, Brant. You're going to be an uncle. You must be so proud."

"I am." He smiled softly. "Zora's going to make a terrific mother. She was probably the only sixteen-year-old girl on the face of the planet who didn't mind babysitting her kid brother."

"She must possess the patience of a saint."

"Funny, that's what *she* used to say."

Samille grinned. "Are the two of you close?"

He joined her on the sofa. "Yeah, we're pretty close. She and my mother make a point of calling me every week. I think they want to make sure I don't forget them or where I came from."

"As if you'd ever forget." Samille smiled, and found that she wanted to know so much more about this enigmatic man, what brought him joy and what caused him pain. What secrets he held beneath that tough, impenetrable exterior. "Wait a minute. Audre and Zora . . . is that a coincidence?"

Brant chuckled. "No coincidence. My mother is named after Audre Lorde and Zora is named after Zora Neale Hurston. Both were christened by my grandmother, who was quite the feminist in her heyday."

Samille grinned. "Way to go, Grandma!"

"I figured you might appreciate that. Speaking of names, yours is a bit unusual."

Samille sighed dramatically. "Alas, I'm afraid I wasn't named after any great feminist authors or poets. My parents named me after themselves—Samuel and Camille. I know it's kind of corny—"

"It's a beautiful name, and perfect for you." Brant smiled at her. "I'm betting that just as your name is a combination of theirs, you're the best of both of them."

Samille gazed at him with a look of indescribable gratitude. "Thank you, Brant," she said around the walnut-sized lump in her throat. *God, please don't let me cry in front of this man and make a complete fool of myself!*

"Hey." He tweaked her nose playfully. "Don't go getting all choked up on me, Broussard."

She laughed, and the sentimental moment passed. As if on cue, the doorbell announced the arrival of their dinner.

They ate their meals on the living room floor beside the hissing fire. Over lo mein and sesame chicken, they talked. They discovered a mutual interest in science fiction and Greek mythology. They talked about their favorite college professors and shared horror stories about the deplorable ones. Samille bragged about attending school in California and taking fun-filled weekend trips to Big Sur with her friends while Brant had to suffer through bone-chilling New York winters. And then he came back with a tale of the lazy summer he'd spent at a beachside cottage in Venice—and Samille grabbed a throw pillow off the sofa and pummeled him with it.

Warding off her blows, Brant wrestled her to the floor and pinned her body beneath his. He dug his fingertips into her ribs, and Samille's head rocked back and forth on the carpet as she howled with laughter and pleaded for mercy. She tried to roll away from him, but he was too heavy and too strong. He tickled her relentlessly until tears slid from the corners of her eyes.

"Who's your daddy, huh?" he taunted.

"You are," she half gasped.

"What? I can't hear you, woman."

"You are, Brant Kincaid! You are! Now will you please . . . stop . . . tickling me!"

"Well, since you asked so nicely." With a chuckle he relented, his dark eyes twinkling with mirth as he smiled down into her eyes. Her cheeks were flushed from their exertions. Firelight gleamed on her heavy hair, which had escaped from its makeshift ponytail and spilled onto the carpet like black silk. All at once he became aware of the heat of her skin penetrating his own, the exquisite softness of her body beneath his.

Samille knew the exact moment the change happened. She watched Brant's eyes grow hooded, the pupils darkening with desire. The smile on her lips faded as a melting warmth started in the pit of her belly and spread outward like a slow, thick liquid. They stared at each other for several charged moments, and Samille knew that if he kissed her, she wouldn't be able to stop him. She wouldn't *want* to stop him.

Brant lifted himself off her and stood. He helped her

to her feet, and in silence they cleaned up and put away the leftovers. He carried her suitcase upstairs to the guest room, pointed out the bathroom in the corridor, and said good night before pulling the door closed behind him.

Samille slowly undressed and climbed beneath the crisp cotton sheets, her body still thrumming with need for a man she couldn't have, and couldn't stop wanting.

CHAPTER 10

Samille was awakened by the muffled ringing of her cell phone. Groggily she opened her eyes and blinked in the darkness of the room. It took several seconds for her mind to register the unfamiliar surroundings, another few moments to remember why she was waking up in a strange, albeit comfortable bed.

She rolled over and groped for her purse on the floor. She answered the phone just before voice mail could intercept. "Hello?" she croaked.

"Broussard, this is Alan Graham." The diversion program manager, in contrast to Samille, sounded wide awake and alert. "Sorry to call you so early, but I wanted to catch you as soon as possible. In light of recent developments in the Georgetown case, we've decided to assemble a task force. You may recall I mentioned this as a possibility on Wednesday?"

Samille's eyes felt as if they had grown a coat of fur overnight. She struggled to formulate a lucid response. "Yes, sir, I do remember."

"Good. We're holding a strategy session this morning after the press conference. Chief Rucker and I will address the media together. We need to put a lid on any rumors before they start."

"I understand. Does Kincaid know about the task force?"

"He's already been briefed. See you both at eight a.m."

"Yes, sir." Samille disconnected and shoved the cell phone back inside her purse. Once again, she was the last to be informed about an important development in the investigation. She told herself not to take it personally, but she couldn't help but wonder if it had anything to do with her being a woman. Immediately she dismissed the rash thought. Her gender hadn't mattered to Alan Graham when he chose her for the assignment, although he'd had plenty of male diversion investigators to pick from. She was selected because Graham believed she was the best candidate for the job.

Anyway, she had bigger fish to fry that morning. She'd spent the entire night tossing and turning, alternately thinking about poor Bradley Whitfield and plotting how she was going to get out of staying with Brant. Both concerns were enough to prevent her from grabbing more than a few winks of sleep.

Exhaustion tugged at her as she flung back the covers and climbed from the bed. The house was silent, and she wondered if Brant was still sleeping. God, she hoped so. The longer she could prolong seeing him, the better.

As she switched on a Tiffany floor lamp, she took a moment to admire the room's simple yet tasteful décor, courtesy—no doubt—of Audre and Zora Kincaid. Pale yellow walls and soft muted colors, a rich bamboo armoire and matching credenza that surrounded a large sleigh bed covered with a thick yellow comforter. Out of habit she made the bed and restored the throw pillows to their previous artful arrangement. She tried not to speculate about other women who may have been overnight guests in that very same room or, worse yet, in Brant's bed.

After rummaging through her suitcase, she scowled at the realization that she'd forgotten to pack her bathrobe. She glanced down at herself and felt scantily clad in the cotton halter and high-cut shorts that were her normal bedtime attire. The last thing she wanted was to bump into her host on the way to the bathroom, or on the way back while covered in nothing more than a towel.

"Get a grip, Broussard," she muttered under her breath. "You're giving this *way* too much thought."

She grabbed a few toiletries and marched to the door. She pulled it open and jumped back with a startled shriek when she found Brant on the other side, poised to knock.

"You scared the crap out of me!" she exclaimed.

"Sorry. I was just coming to wake you up." Brant was ruggedly sexy in black sweatpants and a sweatshirt with torn-off sleeves, exposing powerful arms that glistened with moisture.

Samille's mouth went dry. "You've been out running already? It's barely five-thirty."

"I like to get out early."

"Wish you'd told me. I usually run in the mornings, too."

"You can join me tomorrow. Glad you're already up. I'm going to grab a shower."

As he started away, Samille said, "Listen, about tomorrow—"

He turned around, one heavy eyebrow raised. "Yeah?"

Samille faltered, and was annoyed to find herself somewhat intimidated. It was the sight of all that male flesh, she mentally complained. Never mind that she was constantly surrounded by hordes of testosterone. Nothing and no one could have prepared her for the raw masculinity Brant Kincaid exuded with little or no effort.

"Um, we can talk later," she mumbled, eyes downcast.

Brant reached out, tipping her chin up and forcing her to meet his direct gaze. "If this is about you going back home, you might as well save your breath. You're staying here, and that's nonnegotiable."

"You can't keep me here against my will. In case you haven't noticed, I'm a grown woman!"

"Oh, I've noticed." Slowly, deliberately, Brant let his gaze slide down her body, taking in the simple two-piece pajamas set, admiring the way the skimpy shorts accentuated her sleek, impossibly long legs. It took a supreme effort to drag his eyes back up to her face, although that was no hardship either. Even with the faint dark smudges beneath her eyes that indicated she'd slept poorly, Samille was a vision to behold, especially with all that disheveled ebony hair tumbling about her face and shoulders.

"Believe me, Ms. Broussard," he said softly, "I'd have to be dumb and blind *not* to notice. And therein lies the problem."

"You know very well what I meant," Samille snapped, but her voice was too husky with awareness to successfully deliver the reprimand.

"I'm going to take a shower—one that gets colder the longer I stand here trying not to imagine how much more of a 'grown woman' you are, and debating what I should do about it." He stepped back, his expression faintly amused. "If you get dressed before me, there's fresh coffee downstairs. We can grab breakfast on the way."

He turned and sauntered down the hallway, leaving Samille to stare after him in openmouthed shock at the sexual implication behind his words.

* * *

D.C. Police Chief Charles Rucker was not a happy man. His phone hadn't stopped ringing since that morning's edition of the *Washington Post* ran a story citing "suspicious circumstances" surrounding Bradley Whitfield's death. Because the reporter hadn't been resourceful enough to learn about the note, the article had only fueled speculation and a growing conspiracy theory that the police and feds were hiding something—something the public had a right to know. Suddenly patients at George Washington University Hospital—by far the finest hospital in the entire metropolitan region—were concerned about their safety; some wanted to be transferred to other facilities. As if that weren't bad enough, tensions were mounting between the Georgetown families. Parents of the comatose victims, fearing that their children would meet the same fate as Bradley Whitfield, were demanding that the other teenagers who'd attended the party be marched down to the police station and interrogated until someone confessed. Both sides had contacted attorneys, and a town hall meeting was scheduled for that very same evening.

The press conference had been woefully short on information. They had no solid suspects or witnesses. They had no leads but the note that had been left behind, and Chief Rucker refused to divulge the contents for fear of compromising the investigation. His official statement to the media was that the Metropolitan Police Department, in conjunction with the federal agencies involved, was taking every possible measure to solve the case and welcomed tips from the public that would help lead to an arrest.

It was a god-awful mess, and Rucker had no answers for anyone who called. Not concerned citizens, not the victims' families, not even the mayor—his boss.

As he sat at the head of the table in the precinct's conference room, he could feel the acids tearing a hole through his stomach lining like ravenous piranhas. He'd worn his full dress uniform for the press conference. The sky-blue shirt, freshly starched and ironed by his wife that morning, was now wrinkled and felt like a straitjacket around his expanded waistline. He took a sip of tepid coffee that tasted more like sludge and grimaced. He reached inside his front pocket for a roll of antacids, thumbed one off, and sucked hard. His wife insisted that this new brand was better for his heartburn, but Rucker had never trusted fruit-flavored medicine. Nothing that tasted good could be very effective.

He looked around the table at the people who'd been assembled for the task force. Two of his best detectives, Marc Lopez and his partner, Rick Grimes, who had been pulled off another homicide to lend his investigative expertise to the Georgetown case. Agent Brant Kincaid, the Bureau's top gun, who had spoken very little since the meeting began, observing everyone else with a quiet sharpness that demonstrated he missed nothing. Rucker vaguely recognized two DEA agents, Michael Parham and Jack Burdett, who'd been sent in place of Alan Graham when he was called away at the last minute. Burdett had the most unsettling pair of eyes Rucker had ever seen, so blue and piercing he almost appeared possessed. The intensity of the eyes was offset by Burdett's relaxed, easygoing demeanor.

And last but certainly not least was Samille Broussard. To her credit, she seemed not in the least bit intimidated to be the only woman present. Although she was young enough to be Rucker's daughter, it didn't stop him from wishing he were twenty-five years younger. Not that it would have made much difference. He suspected that the lovely Ms. Broussard's affections lay elsewhere—

namely with Brant Kincaid. The discreet glances that passed between them had not escaped Rucker's notice, nor had he missed the way Jack Burdett's mouth had tightened as he watched the pair enter the conference room together. Kincaid had helped Ms. Broussard into her chair with a gentle solicitousness that reminded Rucker of the way he'd treated his wife when they were courting, and the reminiscence nearly made him smile. But then Rucker saw Burdett's ice-blue eyes narrow with displeasure, and he smothered an impatient oath.

Christ, he hoped he didn't have a love triangle on his hands. It was the *last* thing he, or this task force, needed.

"What do we have so far?" Rucker resumed the meeting once everyone had gotten their coffee refills. He noticed that Kincaid was the only one who had steered clear of the stuff. Smart man. "We've got one dead kid, and another one who may or may not have sold the drugs to him. Lopez, you and Kincaid interrogated Jefferson Spangler, but he denies selling boo to his classmates, although another classmate says he did. Did we check out this witness? Any priors, run-ins with teachers, problems with authority figures?"

Samille answered, "Agent Kincaid and I spoke to the witness and ran a background check on her. Her name is Jillian Carrella. She's a straight-A student at St. Anthony's Prep, no priors. Her teachers claim she's a bright, precocious girl with a chip on her shoulder, but there's no reason to doubt anything she says. One instructor I spoke with said that if anything, Jillian Carrella is honest to a fault."

Rucker gave a satisfied nod and wished, fleetingly, that his eldest son was old enough to be introduced to Samille Broussard. "So our witness is credible. But Spangler, as we all know, is the son of a prominent senator who has already threatened this department with a lawsuit if we pursue his kid without probable cause. What we've got so far is Carrella's word against Spangler's. We've assigned an off-duty uniform to run periodic surveillance on Spangler, but the kid is guarded tighter than the crown prince's jewels. It's impossible to get close to him without blowing our cover, and the last thing this office needs is Senator Spangler charging us with stalking and harassment." He popped another antacid at the mere thought. "Lopez, explain to me this connection to the dead drug dealer. Arthur Cason, was it?"

"*Andrew* Cason, sir," Lopez patiently corrected. "As you know, Jefferson Spangler's name was found in a daily planner belonging to Cason. The handwriting was later confirmed to be Cason's. So we know for a fact that Spangler was supposed to meet Cason on the day he was killed. We—that is, Kincaid and I—don't believe it was coincidence."

"Why not?" Rucker demanded. "Pushers get knocked off all the time, for any number of reasons. This Cason may have owed someone money or stolen a rival's business. Or he may have interrupted a burglary in progress. Didn't you say his computer was missing? Some crackhead may have snatched it—you know those junkies are always looking for something to pawn in exchange for their next fix. Jewelry, TVs, stereos, toasters, it doesn't matter. For all we know, there's some junkie out there who broke into Cason's apartment after the fact and realized he'd hit pay dirt when he found the computer."

"The door was locked when the landlord came," Lopez pointed out. "There was no sign of B and E."

"This was no random burglary," Brant said quietly. "Cason was murdered by someone he knew, someone who wanted to guarantee his silence. Someone he allowed into his apartment and felt comfortable enough to turn his back on. His body wasn't moved from another location to where he'd been found. He was shot at point-blank range while sitting at the desk. Either someone entered the apartment using a key he already had, or Cason himself let the killer into his apartment. The bottom line is that he knew this individual."

The room fell silent as the cold certainty of Brant's assessment settled in. Chief Rucker leaned back in his chair and folded freckled hands across his bulging midsection. "So the Spangler kid fits the bill. Ashton Spangler is a bigwig senator; Jefferson would know what it would do to his father's career and political aspirations if word got out that his own son was selling drugs."

"Jefferson is one plausible suspect," Brant agreed.

"Who else makes sense? Jefferson had motive and opportunity, and he's the only real link between Andrew Cason and those teenagers. Spangler sold drugs to his classmates, Spangler killed Cason to cover his tracks."

"But Cason never made the nine p.m. meeting," Lopez reminded his boss. "He was shot in his apartment that morning."

"We don't know when the transaction took place in which Jefferson Spangler received the drugs he gave his classmates," Rucker countered. "For all we know, he and Cason rescheduled the appointment for the previous night."

"Assuming Spangler got the drugs from Cason," Brant said.

"Back to the 'shooter in the grassy knoll' theory," Rucker grumbled. He sighed impatiently. "We'd have to be looking for another suspect with motive and opportunity. Someone who not only wanted Andrew Cason dead, but deliberately poisoned those teenagers. If, indeed, there is a connection between these two incidents." His skeptical tone made it obvious that he doubted the latter.

Jack Burdett spoke up. "I have to agree with Chief

Rucker. With all due respect, Brant, I think the possibility is too far-fetched. In all likelihood, these cases are unrelated. Whoever offed Cason was probably someone from his past, someone he double-crossed when he was working for the DEA. I've put out some feelers in various prisons to see what the underground chatter has been."

"And what have you learned so far?" Brant asked mildly.

"Well, nothing yet. But that doesn't mean anything," Jack hastened to add. "That was only Friday. These things take time."

Brant shook his head. "Most of the groups Cason rolled on were small-time and have long since disbanded. Some are serving time, but many were killed when the members turned on each other or struck plea agreements with the U.S. Attorney's office. I'm betting that Andrew Cason is little more than a distant memory to those who survived, and certainly not worth the time and trouble it would take to coordinate a hit on him."

Jack's mouth tightened. "I see you've done your research," he murmured, with a sidelong glance at Samille that held a trace of anger and betrayal. Her expression was unreadable.

"I had heard what a thorough investigator you are, Kincaid," Chief Rucker intervened. "Therefore I can't easily dismiss any of your theories. But what are the odds that the same person who killed Andrew Cason also wanted to get rid of a bunch of spoiled rich kids?"

Slowly, deliberately, Brant broke eye contact with Jack to meet the chief's inquisitive gaze. "I think that killing Andrew Cason was little more than a means to an end. The person we're looking for probably had a history with Cason, some unresolved issues. Cason may even have been blackmailing this individual—whether it was about money or illegal activity the person was involved in, something only Cason knew about. This made it imperative to get rid of him."

Brant looked around the table. "My guess is that poisoning those teenagers was the ultimate plan. Our suspect could be someone disgruntled with the system or politics in this town. And what better way to make a statement than to strike out at some of the wealthiest and most prominent citizens through their precious offspring? What better way to wreak havoc on the city than to walk right into a dying patient's hospital room and leave a riddle for the dumbfounded authorities to solve? What better way to keep us all on our toes, wondering if and when he will strike again?

"The person we're looking for has an inferiority complex. He enjoys being the center of attention, and takes immense pleasure in masterminding chaos. He has the financial resources to manufacture or obtain a lethal substance, the likes of which we've never seen before. I don't believe that this individual normally handles or dispenses drugs. This substance was specially created for this purpose—his Frankenstein experiment, if you will. He's cunning and clever, and wants to prove that he can slip beneath the radar. It's a game to him—catch me if you can, he thinks. He's probably getting off on all the media coverage and plotting his next move, something to surpass what he's already done. But make no mistake about it: he's dangerous and not to be underestimated under any circumstances. I can't emphasize that enough," Brant added, looking directly into Samille's eyes.

Once again a heavy silence descended upon the conference table. After a few moments, Chief Rucker exhaled cherry-scented antacid breath. "Christ, Kincaid, you're giving me the heebie-jeebies. That's the problem with you profiler types—you get so entrenched in a subject's psyche that you spook everyone else."

"Sorry," Brant said with a grim smile. "Occupational hazard."

Lopez chuckled. "Agent Kincaid and Ms. Broussard recently located a witness who can identify a man who threatened Andrew Cason. His name's Roy Clark, and right now I've got him in an interrogation room with our sketch artist. We should have a composite within the hour, and we can go from there."

Rucker nodded briskly and made a face. "Something's better than nothing. I have to attend that town hall meeting tonight, and I'll feel a whole lot better going into the lion's den knowing Spangler's golden boy isn't our only lead."

"It may not pan out to anything, Chief," Lopez warned, "so don't get your hopes up."

Rucker scowled at him. "Son, I've been in law enforcement long before you were a flicker in your mother's imagination. You don't have to tell *me* not to get my hopes up." He glanced around the table. "Before we adjourn, does anyone else have any other ideas?"

For a moment no one spoke. And then Samille said in a clear, strong voice, "Actually, I do have one idea."

Six pairs of eyes swung in her direction. Ignoring Brant's suspicious gaze, she forged ahead. "As some of you may know, I work with a group of juvenile inmates at the correctional facility. Yesterday one of the girls told me about her cousin being approached by a man in a nightclub who wanted to sell her drugs. The man was wearing a costume, and I think it was to conceal his identity. He wore a mask and a hooded cloak. He told the girl he would return to the club on Thursday night, in case she changed her mind about buying drugs from him." She paused. "I was thinking that we could set up a sting operation. Someone could pose as a potential buyer, and if this is our perp, we nail him."

Chief Rucker and the others exchanged considering glances. Brant spoke in a low, deadly tone. "No."

Samille glared at him. "Why not?"

"Because I know you're going to volunteer yourself to be the undercover buyer. So the answer is no. Let me clarify that: *hell* no."

"Wait a minute," Rucker interjected. "Let's discuss this for a minute. I think Ms. Broussard may be on to something here."

"I agree," Lopez added quickly. "You said yourself that you don't believe in coincidences, Kincaid. I don't think it's mere coincidence that this information landed right in Ms. Broussard's lap. I definitely think it's a lead we should follow up on. We'd be crazy not to."

Jack jumped into the fray. "Hold on a minute. What's the name of this nightclub?"

"Zydeco," Samille said.

Jack shook his head. "Do you know how many raids I've done at that joint? The whacko who approached your juvie's cousin could have been anyone. Club Zydeco is a freak show, Sammy, and not just because of the rave parties. You'd never fit in."

Samille arched an eyebrow. "I thought the point of going undercover was to *make* yourself fit in."

"You'd have to undergo a radical transformation just to keep from sticking out like a sore thumb. You haven't seen the way these women dress, Sammy—or, more to the point, *don't* dress."

"I think I could handle wearing a skimpy outfit for a few hours," Samille said, stiff with resentment at the implication that she couldn't pull off the assignment.

Her staunch rebuttal was met with stone-cold silence. The expressions around the table ranged from humorous speculation to blatant curiosity. She was suddenly, acutely, aware of being the only woman in the room.

Brant was the first to break the awkward silence. "Be that as it may," he drawled sardonically, "the answer is still no. This isn't a training exercise at Quantico, Samille. What you're proposing is extremely dangerous. You've never gone undercover before."

"There's a first time for everything."

"You lack the training for an undercover assignment. You can't even imagine the things that could go wrong."

"So train me. Give me a crash course in undercover work, take me out on the firing range, and teach me how to shoot a weapon in case I have to use it."

More thoughtful looks passed around the table.

"No." Brant swore savagely. "Didn't you hear a word I said just a few minutes ago, Samille? The individual we're dealing with is incredibly calculating and dangerous. Not to mention the fact that he might already know what you look like!"

When his last statement was met with confused silence around the room, Brant smiled narrowly. "That's right, gentlemen. Ms. Broussard failed to mention that she received a disturbing phone call from the perp last night. How do we know it was him? Because what he said to her is consistent with the message left in Bradley Whitfield's room."

Brant cocked his head to one side as he calmly regarded Samille. "Oh, wait, let me guess. You had no intention of divulging this critical piece of information when you came up with your harebrained scheme."

"It is *not* harebrained!" Samille fumed, ignoring the concerned looks the others were now giving her. "Assuming that the guy in costume is not the person we're looking for, there's no risk of him recognizing me."

"And if this cloaked stranger *is* our man and recognizes you, then what?" Brant challenged.

"Then I guess that's just a chance we'll have to take. If *I'm* willing to do it, I don't see what the problem is."

"The problem is that you could get yourself killed." Brant's expression was downright lethal, and if they hadn't been surrounded by five other men—all of whom were armed—she might have seriously feared for her life.

She turned to Chief Rucker, who seemed increasingly receptive to the plan. "If Jefferson Spangler sold the drugs to his classmates and is on the prowl for more buyers, which I suspect he is, then we have a rare opportunity to catch him red-handed. Once we have him in custody, he might be desperate enough to tell us who gave him the drugs in the first place—which is the person we really want. If Jefferson's not our perp, then he's not the one who called me last night, which means he doesn't have a clue what I look like."

"And if Spangler *is* our perp?" Brant said in a chilling voice.

Samille met his fierce gaze and swallowed. "Then we kill two birds with one stone." She looked around the table for support. "Who else in this room could pose as the undercover buyer? No offense, but all of you *look* like cops. Agents Kincaid and Burdett, in particular, look too intimidating to approach. I'm the best, and most obvious, choice."

Chief Rucker rubbed his chin thoughtfully. "I must confess that I like your plan very much, Ms. Broussard, and I admire your courage and determination. But I also concede that Kincaid's concerns are legitimate, which he articulates rather, uh, forcefully," he added with a knowing look at Brant. "If we proceed with this undercover operation and something happens to you, Ms. Broussard, there'd be hell to pay. Everyone would want to know why we allowed someone without the proper training to participate in such a dangerous assignment.

There have been police officers and agents from the DEA and FBI killed in the course of drug busts gone wrong. Just ask your colleagues around this table."

"When I joined the DEA," Samille said in a low, solemn voice, "I took an oath to carry out my duties to the best of my ability, even if it meant putting my life at risk. I may not carry a gun like the rest of you, but I'm an officer of the law just the same. I take that responsibility very seriously. I wouldn't be here if I didn't."

Rucker's expression registered admiration. Jack and Michael Parham exchanged proud glances. Brant pushed abruptly from the table and stood. Without a word, he stalked out of the conference room.

Samille watched him leave, her heart hammering painfully in her chest.

"If we're going to do this, we need to formulate a solid plan and hash out the details," Lopez said decisively. His dark eyes shone with excitement. "We only have until Thursday."

Rucker hummed a thoughtful note, his gaze still trained on the doorway through which Brant had disappeared. "Let me think about this some more. I need to talk to Alan Graham, get his input. We can reconvene tomorrow. Now if you folks will excuse me, I have a meeting with the mayor that I'm not particularly looking forward to."

Detective Rick Grimes, a short, attractive black man with the sturdy build of a weightlifter, winked at Samille before following Chief Rucker and Detective Lopez from the room.

Michael Parham approached Samille with a lopsided grin. He was medium height and stocky, and showed early signs of developing a paunch at the ripe old age of twenty-seven. "You've got heart, Broussard. Even if I think you're a bit looney tunes at times, I gotta admire your heart."

"Thanks, Irish," Samille murmured absently, using the nickname they'd given him at the office for his shock of curly red hair.

"I thought Kincaid was going to kill you himself," Parham joked.

Samille winced. "That makes two of us."

Parham gave her ponytail a light tug. "Hey, I've gotta run. I'll catch you back at the office, Jack. And I'll see you when I see you, Sammy."

After he left, Jack draped a comforting arm around Samille's shoulder. "Don't worry about Kincaid. He'll come around eventually. He gets like that sometimes, as if some Higher Authority has personally appointed him to defend the weak and downtrodden—kittens, lost puppies, you name it."

"Thanks, Jack. I feel so much better knowing Brant considers me a stray animal." Instead of a woman he cared for and wanted to protect. Irritated, Samille had a sudden urge to shake Jack's arm off. She started toward the door, eager to find Brant and have it out with him.

"I tried to call you last night," Jack said, detaining her with a hand upon her arm. "I kept getting your voice mail. You must have been out late."

"Something like that." For some incomprehensible reason, Samille didn't feel comfortable telling Jack she'd spent the night at Brant's place. Perhaps because she didn't want him to get the wrong idea. She knew how overactive the male imagination could be.

She frowned, tucking an errant strand of hair behind one ear. "Why didn't you try my cell phone?"

Jack shrugged. "I forgot the number. You'll have to give it to me again."

"I'll give you the new one. I'm getting the number

changed once this case is over. In the meantime, Brant thinks it would be a good idea to get caller ID and install a tap-and-tracing device, in case our perp calls again—which I'm almost sure he will." She suppressed an instinctive shudder. "Anyway, Brant's taking the cell phone to his tech guys at the Bureau. I'm using one of his spare ones in the meantime."

"Sounds like Kincaid's got everything under control," Jack said lightly, but his voice sounded odd, strained. He gazed down at Samille, his eyes piercing hers. "Why didn't you tell me about the phone call, Sammy? I thought we were friends."

"Of course we're friends. I guess I didn't want you or anyone else to worry about me. And it wasn't until Brant told me about the note that I made the connection."

"Well, do you need a place to crash? It's probably not very safe for you to stay at your apartment alone."

Samille smiled. "I appreciate the offer, Jackie, but I'll be fine."

"Are you sure? I could at least drop by in the evenings to check up on you. My presence might deter any maniac who may be lurking around, skulking in the shadows."

"You're sweet. But, really, I'll be fine." She hesitated, and decided she owed him the truth. "Actually, I'm staying with Brant for a while. He sort of gave me no choice in the matter."

"I see." Jack's expression tightened.

She bit her bottom lip guiltily. "Jack—"

His face relaxed into the familiar easygoing smile. "Like I said, Kincaid's got everything under control. That's great. He's a good man to have on your side."

"I'm not so sure he's on my side at the moment," Samille muttered sullenly.

Jack laughed. "Go easy on him. For what it's worth, I

understand where he's coming from. No one wants to see you get hurt, Sammy."

"What about the informants we use?"

"What about them?"

"Most of those people are average citizens with little or no law enforcement training. And they go undercover for us all the time, infiltrating dangerous drug rings and ruthless crime families. I'm asking for one night, Jack. *One* night."

He rubbed his chin sheepishly. "I see your point, Sammy. But that doesn't make it any easier to knowingly put you in harm's way. No one's saying you're incapable of handling the assignment. Anyone who's ever worked with you knows better than that."

"Thanks for your support, Jack. You know it means a lot to me."

"*You* mean a lot to me, Sammy. Don't ever forget that."

Samille grinned. "As if you'd ever let me." She curved an affectionate hand against his cheek. "If you talk to Graham, put in a good word for me, will you? Chief Rucker may not go for the sting op if Graham has reservations. And you know how much Graham values your opinion. He'll listen to you."

Jack chuckled, his eyes twinkling. "And what do I get in return for landing you your first undercover gig?"

Samille batted her thick eyelashes and said sweetly, "My undying loyalty?"

"And here I thought I already had that."

Laughing, they walked out of the conference room. Brant and Detective Lopez were standing at the end of the busy corridor, deep in discussion. Brant glanced up, and his expression darkened at the sight of Jack and Samille together.

Samille marched right up to them and, deliberately

ignoring Brant, said to Lopez, "Is Roy Clark finished with the sketch artist yet?"

"Not quite. Should be another hour or so. You sticking around for the results?"

"I would, but I need to keep another appointment. Would you mind doing me a favor, Detective Lopez?"

Lopez eyed her with unabashed male appreciation. "Call me Marc. With a *c.*"

Samille's smile was gracious. "And you can call me Samille, Marc. When you get a positive ID on the composite, would you mind calling me? I'd hate to be kept out of the loop," she added with a pointed glance at Brant. He scowled as she gave the detective the number to the cell phone she was using.

Lopez scribbled the number on a notepad. "No problem at all, Samille. By the way, that is an exquisite name. As beautiful as the woman it belongs to."

Behind Samille, Jack made an exaggerated gagging noise. Even Brant managed to look grudgingly amused.

Samille grinned. "Thanks, Marc. We'll have to give you a nickname. I think Romeo suits you."

"Sweetheart, you can call me whatever you want. Just as long as you call me."

Samille chuckled. She knew she should be offended by the detective's blatant flirtation, but she wasn't. She liked Lopez. During the meeting he'd struck her as intelligent and resourceful, demonstrating a zeal for the investigation that she admired.

Without sparing Brant a second glance, she continued down the corridor and headed out of the police station.

Lopez whistled softly and shook his head in disbelief. "I don't know how you fellas do it. How do you work alongside a woman like that and not want to—"

"Watch it," Brant and Jack warned in unison. Their eyes met and held above the detective's head.

Lopez held up his hands in surrender. "Hey, I'm just curious. It's a perfectly legitimate question. I'm going to check on Clark and Milsner." He beat a hasty retreat.

For a moment Brant and Jack said nothing. They stood inches apart and silently assessed each other. Tension hung thick and heavy between them.

Jack was the first to speak. "Those were some mighty intense fireworks between you and Broussard during the meeting. For a moment it seemed like you'd both forgotten you weren't alone in the room."

"Guess we're both stubborn," Brant said, his voice deceptively soft. "You got something to say to me, Burdett?"

"Not particularly."

"You sure? Because I sensed something back there when we were discussing Andrew Cason."

Resentment flickered in Jack's eyes. "Hey, Kincaid, don't try to give me the shakedown. If I said I'm cool, take my word for it."

Brant regarded the other man in shrewd silence for a moment, watching as Jack's eyes hardened to slits of ice. This wasn't Brant's good-natured drinking buddy, his comrade from the academy. This was a man with a serious chip on his shoulder. A man who could, in the blink of an eye, become an enemy. A force to be reckoned with.

"Whatever you say, Burdett," Brant murmured. He turned on his heel and strode down the corridor and out of the building.

Seated behind the wheel of her Jeep, Samille saw him coming. She'd been waiting for him, and had started to wonder if he would ever show up. They had unfinished business, but she wasn't about to have a shouting match with him in the parking lot of the D.C. police station, with cops coming and going as their shifts changed, as people arrived to file complaints and check on the status of ongoing investigations. She had turned on the heat to ward off the morning chill, but the longer she sat and stewed waiting for Brant, the hotter under the collar she became.

She was glad she'd insisted on driving herself to the meeting that morning. She had no desire to spend a minute longer than necessary in Brant Kincaid's company.

Brant opened the passenger door and slid inside the Jeep without a word. Samille took perverse pleasure in the fact that his legs were too long in the confined space, and he had to adjust the seat or have his kneecaps crushed by the dashboard.

She stared straight through the windshield. "You had no right."

"Tell me something, Samille. Since when is it a federal crime to express concern for a fellow human being's welfare?"

"I don't need your concern, Brant Kincaid. You've been treating me like an incompetent half-wit ever since we met, and I don't appreciate it!"

"And I don't appreciate your cavalier GI-Jane attitude."

"*GI-Jane*? Oooh, I knew it! It's because I'm a woman. If that had been a *male* diversion investigator who suggested the same undercover operation, you would've had no objection whatsoever! You probably would've slapped him on the back and congratulated him on coming up with such a grand scheme!"

"If you really believe that," Brant said in a low, controlled voice, "then you don't know me at all."

"I *don't* know you! And guess what, Brant? You don't know me either! You certainly don't know what I'm capable of, or you wouldn't try to sabotage me every time I want to help with the investigation."

Brant was incredulous. "*Sabotage*? You think I was trying to sabotage you?"

"What do you call it?" Samille demanded furiously.

Brant shook his head. And then, to her utter dismay, he began to laugh—a deep, rumbling sound that rose from his chest and made his broad shoulders shake.

"I don't see what's so funny," she snapped.

"You have so much to learn, Samille. About men, about people, about the world in general. Believe me, if I really wanted to sabotage you, I would."

"So you keep reminding me," she said spitefully. She turned in her seat to face him. "Look, Brant, I know it's a dangerous assignment. I'm not trivializing your concerns or the dire nature of the situation. I just wish you'd give me a chance."

He slanted her a cynical look. "To do what? Get yourself killed?"

She slammed her fist on the steering wheel, then felt stupid when startled passersby stared in their direction at the blast of the horn.

"What are you trying to prove, Samille? That you're one of the tough guys?"

"It works for you."

"Yeah, well, you're not me, nor should you want to be." His eyes and mouth hardened. "Trust me when I tell you that playing the hero isn't all it's cracked up to be."

"I don't want to be a hero, Brant. I want to help. I want to do my job. Why won't you let me?"

Brant gazed at her so long that she had to resist the urge to look away. His eyes roamed across her face, landing on each feature with a feather-light touch before moving to the next. Samille's breath caught in her throat; by the time his gaze reached her mouth and lingered, she felt as if she were suffocating.

Without warning he climbed from the Jeep and

slammed the door. Samille quickly started the ignition so that she could roll down the automatic windows and continue their conversation.

"Where are you headed?" Brant asked.

"To run a few errands."

His expression was dubious. "I think it goes without saying that I prefer to know your whereabouts at all times."

"I'm well aware of that." She obstinately offered no more.

His eyes narrowed on her face. "Don't even think about packing your suitcase and going home."

A defiant chin went up. "And if I do?"

"Then I'll just have to show up on your doorstep, toss you over my shoulder, and drag you back to my place."

Her heart thudded. "You wouldn't dare."

"Try me," he said softly, understated menace in every inflection. With that promise hanging in the air between them, he rapped his knuckle on the roof of the Jeep, turned, and strolled back inside the police station with those relaxed, confident strides.

Samille carefully rolled up the windows and grabbed a spare blanket from the backseat. She buried her face in the cottony folds, waited a beat, then screamed at the top of her lungs until she felt a little better.

"Drumroll, please."

Lopez scowled at Jacob Milsner, a short, wiry man with a cap of dark brown curls and hair that grew copiously from his ears and nostrils. "Enough with the theatrics, Jake. Let's see what you've got."

With a dramatic flourish, Milsner peeled back the opaque protective sheet to reveal the long-awaited composite sketch. The suspect appeared to be in his early thirties and had thick, wavy black hair. His features were prominent: broad forehead and nose, lean cheekbones, and a square jaw. A tiny scar formed a dent in his chin and gave him a stern, hard look. The austerity was softened by dark, fathomless eyes that possessed a keen intelligence.

Brant and Detective Lopez were struck with recognition at the same time.

"Hey, it's that bigwig criminal lawyer," Lopez exclaimed, snapping his fingers. "Sal . . . Sal . . . Christ, what's his name again?"

"Salvatore Carrella." Brant's expression was grim. "Jillian Carrella's father."

CHAPTER 11

Samille spent the remainder of the day running errands and catching up on paperwork at the office before returning to Brant's place. As she entered the empty town house, she was struck by the weirdness of sharing living quarters with a man, especially a man she wasn't dating. She didn't know what to expect. Should she behave as if everything were normal, as if she were back at her own apartment—minus walking around in her underwear?

She lamented her inexperience where men were concerned. She knew women who wouldn't have given the matter a passing thought; savvy, sophisticated women who would find humor in the situation, or would consider forced cohabitation with a gorgeous man a gift from heaven. Samille, unfortunately, was not one of those women.

She scowled at herself. Just because she'd been brought there against her will didn't mean she had to behave like a prisoner. As long as Brant obliged her to remain with him, she would go about her normal business. And the first order of business was to rustle up something to eat.

She entered the immaculate kitchen, pulled open the freezer, and was gratified to discover that it was well stocked. She saw thick steaks, pork chops, some ground beef, and packages of frozen vegetables. She grinned. Did this mean that Special Agent Kincaid could actually *cook*? She gave him bonus points for having domestic potential, opened the other half of the double-sided refrigerator, and was thrilled to find a pair of steaks that were already thawed. She washed her hands and set about the task of seasoning and marinating the meat using basic ingredients, the way Aunt Noreen had taught her.

She set the timer on the broiler and inserted the steaks, then threw a couple of baked potatoes into the oven. She crossed to the living room and turned on the evening news, then decided to build a fire. When the phone rang a few minutes later, she assumed it was Brant and answered it without thinking.

There was a heavy pause on the other end, and then a woman spoke hesitantly. "I must have the wrong number. I'm looking for Brant Kincaid?"

"You have the right number, but Brant isn't here at the moment. Can I take a message?"

"This is Alexandra. When do you expect him back?"

"I'm not sure." Samille glanced around the kitchen for a pad and pencil. "Does he have your number?"

"He'd better." A possessive note crept into the woman's voice. "And who am I speaking with?"

"Don't worry," Samille said, her stomach knotting with an emotion she didn't want to identify, "Brant and I aren't involved. I'll let him know you called."

"You do that," Alexandra said, and hung up.

Samille shook her head as she replaced the receiver. So Brant had other women. It shouldn't have surprised her. A man like Brant Kincaid wouldn't be celibate, not when he could have his pick of any woman. Not that it was any of her business, she told herself. What Brant did in his personal life was his prerogative.

So why did she find herself simmering like the steaks in the broiler?

She went upstairs and changed out of her pantsuit into a pair of black leggings and a Washington Redskins sweatshirt. She had just jammed her feet into a pair of thick wool socks when she heard the garage door open. She returned to the kitchen and was checking the baked potatoes when Brant appeared. Hands thrust into his pants pockets, he leaned in the doorway and said nothing for several moments, watching her with the oddest expression on his face.

Unsettled by the intensity of his dark gaze, Samille said the first thing that came to mind: "Don't tell me you've never had a woman in your kitchen before?" The instant the words left her mouth, she wanted to retract them. Heat flooded her cheeks when Brant's mouth curved upward in a slow pirate's grin.

"Why, Ms. Broussard," he drawled, "a gentleman should never kiss and tell."

"Oh, you know what I meant," she snapped.

He chuckled. "Something smells wonderful in here."

"I figured since you're letting me stay here rent-free," she said sardonically, "I might as well earn my keep."

"Don't earn it too well," Brant warned softly, "or I may never let you leave."

Her pulse skipped dangerously. She strove for aloofness. "Oh, I don't know about that. I wouldn't want to cramp your style. You know, with the ladies and all. Which reminds me: Alexandra called."

"Alexandra?"

"Yes, Alexandra." She brushed past him and stalked into the living room, suddenly and inexplicably aggravated.

Brant followed her, his expression baffled. "Is something wrong?"

"Of course not. Why would anything be wrong? And before you ask, the only reason I answered your phone is that I thought it was you."

"I tried to reach you on the cell. Twice."

She frowned. "I had it with me the entire day."

Brant's eyes landed on the cell phone in question. He walked over, picked it up from the dining room table, and scowled. "No wonder. It was turned off."

"Oh." Samille felt stupid, and it showed in her abashed expression. "That would explain why I never heard from you."

"Why didn't you call me?"

"I got preoccupied. Did you get a positive ID on the composite sketch?"

He nodded. "I'll fill you in over dinner. I'm going to take a shower first—I just came from the morgue."

Brant returned twenty minutes later wearing jeans and a Syracuse University T-shirt. He was pleasantly surprised to discover that Samille had set the dining room table using chinaware and linen napkins he didn't remember owning—courtesy of his mother and sister, no doubt. Candles were lit on the table, flickering against the glossy mahogany and adding to the cozy warmth created by the roaring fireplace.

For a split second, the inviting allure of the scene made Brant forget all about the investigation and sadistic predators who preyed on gullible teenagers. He suddenly wished different circumstances had brought Samille Broussard to his home. He wished he could pretend, even for just a few hours, that they were two people without a care in the world, who simply wanted to spend time getting to know each other. When he'd arrived home that evening to the mouthwatering aroma of grilling steaks and the sight of her moving about his kitchen with familiar ease, he'd found himself wondering what it would be like to come home to her every day, to have her greet him with a warm smile and one of those deep, intoxicating kisses. A wave of longing had washed over him, shocking in its intensity.

Samille emerged from the kitchen carrying a vibrantly colorful garden salad arranged in a large glass bowl. She paused at the sight of him just standing there with what he assumed was a look of numb paralysis. "Is something wrong?"

He shook his head, dismissing the torturous image for the second time that evening. It was pointless to allow himself to want things he could never have. "Everything looks good," he said appreciatively. He managed a smile. "Thanks, Samille."

"No big deal. Let's eat."

Brant groaned after taking his first bite of succulent steak. "Oh, man, this is good."

Samille's mouth curved with pleasure. "Glad you approve."

"You've sealed your fate. You're never leaving here."

She laughed huskily, buttering her potato. "Last I checked, kidnapping was a federal offense, Agent Kincaid."

His eyes danced with mirth. "I'll try to remember that."

"Tell me about the composite sketch."

Reluctantly Brant abandoned his hopes for light dinner conversation and allowed her to switch gears. "It was Salvatore Carrella."

Samille froze in the middle of cutting a piece of steak. Her stunned gaze flew to his face. "Jillian Carrella's father?"

"One and the same. Detective Lopez and I went to his office, but he wasn't there, and no one answered at his home. The secretary said there was some kind of family emergency, but she expected him back tomorrow."

"What possible connection could Andrew Cason and Salvatore Carrella have?"

"Guess we'll have to wait until tomorrow to find out. That is, if Carrella cooperates."

While they finished their meal, they discussed the investigation, tossing theories back and forth in a fluid, energetic exchange. The brainstorming session continued as they cleared the table and loaded the dishwasher, as Brant opened a bottle of vintage Cabernet Sauvignon and filled two crystal wineglasses—items his mother had casually supplied on a previous visit to his home.

Sipping their wine, they crossed to the living room and sat on the sofa. "You mentioned being at the morgue," Samille said. "What were the results of the autopsy?"

Brant had hoped to delay telling her for as long as possible. His time was up. "Bradley was poisoned with cyanide. It sent him into cardiac arrest almost immediately."

"Oh my God," Samille breathed.

"It was administered intravenously between his toes. The ME must have missed it during his initial examination of the body."

Samille shuddered. *The body*. The description sounded so cold and detached, so clinical. Bradley Whitfield had been someone's son and brother. Just twenty-four hours earlier he'd been alive, and there had been hope, however slim, that he might fully recover. The cruel whim of an unknown predator had put an end to that.

"Does the family know?" she asked quietly.

"They were notified this evening."

Samille nodded, swallowing around the knot of

sorrow wedged in her throat. "I can't believe someone just waltzed into a hospital room, injected a patient with cyanide, and walked right back out—and nobody saw a thing! How can that be? *How?*"

Brant stared into the twinkling contents of his wineglass and said nothing. He wanted to give Samille the routine spiel about the importance of maintaining professional objectivity and emotional detachment during investigations, lessons that were rammed down the throats of those in law enforcement. Lessons that were vital to retaining one's sanity, that kept one from walking off the job and never looking back when the horror became too much. But he didn't utter a word. He knew Samille would eventually learn on her own—she had no choice. It was a matter of survival, and this woman was a survivor. She possessed incredible strength and courage, an intestinal fortitude that commanded the respect and admiration of every man she worked with, including him.

Still, her vulnerability beckoned to him, stirring something deep within him. He was driven by a fierce instinct to protect her, whether she welcomed it or not.

"I want to get this bastard," she whispered fervently. "I want to find him and nail his hide to the wall."

"I know, Samille." Brant shoved out a deep breath and rolled his cramped shoulders. "It's been a long day. What do you say we drop this for tonight?"

Samille gave a distracted nod. She drew her knees up to her chin and stared into the hissing flames. Her expression remained gloomy.

Brant took a sip of his wine, set the glass on the table, and stood. "I can't believe I'm about to do this," he muttered under his breath.

Samille's gaze lifted from the fire to follow him across the room to a closet. Intrigued, she watched as he withdrew a guitar encased in black leather. He closed the door and returned to the living room.

Samille gave him a surprised look as he rejoined her on the sofa. "Do you play?"

"Not anymore."

"You mean you used to?"

Brant chuckled at her pleased tone. He ran his hands along the leather case, slightly worn and faded with time. "It was a long time ago. My grandfather taught me when I was a kid. He was the guitarist in a blues band during the fifties and sixties. They called themselves the Pickled Blues."

"The *Pickled Blues*?"

"In honor of their fallen comrade who died in World War Two. His name was Jesse Bridges, but the fellas called him 'Pickles' because he loved pickles so much." A reminiscent smile curved his lips. "My grandfather used to tell me these stories that made me laugh so hard I cried."

Samille found herself smiling. "Is your grandfather still alive?"

"No," Brant said quietly. "He died several years ago."

"I'm sorry. You must miss him a lot."

"I do. We all miss him. But we take comfort in knowing that he enjoyed a long, rich life. He did everything he ever set out to accomplish. He traveled around the world, married his childhood sweetheart, and lived to help raise his grandchildren. Not to mention the night his band opened for B.B. King. He'd never admit it," Brant added with a grin, "but I know that night meant almost as much to him as receiving the Purple Heart."

"Your grandfather was quite an extraordinary man, wasn't he?"

"That he was. He's buried at Arlington National Cemetery, so I visit him often. Living here makes me feel closer to him." His expression softened as he gazed down at the guitar in his arms. "He gave this to me before he died. It was his very first guitar."

Samille smiled, touched by the poignancy of the gift and the special bond Brant had shared with his grandfather. She was struck, once again, by his uncharacteristic willingness to confide in her, to share such deeply personal details about himself. It was downright endearing. "Play something for me."

Brant sent her a wry look. "I was afraid you'd say that. This guitar hasn't seen the light of day in ages, Samille. It probably needs a lot of tuning."

"Come on, Brant. Do it for me. Pretty please?" Samille made an exaggerated show of batting her eyelashes at him.

Brant chuckled. "Uh-huh, I see how you operate, pulling out the feminine wiles when you want something."

Samille offered a coquettish grin. "Does it work?"

"Oh, you have no idea." Shaking his head at her, Brant unzipped the leather case and carefully lifted out a guitar that was in surprisingly good condition. He pulled the strap over his shoulder and balanced the guitar over his knee, and instantly appeared to become one with the instrument. His fingers glided slowly, almost reverently, across the rich maple back and solid walnut neck. "Isn't she beautiful?"

"She is," Samille agreed, admiring the guitar's fine craftsmanship. She knew, without being told, that she was looking at a vintage collector's item. She wrapped her arms around her legs and sent Brant a teasing smile. "What're you going to play for me? B.B. King? Stevie Ray Vaughan?"

"Yeah, right. I'm nowhere near *that* good."

Samille laughed, sipping her wine and watching his

strong fingers stroke the guitar strings as he plucked out a few practice notes. She marveled at his transformation from the stern, brooding FBI agent she'd grown accustomed to, to this relaxed stranger who seemed as at ease with a guitar as he was wielding a Glock. She knew Brant didn't share himself easily with others; she doubted there were many who'd ever witnessed this side of him. She felt incredibly privileged, as if she'd been entrusted with a cherished secret.

"This first number is a Pickled Blues original," Brant announced as if he were onstage, introducing the band in a dimly lit, smoke-filled Brooklyn nightclub. She stared at his handsome face, so dark and wicked and fine. He winked at her, and Samille's heartbeat actually accelerated. He couldn't have been more sexy if he tried. "It's called 'Comin' Home.' "

He began the song, his voice low and smoky, the gentle strum of the guitar melodious and transfixing. Samille listened in rapt attention as he regaled her with a gritty tune about a black soldier returning home from the war to find his world unchanged. A soldier who, despite his valiant efforts on the battlefield, was confronted with racism and the cruel reminder that he remained a second-class citizen in his own country. The lyrics were hauntingly profound, a scathing indictment that was equally mournful.

By the time Brant struck the last note, tears had welled in Samille's eyes. She blinked to clear her vision and blew out a deep, shaky breath. "Wow," she murmured. "That was amazing, Brant—your playing *and* the song. Did your grandfather write that?"

"Yeah." Brant wore a faraway expression as he continued strumming a few errant chords, lost in a distant memory.

Just when it seemed he'd forgotten her presence, he

looked up and saw the shimmering moisture in her eyes. He started another song, this one more upbeat than the first, a lively ragtime tune that had Samille's toes tapping in no time at all. She laughed and clapped as Brant crooned about an unfaithful gambler and the no-nonsense woman who put an end to his cheating ways. The colorful song segued into another, and unable to resist, Samille jumped up from the sofa and began dancing. She honestly couldn't remember the last time she'd had so much fun or felt so uninhibited. It was wonderfully exhilarating, and when Brant struck up B.B. King's famous "Is You Is, Or Is You Ain't," Samille joined right along as he belted out the lyrics. Without missing a beat on the guitar, Brant stood and danced with her, and they were transported from his living room to a smoky night-club pulsing with live music and gyrating bodies.

When the song ended, they collapsed against the sofa and howled with side-splitting laughter. "Oh my God," Samille gasped. "That was so much fun!"

Brant grinned at her. "Beats sitting around singing campfire tunes, huh?"

"Most definitely!" Dark eyes glittering with mirth, Samille slanted him a sidelong look. "You're pretty good, Kincaid. Ever think about retiring from the Bureau and launching a solo career?"

He laughed. "Not a chance." He gazed at her, noting how relaxed and content she looked. Not a trace of tension or anxiety remained, and he felt a mixture of tenderness and amazement that something as simple as their playful antics could bring her so much pleasure. Her throaty laughter was the sweetest sound he'd ever heard in his life. He found himself thinking of other ways to make her happy, to keep the glow in her cheeks and the infectious smile on her face.

"How about another selection?" she suggested.

Brant feigned exasperation. "Doesn't the musician get a break between sets?"

"Just one more song, Brant, and then I promise you can retire from your playing days—although I think you're depriving the world of an extraordinary gift."

He grinned. "Stop trying to butter me up, Broussard. You'll get your encore performance."

He sat up, adjusted the guitar across his knee, and strummed a few mellow notes. Samille's breath hitched when he began Eric Clapton's "Have You Ever Loved a Woman?"

"Have you ever loved a woman so much you tremble in pain . . ." His fingers caressed the guitar strings as his deep voice poured out the lyrics—and all the time his eyes remained locked on hers. She was caught in the beam of that intense gaze, held captive, mesmerized. The experience was undeniably seductive, intimate to the point that she felt naked and utterly exposed before him.

And suddenly she knew she was in big trouble. She had allowed the unthinkable to happen.

She had fallen in love with Brant Kincaid.

Her first inclination was to deny it. It had been an emotionally trying day. Brant had been a sounding board, giving her a much-needed opportunity to vent her frustration and anger about the case. He'd lifted her spirits by playing the guitar for her, and now he was serenading her with an incredibly romantic ballad. A drowsy fire was crackling in the fireplace, and her insides were warm with good wine. What woman in her right mind *wouldn't* be feeling amorous at that moment?

But no matter how hard Samille tried to rationalize her feelings, she knew she couldn't outrun the truth. She was in love with Brant, deeply and irrevocably. She couldn't pinpoint the exact moment it had happened. Perhaps she'd been halfway in love with him for the past six months, ever since she'd first laid eyes on him at the academy. Or perhaps it had happened after that first explosive kiss they'd shared in her apartment. It didn't matter. She loved him, and there was nothing she could do about it. The revelation rocked her to the core of her being and left her feeling excruciatingly vulnerable.

Brant trailed off at the expression on Samille's face. It was a fascinating mixture of terror and yearning. Slowly he slid the guitar strap over his shoulder and returned the instrument to its case. Samille continued to stare at him in that odd, transfixed manner.

"Samille," he said quietly, "is something wrong?"

She swallowed and shook her head quickly. "Thanks for taking my mind off the case, Brant. It was just what I needed." Hastily she rose from the sofa. "Tomorrow's going to be another long day. We should really get to bed—not together, of course. I meant separately."

His mouth twitched as he stood. "I know what you meant."

"Um, I'll just take these into the kitchen—" She bent to retrieve their empty wineglasses and was forestalled by his gentle hand upon her shoulder.

"I'll get them," he murmured.

"All right. Well, good night, Brant."

As she started away, he reached out and caught her wrist. She turned, her chin tilted at a defensive angle. He watched her through slumberous eyes, his lids at half-mast. When he lifted a hand slowly to touch her face, she closed her eyes as if to brace herself.

"Samille—"

The phone rang, intrusively announcing the existence of an outside world. Samille looked relieved by the interruption. "Good night," she mumbled before beating a hasty retreat upstairs.

Brant watched her go before grabbing the cordless phone and answering brusquely, "Hello?"

"Hello there, stranger," a smooth, cultured voice purred. "Long time no speak."

A warm smile of recognition spread across Brant's face. "Hey, Alex. How are you?"

"Oh, I've been better." She paused. "I'm sure your mother told you about my recent breakup with Dennis."

"She may have mentioned it. I'm sorry, Alex."

"Don't be. It was for the best. Dennis and I weren't as compatible as we thought we were. Getting married would have been nothing short of a disaster." Her soft laugh held a tinge of self-deprecation. "Your mother has been a godsend. She sent me to Paris in her place, and it was just the cure I needed. I had a fabulous time."

"Glad to hear it," Brant said, cradling the phone to his ear as he gathered empty wineglasses and carried them into the kitchen.

"Of course," Alexandra drawled, "I probably would've enjoyed the experience even more if there had been someone to share it with. As they say: *Paris est pour des amoureux*—Paris is for lovers."

"Hmm," Brant murmured noncommittally. He cast a glance toward the staircase and wondered if Samille had already gone to bed.

"I called you earlier. Some woman answered the phone. Did you get the message?"

"Yeah."

"I didn't know you were seeing anyone special, Brant. Your mother and sister will be thrilled. You know how desperately they want to see you married."

"Don't remind me," Brant muttered darkly.

The phone line was filled with a low, sultry chuckle. "Do you remember what I used to tell you when you were just thirteen, and all the girls had crushes on Bryan because he was the outgoing, popular athlete? I held your handsome little face in my hands and promised you that one day all those silly young girls who dismissed you as too 'brainy' or 'serious' would come to their senses and realize how amazing you are, and then you'd have to beat them off with a stick. And I was right! By high school you had those females eating out of the palm of your hand, sighing and carrying on about how *intense* you were, how your intelligence made you *so* sexy and fascinating." Alexandra laughed lazily. "I still remember how upset Bryan was when *you* slept with the home-coming queen before he got the chance. That's when he started warning everyone to watch out for you. He said you were way more dangerous than he was, because you were so smart you could talk a woman out of her panties without her even knowing it!"

Brant smiled slightly as he leaned in the kitchen door frame. "My brother had a tendency to exaggerate."

"I don't think so, baby boy. Zora says the same thing about you. How many hearts have you broken down there? You've probably lost count. And what about this new woman? What's her name, by the way?"

Brant hesitated. "Samille. And before you go broad-casting news of my pending nuptials to my family," he added dryly, "you should probably know that Samille and I aren't involved."

"Interesting," Alexandra murmured. "She said the same thing when I called earlier. I wonder what *that* means."

"It means we're not involved."

"All right. I'll take your word for it."

Brant wondered if he'd only imagined the note of relief in Alexandra's voice. Smoothly she continued, "Anyway, the reason I called is that I'll be at Howard University next weekend to attend a fund-raiser sponsored by my sorority. If you weren't such a workaholic, Brant

Kincaid, I would have asked you to be my escort. Appearing on the arm of a gorgeous man would give my self-esteem a welcome boost—not to mention how it would make those hussies green with envy." She issued a plaintive sigh. "But your mother tells me you're working on a big case, so I won't lay a guilt trip on you. However, I *will* expect you to set aside some free time to have dinner with me. Can you promise me that?"

"I'll see what I can do," Brant said easily. "How long will you be in town?"

"Just for the weekend. I'll call you when I arrive next Friday, and we can set up a date. How does that sound?"

"Works for me. Talk to you then."

"Good night, Brant." Her tone softened. "Can't wait to see you again."

"Same here." As Brant hung up the phone, Audre Kincaid's sage prophecy echoed in his mind: *I honestly believe she's been carrying a torch for you all these years, and that's why her relationships fail.*

God, he hoped his mother was wrong. He didn't need any more complications in his life. Lord knew he could barely handle the unpredictable woman residing under his roof now. One minute she'd been carefree and exuberant, tossing her head in laughter as she boogied with him. Then without warning her mood had changed, and she couldn't get away from him fast enough.

Brant scowled as he turned off the lights and headed upstairs. The man who unlocked the key to understanding the female psyche definitely deserved the Nobel Prize.

He paused outside Samille's room, fighting the temptation to knock, to go in and apologize for whatever wrong he'd committed against her. He listened at the door, but there was no movement from within. She was probably fast asleep. Good, he thought. He didn't need another eyeful of her in the skimpy halter and shorts she considered sleepwear. It had already taken most of the day to erase the image from his mind.

He turned and continued down the hall to his own room, the door closing behind him with a decisive click.

Samille heard him stop outside her room and waited, heart hammering violently in her chest. She didn't want to face him again after the self-discovery she'd made; she *couldn't* face him. It was only when his bedroom door closed that she breathed again, her fists unclenching on the coverlet she'd seized in panic. She stared at the dark ceiling in abject misery.

God, what a mess she'd made. For all her pontifications about not getting involved with men she worked with, she'd gone and fallen in love with Brant Kincaid. And it had taken all of six days. *Six days,* she thought in self-disgust. She'd taken longer than that to choose a new car!

This case was her first criminal investigation. She needed her wits about her, needed her mind clear and free of distraction. How was she supposed to put aside her feelings for Brant Kincaid and carry out her responsibilities when her body couldn't stop clamoring for his next kiss, when all she wanted to know was whether he felt the same about her? She'd even found herself enjoying their relaxed domesticity as they cleared the table after dinner and loaded the dishwasher together. She had wondered how such an ordinary task could feel so special, so *right.* How insane was that?

On her way to the bathroom to brush her teeth, she'd caught a fragment of his phone conversation, had heard him tell another woman that he and Samille weren't involved. And then she'd spent the next half hour torturing herself with mental images of Brant and the mystery woman locked in a torrid embrace.

"What a colossal fool you are, Samille Broussard," she whispered into the darkness.

Punching the pillow in frustration, she rolled onto her side and squeezed her eyes shut, determined to put Brant Kincaid—and her foolish love for him—out of her mind.

CHAPTER 12

"Life is good, B.K. The school year's finally over, we're heading to Syracuse University on full scholarships—you for your brains, me for my athletic prowess—"

Brant nearly choked on a laugh. "Athletic prowess?"

"That's what all the newspapers are saying about me. Do I need to show you the article from yesterday's Post? I think there's another copy in the backseat." The Buick teetered between lanes as Bryan Kincaid reached behind him for the newspaper in question.

"Hey, watch the road before you get us killed!" Brant warned.

Bryan flashed a mischievous grin at his brother. "Relax, B.K. Need I remind you who got his driver's license first?"

Brant rolled his eyes. "It was one day, Bryan. And that's only because I kept my word about helping Mom move her office furniture—unlike some people I know, who made up a bogus story about having basketball practice so he could sneak to the DMV in his buddy's car and take the test."

Bryan chuckled. "I'll never live that down."

"Not any time soon," Brant retorted, then grimaced as his brother veered into a tight parking space outside the corner convenience store and came within inches of clipping the car in front of them. Brant tried not to think about their father's part-

ing words as they left home that afternoon: "Brant, I'm holding you accountable for returning that vehicle in the same condition. Take good care of it, son, or it'll be the last time you or your brother get behind the wheel again."

Bryan had snatched the keys and raced to the Buick before Brant could utter a word of protest. But he planned to remedy that as soon as Bryan went inside the store.

But Bryan had not moved a muscle. He was watching Brant expectantly. "What're you waiting for?"

Brant frowned. "What do you mean? I'm not going in there. It wasn't my idea to stop at the store first."

"I told Michelle we'd bring some sodas. We can't show up empty-handed."

"So there's the door."

"Come on, B.K. I'm the driver. The driver always waits in the car. It's an unwritten rule." When his brother didn't budge, Bryan heaved a sigh of resignation. "All right. I'll call you for it."

Reluctantly Brant agreed to settle the matter the old-fashioned way: in a round of rock, paper, scissors. When he lost three out of five, Bryan whooped in delight. "I can't believe it! I finally beat you!"

"I'm having an off day," Brant muttered darkly as he climbed from the car.

"Get some mints too," Bryan called after him. "Michelle promised to give me a nice going-away present after the cookout, and I don't wanna be caught with potato salad breath!"

"Yeah, yeah, yeah." Brant entered the tiny convenience store and nodded a greeting to the West Indian store owner, who gave him a gold-toothed grin. Bob Marley was crowing from a portable radio behind the counter, and a rickety oscillating fan recirculated sticky summer air.

Brant grabbed two cases of Pepsi and headed for the checkout counter. He was reaching for Bryan's favorite brand of mints when a sudden crack of gunfire exploded outside. His blood turned to ice. He dropped the armload of sodas and rushed from *the store just as a blue Mustang with gleaming rims sped away on screeching tires.*

Brant's eyes swung to his father's Buick parked at the curb. His heart plunged to his stomach at the sight that greeted him.

No! he shouted soundlessly.

He raced around to the driver's side and yanked open the door. Bryan Kincaid's lifeless, bullet-riddled body spilled from the car and into his brother's arms. He'd been shot once in the head, twice in the chest. Immediately Brant began to apply pressure to the gaping wounds, desperately hoping to stem the tide of bright warm blood even as he knew it was too late.

The store owner appeared in the doorway. "What happened?"

"Call 911!" Brant roared at him. Cradling his brother's body in his arms, he collapsed onto the street, alternately cursing and screaming Bryan's name.

Brant bolted upright in the darkness of his bedroom. His heart pounded painfully against his rib cage, choking the air from his lungs. He tossed the covers aside and swung his legs over the side of the bed. He sat there for several moments, allowing his mind to accept that it had been another dream—even if his heart never could.

"Christ," he muttered, holding his head in his hands. Grief and nausea churned in his stomach until he thought he would be sick. He stood and crossed to the adjoining bathroom, splashing cold water onto his face and bare chest. He dried off with a towel before returning to bed. Lying on his back with his hands clasped behind his head, he stared at the ceiling and knew sleep had once again deserted him.

A soft knock sounded at the door. Frowning, he sat up and called, "Come in."

The door opened slowly to reveal Samille's shadowy

silhouette. "Brant?" His name came to him quietly, her voice soft and tentative.

"What is it? Is something wrong?"

"No. Actually, I came to see if you were all right." She hesitated. "I heard you shouting in your sleep."

"It was just a nightmare," he mumbled. "Nothing for you to worry about."

"Are you sure?"

"Yes. Go back to bed, Samille." But as the door began to close behind her, he reconsidered. He called in a low voice laced with urgency, "Come here."

She turned back. "Excuse me?"

"I won't try anything. You have my word. I just . . . I just want you beside me for a while."

Samille's heart melted at the vulnerability in his voice. Knowing there was nothing she would deny this man, she started across the large room toward him. A sliver of moonlight seeped through the curtained window, guiding her path. When she reached the enormous bed, Brant pulled back the covers for her.

Her mouth went dry. "You're not, um, naked under there, are you?"

She thought he smiled a little, but it was too dark to be certain. "No," he murmured. "You're safe."

Samille climbed into the bed and quickly pulled the covers up to her chin. She was immediately enveloped in Brant's clean-scented warmth. She lay flat on her back and stayed as close to the edge of the bed as possible.

"Are you cold?" he asked softly.

She shook her head. "A little nervous," she admitted. "This is dangerous, Brant. Lying together in your bed like this."

"I know. I want to kiss you," he said huskily. "But I won't."

She didn't know whether to feel relieved or cheated.

She closed her eyes and willed her thudding pulse to return to its normal rate.

"Is everything all right now?"

She turned her head on the pillow to give him a quizzical look. "What do you mean?"

"You seemed a little upset earlier. I thought something was wrong."

"Oh." Samille swallowed at the tightness in her throat. *If only he knew!* But he would never know, she resolved. She wouldn't put her heart on the line like that. She wouldn't give him the opportunity to destroy her, to shatter the protective shield she'd spent a lifetime erecting around her emotions.

"It's nothing for you to worry about," she said quietly, echoing his earlier words to her. She sat up and propped her head in her hand as she faced him in the bed. He wore no shirt, and even in the shadowy darkness she could tell his chest was planed with hard, sinewy muscle. She forced the thought from her mind and concentrated on what had brought her to his room in the first place. "Brant?"

"Yeah?"

"Who's Bryan?"

She felt him tense, and wished she could discern his expression. She immediately knew she'd struck a raw nerve and should probably drop the subject, but she couldn't. "You called his name in your sleep," she gently explained. "Several times."

Brant eased back against the pillows. He was silent for so long that she wondered if he intended to ignore her. When he finally answered, his voice was so low she could have imagined it. "He was my brother."

She stared at him. "Your brother?"

"Yes."

Comprehension slowly dawned. "The boy in the high school graduation photo . . . That isn't you, is it?"

"No. Bryan was my twin."

Samille grew very still. "What happened to him?"

And just like that, Brant knew he was going to tell her everything. But he didn't want to examine the myriad feelings that were compelling him to do it. He swallowed hard. "He was killed when we were seventeen."

Samille's heart constricted. "Oh, Brant," she whispered. "I'm so sorry."

"It was a long time ago," he said gruffly.

"But you still dream about him and call out for him. You haven't really healed, have you?"

She spoke with such certainty, and with such tenderness, that Brant found it impossible not to confide in her. "It was two months after our high school graduation. We'd been invited to a friend's cookout and stopped at the store first. Bryan waited in the car while I went inside." He stopped and reflected, as he'd done countless times over the years, on the game of chance that had determined their fates. Brant had always beaten his brother at rock, paper, scissors.

Not on that fateful afternoon.

He closed his eyes against the familiar all-consuming guilt. "While I was inside, Bryan was shot by someone in a passing car."

Samille couldn't suppress her horrified intake of breath. "Oh my God."

"He never stood a chance. He died almost instantly." When the paramedics arrived, they had found Brant slumped against the Buick with his brother cradled in his arms, his face and clothing smeared with Bryan's blood. It had taken three EMTs to pry Brant away from his twin, and then he'd simply gone into shock. He'd remained catatonic for three days.

"Oh, Brant." Without thinking Samille wrapped her arms around his wide chest and drew him close. He automatically tensed, and for a moment she feared he would pull away. But he didn't. After a while his body relaxed, and he curved his arms around her waist and held on to her.

Gently she asked, "Did your brother know the person who shot him, or was it random?"

"He knew him." Brant's tone was hard, brittle. "The kid was a rival basketball player from another school. He and Bryan got into a fight the month before when Bryan started dating his ex-girlfriend." Fury tightened Brant's features at the sheer senselessness of the tragedy. Years later, he still couldn't believe that his brother's life had been cut brutally short over something so trivial.

"God, I'm so sorry, Brant."

"Yeah," he whispered bitterly, "me too."

"What happened to the other boy?"

Again Brant tensed. When he answered, his voice was chillingly succinct. "He served six years at Rikers and got out on a technicality. Not long after, he hooked up with some of his old buddies who were deep into money laundering." His jaw hardened. "He was killed less than a year later."

Something in his lethal tone made Samille shiver. She knew, from personal experience, that the death of Bryan Kincaid's murderer had brought little consolation to the family. She started to ask Brant how the boy had died, then decided against it. It wasn't important.

"I've always heard that twins possess some sort of tele-kinetic link to each other," she said. "Did you ever feel that way about Bryan?"

"I don't know." His chest lifted beneath her cheek as he drew in a deep breath and slowly expelled it. "I feel as if a big part of me is missing, but so does anyone who has ever lost a loved one. You know that as well as I do."

"Yes," she said softly, lifting her head and searching his face in the moonlight, "but somehow I think it must be different for twins." Suddenly she remembered what she'd asked him on the night they discovered Andrew Cason's body: *You didn't get sick at your first crime scene?*

His first crime scene had been that of his brother's.

Her heart swelled with sorrow. Laying her hand against Brant's face, she cradled him protectively to her chest and brushed her lips across his forehead. But she didn't stop there. She kissed his closed eyelids, the strong bridge of his nose, the hard line of his cheekbones. She skated her open mouth along his jaw, and when he turned his face into hers, she covered his lips hungrily with hers. Brant made a sound deep in his throat, pure masculine hunger. His arms banded around her waist as he matched the urgency of her kiss, and Samille experienced a surge of euphoria like nothing she'd ever felt before. She wanted this moment, needed it like her very life depended on it. She would save the recriminations for tomorrow. Tonight, her body and soul belonged to this man whom, she was now convinced, she'd been destined to love from the beginning of time.

She caught his sensuous bottom lip between her teeth and gently suckled, and was rewarded with the gasp of his indrawn breath. He sank his fingers into her hair as his tongue delved into her mouth, tangling with hers, plunging and retreating in blatant imitation of what he wanted to do to her with his body. This time it was Samille who moaned in mindless pleasure.

Her heart thundered furiously as she trailed her fingertips over the thick cords of his shoulder, then lower along the rigid planes of his muscular chest. His skin was warm and smooth as satin over granite, and when she leaned forward and kissed his chest, the muscles contracted reflexively. Heady with her newfound power, Samille sat up and straddled him. Bracing her palms on his taut abdomen, she bent and licked his flat, dark nipple, then trailed a long, seductive kiss downward toward his waist.

Brant groaned and closed his eyes against the staggering onslaught of sensation: Samille's silken thighs as she straddled him, the way her hair teased his flesh as she leaned over him, the erotic boldness of her kisses. His blood was roaring in his ears. He wanted to crush her in his arms and bury himself deeply inside her exquisite sweetness. He was fast losing control, and he knew it.

Samille's exploring hands were roaming over him, gliding beneath the waistband of his shorts. His breath caught sharply when she brushed her fingers over his rigid arousal. The moment she took him in her hand, her eyes widened in surprise. But Brant was too far gone to care or feel flattered that she'd been taken aback by his size and, judging from the demure smile on her lips, was obviously impressed.

Her warm fingers stroked and caressed him until he was on the verge of exploding in her hand. He tossed back his head and swore in a low, guttural voice he hardly recognized.

"Let me love you," Samille whispered to him.

At those sultry words, his restraint finally broke. With an agonized groan, he rolled her onto her back and crushed his mouth to hers with a reckless desperation that made Samille feel at once powerful and helpless. His hands and mouth claimed her, sliding over her breasts and waist, then reaching beneath her body to grasp her buttocks and hold her tightly against his straining erection.

Samille slid her arms around his neck and kissed him with all the passion building inside her, pressing herself against his solid length, exulting in the shudder that racked his body as his mouth opened and closed over hers in a kiss that was both rough and tender. She wrapped her legs around his hips and reached frantically for the waistband of his shorts.

The sudden jangling of the phone was like the sharp crack of a rifle. With a savage oath, Brant tore his mouth away and rested his forehead against hers. Samille gazed up at him, heart hammering in contralto with his as she awaited his decision.

She almost sobbed in frustration when he reached across the nightstand and grabbed the phone on the last ring.

"Hello?" he rasped impatiently. He frowned when he was greeted with a dial tone. Angrily he replaced the receiver and, after a slight hesitation, rolled away from Samille.

She raised herself on one elbow and looked at him. "Who was it?"

"Wrong number." Brant ran his hands over his face and dragged air into his lungs to steady his erratic breathing. He was shaken by how close they'd come to making love. He'd never wanted another woman as badly as he wanted Samille—still wanted her.

He turned his head to look at her and said quietly, "That was a mistake."

"Somehow I knew you'd say that."

"And you don't think it was?"

"Obviously not. I started it this time."

"My point exactly." His tone hardened. "Don't give yourself to me out of pity, Samille."

She gaped at him. "Is that what you think I was doing?"

"I didn't tell you about my brother to make you feel sorry for me."

"You honestly think—" She broke off abruptly. She couldn't let him believe such a ludicrous thing about her. But what was the alternative? To tell him the truth? That she loved him and wanted nothing more than to be loved in return—mind, body, and soul?

How quickly falling in love had changed her. She couldn't remember the last time she'd felt so unsure of herself, so vulnerable. So *needy*. It was unnerving, and downright terrifying.

She climbed from the bed and started for the door. She'd barely taken two steps before Brant was upon her, towering over her, his broad shoulders blocking what little moonlight there was.

"I'm sorry," he said huskily. "You came in here tonight out of concern for me, and I appreciate that. Thank you for being so sensitive and compassionate."

Samille swallowed hard and focused on a point beneath his collarbone. "You don't have to thank me."

"Yes," Brant murmured, brushing his knuckle tenderly across her cheek, "I do."

"All right then. You're welcome." She took a step backward. "Good night, Brant. See you in the morning."

He nodded slowly. "I run at five. Still want to join me?"

"Yeah. I'll be ready."

Brant stood rooted to the spot long after she had left his room. Samille Broussard was not the same woman he'd met less than a week ago. Something about her had changed, although he couldn't put a finger on what it was. He sensed it in the subtle nuances of her voice, in her softened demeanor toward him.

As he returned to bed, another possibility whispered in the back of his mind.

Maybe, just maybe, Samille wasn't the only one who'd changed.

Ivy Billingsley was not having a good day. Nothing had gone right since she'd arrived at work at six-thirty a.m. First she'd burned the coffee that she prepared for the senior associates every morning, the coffee they demanded the minute they stepped through the lacquered double doors in their pressed Italian suits and polished wing tips. She'd gotten tied up on a phone call with her nephew, whose behavior had been very erratic lately, and who now wanted to borrow an exorbitant sum of money from her, for reasons he wouldn't disclose. Ivy suspected he was in trouble and had been trying to wring the truth out of him when the stench of scorched coffee reached her nostrils. She'd raced to the small kitchen at the end of the corridor, but it was too late. Neither the coffee nor the ancient coffeepot could be salvaged. Ivy discarded both and took some comfort in the fact that now, perhaps, her notoriously frugal employer would spring for a new coffeemaker. One of those fancy Cuisinart machines with a built-in timer so that she'd never again have to worry about burning coffee. She couldn't understand why Salvatore Carrella was too cheap to buy a decent coffeemaker for the office. She knew how much money the firm raked in every year. *She* processed their billable hours, for heaven's sake.

The more she thought about it, the more convinced she became that burning the coffee had been a blessing in disguise. She ordered a ton of espressos from the gourmet shop across the street and sprayed air freshener to mask the bitter odor of burned coffee. At half past seven, the senior associates began to trickle into the office. She handed each a cup of espresso and ignored their wrinkled noses as they asked, "What's that smell?"

When her boss arrived, she braced herself for a lecture about the burned coffee, but Salvatore Carrella seemed to be in good spirits. He took her apology in stride and joked that *he* would take credit for the espresso idea, since he'd left some of the attorneys in a lurch yesterday while he tended to personal matters.

"How's Jillian?" Ivy asked.

"Feeling a little under the weather, but she's a tough cookie. She'll be fine. Why don't you go ahead and order another coffeemaker? We were past due for a new one anyway," he added with a rare self-deprecating grin. "Get whatever brand you like, Ivy. I trust your judgment."

Ivy beamed. "Why, thank you, sir. I put your messages through to your voice mail. Oh, and before I forget, Mr. Cason stopped by yesterday afternoon."

The relaxed grin slid from Salvatore Carrella's face. He blanched a little. "Did you say *Cason?*"

"Yes. Andrew Cason, sir."

"You must be mistaken."

She frowned. "I don't believe so. The gentleman identified himself quite clearly. He was with another man—"

With a muffled curse Salvatore Carrella stalked off to his office, leaving Ivy to wonder what she'd said or done wrong. But then the phone lines started ringing, signaling the start of another hectic day, and she settled into her normal routine.

Salvatore remained behind closed doors in his office. He canceled the weekly staff meeting and tersely instructed her to hold his calls until further notice. When one of his major clients insisted on speaking to him, Ivy reluctantly buzzed his intercom—and got a scathing earful about not being able to follow simple directions. Salvatore took the call, but as soon as he finished with the client, he called to reprimand her some more. Ivy was so traumatized by his unexpected fury that she accidentally hung up on two other callers and misfiled an invoice, a mistake she didn't realize until she'd already sent the file to accounting.

By the time Brant and Samille walked through the doors, Ivy Billingsley was so flustered she didn't know up from down. She barely glanced at the newcomers as she transferred calls and tried to locate an address for one of the paralegals.

"I'll be with you in a minute," she told the visitors.

"Take your time," drawled a deep, distinctly familiar voice.

Ivy's head snapped up, and her eyes narrowed at the sight of the tall, handsome black man who'd been there the day before. "It's you!" she blurted without thinking.

Andrew Cason had the grace to look vaguely amused. "You remember me."

"Of course I remember you, Mr. Cason. So does my boss, apparently."

His lips quirked. "Rough morning?"

"You don't know the half of it," Ivy retorted, then wondered what had compelled her to divulge so much information to a complete stranger. A stranger whose mere name had rattled Salvatore Carrella senseless. No one rattled Salvatore Carrella.

She sensed that Andrew Cason was watching her carefully, seeing everything and missing nothing. "It's a busy law firm," she offered by way of explanation. "*Every* morning is a rough morning. What can I do for you, Mr. Cason?"

"We're here to see Mr. Carrella."

"I'm afraid Mr. Carrella isn't taking any appointments this morning."

"He'll see us," Andrew Cason said in a tone that brooked no negotiation. He flipped open a billfold with a practiced flick of his wrist, and Ivy's eyes widened. She ignored the ringing telephone.

"You . . . you're an FBI agent?"

"Special Agent Brant Kincaid, and this is Ms. Samille Broussard. We need to ask Mr. Carrella a few questions."

Ivy's stunned gaze flew to the unsmiling young woman beside him, then back to Brant Kincaid. "But yesterday you said your name was—"

"Ivy!" Salvatore Carrella stormed into the reception area. "What the hell's going on out here? Why aren't you answering the—" He stopped abruptly at the sight of Brant and Samille. His dark eyes narrowed suspiciously. "Yes, may I help you?"

Brant flashed his credentials again and briskly introduced himself and Samille. "We'd like a few minutes of your time, Mr. Carrella."

Carrella frowned. "What is this about? Ivy, would you please answer that phone," he snapped. "I'm trying to run a business here."

Samille sent the woman a sympathetic look as she quickly returned to the switchboard. She wondered if Salvatore Carrella's law firm had a high turnover rate. It wouldn't surprise her in the least, not if he treated all of his employees with such blatant disrespect.

"Is there somewhere we could speak in private?" Brant said. "Your office, perhaps?"

"Fine, but I can only spare a few minutes." Carrella led them down a long corridor to the corner office suite.

He closed the door and gestured his visitors toward a pair of oxblood leather chairs opposite the cherry-wood island of a desk. A photograph of a much younger Jillian Carrella, sporting pigtails and a gap-toothed smile, occupied one corner of the desk.

Carrella reclaimed the leather executive chair behind the desk. At five minutes to ten, he was already in shirt-sleeves. His dark, shiny hair looked as if he'd been combing agitated fingers through it. Either Salvatore Carrella was a prime candidate for burnout, or something else had gotten to him that morning. Samille bet on the latter.

"What's this about?" Carrella demanded.

"What's your association with Andrew Cason? And before you deny knowing him," Brant said dryly, "your receptionist already gave us a different impression."

A solitary muscle ticked in Carrella's jaw. "My receptionist is bordering on incompetent. You witnessed that yourself this morning."

"What we witnessed," Samille countered coolly, "was a woman under immense pressure to perform her duties, despite being humiliated and shouted at by an overbearing boss. With all due respect, Mr. Carrella, I would say you're rather fortunate to have such 'incompetent' employees."

Carrella looked at her, and in the second before his expression grew shuttered, Samille detected recognition. He knew who she was. Had they met before? She racked her brain trying to remember if she'd ever testified against one of his clients in court. She drew a blank.

"I concur with Ms. Broussard," Brant said mildly. "Your management skills need some serious work, Carrella. Fortunately for you, we're here to discuss a different matter. I believe you were going to explain your association with Andrew Cason."

Carrella shrugged. "I may have provided Cason with some legal counsel in the past."

Brant appeared bored. "Either you did or you didn't."

"It was a long time ago. He came in, said he needed some legal advice. I helped him the best I could, and that was it. Of course you understand that I can't disclose the specifics of our discussion. Attorney-client privilege."

"Were you paid for your services?"

"Of course." Carrella's tone turned coldly mocking. "We don't do pro bono, if that's what you're asking. My Sicilian ancestors worked too hard and sacrificed too much to migrate to this country, for me to simply give away what took blood, sweat, and tears to build."

"Allow me to say how relieved I am that more people don't share your views," Samille murmured with thinly veiled disdain.

Salvatore Carrella sent Brant a crooked grin. "She's a pistol, isn't she?"

"You don't know the half of it," Brant agreed.

Samille resisted the urge to kick him with the pointy toe of her leather boot. She crossed her legs and watched Salvatore Carrella's dark eyes follow the movement. Her hackles rose. She sat up straighter in the chair, cursing her decision to wear a skirt that morning.

"So all you did was give Cason some legal advice?" she said, her tone cynical.

"That's right."

"What happened? Cason didn't follow your wise counsel, so you got mad at him?"

Carrella's mouth tightened. "What are you talking about?"

"We have a witness who heard you threaten to kill Cason," Brant said. "Less than a month later, Cason turns up dead." He paused, his eyes narrowing on Carrella's face. "You don't look surprised. I take it you already knew about his untimely demise?"

"Word gets around. Anyway, I never threatened the man. Why would I do that?"

Brant shrugged. "You tell us."

"I didn't threaten Andrew Cason, or anyone else for that matter. Your so-called witness is delusional."

"You ever been to Hot Flicks? It's an adult video store in southeast D.C."

"Never heard of it."

"That's interesting."

"Why?"

Brant reached inside his suit coat pocket and withdrew a videotape. "I have a surveillance tape showing a customer who bears a striking resemblance to you. You can see for yourself." He glanced around the luxurious office suite. "Got a VCR?"

"No." Carrella drummed his fingertips against the desk and studied Brant's face as if to gauge whether or not he was bluffing. Brant's deadpan expression gave nothing away.

"All right," Carrella conceded, "so I've rented a few porno flicks. Last I checked, it wasn't against the law. Or has the omnipotent FBI decided it should be?"

Brant took the barb in stride. "Why did you lie in the first place?"

Carrella shrugged. "Who doesn't lie about watching porn? It's a guilty pleasure, and no matter how liberal our society has become, pornography will always be frowned upon." He sounded as if he were delivering a closing argument. He offered an indulgent smile. "I'm a father. I have to set a good example for my daughter."

"Of course," Brant said smoothly. "Speaking of your daughter, how is she doing?"

"Jillian is fine," Carrella said tightly.

Brant nodded thoughtfully. "Ms. Broussard and I had an opportunity to meet her when we visited St. Anthony's Prep last week to speak to the students about what had happened to their classmates. Jillian was gracious enough to come forward with pertinent information about the case. Did she tell you about our visit?"

"No, she didn't mention it. And quite frankly, I don't know how I feel about you interrogating my underage daughter without my permission. Perhaps I need to give the school a call."

"Relax, Carrella," Brant said dryly. "No one interrogated your daughter. As I said, Jillian voluntarily came forward with information pertaining to the investigation. We appreciated her courage and honesty." He paused, his eyes narrowing on the other man's face. "I would think you would as well."

Carrella's mouth tightened. "Jillian's a very bright, conscientious girl. I'm not at all surprised by her willingness to help you out. That's the kind of person she is. It's my responsibility to make sure no one else takes advantage of her or hurts her."

"Such as her classmates?" Samille inquired. At Carrella's dark look, she elaborated, "When we spoke to Jillian, she told us that some of her classmates tease her because she's Italian American, and they think you have ties to the Mafia. That must hurt a great deal."

"Jillian's a survivor," Carrella said tersely. "She doesn't let those things get to her."

"What about you?" Brant prodded. "You seem like a devoted father. It must bother you to know that your daughter is being subjected to such cruelty and ignorance simply because her ancestors didn't arrive on the *Mayflower*."

"Of course it does. But it's nothing new to me, Agent Kincaid. I grew up in a lily-white Maryland suburb. I've been dealing with racism my entire life." He smirked. "I'm sure the two of you can relate. You're not exactly in the majority at your respective agencies, now, are you?"

"No argument there," Brant concurred, recognizing

the lawyer's ploy to put them on the defensive. They didn't rise to the bait. "As you know, we're trying to establish a link between the person who killed Andrew Cason and the one who provided drugs to Jillian's classmates. I must admit, Carrella, you're looking more and more like a possible suspect to me. You have the basics: motive and opportunity."

"You can't be serious," Carrella said angrily. "Do you actually think I would jeopardize my career, not to mention my *freedom*, to sell drugs to my daughter's classmates simply because they ostracized her?"

Brant's expression was deadpan. "Would you?"

Carrella shook his head in disgust. "You people must be more desperate than I thought. That's the craziest thing I've ever heard, and in my line of work, I've heard just about everything you can imagine. Let me spell this out for you: I did not threaten Andrew Cason, nor did I sell drugs to Jillian's classmates. Now if you'll both excuse me, I have phone calls to make and appointments to keep."

Neither budged. If anything, Brant seemed to settle more comfortably into his chair. "Indulge us a few more minutes, Sal."

Carrella's jaw tightened at Brant's cavalier use of his nickname, but he said nothing.

"Can you vouch for your whereabouts on the morning of November sixth?"

"I'm sure I was with a client, but Ivy can verify that. She keeps my schedule."

Brant nodded. "Before we leave, I want to give you another opportunity to come clean about Andrew Cason."

Carrella scowled. "I don't know what you're talking about. I already told you the nature of our association, and I can't imagine why anyone would accuse me of threatening him."

"You know," Brant began casually, "the owner of Hot Flicks is a bit of a techno geek. A few months ago he installed a second surveillance camera outside the store. It's a bad neighborhood, as you well know, so he wanted as much security as possible. According to our eyewitness, you threatened to kill Andrew Cason about a month ago. I've subpoenaed the rest of the store's surveillance tapes. Think I'll find anything interesting?"

The color leached out of Salvatore Carrella's olive-toned face. "Even if I did threaten Cason," he said in a low voice, "it doesn't mean I killed him."

"Now you're admitting to threatening him?" Brant tsk-tsked and shook his head in mild disapproval. "I don't know about you, Sal. A man who changes his story as often as you've done leads me to believe you're hiding something." He cocked his head to one side. "Now what could that be, I wonder?"

"I'm not hiding anything, Kincaid. I threatened Cason because he owed me money. Ask anyone in this office how I am about receiving payment for services rendered."

"Is that right?" Brant exchanged perplexed looks with Samille. "But earlier you told us that Cason paid you for the legal advice. Let me guess: you were lying then, too?"

Carrella looked like he wanted to put a bullet between Brant's eyes. "I think you'd both better leave now," he said coldly. He rose stiffly to his feet and prepared to escort them from the office.

Samille paused at the door, her gaze landing on the hooded black parka that hung from the hook. Her blood froze.

Salvatore Carrella reached around her impatiently and yanked the door open. He walked them to the reception area.

"We'll be in touch," Brant told him in a voice hard with promise.

Carrella's expression darkened. "I wouldn't expect otherwise."

"That went well," Samille remarked once she and Brant were back inside his Expedition. "You know, before we arrived this morning, I thought it was a stretch to consider Salvatore Carrella an actual suspect. Now I'm almost convinced he's somehow involved."

"He's definitely hiding something," Brant agreed, sliding on his mirrored sunglasses and pulling out of the narrow lot. "He was careless. He would've been more on the defensive—and perhaps better prepared—if Detective Lopez and I had questioned him. A macho man like Salvatore Carrella feels threatened by other men."

Samille slanted him a knowing look. "Is that why you insisted that I accompany you this morning instead of Lopez? Because you counted on Carrella being distracted by a woman?"

"Maybe," Brant said without a trace of apology. "You saw what a hard time he had keeping his eyes off your legs."

Samille rolled her eyes in disbelief. "And I walked right into your little strategy by wearing a skirt."

"It certainly didn't hurt. But, no, I wouldn't intentionally use your sex appeal against a suspect." He sent her a sidelong look before adding softly, "Believe me, Samille, no man deserves to be tortured in such a manner."

Heat stung her cheeks. "You don't have to resort to such measures anyway. You're one hell of an interrogator, Brant. And telling the receptionist yesterday that your name was Andrew Cason was a brilliant way to get him flustered. I'm quite impressed."

He inclined his head in a simple nod. "*Grazie.*" He smiled at her. "I think we work well together."

Samille's heart skipped several precious beats. "Yeah," she said softly, "I think so, too."

Both fell silent for a few moments.

"I'm curious," Samille continued with a tiny smile. "When did you obtain a copy of Roy Clark's surveillance tape?"

His mouth twitched. "I didn't."

"Of course you didn't. What exactly *is* on that tape?"

"An old training video from the Bureau."

"I see. And if Carrella had agreed to watch the tape?"

A slow grin curved his mouth. "I would've chalked it up to an honest mistake. You've never seen my 'overworked, underpaid public servant juggling a million cases at once' shtick. It's pretty good."

Samille burst out laughing.

Brant chuckled, enjoying the sound of her laughter. She'd been distant all morning, speaking to him only as necessity warranted. They'd hardly exchanged three words during their predawn run, and even when he'd teasingly challenged her to a race, she hadn't so much as cracked a smile as she politely declined. When he stopped at the field office to retrieve her cell phone, equipped with the new tap and tracer, Samille opted to wait in the truck. Brant had secretly hoped to introduce her to some of his colleagues—a compulsion even *he* didn't understand. He'd never been one for introducing women to his friends, but he'd very much wanted them to meet Samille.

Brant knew her distant behavior was a result of what had transpired between them last night. He wanted to assure Samille that he hadn't rejected her, that he'd wanted very much to make love to her—too much. But he feared that anything he said to her would only make matters worse.

He found a certain ironic humor in his predicament. He wasn't an awkward teenager with his first crush. He was thirty-four years old, experienced with members of the opposite sex and no stranger to adversity. He had survived a brutal sixteen-week training program at Quantico that had sent quite a number of new agent trainees packing after the second week. Against the counsel of many well-meaning individuals, he'd balanced the demands of his job with the academic rigors of pursuing a doctorate degree. Brant never backed down from challenges; he tackled them with a relentless ferocity that usually guaranteed success.

He'd never met a challenge like Samille Broussard.

He glanced at her profile and had to suppress the urge to touch her cheek, to caress the delicate nape of her neck, to curl his finger around the errant strands of hair that had escaped from her loose twist.

"What did you see back there?"

Samille gave him a surprised look. "You really don't miss anything, do you?"

"Oh, I don't know about that," he drawled, thinking he'd give anything to divine the reason for her hasty retreat from him last night, right after he'd finished playing the guitar for her.

"It was the parka hanging on the back of Carrella's door," Samille explained. "Yesterday when I stopped at my apartment to pick up a few things, there was a man waiting outside to ask for directions. He wore a black parka just like the one in Carrella's office."

Brant looked at her, but she couldn't read his expression behind the sunglasses. "What are you thinking?" she prompted.

He shrugged, slowing for a traffic light. "I noticed the parka, too. Odd, isn't it? A man with Salvatore Carrella's wardrobe wearing a parka. Doesn't quite go with Armani and Bruno Magli, does it?"

"No, it doesn't." Samille paused, her brows furrowed in thought. "It was cold, and I couldn't see the man's face very well because he wore a scarf and dark sunglasses. Now that I think about it, he could have been Carrella's same height and build. And there was a moment back there when I could have sworn that Salvatore Carrella recognized me. I've never testified against one of his clients, but I can't think of anywhere else he may have seen me outside of the courtroom."

"Interestingly enough," Brant murmured thoughtfully, "he just happened to be out of the office yesterday."

Samille stared at Brant. "Do you think it's just coincidence?"

"You already know how I feel about coincidences. I think we need to pay a visit to Carrella's ex-wife."

Samille frowned. "But Jillian said her parents haven't spoken to each other in years."

"That, in and of itself, is very telling." Brant pulled out his cell phone, called directory assistance, and was patched through to National Geographic headquarters in D.C. He was told that Sophia Carrella was out of the country on assignment until the following Monday. He thanked the secretary and disconnected.

"That'll be our first stop on Monday," he told Samille.

She nodded. "I can only imagine what she'll have to say about her ex. We've already seen that he's arrogant, self-absorbed, hot-tempered, and callous—and that's the *least* of his offenses."

"Don't hold back," Brant teased.

Samille bit her lip guiltily. "I probably could've done a better job of curbing my tongue back there. I wasn't

prepared to encounter such a jerk—even one who may
be a murderer. I mean, if he doesn't believe in doing pro
bono work, that's his prerogative. But to mention it as if
it were a source of pride, as if being uncharitable to
others is something to be commended for? Give me a
break! And did you see the portrait in the lobby of all the
senior associates? Not a single woman, Brant. Not one!"
She shook her head in utter disgust. "Sexist pig. I hope
Jillian grows up to become president of the United
States."

Brant chuckled softly. "I sense a tirade coming on."

"Don't make fun of me."

"I wouldn't dare."

Her cell phone rang. Immediately she tensed, her
wary gaze flying to Brant's face. He nodded for her to
answer the phone.

"Hello?" she said tentatively.

"Hey, beautiful," Jack greeted her cheerfully. "I see
you've got your phone back."

"Hey, Jack. Yeah, we picked it up this morning. Are
you at the office or in the field?"

"I'm just leaving the office. I don't know if you've already been contacted, but the task force is meeting at
the station this morning. Chief Rucker wants to hammer
out the details of Thursday's sting op."

Samille's eyes widened. "Graham went for it?"

Jack chuckled. "He had no choice after I got through
with him."

"Oh, Jackie, I love you! Thank you so much." She
glanced at Brant. His profile was impassive as he skillfully
maneuvered through dense D.C. traffic.

"Where's Kincaid?"

"Right here. Do you want to speak to him?"

"No. I guess you can give him the news. He won't be

too happy about it, but he'll get over it." Jack hesitated. "How's the living arrangement working out?"

"Um, fine." She unconsciously lifted a hand to her flushed cheek.

"I hope Kincaid's been behaving like a gentleman," Jack teased.

"A perfect gentleman," Samille murmured, a touch regretfully. "Listen, Jackie, we're about fifteen minutes from the station, so we'll see you then."

She disconnected and waited a beat before looking at Brant. She was suddenly and unaccountably nervous. "I guess you gleaned from my conversation that the undercover operation has been approved."

"Yes."

"Brant—"

"Don't worry, Samille. I'm not going to lecture you. I've said all I'm going to say on this subject."

She didn't know whether to be relieved or concerned. "But you still have reservations."

"I do, but I've been given my marching orders, and I intend to follow them. Case closed."

Samille turned her head to stare out the window, wishing his opinion didn't matter so much to her. But it did. *He* mattered to her. She'd been trying all morning to forget that she loved him, to keep things strictly professional between them. But it was so hard. After the tragic story he'd shared with her last night, she felt that she knew and understood him better. Like her, he had experienced a tremendous loss in his life and still bore the scars. She wasn't idealistic enough to think she could heal him, or ease the pain and self-imposed guilt he carried around. She simply wanted to be there for him, wanted to be his sounding board whenever he needed one.

She'd come to enjoy the relaxed camaraderie they shared. At times he infuriated her, but he could also make her laugh until her sides ached. He intrigued and inspired her, and made her feel like she could accomplish anything she set her mind to. When she was with him, she felt incredibly safe and protected, like nothing or no one could ever harm her. She knew it was dangerous to surrender so much of herself to another—and that was why she could no longer stay with him.

"I didn't realize how close you and Burdett are," Brant said, the quiet words breaking into her tumultuous thoughts. "He lets you call him Jackie."

"Yeah." She grinned in spite of herself. "I consider myself privileged. I've heard horror stories about what happened to other people who called him that."

"You're not other people, Samille. You're special."

Am I special to you? The question rose, unbidden, and was on the tip of her tongue the second before she retracted it. And it was then that she knew, like never before, that she was in serious trouble. It was time to get out of Dodge. While she still could.

"I called Amanda earlier," she blurted before she lost her nerve. "She's going to let me crash at her place for as long as I need to."

Brant's expression didn't change. Slowly, deliberately, he turned his head to look at her. "I never figured you for the type."

"What type?"

"The type to run away."

Her temper flared. "I'm not *running* away."

"Oh, really? What do you call it then?"

"Wait a minute," she snapped, "don't try to psychoanalyze me, Dr. Kincaid. Don't try to make this about some perceived weakness of mine. I am *not* running away from you—"

"Don't kid yourself. You're running so fast you can hardly breathe."

She *was* having difficulty breathing. "And what about you?" she choked out furiously. "Aren't you doing a little running yourself?"

He scowled. "Don't turn the tables on me."

"Why not? Are you untouchable? Oh, wait, I think I already know the answer to that question."

"What's that supposed to mean?"

"It means— Oh, just forget it!" Samille drew a deep breath and said with forced composure, "You can't hold me at your place against my will, Brant. I'm staying with Amanda, and that's all there is to it."

Other than the tightening of his jaw, Brant showed no visible reaction to her declaration.

They arrived at the police station in mutinous silence.

CHAPTER 13

"Do you want to talk about it?"

Samille glanced up from the course catalog she'd been perusing as she reclined on the bright orange sofa in Amanda's living room. A matching pair of salt lamps set in hand-blown glass adorned the wicker center table. A cluster of Austrian crystal prisms hung from the vaulted ceiling and window frames, reflecting dancing rainbows against the walls every time the heater sighed on. The crystal prisms, which were used in feng shui to balance and circulate ch'i, made a soft tinkling sound that Samille found rather relaxing.

They had gorged themselves on a large pizza loaded with pepperoni, sausage, ham, and mushrooms, before topping off a pint of Häagen-Dazs ice cream. "Eating like this will force us to get up and run in the morning," Amanda had reasoned around a mouthful of Rocky Road. "We'll feel so guilty for overindulging that we'll have no choice."

Samille laughed. "Whatever motivates you, Winters."

Afterward they settled down to watch *Survivor* on Amanda's thirty-two-inch plasma television. Between commercial breaks, they debated which contestants possessed the best strategy and who would be voted off the island next. They cheered and high-fived each other when, at the end of the hour, a despised contestant was booted off the show.

While Amanda went to apply her cucumber facial mask, Samille pored through the course catalog she'd requested from Virginia Commonwealth University. She had decided it was high time to get serious about pursuing her Ph.D. in forensic science. If Brant Kincaid could earn his doctorate while giving his all to the FBI, so could she.

At the reminder of Brant, her heart sank. They hadn't exchanged a single word after their heated argument that morning. The strategy session at the police station had only lasted one hour. Brant and Samille sat on opposite sides of the conference table and did their best to ignore each other, a performance they'd be required to repeat, ironically, in their respective roles for the sting operation. Samille would pose as a buyer for the anticipated drug deal. Brant's role, arranged via his own undercover connections, was to head the security detail for a popular hip-hop star who would be at Club Zydeco on Thursday night. The remaining members of the task force would conduct surveillance from a commercial van parked in an alley adjacent to the club—near enough for them to move in swiftly for an arrest, but inconspicuous enough not to arouse suspicion from partygoers.

Samille felt good about the simple yet well-constructed plan. If she had any qualms or reservations about her own involvement and the possibility of something going wrong, she didn't let on—not even to herself.

After the meeting, Jack had volunteered to take her to the office so that she could finish some paperwork. Afterward Amanda had driven her to Brant's town house to retrieve her belongings and her Jeep.

When they arrived to find the house dark and empty, Samille hadn't known whether to weep or rejoice. She soon decided that Brant's absence was a blessing; she didn't completely trust herself not to capitulate if he put up the least resistance to her leaving.

She quickly packed her suitcase and sprinted downstairs, then lingered before the cold fireplace where they'd talked late into the night, where they'd wrestled like a couple of teenagers, where he'd sung to her and played the guitar and made her realize there would never be another man for her. She'd found herself wondering if she would ever return to Brant's place, if different circumstances would ever bring her there. When her throat tightened with emotion, she turned and fled from the town house as if it were on fire.

You're running so fast you can hardly breathe.

Amanda was still awaiting her response, her arms folded expectantly across her chest. She had changed into her pajamas and swept her wheat-blond hair into a ponytail. Only her eyes and mouth were visible beneath the green facial cream she'd slathered on.

Samille feigned innocence. "Do I want to talk about what?"

"For starters, let's discuss the reason you haven't turned a single page since you opened that catalog."

"It's not a novel, Amanda. I'm reading the course descriptions and taking mental notes."

"Mental notes, huh?" Amanda crossed the living room and joined Samille on the sofa. Gold-flecked hazel eyes searched Samille's face. "Why don't you tell me what you're really doing here?"

"I already did. I needed a place to crash—"

"You *had* a place to crash. A perfectly good place. And, might I add, a perfectly good body to crash *with.*"

"And therein lies the problem." Samille snapped the

course catalog shut and pushed out a deep breath. A dull headache was starting at the base of her skull. She'd hoped to avoid having this conversation with Amanda. When she'd called earlier, Amanda had agreed to the arrangement, no questions asked. Samille should have known it wouldn't last.

"What happened, Samille?" Amanda gently probed. "Why did you leave Brant's place?"

"I couldn't stay there any longer. It wasn't a good idea." She hesitated, deliberating whether to share the whole truth with Amanda. Before she knew what was happening, the words were tumbling out of her mouth. "Things got a little out of hand last night. Suffice it to say that if the phone hadn't interrupted us, I would have found it a little hard to face myself in the mirror this morning."

"Ohhh." Amanda nodded as a slow grin tugged at the corners of her mouth. "I wondered about that when you first told me you'd be staying with Brant. I knew something might happen between you two."

"Gee, thanks for the vote of confidence."

"Girl, please! I would have thought something was seriously wrong with you if *nothing* had happened!" Amanda laughed at Samille's pained grimace. "You shouldn't be so hard on yourself, Broussard. I don't know too many women in your position who would've been able to resist *that* kind of temptation. We are talking about Brant Kincaid here."

"That doesn't matter," Samille said miserably. "We almost crossed the line, and *I'm* the one who initiated it. I compromised my own rule about not getting involved with colleagues—and this wasn't the first time! Brant and I have been playing with fire from day three. Last night was the closest we came to getting burned."

Amanda's eyes widened. "Samille Broussard! You've been holding out on me!"

"Well, now you know." Samille slapped her forehead with the course catalog and groaned. "I'm so stupid, Amanda. How could I be so stupid?"

"Stop beating yourself up. You're not stupid. You're a red-blooded woman with normal, healthy needs just like the rest of us."

"My *needs* have no place in a criminal investigation."

"Why not? What would have been so terrible about you and Brant taking comfort in each other's arms? It's a depressing and frustrating case. I'm sure you could both use some stress relief."

"Believe me, Amanda," Samille said quietly, "last night had nothing to do with stress relief. At least not for me."

Amanda grew still. Above their heads the crystal prisms chimed softly as the heater kicked back on. Samille stared at the floor until her vision blurred.

"Oh my God," Amanda finally whispered. "You're in love with him, aren't you?"

Samille leaned her head back against the sofa and closed her eyes. "He's the most incredible, compelling man I've ever met. He's so multifaceted that I could know him a lifetime and still learn something new about him. On one hand I see this tough, rugged maverick who couldn't care less what the world thinks of him, and it takes my breath away. And then in the next instant he can be incredibly kind and endearing, and so sweet and boyish that my heart melts."

Amanda stared at her. "Those are pretty intense feelings, Broussard."

"I know." A soft, reminiscent smile touched her lips. "He played the guitar for me, Amanda. And he plays so beautifully it would make the devil himself weep." She told her friend about Brant's grandfather and the Pickled Blues, about dancing to B.B. King and feeling as if her heart would burst from the sheer exhilaration.

Amanda issued a lusty sigh when Samille recounted the sinfully romantic serenade that had been her undoing, then listened in rapt absorption as the rest of the tale unfolded. She laughed at Samille's glee upon discovering that Brant remembered her from the academy; fanned herself at Samille's brief description of the explosive kiss they'd shared in her kitchen; and sighed some more when she heard about Brant's volatile behavior during the preliminary task force meeting. Amanda believed his actions demonstrated just how much he cared about Samille, but Samille disagreed, offering the same rationale Jack had given about Brant's hero complex.

By the time she finished sharing everything with Amanda, two hours had passed. Amanda's cucumber mask had dried to a hard crust, which Samille discovered by touching her face. She laughed. "I can't believe I just spilled my guts to a woman wearing a vegetable by-product on her face!"

Amanda grinned, but she was still dazed from everything she'd heard. "I can't believe how much has happened between you and Brant in seven days. Seven days!"

"Tell me about it," Samille mumbled disconsolately.

"Well, technically, it's been longer than that, because I'm convinced it was love at first sight when you first saw him at the academy six months ago."

Samille sighed, drawing her knees up to her chin. "I never thought I'd say this, but I think you may be right, Amanda. I always believed love at first sight was such a preposterous, impossible notion—until it happened to me."

Amanda eyed her sympathetically. "What are you going to do? You have to tell him how you feel."

"I can't. Not now, not in the middle of this case." She bit her lip and stared into space for a moment. "Maybe when it's all over . . . I don't know. What if he doesn't feel the same? He doesn't strike me as a man seeking a serious relationship—he seems to want just the opposite, in fact. Oh, it's not anything he's said outright. It's the way he is, the way he lives. I get the distinct impression he could just as easily spend the rest of his life alone, indulging his needs whenever necessary, but never settling down with one particular woman."

"People change," Amanda countered softly. "You did."

"Yeah, for all the good it'll do me." Samille managed a wobbly grin. "Got any more Rocky Road?"

Over the next two hours, they talked about everything from their families and childhoods to careers and relationships. Amanda confessed to enjoying the same sexual freedom that had been historically reserved for men. "I know there's a big part of me, deep down inside, that wants something more permanent and meaningful out of relationships. When I find it, I know I'm going to grab on to it with both hands and never let go. But in the meantime, I plan to enjoy the single life. There's something to be said about the thrill of meeting someone new every other week. It's like going on a roller-coaster ride for the first time over and over again." She paused, wriggling her eyebrows suggestively. "Okay, how sexual did *that* sound?"

Laughing, Samille launched a throw pillow at Amanda's head. "You're crazy, girl."

"I know. What're you going to do without me when I leave the DEA?" Amanda had recently decided to apply for a legal position in the criminal division of the Department of Justice. She had the skills, qualifications, and, perhaps more importantly, the right connections. Working for the DEA had given both women such connections.

"I still can't believe you're deserting us," Samille grumbled playfully.

Amanda grinned. "The current DEA administrator

started her career as an assistant U.S. attorney. If I hope to land that job one day, I have to put things in place. After earning my law degree, I swore I never wanted to practice law, but it's time I reconsidered. I've got eight years of diversion investigation under my belt, which has helped me learn a great deal about the DEA and really get a foot in the door. But it's time for me to broaden my horizons. I figure I can gain some litigation experience over at the DOJ, work my way up through the ranks, pick up a presidential citation or two, then loop back over to the DEA and snag the chief counsel position." She grinned. "From there it's only a matter of greasing the right wheels and patiently biding my time until the next elected president nominates me for appointment to administrator."

She sounded so self-assured and determined that Samille could only smile proudly. "I have no doubt that you can, and will, accomplish everything you set your mind to, Winters."

"Thanks, Samille." Amanda chuckled. "Guess I'd better start leading a chaste lifestyle. Wouldn't want any embarrassing indiscretions or sexual exploits coming back to haunt me later."

Samille laughed. "No, that wouldn't be good. As for what we're going to do once you defect to DOJ, we're going to make sure we have lunch together on a weekly basis."

"And on top of that, we'll schedule a sleepover at least once a month. That is, if your husband will allow it."

"My husband?"

Amanda grinned. "Why, Special Agent Brant Kincaid, of course. Whom you'll likely join at the Bureau once you two are married. You think I don't know about your secret aspirations to work at the FBI Laboratory? You'll be Drs. Brant and Samille Kincaid, and you'll solve high-

profile cases together and coauthor a best-selling book
on criminal psychology. Right before you start hatching
little Brant Juniors and Samilles."

Samille laughed and tried to ignore the pang of longing wrought by Amanda's words. "On that note," she
said, rising from the sofa and stretching, "we'd better
take our butts to bed if we hope to accomplish anything
tomorrow—starting with the morning run we can't
afford to miss after the way we pigged out tonight."

Amanda made a face. "Don't remind me." She bright-
ened as she led Samille to the spare bedroom in her spacious apartment. "Hey, I *am* looking forward to dragging
you shopping to buy your hoochie gear for the undercover op. Jack instructed me to make sure you get the
skimpiest outfit possible so that you'll blend right in with
the club crowd."

Now it was Samille's turn to scowl. "Don't remind me."

It was after eight p.m. by the time Brant arrived home
with the scent of pastries and another woman's perfume
on his clothes.

After leaving the police station that afternoon, he'd
gone to the office to retrieve his messages and check on
the status of a few ongoing cases. He'd been in the office
of Assistant Director in Charge Bruce Masden when the
receptionist informed him that Angel Hart was on the
phone.

Masden lifted bushy black eyebrows at him. "Angel
Hart? Sounds like a porn star's stage name."

Brant was still chuckling when he took the call in his
cubicle. "Special Agent Kincaid."

"Hello, Special Agent Kincaid. This is Angel Hart from
Sweet Nothings Bakery. Do you remember me?"

"Of course. What can I do for you, Ms. Hart?"

"Call me Angel," she said smoothly. "I thought you should know that one of Andrew Cason's homeless friends was just in here looking for him. He thinks something bad happened to him, but I couldn't confirm anything because you were so hush-hush about Andrew when you were here."

Brant straightened in his chair. "Is he still there

"Who, the homeless guy? No, he just left. I got on the phone and called you right away."

"You did the right thing. Listen, Angel, I need you to get him back for me. Can you see if he's still hanging around outside the shop?"

"All right," Angel said. "Hold on."

Brant stood and paced the floor while he waited. He nodded briefly to two agents who greeted him as they passed his cubicle.

Angel came back on the line sounding a little breathless. "I found him. What should I do with him?"

"Keep him there. I'm on my way."

"How am I supposed to hold him here?"

"Give him hot coffee and pastries, whatever he wants. I'll pick up the tab when I get there."

"But what if he doesn't want to stay?"

"You're a beautiful woman, Angel Hart. I doubt you'll have any trouble holding his attention until I get there."

Angel's voice softened with unmistakable pleasure. "You'd better believe it."

Suppressing a grin, Brant rattled off his cell phone number. "Call me if he tries to leave. I'll be there in ten minutes."

He arrived at the Wisconsin Avenue bakery to find an er black man who reminded him of Whitman Mayo, actor who'd played Grady Wilson on *Sanford and Son*. s coat was a sturdy brown tweed and slightly shabby. neath the grungy knit cap he wore, his woolly hair was almost as white as the smile he bestowed upon Angel Hart as she refilled his coffee cup. Before returning to the counter to help other customers, she gave Brant a tight-lipped smile that said he owed her big time. He grinned at her.

"It's nice to be treated well by such a beautiful young woman," Whitman Mayo's look-alike remarked as Brant slid into the chair across the table from him. "Even if I know she's only being nice to me as a favor to *you*." He sighed. "We may as well get the formalities out of the way. My name's Willie Brooks."

Brant shook his hand. "A pleasure to meet you, Mr. Brooks. I'm Special Agent Brant Kincaid." He flashed his creds. "I'd like to ask you a few questions about Andrew Cason."

"Andrew's dead," Willie said mournfully. "I can feel it in my bones. A real shame, too. He had a good heart, no matter what you might think about him."

"He was a drug dealer, Mr. Brooks. I'm not inclined to think much of anyone who earns a living that way. How did you meet Andrew Cason?"

"So it's true then. He *is* dead."

"I didn't say that."

Astute gray eyes studied him over the rim of the coffee cup. "If he wasn't dead, you'd have said so. You don't strike me as the sort of fella to lie to an old man just to get information out of him. As for *other* feds . . . well, I don't trust them as far as I can kick them."

Brant's mouth twitched. "How long have you been homeless, Mr. Brooks?"

"Fifteen years, off and on."

"Off and on?"

"Sometimes my daughter calls the authorities and has me brought back to live with her. She's been trying, unsuccessfully, to have me declared mentally incompetent

so that she can keep me locked up in the sanitarium—
for my own protection, she says." A rueful smile touched
his mouth. "She means well."

"I don't doubt that," Brant said, thinking that Willie
Brooks was no more mentally incompetent than he was.
"Why does your daughter think you're crazy?"

"I choose to live on the streets when I don't have to.
Doesn't that sound crazy to you?"

"No argument there. Where'd you meet Andrew
Cason?"

"A few blocks from here. He stopped right in front of
me one morning and offered me a bagel. He was the
first person in a long time who'd looked at me as if I actually mattered as a human being. We got to talking and
became good friends."

"Have you ever been to his apartment?"

Willie frowned. "No. He always came here. I didn't
even know where he lived."

"What kind of favors did you do for him?"

Willie glanced toward the counter where Angel Hart
was ringing up orders. An elderly white woman waiting
in line stared at Willie as if he'd crawled from a sewer.
He winked at her, and she recoiled as if she'd been
slapped. Angel glared at him as the woman turned on
her heel and hustled out of the bakery without buying
a thing.

"Poor Miss Angel," Willie lamented. "She's losing business on account of me. Folks around here don't want to
patronize an establishment that serves free food to
homeless people."

"She'll be reimbursed. You're avoiding my question,
Mr. Brooks."

"I'm not avoiding it. I'm trying to decide how to
answer you."

"Try starting with the truth."

"And what will I get in return for my honesty? If it's all the same to you, Agent Kincaid, I'd rather not spend the night in jail. I've been down that road before and, believe me, I'd much rather sleep on the cold street than in a D.C. jail."

"Jail is for criminals. Are you a criminal, Mr. Brooks?"

He chuckled. "Depends on who you ask. Tell you what, Kincaid. You seem like a sharp young man. I suspect you'll lift my fingerprints off this cup the second I leave so you can take it back to your people at the Bureau and confirm my identity. I'll save you the trouble and play it straight with you. My real name *is* Willie Brooks—William if you go by my birth certificate. I was born and raised right here in the nation's capital. My wife died several years ago and we only had one child, the daughter who's trying to have me committed. The only thing I ever did for Andrew Cason was make deliveries, which he paid me generously for."

"What kind of deliveries?"

"I never asked, and he didn't tell—just like the military. He gave me packages and cab fare, and I delivered the packages to their intended recipients."

"Who were these recipients?"

"Can't remember their names. A few local businessmen."

Brant withdrew two small photographs from his breast pocket. "Do you recognize either of these individuals?"

Willie examined the photos for a moment. He shook his head at Jefferson Spangler. "Never seen the kid before, but I definitely recognize the lawyer. His name is Salvatore Carrella."

"Cason did business with Carrella?"

"That's what Andrew called it—business. Come to think of it, most of the deliveries I made were to Carrella. Not to him personally, of course. I was always instructed to leave the package with his receptionist. One day my curiosity got the better of me, and I hid around the corner to get a peek at Carrella when he came out of his office." Willie shook his head, his expression grim. "Meanest-looking S.O.B. I'd ever seen. And that's saying a lot considering I was in Nam, and *nobody* could look meaner than the Vietcong."

"And you don't know what the packages contained? Were they heavy? Light?"

"A little heavy. Solid." Willie shrugged. "Could have been money."

"Or drugs."

"Nah. Salvatore Carrella wasn't buying drugs from Andrew."

Brant's eyes narrowed on the other man's face. "How can you be so sure if you didn't know what the packages contained?"

"Andrew didn't have bigwig buyers. He was small-time, and he liked it that way." Willie glanced around the half-empty bakery before leaning toward Brant to whisper, "Just between you and me, I think he had something much bigger brewing on the back burner."

"Is that right?" Brant feigned only mild interest when, in fact, his investigative instincts were buzzing with excitement. "Did Cason give you any idea what that might have been?"

"Nah, but I could just tell. He seemed pretty tense, and he looked over his shoulder a lot, like he thought someone was following him."

"If you and Cason were such good friends, why didn't he confide in you?"

"I never asked. Every man has secrets, Kincaid. Sometimes it's better not to know what those secrets are." He peered closely at Brant. "I bet even *you* have secrets."

"Be that as it may," Brant drawled, "do you have an idea who may have been following Cason?"

Willie took a long sip of coffee. "Could have been anyone. Andrew once mentioned that the feds were watching him."

"The FBI?"

"Nope. He thought some folks from the DEA had it in for him."

"He actually told you that?"

"Yep. He didn't say who though. He just said they were waiting for him to slip up and make a wrong move, but he would outsmart them."

"By flying beneath the radar," Brant said softly.

Willie grinned. "That was Andrew all right. Mr. Low Profile himself." He scratched his chin thoughtfully. His fingernails were short and immaculate. "They killed him, didn't they?"

"Someone did," Brant said grimly. "I intend to find out who, and why."

Willie nodded, his solemn gaze skipping to the window. "That's why I agreed to wait for you," he said quietly. "I had to know for sure if Andrew was dead. I'd been out of town for a few weeks. When I came back to D.C. I couldn't find Andrew anywhere, and no one knew anything. I finally decided to try the bakery."

"I'm glad you did."

Willie shrugged. "Not sure if I was any help to you. Like I said, Salvatore Carrella's the only person I could definitely remember delivering packages to." He stared hard at Brant. "Do you think he killed Andrew?"

"Anything's possible, Mr. Brooks. Is there somewhere I can reach you if I need to speak with you again?"

"Here's as good a place as any. The food's great, and Miss Angel Hart ain't too bad on the eyes." He chuckled. "If I were thirty years younger—and smelled a little

better—I'd give you a run for your money, Kincaid. That
pretty gal hasn't taken her eyes off you since you walked
through that door. I bet she'd like nothing better than
to take you home and sop you up like a bowl of whipped
cream, you lucky son of a gun. Say, where are you from?
I detect a Brooklyn accent in your voice, unless my hearing is failing me."

"Your hearing is just fine. I was born and raised in
Brooklyn."

Willie grinned. "I used to know some fellas up in
Brooklyn. They played in a local blues band during the
sixties—way before your time, Kincaid. They were called
the Pickled Blues, and boy, were they good! Everyone
thought they'd blow up big time, but they never did. A
real shame."

Brant's mouth twitched. "I heard the guitarist wasn't
interested in fame or fortune."

Willie's eyes lit up. "So you've heard of them before?"

"A little something. They were a local legend." He
smiled at Willie Brooks. "Why don't you reconsider staying with your daughter? I don't know if you're safe on
the streets with Cason's killer on the loose."

"Nah. One thing years of combat taught me was how
to be incognito. I know how to disappear and resur-
face whenever necessary. They didn't call me a chameleon for nothing." He drained his coffee and rose from
the table.

"Thanks for your time, Mr. Brooks," Brant said. He
reached inside his breast pocket for a business card and
passed it to Willie. "Let me know if you think of anything
else, or if there's anything I can do for you."

"Will do. It was a pleasure meeting you, Special Agent
Brant Kincaid. Too bad they don't make young fellas like
you anymore." With a lazy salute, Willie Brooks shuffled
out of the bakery, his shoulders stooped beneath the

shabby tweed coat, his cap pulled low over his head. Brant watched through the window as the old man made the seamless transformation into an invisible homeless person at whom no one would look twice. Like a chameleon, Brant mused.

Shaking his head, he removed a small plastic bag from his breast pocket. Using the very tips of his fingers so as to preserve Willie Brooks's prints, Brant lifted the empty coffee cup and dropped it inside the bag.

One could never be too sure.

Angel walked over and perched a shapely hip against the table. "Did you have a productive talk with the homeless guy?"

"Willie Brooks?" Brant said, pointedly providing his name. "Yeah, it was very productive. Thanks for calling me and keeping him here."

"No problem." She gave him a demure smile. "I knew on Saturday that I'd be seeing you again, Agent Kincaid. I even went home and told my roommate."

"Is that right? You must be clairvoyant." Brant stood and pulled a crisp fifty-dollar bill from his wallet. He held it out to her. "Thanks for feeding Willie."

"I can't take your money."

"Of course you can." When she hesitated, he drawled, "Don't worry, I'll write it off as a business expense."

"Well, in that case . . ." Angel made a point of gliding her hand across his as she took the cash. Her nails were long and painted a deep scarlet. Dark, gleaming hair spilled over her shoulder and drew attention to the scooped neckline of her blouse.

"That settles our *business* arrangement," she said, green eyes locked onto his. "What about your personal obligation to me? I did you a favor out of the kindness of my heart, Agent Kincaid. What will you give me in return?"

"That depends," Brant said slowly. "What do you want?"

She gave a low, sultry laugh. "Give me a ride home while I think about it."

"I suppose I could manage that."

"Good. Just let me settle the cash drawer and get my things, and we can be on our way."

Angel lived in an apartment complex twenty minutes from the bakery. She talked during the whole ride, telling Brant about her part-time modeling assignments, the various celebrities she'd met, and the exotic locales she'd visited over the years.

"I'm saving money to buy the bakery," she announced, segueing to yet another topic. "The current owner wants to retire next year, and I have a lot of great ideas for running the place. I think—" She stopped abruptly and began to laugh. "Oh my God. I can't believe I've been rambling on and on like this! I'm not usually such a chatterbox. It's only when I'm nervous."

Brant slid her an amused look. "Do I make you nervous?"

"Are you kidding? I've never been more nervous in my life!"

He chuckled. "Relax. I won't bite."

"Not even if I want you to?" Just like that, the sex kitten was back. She sent him a seductive smile that left no doubt what she wanted.

"Would you like to come inside for a drink?" Angel purred when they arrived at her apartment building. "My roommate is out for the evening, so we can have all the privacy we want."

"As tempting as the offer sounds, I'm afraid I'll have to pass."

"What about a rain check, then? I could fix you dinner, or we could go out somewhere? Tell you what," she hastened to add before he could refuse a second time, "I have your cell phone number, so I'll call you in a couple of weeks to see if you're available. I know how busy your job keeps you. My grandmother—God rest her ornery soul—used to say criminals never sleep, and neither should those who fight them."

Brant grinned and shook his head at her. "You're really something, know that?"

Angel smiled, then leaned over and hugged him, pressing her warm body tightly against his. The cloying musk of Opium filled his nostrils. "Thanks for the ride, Agent Kincaid," she murmured as she pulled slowly, deliberately, away. "We'll be seeing each other again real soon, mark my words."

"Just don't start stalking me," Brant warned lightly. "The FBI is pretty tough on people who stalk their agents."

She laughed in delight and climbed out of the truck. She waved and blew him a kiss before disappearing inside the apartment building.

And Brant drove home wondering if he'd ever be able to look at another woman without thinking of Samille.

He was struck by her absence the moment he entered the dark, silent town house. She'd been in his life a little over a week, had spent just two nights under his roof, yet he couldn't remember what his world had been like without her.

She'd become part of him.

Shaken by the revelation, Brant jerked his tie loose and headed into the kitchen to find something for dinner. He heated up leftover Chinese food and watched a basketball game on ESPN while he ate. But his thoughts kept returning to Samille and the heated words they'd exchanged that morning. After the meeting, he'd considered pulling her aside to call a truce, but Jack had intercepted her and offered to give her a ride back to the office. Samille readily agreed, and as they left the room together, Jack sent Brant a triumphant look over his shoulder. Brant was seized with an urge to put a fist through Burdett's smug face—before he remembered his cardinal rule against fighting over women. Ignoring Chief Rucker's knowing gaze, he strode out of the room.

Brant returned his empty plate to the kitchen and grabbed a beer from the refrigerator just as his phone rang. "Hey son," his father greeted him warmly.

"How's it going, Dad? No late-night sessions this evening?"

"Luckily, no. And your mother and grandmother are at the beauty salon, so I have the place all to myself. I've got a nice Italian hoagie in one hand, a cold beer in the other, and the Knicks on ESPN. You watching the game?"

"You know it." From the time Brant and his brother were old enough to palm a basketball, it had been tradition for the Kincaid men to attend New York Knicks games. Brant remembered the way he and Bryan had ducked their heads in embarrassment as their grandfather shouted insults at the referees. They'd always feared that his antics would get them escorted from Madison Square Garden, and save for the fact that Maurice Kincaid was old friends with the team owner, they likely *would* have been tossed out.

Brant grinned at the bittersweet memory. "A hoagie, huh? You'd better hide the evidence before Mom gets home. You know how she feels about you eating junk food with your high cholesterol."

Maurice Kincaid chuckled. "Believe me, the 'evidence' will be in my stomach and long digested by the time your mother walks through that door. You know how many hours they spend at the beauty salon. No wonder your sister decided to grow dreadlocks—after years of being dragged down to that place to get her hair done, she finally decided enough was enough. Speaking of Zora, has she called you this week?"

"Not yet. Why?"

"I understand Alex will be visiting you next weekend?"

"Yeah. She said she'll be in town for a fund-raiser at Howard. We're supposed to get together for dinner." Brant smiled as he returned to the living room and sat down. "What's going on, Dad?"

His father hummed a thoughtful note. "Those women are up to something, I just know it. Including your mother. Did she tell you that she'll also be in town next week?"

"No."

"That doesn't surprise me. She said she's meeting an old friend to discuss art-related business, but I think there's more to it than that."

Brant grinned. "Mom's not having an affair, Dad, if that's what you're worried about."

Maurice laughed. "I'm not worried, son, but maybe *you* should be. I overheard your mother on the phone asking her friend all these questions about her niece. If you ask me, I think Audre is going to Maryland to satisfy her curiosity about this young lady."

Suddenly Brant made the connection. He closed his eyes and groaned. "Mom's friend wouldn't happen to be Noreen Broussard, would she?"

"That's right. How'd you know?"

"I had dinner at her house on Saturday. Her niece and I work together."

"Is that so?" Again Maurice laughed. "Small world, isn't it? No wonder your mother's been so secretive. She knew if I found out I'd try to talk her out of whatever matchmaking scheme she and her friend are hatching. I can't tell you how many times I've asked your mother, grandmother, *and* Zora to leave you alone, to let you

settle down with a wife when *you're* ready." He chuckled.
"For your sake, son, I hope Noreen Broussard's niece is
at least easy on the eyes."

"Very easy," Brant murmured.

"You're lucky, then. Nothing's worse than being fixed
up with a woman you find unattractive. So you and this
young lady work together? What's her name, by the
way?"

"Samille Broussard. We're working on a case together.
She's with the DEA."

"Hmm. Your mother won't like that. You know she
wants you to settle down with a woman who'll take your
mind *off* your job, not help you do it." He laughed.
"Since Audre won't approve of you marrying someone
in law enforcement, I guess you're off the hook—this
time anyway."

Brant said nothing.

"That's a good thing, right?" Maurice prompted.

Slowly Brant replied, "Dad, I think you know me well
enough to know that as much as I love Mom and value
her opinion, when it comes to my personal life, I make
my own choices."

"Of course. You've always been your own man. We
wouldn't have it any other way." If he hadn't before,
Brant now had his father's undivided attention. "What
aren't you telling me, son?"

Brant moved to the edge of the sofa. His hands, which
hung between his legs, suddenly felt clammy. He and his
father had always been close. Brant admired and respected Maurice Kincaid more than anyone, and he'd
never had difficulty confiding in his father and seeking
his counsel.

So he shouldn't have been at all surprised when the
quiet admission slipped from his mouth: "I think I'm in
love with her, Dad."

Maurice Kincaid grew silent. He'd never heard those words leave Brant's mouth before. Zora had gone through the requisite teenage crushes and, before getting married, had believed herself to be in love more times than Maurice cared to remember. Even Bryan Kincaid, notoriously fickle, had proclaimed his undying love to every pretty girl who crossed his path.

But not Brant.

Brant had always been so immersed in his studies and extracurricular programs that at times he'd seemed oblivious of members of the opposite sex. Even the relationships he'd indulged in had been short-lived and inconsequential.

Now, at thirty-four, he'd finally fallen in love.

"Wow," Maurice said after a lengthy pause. He chuckled. "That was the *last* thing I expected to hear when I called you this evening."

"Believe me," Brant said ruefully, "I'm as shocked as you are."

"How long have you known Ms. Broussard?"

"You wouldn't believe me if I told you."

"Try me."

"I met her last Wednesday."

Maurice whistled softly through his teeth. "She must be really special, son. Tell me about her."

Brant blew out a deep breath. "I don't even know where to start, Dad. She's the most amazing woman I've ever met. She has a brilliant mind, she's talented, ambitious, and deeply compassionate. And she has a great sense of humor. God, I love to hear her laugh. You know how you can hear someone laugh, and it just sounds like it's coming from the very depths of their soul? That's how Samille laughs; it's an incredible sound."

There was a warm smile in his father's voice. "You don't say?"

"We like the same books and music. Even our professional interests are similar. We could talk for hours at a time on the same subject." He grinned and shook his head. "But she drives me crazy, Dad. She's so feisty and stubborn that I never know whether to kiss her or take her across my knee."

His father chuckled. "She should fit right in, then. Your grandmother, mother, *and* sister are three of the most headstrong and opinionated women we know."

Brant laughed in agreement. "Samille can launch into these tirades at the least provocation. One minute you're having a perfectly normal conversation, and the next minute she's going off on a tangent. But I think I'm finally learning what makes her tick."

"Then you're ahead of the game. It took me years to figure out your mother's minefields, and I'm still no expert, not by a long shot. Every day is a new journey."

"Well, I'm enjoying the journey so far. I want to know everything about Samille, and I mean *everything*." His voice grew husky with emotion. "I won't lie, Dad. It's scary as hell."

"It is," his father agreed, "but it's worth every scary moment if you've found the right woman. And it seems that you have. So what are you going to do about it, son?"

"I don't know, Dad." Brant leaned back against the sofa and stretched out his long legs. Wearily he pinched the bridge of his nose. "I just don't know."

His father said quietly, "You owe it to yourself to be happy, Brant. I don't have to tell you that."

Brant closed his eyes. "I know."

"Do you really?"

"Dad—"

"I already know what you're going to say. You're going

to tell me that you can't get involved with Samille Broussard because you work together and you can't afford the distraction, and it's unprofessional to mix business with pleasure. But even if she weren't your colleague, son, you'd still have an excuse for not becoming involved with her. You see, you've had a built-in excuse for years, long before you joined the FBI. I want you to listen to me, Brant. Do you promise not to interrupt until I've said what I have to say?"

"Yes, sir."

"Good." Maurice Kincaid took a deep breath. "Not a day goes by that I don't think about your brother, and wonder what kind of man he would have become. Every time I watch a Knicks game, I wonder if Bryan would have been out on that court playing like he always dreamed, like he always vowed. You and Bryan were two peas in a pod, yet you were as different as night and day. Let's face it: you always had more sense than your brother. You were more mature, more sensitive and conscientious. You always accepted responsibility for him, and for that I feel largely to blame. I put that weight on your shoulders long before you were ready.

"When Bryan died . . . when he died I knew you felt responsible for not being there to protect him—as if you could have prevented what happened. We all watched you at the funeral, son. We knew if you could, you would've traded places with Bryan in a heartbeat. How many times have you replayed that afternoon in your mind, wondering if the outcome would have been different if *you'd* been the one behind the wheel and your brother inside the store? And then you realize that it wouldn't have made an iota of difference because you were twins, and the animal who killed him wouldn't have known it wasn't Bryan in the car, nor would he have

cared. You've convinced yourself that you don't deserve
happiness because your brother isn't here to share it
with you. So you've spent the last sixteen years depriving
yourself, punishing yourself, and it has to stop, son. It
has to stop."

"Dad—"

"Your brother wouldn't want you to spend the rest of
your life this way. He loved life, and he believed in enjoying it to the fullest. You want to honor his memory?
Live, Brant. Live, and be happy. Otherwise . . ." Maurice's
voice hitched. He cleared his throat before continuing
thickly, "Otherwise it's as if your mother and I lost both
of our sons in that car."

Brant swallowed at the tightness in his throat. He
drew a deep, ragged breath and slowly exhaled. For a
long time neither man spoke. Both recognized the significance of the moment. As close as father and son
were, the subject of Bryan Kincaid had always been off-
limits. For years Brant had deflected the concerns of
his family and friends. After Bryan's death he'd attended Syracuse University as planned. When people
whispered and pointed him out on campus as the twin
brother of the slain star recruit, he'd pretended not
to notice. When friends judiciously avoided mentioning the basketball team and attended games without
him, he'd pretended not to mind. No one had to know
that he felt less than whole without Bryan, that he was
slowly being ravaged by rage and guilt, that by the time
he graduated summa cum laude from the university,
he was little more than a shell of his former self. He'd
spent years honing the skill of hiding his anguish from
others, protecting it with a ruthlessness that no one
could penetrate.

But he hadn't fooled Maurice Kincaid.

"If this is your way of lobbying for more grandchildren, Dad," Brant said at last, "Zora's already got it covered."

Maurice Kincaid laughed, but it was a shaky sound. "Speaking of family, your mother and I were thinking that we could all come down there for Thanksgiving, Zora and Kenny included. There's no reason we have to spend every holiday in New York. Besides," he added slyly, "once you and Samille are married, we'll have to get used to sharing you with her family anyway."

"Nice try, Dad," Brant drawled. "Did anyone ever tell you you'd make an excellent politician?"

"Very funny. I think I'll wait before sharing this wonderful news with your mother. I'd like to see how far she plans to go with her matchmaking scheme. And, hey, maybe we'll even let her take credit for bringing you and Samille together." He hesitated, a distinct smile in his voice. "Well, maybe not. She'd never stop gloating and patting herself on the back. Do you promise to give serious thought to what I told you?"

"I will, Dad."

They watched the game together for a few minutes before Brant got off the phone. Slowly he rose from the sofa and walked to the entertainment center. He stopped in front of Bryan Kincaid's photograph and cocked his head thoughtfully to one side.

Live, Brant. Live, and be happy.

On the television the buzzer sounded as the Knicks iced their opponent. With a half smile, Brant lifted his beer bottle in a silent toast to his brother. Bryan's grin seemed to widen in response.

"Cheers," Brant whispered. He took a sip of beer, then walked to the kitchen and poured the rest down the drain. He turned off all the lights and headed upstairs.

As he paused in the doorway of the empty guest bedroom, he almost imagined Samille's light citrus fragrance still clung to the air. God, he missed her. Somehow he had to convince her to come back to him. After all, it was a matter of her own safety.

He refused to admit, even to himself, what else was at stake.

CHAPTER 14

Samille was accosted by a blast of sunshine the minute she opened her eyes the next morning. She groaned and shoved her head beneath the pillow. She'd spent yet another restless night tossing and turning, and had only drifted off to sleep in the early hours before dawn.

She lifted her head and peered around the small room, scowling when she couldn't find a clock. She climbed out of bed and checked her watch. She swore when she saw that it was eight-thirty.

She shuffled across the hall and pounded on Amanda's bedroom door. "Winters! Time to get up!"

She heard a muffled curse, a dull thud, and then Amanda's bleary-eyed face appeared in the open doorway. "Must you shout?"

"You were supposed to set the alarm for five so we could get out and run," Samille accused. "What happened?"

Amanda grinned sheepishly. "Oops, guess I forgot."

"Likely story. I'm going to hop in the shower. Think you can fix a pot of coffee?"

"I think I can handle it. Sheesh, Broussard, I had forgotten how bossy you can be in the morning."

Samille muttered something unintelligible as she

headed for the bathroom. She showered quickly and threw on a pair of boot-cut jeans and a U.S. Air Force sweatshirt that belonged to Jared. She scooped her hair into a makeshift ponytail before heading for the small kitchen. Amanda sat on the Formica countertop sipping coffee and watching the *Today* show.

"I swear Katie Couric defies the laws of gravity," Amanda muttered enviously. "Would you just look at her legs? I hope *I* look that hot when I'm fifty-five."

Samille laughed as she poured steaming coffee into a pink Hello Kitty mug. "She's not even fifty, Amanda."

"Well, she looks great. Why'd you take a shower? I thought we were going to run first."

"We can run this evening. I want to get out and about—it feels like the day is already half over."

"That's because you don't know how to sleep in. Wait until you have a hangover or, better yet, spend the whole night romping between the sheets with a man possessing the stamina of the Energizer Bunny." She winked. "*Then* you'll appreciate the luxury of sleeping in late."

Samille shook her head. "I worry about you sometimes, Winters."

"Funny, that's what I always say about you."

When the doorbell rang, the two women exchanged curious glances. "Expecting someone?" Samille asked.

"Nope." Amanda hopped off the counter and went to answer the door. She was totally unprepared for the sight of Brant Kincaid on her doorstep. So unprepared, in fact, that she panicked and promptly closed the door in his face.

Samille stepped from the kitchen and stared at Amanda's shocked face. "Who is it?"

Your future husband, Amanda mouthed before turning and reopening the door. She gave Brant a meek grin. "Sorry about that. I don't usually answer the door without combing my hair and applying makeup first. You caught me by surprise."

"My apologies." Brant's mouth quirked as he slowly removed his mirrored sunglasses. "I'm looking for Samille."

"Then you've come to the right place." She thrust her hand forward. "Amanda Winters, by the way."

Brant shook her hand. "Brant Kincaid. Nice to meet you, Amanda."

"Oh, you have no idea." Grinning, she opened the door wider and waved him inside the apartment. "Would you like some coffee, Brant? I just made a fresh pot."

He shook his head distractedly as his dark gaze landed on Samille. "No, thanks."

They stared at each other across the room. The moment stretched into two. Samille was the first to break the silence. "Hey," she said softly.

"Hey yourself."

"What're you doing here?"

"Came to take you to the firing range."

"The firing range? Really?"

He raised an eyebrow. "Isn't that what you proposed during the first task force meeting? When you volunteered for the undercover assignment?"

"Yeah. I just didn't think anyone would take me up on the suggestion."

Brant shrugged. "Now that you're officially going undercover, you should at least be comfortable with a firearm."

"Absolutely," Samille agreed. Amanda stood just beyond Brant's left shoulder giving him a slow, appreciative once-over. She gave Samille a thumbs-up sign and mouthed: *Nice butt.*

"You coming?"

Samille's gaze snapped back to Brant's face. "Of

course." She grabbed her purse from the sofa and walked to the front door.

"Don't keep her out too long," Amanda admonished Brant. "We still need to go shopping for an outfit for tomorrow night."

"Yes, ma'am," Brant drawled as he held the door open for Samille. Before following her out, he tossed over his shoulder, "Oh, and thanks for the compliment."

Amanda looked momentarily baffled. As comprehension dawned, her eyes widened in shock. She burst out laughing.

Samille chuckled as she and Brant walked to the parking lot. "I should have warned her."

"About what?"

"That Super Agent Brant Kincaid sees and hears *everything*."

He grinned lazily. "And don't you forget it."

Amanda's gaffe had broken the ice between them. Once on the beltway Brant told Samille about his conversation with Willie Brooks the day before.

"So Salvatore Carrella lied to us about the extent of his dealings with Andrew Cason." Samille shook her head in patent disgust. "Why doesn't that surprise me? And Willie Brooks has no idea what the packages contained?"

"That's what he said." It didn't escape Brant's notice that Samille used Willie Brooks's name instead of referring to him as the "homeless guy," as Angel Hart had repeatedly done. His appreciation for Samille grew.

"I wonder what Cason was giving him," she ruminated aloud. "I suppose it could have been anything, although I'm inclined to agree with Mr. Brooks that it wasn't drugs. Salvatore Carrella may be a lot of things, but he didn't strike me as a drug dealer."

"Me neither," Brant agreed. "And I can't imagine that Cason was settling his financial obligation via packages delivered to the law firm. If, in fact, he *did* owe Carrella any money."

"Roy Clark overheard Carrella telling Andrew that he owed him something. If not money, then what?"

"It's highly possible that Cason was blackmailing him. Willie suspected Cason had a big score in the works. I'm willing to bet he had dirt on good ol' Sal, and if anything, Carrella was paying *him* off."

Samille nodded. "Maybe the packages contained incriminating photographs. Every time Cason sent another batch, Carrella shelled out more dough."

"Exactly. So I'll be digging into Carrella's background and researching some of his cases to see if anything interesting turns up."

"I'll help you," Samille said in a tone that left no room for debate.

"I wouldn't have it any other way." Brant slanted her a speculative look. "Cason thought someone from the DEA was after him. What are your thoughts on that?"

Samille's eyebrows knitted together. "I suppose anything's possible, but I can't imagine who would have been after him. As far as the DEA is concerned, that whole trial fiasco is ancient history. Yes, it was a PR nightmare and Cason's testimony helped a bunch of drug dealers walk, but it happened three years ago. Everyone just wants to move on."

"What about Burdett? Does he want to move on?"

Samille was silent a moment. "I don't doubt that Jack had residual feelings of resentment for Andrew Cason," she answered carefully. "As I told you before, that case nearly ruined his career. But at the end of the day, I'm sure Jack can admit to himself that he was as much to blame for what happened as Cason was. He made a grievous error by not checking Cason's background. He

Maureen Smith

learned from that experience, and he's redeemed himself twenty times over."

"Is that a fact?" Samille's vehement defense of Jack Burdett bothered Brant almost as much as hearing her tell Jack that she loved him. That had made him see red.

"How well do you know Jack?" he asked.

"What do you mean? We've been friends ever since I joined the DEA six years ago. He took me under his wing and showed me the ropes."

"I'll just bet he did," Brant muttered under his breath.

Samille frowned. "What's this about, Brant? I thought you and Jack were friends, but I get the distinct impression you're trying to implicate him in Cason's murder. Why would you want to do something like that?"

"It's not a matter of what I *want*, Samille. The truth is that Jack had motive and opportunity to kill Andrew Cason. We both know it."

"Even if that were true," Samille challenged, "what's Jack's connection to the Georgetown kids? According to your theory, the person who murdered Cason also drugged those teenagers *and* poisoned Bradley Whitfield. Do you really believe Jack is capable of these crimes?"

"It doesn't matter what I believe, Samille," Brant said through clenched teeth. "My opinion or personal bias has no place in this investigation, and neither does yours."

"Fine," she snapped. "But I think our time would be better served focusing on a more plausible suspect—i.e., Salvatore Carrella."

Brant shook his head, torn between frustration and incredulity. "I don't believe this."

"What?"

"Do you realize that every time we discuss Jack Burdett, we end up arguing? Why is that?"

"Maybe because you insist on impugning his character," she retorted hotly.

"And you insist upon defending him as if your very life depends on it." Brant paused, anger pumping hard through his veins. "Are you in love with him?"

"*What*?"

"It's a simple question, Samille. One that requires a simple yes-or-no response."

"How dare you! What business is it of yours who I'm in love with?"

"If your feelings for Jack Burdett prevent you from remaining objective," Brant answered evenly, "then it's very much my business. I'm trying to conduct a criminal investigation, and that entails examining each and every one I deem a potential suspect. If you have a problem with that, perhaps you need to be reassigned."

"You'd like that, wouldn't you? You've been trying to get me off this case from day one!"

"Believe me, Samille," Brant said darkly, "that's the *last* thing I want."

Samille opened her mouth with a scorching comeback—and promptly snapped it shut when his words registered. He wasn't looking at her, but was scowling ferociously at the road ahead. A telltale muscle ticked in his jaw.

She suddenly felt like a balloon that had been pricked with a needle and was slowly deflating. She felt physically and emotionally drained, and half crazed. This was utterly ridiculous. Why was she arguing with Brant Kincaid about her nonexistent feelings for another man? She loved *him*, for God's sake. Didn't he know that? How could he not?

Gloomily she stared out the window. "Just out of curiosity, where exactly are we going?"

"Quantico," he said tersely. "I obtained clearance for private access to one of the firing ranges."

"Oh." Another ounce of air left her body. Quantico, Virginia was an hour and a half from Silver Spring, Maryland. Brant had left his town house and come all the way out to Amanda's apartment, only to drive right back to Virginia to take her for shooting practice.

She turned partially in the seat to face him. "Look, Brant, I didn't mean to argue with you."

"Neither did I." His mouth curved cynically. "Matter of fact, I was going to suggest a cease-fire from *yesterday's* argument."

She grimaced. "About yesterday—"

"I shouldn't have said what I did."

"No, you were right." She hesitated, moistening her dry lips. "I *was* running from you, Brant. I didn't think we should risk another encounter between us. It wouldn't be wise for us to . . . become lovers."

He gave her a long, probing look that sent frissons of heat licking through her. When he spoke, his voice was low and husky. "That's what we keep telling ourselves, isn't it?"

She stared at him. "What are you saying, Brant?"

"Nothing. Forget it." He switched lanes to cut in front of a crawling Volkswagen Beetle. His eyes slid from the rearview mirror to return to hers. "Truce?"

"Truce." She settled back against the leather seat and folded her arms across her chest. Striving for a casual tone, she said, "I bet Angel was happy to see you again."

Brant grinned. "You trying to pick another fight with me?"

"No, I'm merely making an observation. I seem to recall her ogling you the entire time we were at the bakery. I knew she couldn't wait to sink her lovely claws into you."

"I'm happy to report that Ms. Hart kept her lovely claws to herself."

"Wait a minute. What's her last name?"

"Hart—no *e*."

"*Angel Hart*?" Samille rolled her eyes derisively. "Give me a break."

Brant chuckled. "Now, Samille. I'm sure she had no more control over her name than we have over ours."

Samille only rolled her eyes again. It was so unlike her to be catty toward other women. Yet another thing to blame on Brant: this newfound possessiveness. She wanted to lay claim to him in a way she'd never felt about any man before.

Shoving the thought aside, she sent Brant a ghost of a smile. "Tell me more about Willie Brooks. He sounds like quite a character."

Brant laughed. "Most definitely. You know, Samille, he reminded me a little of my grandfather."

Half an hour later, they exited at the turnoff for Quantico and drove for fifteen minutes through a densely wooded area where Marines jogged in precise formation along the edge of the blacktop road. They passed a number of nondescript buildings as they headed deeper into the Marine base.

The FBI Academy was located behind the Marines' facilities. As they approached the guard post, Brant suddenly stopped the truck.

Samille stared at him. "What are you doing?"

He turned to face her. "I want you to come back to my house."

"I can't stay with you, Brant. I thought we already discussed this."

"We agreed to a truce," he corrected. "We didn't discuss your coming home with me."

"There's nothing to discuss," said Samille, checking the passenger-side mirror for oncoming traffic. A blue Crown Victoria appeared in the distance. "I can't go home with you, Brant."

"Can't or won't?"

"Both. Now will you keep moving? We're sitting in the middle of the road!"

"Samille, there's a very real possibility that your life may be in danger. Under the circumstances, I'd feel a whole lot better keeping an eye on you myself."

Samille crossed her arms, her expression obstinate. "I don't need a bodyguard, Brant. I'm perfectly safe at Amanda's apartment. Some of her neighbors are cops. I met one of them yesterday, as a matter of fact. He seemed tough enough."

"Did you tell him about the investigation and the threatening phone call you received?" Brant challenged.

"Of course not. That's not public information."

"Then he has no reason to be on the lookout for you, does he?"

He had a point there. "It doesn't matter, Brant. I'm staying with Amanda, and that's all there is to it. Now would you please move this truck? There's a car coming down the road, for God's sake!"

"Tell you what," Brant said unhurriedly, inclining his head toward the guard post that loomed ahead, "if I can make the security guard laugh, you come home with me. If not, you stay with Amanda and I'll never raise the issue again."

"You must be crazy." Samille glanced anxiously at the mirror again. The Crown Vic was drawing closer. "You know very well that no one makes those guys laugh,

Brant. They're like the Buckingham Palace guards. I don't even think they're capable of cracking a smile."

"Then the odds are in your favor," Brant said reasonably. "Is it a deal?"

She threw up her hands in exasperation. "All right, fine! Now can we get moving before these people think we're terrorists staking out the academy?"

With a devilish grin, Brant continued down the road to the guard post. He slowed to allow the stony-faced security officer to see his identifying window sticker. The man nodded and signaled for Brant to proceed through the checkpoint.

Instead, Brant stopped and rolled down his window. "Hey, Sergeant Harding, how many FBI agents does it take to change a lightbulb?"

The man's expression remained stoic. In a voice without inflection he answered, "How many?"

"Depends on how far away the lightbulb is. Everyone knows how cheap the Bureau is when it comes to authorizing travel expenses."

For a moment the guard said nothing. Then suddenly, miraculously, the corners of his mouth twitched. A low chuckle escaped before he caught himself. The stony mask slid back into place. "Please proceed, Special Agent Kincaid."

Brant pulled off with a mock salute. He slanted a triumphant grin at Samille. "You lose, Broussard."

"I can't believe he laughed at that!" Samille complained. "That was an awful joke, Brant, really awful."

His grin widened. "What time shall I expect you this evening?"

"Wait a minute! He knew your name." Her eyes narrowed suspiciously on his face. "How do I know you and Sergeant Harding aren't old buddies?"

"Nah. I'm at Quantico often enough for him to

recognize me. I'll expect you by eight. And don't make me come looking for you, Samille, because you know I will."

Samille muttered an obscenity under her breath that made Brant throw back his head and roar with laughter.

He parked in the outdoor lot next to the firing ranges, waving at two agents who called greetings to him. He and Samille walked to the empty range reserved for their private use. Samille donned protective goggles, earphones, and a holster while Brant loaded a nine-millimeter semiautomatic and gave her instructions. Once she was ready, he helped her into position. As he stood behind her and spoke close to her ear, Samille had to squelch the urge to lean her head against his shoulder, curve an arm around his neck, and bring his mouth down to hers. Instead she focused on the "Q" target ahead of her, on the solid weight and feel of the semiautomatic in her hands. On his command, she drew and fired two rounds, then repeated the drill. Her first attempts were less than spectacular, but Brant didn't ridicule or patronize her. Patiently he repositioned her arms and gave her some pointers, then instructed her to repeat the course of fire.

She witnessed firsthand his excellent marksmanship when he performed a series of demonstrations for her, hitting the target dead-center with a lethal accuracy that seemed second nature to him. He didn't pause to indulge her awed exclamations, but jumped right back into the drills. He taught her how to unload and reload her weapon in under twenty-five seconds, how to fire six rounds using her strong hand, and then to shoot from the weak-hand barricade position. He was a patient instructor, remarkably knowledgeable and tough.

Afterward they ate lunch in a nearby little town. Over steaming crab bisque and roast beef sandwiches, Brant answered Samille's questions about marksmanship fundamentals and the rigorous firearms training provided by the FBI Academy. He was amused to learn about her thwarted attempt to sneak into the firearms course during her previous visit to Quantico.

"If you're interested in joining the Bureau," he said with a chuckle, "let me know and I'll put in a good word for you."

"Would you really?" Samille stirred sugar into her iced tea and added almost shyly, "Actually, I *am* kind of interested in working for the FBI Laboratory."

"Really? I didn't know that."

"You never asked."

"I'm asking now. So you're serious about this?"

She nodded, sipping her oversweetened tea. "I'm a scientist who enjoys criminal investigative work. I think working for the lab would be a great fit for me." She grinned. "So you'll put in a good word for me?"

"Absolutely. I think the Bureau would be very lucky to have you, Samille."

"Thanks for saying that, Brant. I really appreciate it." They exchanged warm smiles across the table. Samille tilted her head to one side and studied his face. "Have you always wanted to be an FBI agent?"

"Not exactly. I always thought, as did everyone in my family, that I'd earn a law degree and go into politics like my father. But after Bryan died, things changed for me." He shook his head and stared into his glass of iced tea. "I became obsessed with understanding the criminal mind, with learning what drove seemingly normal people to kill. I enrolled in criminal justice courses and did a few internships. But soon learning wasn't enough. I needed to be on the front line, so after getting my master's degree I joined the FBI."

"Was your family surprised?"

"A little. But I think they understood my decision."

"Yeah," Samille said softly, "I think I do, too."

Brant lifted his head to meet her gaze. Gently he smiled. "I know you do, Samille." He reached over and tucked an errant strand of hair behind her ear. She gave him a shy smile.

"Are you going home for Thanksgiving?" she asked.

"No. Actually, my family is coming here."

"Oh, that's wonderful, Brant." She grinned. "At least you don't have to worry about Aunt Noreen pressuring you into joining us for Thanksgiving dinner."

Brant chuckled. "No hardship there. Your aunt is one helluva cook."

"She's always made the holidays pretty special. She's from a huge New Orleans family, and let me tell you, you haven't experienced holiday festivities and summer cookouts until you've experienced them with the Broussards. To say they're a 'lively' bunch is a major understatement, and I love each and every one of them."

Brant smiled, watching her with complete absorption. "What's your favorite holiday, Samille?"

"Christmas, hands down." A nostalgic smile touched her mouth. "When I was little, my parents always took me ice skating at Rockefeller Plaza in New York. They were both busy surgeons, but no matter what was on their schedules, they always took me to New York during Christmastime. You being from Brooklyn, I don't have to tell *you* what a magical place the city is during the holidays. All the bright lights, the storefronts with their elaborate displays—FAO Schwartz was downright mesmerizing. But Rockefeller Plaza was always my favorite. The last time my parents took me ice-skating there, it started snowing. It was like a Norman Rockwell painting, Brant."

His smile was tender. "Sounds incredible."

"It was." A melancholy note crept into her voice. "They died the following year, and Aunt Noreen and

Uncle Gabe thought it would be too painful for me to go back to New York without them. And they were right. It was a long time before I could return there and enjoy those festive sights and sounds once again. The city holds special memories for me that I'll always cherish."

She grinned self-consciously. "Don't worry, Brant, I'm not going to launch into a Broadway rendition of 'I Love New York.' I'm not as musically gifted as you are." She consulted her wristwatch and said regretfully, "I guess we'd better start heading back before Amanda sends a rescue squad after me. She's so excited about this shopping mission that you'd think she won the lottery."

Brant chuckled as he signaled the waitress for the check. "She's quite a character. Her apartment is rather . . . interesting."

Samille grinned. "It's feng shui. And I don't expect *you* to appreciate it, Mr. Minimalist Décor."

Late that night as Samille slept in the guest bedroom, Brant pored over paperwork. Files covered every available surface of his desk. He'd gone through the court dockets to retrieve information about Salvatore Carrella's cases over the last two years. Carrella's clientele ranged from CEOs accused of embezzlement to prominent physicians charged with murder. If Andrew Cason had uncovered something incriminating about Carrella, Brant was determined to find out what it was.

Just as he was determined to learn what Jack Burdett was hiding.

According to Willie Brooks, Andrew Cason had believed someone in the DEA was following him. Samille thought the DEA had lost interest in Cason. Who was right? Was Cason simply paranoid? Or was Samille in denial? Cason had struck an immunity agreement with the U.S. Attorney's office in exchange for his testimony. He was untouchable. In all likelihood he *had* been written off. The DEA had far bigger fish to fry than a small-time drug dealer who couldn't keep his lies straight. The only one who had motive for going after Cason was Jack Burdett.

Brant wondered if Willie Brooks would recognize Jack if shown a picture. Frowning, Brant reached for the photographs he'd retrieved from the law enforcement database. One was as recent as last year, and the other had been taken when Jack first joined the DEA. He'd only been twenty-three years old, a fresh-faced southern kid who'd come to D.C. in search of life in the big city. His blue eyes practically sparkled with excitement and an eagerness to establish a name for himself.

Brant froze.

Quickly he rummaged through the papers littering his desk until he found Jefferson Spangler's photograph. He held the two photos side by side. The resemblance between Jefferson Spangler and Jack Burdett was jarring, and so unmistakable that Brant wanted to smack his forehead. No wonder he'd been struck with an uncanny sense of recognition the night he met Jack for drinks. He'd just come from interrogating Jefferson at the police station. He'd recognized the likeness between the two men, even if his mind hadn't made the connection.

Jefferson Spangler was Jack Burdett's half brother.

Was it possible?

Senator Ashton Spangler was from Baton Rouge, Louisiana. So was Jack. Jack had never known his real father. He'd been raised by a single mother who devoted her life to serving the Lord in the hopes that He would deliver them from abject poverty. Jack had grown up hating God almost as much as he'd hated the faceless man who had abandoned him and his mother.

Was Ashton Spangler Jack's long-lost father?

Brant carefully scrutinized the photos. The resemblance between Jack and Jefferson was too strong to be dismissed as mere coincidence. Did Jack know? Had he deliberately followed his father to Washington, D.C. to confront him? To blackmail him?

Brant felt a tightening of nerves as another scenario occurred to him. If Jack knew the identity of his real father, then it was entirely possible he'd given Jefferson Spangler the deadly drugs. What better way to exact revenge against the man who'd deserted him than to ruin him? Brant had always insisted that the individual who killed Andrew Cason had also poisoned Jefferson's classmates. Theoretically Jack fit the profile of their suspect: he had personal history with Cason *and* he had a connection to Jefferson Spangler—if indeed they were brothers.

Brant frowned, chilled by the direction of his own thoughts. They were no longer looking for a person who'd murdered a drug dealer to settle a vendetta. The individual they sought was a methodical, cold-blooded assassin who'd masterminded a sadistic plot to harm innocent teenagers and terrorize an entire community. Would Jack's malevolence toward his father have such far-reaching tentacles? Could he have walked into that hospital room and calmly injected Bradley Whitfield with cyanide?

Brant rose from his chair and crossed to the French doors overlooking the large backyard. His expression was grim as he contemplated the darkness. He'd always liked and respected Jack Burdett. But if Burdett was responsible for these crimes, Brant had no qualms about taking him down.

First thing tomorrow, Brant decided, he'd go find Willie Brooks. Something told him Willie knew more than he was letting on.

* * *

Willie Brooks knew someone was following him.

He had emerged from his hiding place that night to reach the Wisconsin Avenue bakery before closing time. He had to get a message to Special Agent Kincaid. Willie had suddenly remembered the name of another recipient of Andrew's "packages," and he knew it was someone Kincaid would definitely recognize.

But Willie feared he'd waited too long.

He ducked down another dark alley littered with broken bottles and scattered trash. Just a few more blocks to the brightness of Georgetown and its upscale clothing stores. He could see the lights in the distance, beckoning to him like a beacon rising above a dark, murky sea.

But his predator was getting closer. Willie turned his head just enough to see the advancing shadowy figure with his peripheral vision.

He hurried down the alley. The cold night air burned in his lungs and stiffened his joints. He'd kept himself in good shape over the years, but at sixty-eight, he knew it was only natural that age had slowed him down. The years had definitely taken a toll on the instincts and lightning reflexes that had helped him survive the unforgiving jungles of Vietnam.

He'd be okay once he reached Georgetown, where he could lose himself in the foot traffic. Just a few more blocks.

Perhaps Kincaid was right, Willie thought. Perhaps it *was* time for him to give up this crazy lifestyle and live with his daughter. If he could convince her of his sanity, just maybe she'd stop trying to have him committed to a mental institution.

Yeah, maybe he'd pay her a visit tomorrow. Maybe

they could finally talk things over. He knew she was still hurting from her mother's death. Neither of them had ever recovered—Willie had yet to stop running from his own grief. If anything ever happened to him, he knew his daughter would be devastated. She would stupidly blame herself for not doing more to keep him off the streets. He couldn't let that happen. He owed it to her to keep himself alive.

Willie suddenly realized that the alley had grown silent. He no longer heard the ominous approach of footsteps behind him. He stopped and peered cautiously around. The alley was empty save for the lone figure huddled beneath the shelter of a cardboard box. Had his stalker given up the chase? Willie wondered. He waited, air stalled in his lungs, head tilted to one side as he listened. All he heard was the wind sighing through the trees and the motor of an occasional passing car.

He turned and hastened toward the end of the alley. He had to get to that bakery—

He stopped dead in his tracks when the hooded stranger appeared in his path, a .32 aimed straight at Willie's chest. His final thought was of his daughter and how he'd failed her miserably as a father. He hoped, in time, she would learn to forgive him.

Blackness enveloped him as his body fell to the cold concrete.

CHAPTER 15

"I'm going to kill you."

Amanda blinked innocence. "Why?"

"*Why?* For making me buy this ridiculous getup! I look like a two-bit tramp!" Unhappily Samille regarded her reflection in the full-length mirror. She hardly recognized herself in the black leather bustier and leather micro-miniskirt Amanda had selected for her undercover attire. As if the skimpy outfit weren't scandalous enough, she wore a pair of black leather stiletto boots that climbed all the way up to her thighs. All she needed were handcuffs and cat-o'-nine-tails to complete the dominatrix look.

"You don't look like a tramp," Amanda countered calmly. "You look sexy. There's a big difference. And will you stop tugging at that? Trust me, your boobs aren't going to fall out."

"Easy for you to say. *You're* fully clothed. And what in the world did you do to my hair?" Her poor hair had been teased, spritzed, and feathered into a style that made her look as if she'd just emerged from a wind tunnel. She raised her hand to smooth it down; it was stiff to the touch.

"You'd better get comfortable with what you're wearing, Samille," Amanda admonished, "or you're going to find yourself distracted from the assignment. You need to be focused."

"I know," Samille grudgingly conceded. "It's just that I'm not used to being so . . . *exposed.*"

Amanda grinned. "Just pretend you're at a costume party. Believe me, once you get to Club Zydeco and see what everyone else is wearing, you're going to feel right at home. Work it like you own it, baby."

"So you keep telling me."

Samille knew her apprehension extended beyond her clothing, or lack thereof. She was nervous about tonight's sting operation. So many things could go wrong—a missed cue here, a blunder there, and it could all blow up in their faces. She'd fought tooth and nail for this opportunity. It was sobering to realize that the success of the outcome ultimately rested on her shoulders.

Be careful what you ask for, Broussard.

Samille took one last look at her reflection in the mirror, drew a deep, fortifying breath, and turned to Amanda. "Showtime."

The other members of the task force awaited her in Amanda's living room. Marc Lopez, Rick Grimes, and Michael Parham were glued to a college football game on the wide-screen television. Brant and Jack stood by the window, deep in conversation. At her appearance all five men looked over in unison.

A stunned silence fell over the room. Samille swore she could have heard a pin drop.

And then Lopez exclaimed softly under his breath, "*Ay dios!*"

Michael began whistling the popular eighties song "Centerfold," which drew hearty male laughter from Lopez and Rick Grimes.

Brant and Jack exchanged tense glances.

Resisting the overwhelming urge to run and cover herself, Samille defiantly stood her ground. "All right, fellas, go ahead and get in all your lewd jokes before we leave. But you see these spiky six-inch heels I'm wearing?" She paused as five pairs of eyes lowered to her boots. She wagged her finger as she continued, "Once we leave this apartment, anyone who so much as *looks* at me wrong will get a heel right where the sun don't shine. Do you boys catch my drift?"

The threat was met with muffled male groans and more laughter. Only Brant was not amused. His face had that masklike quality that always made Samille nervous— carefully blank, deliberately expressionless. But his displeasure was palpable enough to reach out and touch.

She found herself holding her breath as he crossed the room toward her. Dressed in an open-necked black shirt, a well-cut black blazer, and black trousers, he exuded a raw, dangerous masculinity that Samille found utterly compelling.

When he stopped in front of her, she held perfectly still as his dark, potent gaze raked over her body in frank appraisal. "I don't suppose there's anything I can say to talk you out of this," he said in a deceptively soft voice.

She feigned insouciance. "The outfit or the undercover op?"

"Both."

"Absolutely not."

Smoothly Amanda intervened, "Everything's all set, Brant. Samille is properly wired, and her weapon is concealed in the lining of her right boot. The fur trim should hide the bulge, but thank God for compact pistols."

Brant nodded without breaking eye contact with Samille. "Thank you, Amanda. You've been most helpful."

She grinned. "Just doing my job as special operations

wardrobe consultant—my new self-dubbed title, by the way. What do you think, Jack? Think our gal will have any problems blending in with the crowd?"

"None whatsoever." Jack winked at Samille. "Now as to whether these fellas will be able to get any sleep tonight, that's a different story."

Michael began whistling "Centerfold" again. Samille shot him a withering look. "We get the point, Irish."

"Time to go," Brant said authoritatively. He rattled off instructions like a man who was used to giving orders and being obeyed without question. "Samille, you're following me to the club, but give me a few minutes to go inside and settle in before you get in line. Jack, the rest of you hang back a little. We can't risk raising suspicion by arriving together at the same time. Everyone clear? Good, let's go."

Club Zydeco was located in a two-story building on K Street in northwest D.C. By nine o'clock the line was nearly wrapped around the corner. One look at the revelers effectively put to rest any lingering doubts Samille may have had about her own state of indecency. She saw girls clad in psychedelic minidresses, micro-miniskirts, and scraps of spandex that barely concealed vital body parts. Standing in clusters, they teetered in high-heeled platform shoes and tried not to look cold. With cars parked in every direction, traffic was jammed. Music blared from elaborate stereo systems, hip-hop colliding with rock and a smattering of reggae.

Samille didn't bother trying to find a spot; she relinquished her Jeep to the valet attendant and coolly strolled to the end of the line, praying she wouldn't trip and fall flat on her face in the ridiculous stiletto boots she wore. *Work it like you own it*, she mentally recited

Amanda's earlier words to her. She held her head high as she walked, ignoring the rowdy whistles and catcalls that followed her.

A group of giggling college students brought up the rear of the line. Combined they wore just enough material to clothe one person, and their faces were so heavily made up they looked as if they'd just raided a cosmetics factory. Brant had instructed Samille to assimilate with a group of girls so that she would appear less conspicuous.

Samille sidled up to one of the girls and beamed a smile. "*Love* your shoes."

She didn't, really. They were horrendous and looked terribly uncomfortable with leather straps woven between the toes. Why, Samille wondered, did women subject themselves to such torture in the name of so-called fashion?

The petite brunette appeared slightly startled. And then, to Samille's surprise, she offered a shy smile. "Thanks. I love *your* boots. Where'd you get 'em?"

As Samille and the brunette struck up a friendly conversation, the other girls eyed her suspiciously, as if they felt threatened by her presence. Amused, Samille wanted to assure them that she had no intention of competing for dance partners. She was there for one purpose, and one purpose only.

To catch a killer.

Just then the club's doors swung open and two burly bouncers emerged. Slowly the line began to move forward as people were allowed inside after showing their ID.

"We're not going to get a good table," complained one of the brunette's friends, a beautiful girl of biracial descent. She stamped her foot impatiently. "I told you guys we should have left campus earlier!"

Samille was just as eager to get inside and grab a good table, one that gave her an unrestricted view of everyone who entered and left the club. She watched as Brant emerged and joined one of the bouncers on the sidewalk. They stood laughing and talking for a few minutes, and then the bouncer looked toward the end of the line. He left Brant and walked right up to Samille's group.

He grinned at her. "Seems you have a secret admirer. The head of security says I should let you and your friends inside now."

Samille swallowed a grin. "My friends? Oh, but I just met these—"

"Don't be silly! Of course we're friends!" The biracial beauty grabbed Samille's hand and followed the bouncer before Samille could utter another word of protest.

When they neared the front entrance, Samille sent Brant a coquettish smile of gratitude and said loud enough for her companions to hear, "Thanks, handsome. I've always wanted a secret admirer."

"Oh, I'm sure you'll have many more before the night's over," Brant drawled in the thickest, sexiest Brooklyn accent Samille had ever heard. She practically felt the girls swooning behind her.

Club Zydeco featured high-tech lighting, a full wraparound bar, and a large dance floor that was starting to fill with bodies gyrating to techno music. The club attracted an interesting blend of patrons ranging from college students to those in their late twenties. Samille and her companions snagged a table that afforded them an unobstructed view of the door and a clear path to the bar. While the rest of the girls made a beeline for the liquor, Samille and the brunette remained at the table.

"You don't drink?" Samille shouted above the pulsating music.

"Not really. I'll probably get something in a little while

though, or I'll never hear the end of it. Especially from Zaria." She rolled her eyes and laughed.

Samille presumed Zaria was the leader of the pack, the one who'd been only too willing to welcome Samille into the fold as long as she benefited from doing so. "What's your name?"

"Amber. Yours?"

"Erika," Samille answered, the alias rolling smoothly off her tongue. "Nice to meet you, Amber. You guys come here a lot?"

Amber shrugged. "Every other weekend. We're seniors at the University of Maryland. What about you?"

"Grad student at Georgetown. What're you studying at Maryland?"

Zaria and the others returned with their drinks just as a minor commotion near the entrance signaled the arrival of hip-hop star Damien "Da Omen" Johnson. As people paused on the dance floor to point and scream his name, he and his entourage of friends and bodyguards were led to the VIP lounge located on the club's second floor.

"Man, I'd give anything to meet Da Omen tonight," one of Amber's friends said with a dreamy smile.

Zaria snorted. "Forget *him*. What about that fine security guard who let us into the club? Give me a night with him anytime!"

Her friends giggled and nodded vigorously in agreement. The tiny microphone hidden inside Samille's earlobe was filled with Detective Lopez's amused voice: "Looks like Kincaid's gonna get laid tonight. We're in place, by the way. So far no sign of our cloaked friend. Ask your new buddy if she'd settle for a lowly cop."

Samille nearly grinned when she heard Brant's low, acerbic response to the detective. Brant's "cover" as head of the security team enabled him to wear an earpiece without arousing suspicion. He could simultaneously monitor the club and the undercover operation.

"Ladies," Zaria announced, rising from the table, "it's time to hit the dance floor and show these freaks how it's done."

Samille swallowed an instinctive groan. She'd hoped to avoid this particular aspect of the assignment. She couldn't remember the last time she'd danced in public, and she had serious reservations about attempting it now in these boots.

Work it like you own it.

Amber grabbed her hand and led her from the table as the summertime hit "Crazy in Love" cued up.

Brant stood on the second-floor balcony enclosed in clear Plexiglas. His gaze was trained on the crowded dance floor below where bodies writhed to music that seemed to pound from every crevice of the building. Scantily clad women and men gyrated in steel cages suspended from the ceiling, and the blinding flash of strobe lights made the dancers appear electrified.

For all that activity, Brant may as well have been viewing worshippers at mass. He only had eyes for Samille. Samille, who looked like an erotic fantasy in skimpy black leather that rode her lush curves like oil gliding over silk. And her legs, those incredible legs that had tantalized him from the moment he met her, went on for miles in those obscene thigh-high boots. Brant had always prided himself on possessing an inordinate amount of self-control. He didn't get off on watching half-naked women mud-wrestle in beer commercials, and he wasn't particularly titillated by Victoria's Secret models strutting down runways in scraps of lingerie. He hadn't so much as peeked at a *Playboy* magazine since college, nor had he felt compelled to.

Now, watching Samille on the dance floor, he may as well have been a horny adolescent. He'd been battling an erection ever since Samille first made an appearance in the dominatrix getup, her lips slicked a sinful red and her hair looking as untamed as if she'd just indulged in a night of unbridled sex. Brant didn't know whether to march downstairs and cover her up with his blazer, or join every other male in the club who was openly ogling her as she moved to a fast, edgy number on the dance floor. Her movements were fluid and primitively sensual. Brant's gut clenched as he watched her dance partner lean close to murmur something in her ear. When Samille threw back her head and laughed, Brant felt positively murderous. He'd instructed her to act natural and at least *appear* to enjoy herself.

Did she have to be so convincing?

Unfortunately, Damien "Da Omen" Johnson, who stood at the balcony observing the dancers, had also noticed Samille. "Man, who *is* that chick working it out on the dance floor?"

Beside him, his homeboy laughed. "Which one?"

"The one in the skintight black leather and wild hair." Johnson pointed. "She is hot as all get out."

"Yeah, I've been scoping her, too."

"I wanna meet her. Yo, Dre," Johnson called, signaling to the muscle-bound bodyguard who stood nearby, "send Tips downstairs to get her. Tell her Da Omen requests the honor of her presence in the VIP lounge."

Brant smothered a violent oath as the bodyguard disappeared to do his employer's bidding. Now was not the time for indulging Damien Johnson's libido. Samille needed to be in place when—and *if*—their perp decided to make an appearance.

A HEARTBEAT AWAY   309

His Glock rested comfortably in the shoulder holster beneath his blazer. He hoped Johnson wouldn't force him to use it.

Samille and her companions had returned to their table when Johnson's buddy approached. Brant watched Samille smile and demurely decline the offer, then grow visibly irritated when Tips wouldn't take no for an answer. Brant silently willed her to accept the invitation, knowing she couldn't afford to cause a scene. Heads had already turned in their direction as people recognized Tips, who made a regular appearance in Damien Johnson's music videos.

Finally Samille acquiesced. Her companions looked on in astonished envy as Tips escorted her from the table and upstairs to the VIP lounge.

Samille walked into a luxurious suite done in glass and gleaming black marble. It was equipped with a private bar and a wide-screen television mounted against the wall. Slow jams drifted from a state-of-the-art sound system. A sideboard table was laden with gourmet cheeses, buffalo wings, pineapple turkey meatballs, shrimp cocktail, crab cakes, and several bottles of Cristal champagne. Members of Da Omen's entourage stood around in clusters, laughing and watching the action below. Samille counted only two other women in the room. Oh well. The night was still young. She knew how these things worked. She knew musicians amassed groupies the way some people collected coupons.

Still, she didn't appreciate being summoned by Da Omen's lackey. The hip-hop star's arrogance rankled, and she had a mind to tell him just what she thought of him *and* his corny rap songs.

She noticed Brant in a corner of the room conversing with another man. He didn't glance in her direction, but she knew he was keenly aware of her presence and was more than ready to step in if necessary.

Damien Johnson approached her with the suave megawatt smile that drove his female fans crazy. He was brown-skinned and good-looking, although a lot shorter than he appeared on television. He was decked out in a velour athletic suit from his recently launched urban clothing line. A rope of gold circled his neck.

"Hey, beautiful," he greeted her in a low, intimate tone. "You were playing hard to get down there, but I ain't mad atcha. I enjoy a good chase, especially when the prize is as fine as you are."

Samille resisted the urge to roll her eyes. "Look, Mr. Omen—"

He chuckled. "Call me Damien. Why don't we have a seat over here? Would you like something to drink? We got some Cristal, Moët—whatever your lovely heart desires."

"No, thank you. I'm fine." Damien guided her over to a U-shaped leather sectional. His hungry gaze latched onto her thighs as she sat and crossed her legs. He eased down beside her, closer than she would have preferred, but at least on the opposite side of her microphoned ear.

He licked his lips and smiled into her eyes. "What's your name, beautiful?"

"Erika."

"Really? You don't look like an Erika."

She arched an amused eyebrow. "I don't?"

"Nah, your name should be something different, something more exotic."

"I'll take that as a compliment."

"You should. Definitely. Do you have a boyfriend, Erika?"

"Not at the moment. Why? Are you offering to be my boyfriend, Damien?"

He grinned, leaning closer until his minty breath fanned her face. "I'd like nothing better than to be your boyfriend," he said seductively. "As a matter of fact, I was just thinking that the two of us could go back to my hotel room and get to know each other a little better, know what I'm saying?"

"Oh, I know *exactly* what you're saying." Out of the corner of her eye Samille saw Brant move toward them, looking none too pleased.

Damien consulted his diamond-encrusted Cartier wristwatch. "I've got an executive suite at the Hotel George and a Hummer limo parked right outside. We could be back at the hotel in no time at all."

"Is that right?" Samille leaned into him and whispered throatily, "You've obviously got me pegged as the sort of gal who jumps into bed with men I hardly know."

He licked his lips again and stared at her cleavage. "I'm *hoping* you are."

"Mmm," she purred. "Well, I'm hoping you're into threesomes."

His eyes snapped to her face. "What?"

"You heard me, Damien. I want to have a threesome with you." Brant stood near the door with his arms folded across his chest. At her words, his dark eyes narrowed and zeroed in on her face. A low whistle emanated from the microphone in her ear—Lopez again.

Damien grinned as if he'd struck gold. "Hey, that's cool with me. What about that little hottie you were with? The one with the long pretty hair and—"

Samille bit her lip and gave her head a naughty shake. "Actually, I had someone else in mind."

"Who?"

She inclined her head toward Brant. "Him."

Damien looked over at Brant. Brant's expression was

inscrutable—except for the steely glint in his eyes that clearly warned: *don't even think about it.*

Damien turned quickly back to Samille. "I don't think so."

She pretended to pout. "Are you sure, Damien? The three of us could have a *really* good time."

Damien gave Brant another assessing look before shaking his head firmly. "Nah, baby girl. I ain't into that kinda stuff, know what I'm saying?"

What's wrong, Da Omen? Afraid you'll be outperformed?

Samille swallowed a knowing grin and said sweetly, "I understand, Damien. It's not for everyone." Smoothly she uncrossed her legs and stood. "I'm going to head back downstairs to my girlfriends. Maybe next time you're in town we can hook up."

"Most definitely." But Damien's ardor had cooled considerably.

Samille passed Brant on her way out of the suite. Briefly their eyes met. She knew he hadn't appreciated her little stunt, even if it *had* rescued her from Damien Johnson's clutches. Samille thought she deserved points for ingenuity.

Brant's eyes communicated that he would deal with her later.

She was still congratulating herself as she descended the stairwell to the first floor. She scanned the crowded room to locate her table, and froze.

There, seated alone at the bar, was a masked figure cloaked in black.

Her pulse quickened.

"The eagle has landed," she spoke aloud, using the signal the task force had agreed upon. "He's wearing a black mask and hooded cloak, just as Portia Dawkins described."

"So much for thinking he might show up at the club

already in costume," Lopez grumbled. "We didn't see anyone matching that description. Whoever he is, he slipped right past us. Maybe Burdett saw something."

"Where's Jack?" Brant demanded.

"Stepped out a few minutes ago. Said he was getting cagey locked up in the van. He wanted to be closer to the action."

Brant swore colorfully under his breath.

"What was I supposed to do?" Lopez said defensively. "Make him ask for a hall pass before he could be dismissed?"

"I hate to interrupt, fellas," Samille interjected dryly, "but our suspect is waiting."

"Are you ready?" Brant and Lopez spoke in unison.

Samille's mouth quirked at the corners. "As ready as I'll ever be. I'm going in. Over and out."

"Be careful," Brant warned brusquely.

Samille took a deep breath and wended through the vibrating throng of bodies to the bar. She slid into the empty seat beside the masked stranger and signaled the bartender. He materialized almost at once with a flirtatious smile.

"What're you drinking, beautiful?"

"Cosmopolitan," Samille answered, returning his smile. As he moved away to fix her drink, she reached into the folds of her leather boot and withdrew a slim pack of cigarettes. She made a show of digging around for a concealed lighter and swearing profusely when she couldn't find it.

She looked at the cloaked figure beside her. He had not moved an inch since her arrival. His gloved hands were wrapped around a glass of beer. The drink was untouched.

Samille leaned toward him. "Got a light?"

For several moments he showed no reaction to her question. He continued staring into the foamy contents of his glass without moving. She was about to repeat herself when, with a quick flick of his wrist, he produced a lighter.

Samille grinned at his dexterity. "Hey, thanks," she said gratefully. As he held the flame to her cigarette, she tried to get a better look at him, but the cloak and mask made it impossible. She couldn't even discern the color of his eyes through the narrow slits in his mask. He pocketed the lighter and turned away without a word.

Samille took a slow drag on the cigarette and tried not to gag. She hadn't smoked since college, when she'd experimented with her roommate and found the taste of nicotine appalling. Nothing had changed.

The bartender returned with her cosmopolitan and a sexy wink. Samille thanked him and sipped just enough of the cocktail to wet her tongue. The *last* thing she needed was to get drunk while on assignment.

She smiled at her silent companion. "What's with the disguise?" she teased, not really expecting an answer.

She was totally unprepared for his quiet response. "I've been waiting for you."

Samille tensed. Was her cover blown? Did the stranger recognize her, as Brant had feared?

She forced a dry laugh. "Is that right?"

Slowly he nodded. "I was watching you on the dance floor. You're a good dancer. Hypnotic."

"Hypnotic, huh?" Samille pondered the word a moment, then grinned approvingly. "That's one of the best pickup lines I've heard all night. My name's Erika, by the way. And you are?"

He fell silent again.

Watching him, Samille puffed on her cigarette and released twin curls of smoke through her nostrils, a trick she'd learned from watching old Doris Day films. "Wanna dance?"

He shook his head. "I didn't come here to dance."

"Really? What'd you come here for?"

Once again he ignored her.

Samille swiveled around on the bar stool and swept her eyes around the club. Amber sat alone at the table looking lonely and miserable. Zaria and the others had returned to the dance floor. As Zaria gyrated to a bass-heavy remix of Da Omen's chart-topping single "Laid Back," she kept glancing toward the second-floor balcony—no doubt hoping Damien would summon her to the VIP suite.

Samille glanced discreetly toward the balcony. Brant was nowhere in sight.

She took another drag on the cigarette and spun around on the bar stool. "I need something stronger than this," she muttered, crushing out the cigarette in an ashtray shaped suspiciously like a member of the male anatomy.

"What did you have in mind?"

"What? Oh, I was just thinking out loud." Samille regarded the stranger with mild interest. "Why? What did *you* have in mind?"

Slowly he lifted his head and glanced over his shoulder as if to check for eavesdroppers.

And Samille knew she had him.

"I may have just what you're looking for," he said casually.

"Is that right?" Samille lifted her glass and sipped her tangy cocktail, trying not to appear eager. Her heart was racing a mile a minute. "What're we talking about here?"

"If you step into the back with me, I'll show you what I'm talking about."

Samille eyed him skeptically. "Look, pal, if this is your way of luring me to the bathroom for a private peep show, forget it. I'm not that kinda girl."

He chuckled. "That's not what I had in mind."

"Then let's step outside instead. I need some fresh air anyway."

He hesitated, and for a moment she feared he would refuse. But then he stood and, without another word, headed toward the corridor. Samille followed him out a back door that opened onto a dark alley that dead-ended on the right. Parked alone at the opposite end was the commercial van containing the members of the task force. Unbeknownst to the masked stranger, Brant had arranged for the club's back door to lock from the inside. Once the sale occurred, Detective Lopez and the others would close in for the arrest. The suspect had no escape route.

The chilly night air was like an arctic blast after the heat from the packed club, but Samille scarcely noticed. Adrenaline surged through her veins, making her feel a little light-headed. This was it. The moment of truth.

She faced the stranger in the dark alley. He was tall, at least six feet, and beneath the black cloak his shoulders were broad enough to partially obscure the moonlight behind him.

Ignoring a flicker of unease, Samille asked, "What've you got?"

He reached inside his cloak and withdrew a small plastic bag. "It's called Utopia," he said in a low voice.

"Utopia? Never heard of it. Is it new?"

"You could say that." He stared at her. "It's pretty intense."

"Really?" Samille hesitated, chewing her bottom lip with a pensive expression.

The stranger waited in silence.

She shrugged. "Why not? I'll live dangerously. How much?"

"Sixty bucks."

Samille reached into her bustier and pulled out a rolled wad of bills. She peeled off three twenties and paid the stranger, muttering about money she'd intended to spend on a new pair of boots.

He glanced over her shoulder to the silent van parked near the mouth of the alley. Samille's throat went dry. She panicked. *Oh no.* Had he seen movement from within the vehicle? No one was supposed to budge until money and drugs had exchanged hands. The fellas knew that—it was standard procedure.

She held out her hand. "Merchandise, please."

Slowly the stranger passed the small bag to her. Inside was a clear plastic vial containing at least ten oblong tablets imprinted with the name UTOPIA.

Bingo.

Samille backed slowly away from the stranger. "Can't wait to try it," she said, delivering the cue. At the same time she spied a shadowy figure standing atop the brick wall at the end of the alley.

Detective Lopez and the others spilled from the van and charged toward them. "Police! Freeze!"

A savage oath erupted from the stranger's mouth. "You set me up!"

Too late, Samille jerked her gaze from the shadowy silhouette on the wall as the stranger seized her roughly. She cried out as he twisted both arms behind her back and positioned her as a human shield before training a semiautomatic on the approaching group of men.

"Stay back!" he shouted, enraged. "Don't come any closer, or I swear to God I'll blow her brains out!"

Detective Lopez and the others came to an abrupt halt. "Look, man—"

The club's back door burst open as Brant barreled into the alley. His expression was lethal, his Glock drawn and aimed at Samille's captor.

"FBI! Drop your weapon!"

The nose of the stranger's gun swung toward Brant. Samille felt his body tremble against hers. "Special Agent *Kincaid*?" he said in a thin, shocked voice.

Brant's blood turned to ice as recognition dawned. "Drop your weapon, Jefferson," he said quietly. "You're under arrest."

CHAPTER 16

Jefferson Spangler took a step backward, pressing the semiautomatic into Samille's temple. "No," he said flatly. "You can't arrest me. She tricked me!"

Brant didn't lower his weapon. His gaze was locked on Jefferson Spangler's masked face with a calm he was far from feeling. He'd been detained inside the club by a member of the security team who needed assistance with an unruly patron. The guy had had one too many drinks and started groping women on the dance floor. When approached by security, he became belligerent and began throwing punches. He was a big man, and it had taken three bouncers to restrain him and escort him from the building. The distraction had cost Brant precious minutes. By the time he reached the alley, the situation had already escalated to the hostage crisis he now faced.

His heart jammed at the base of his throat as he stood watching Samille imprisoned in Jefferson Spangler's arms, the nose of a gun pointed at her head. Their gazes connected, and Brant willed Samille to remain strong, to have faith in him. He had no intention of letting anyone hurt her.

God, if anything happened to her . . .

"Drop your weapon, Jefferson," Brant ordered calmly. "You have nowhere to go. We have the entire building surrounded."

"No!" Jefferson roared. He shifted, wrapping his arm around Samille's neck and dragging her tighter against him. She flinched as the gun quivered in his hand. "This wasn't supposed to happen! I wasn't supposed to get caught. She *lied* to me!"

"She was just doing her job, Jefferson," Brant countered. "She's a federal officer. If you hurt her, you'll be in even deeper trouble. Do you understand that?"

"Don't! Don't take another step, Agent Kincaid, or I swear I'll kill her!"

"Listen to me, kid. You don't want to do this."

"Lower your gun to the ground!" Jefferson shouted. "Do it now!"

Slowly Brant complied, keeping his gaze trained on the boy's masked face. He kicked away the weapon to demonstrate his full cooperation. "Let her go, Jefferson. We can talk about this."

"Bull! You don't want to talk! First chance you get, you're gonna blow a hole through my head! You, or one of your buddies over there." Jefferson inclined his head toward Michael Parham and Detectives Lopez and Grimes. Jack was nowhere to be found.

"No one's going to shoot you, Spangler," Lopez said calmly. "We'd like to take you down to the station and ask you a few questions."

"You think I'm stupid, Detective? You're not going to ask me a 'few' questions. You're going to toss me in jail and throw away the key! I can't let you do that!"

"You don't have a choice, Jefferson." Brant spoke tersely, striving for patience. "You broke the law. You sold drugs to an undercover federal officer. You know we can't let you walk away scot-free."

"I can't go to jail, Agent Kincaid. My father—" His voice broke before he continued querulously, "My father would disown me."

"Think how much worse it will be if you kill a hostage," Brant said quietly. "Not only would your father's political career be ruined, but you'd be sent to prison for a very long time, Jefferson, probably for the rest of your life. Think about that."

Jefferson said nothing. His arm tightened convulsively around Samille's neck. She closed her eyes and swallowed hard. She wished she could reach the pistol tucked inside her boot, but it was a long shot. One false move could spell immediate disaster.

"It's not too late to get help, Jefferson," Brant continued evenly. "I want you to tell us who gave you these drugs. If you cooperate with us, we'll try to help you as much as possible. But if you hurt Ms. Broussard, we can't help you."

"My father is never going to forgive me for this," Jefferson cried. "So I'm screwed either way!"

Brant's heart thundered in his throat. The boy was on the verge of hysteria. Hysterical gunmen were always the most difficult to negotiate with—and the most dangerous.

"That's not true, Jefferson. You still have a chance to rectify the situation. Let Ms. Broussard go. We'll take you down to the station and talk. We want to hear your side of the story."

"There's nothing to tell! You said it yourself: I sold drugs to an undercover fed. I'm in big trouble, and there's nothing you can do to help me!"

Brant and Lopez exchanged wary glances. Both knew that the situation was spiraling out of control. The rising desperation in Jefferson's voice was alarming.

"Listen, kid—"

"Don't come any closer, Agent Kincaid!" Jefferson

warned. He yanked Samille's head to one side and shoved the nozzle against her jugular vein. She gritted her teeth against the pain. Police sirens wailed in the distance.

"Look, Jefferson," Brant tried again, "I know how hard it can be when your father is a prominent public figure. My old man is a city councilman in New York, and although that's not quite the same as being the son of a U.S. senator, I can definitely relate to a lot of the pressures you face. I know what it's like to grow up under a microscope, having to watch your every move so that you don't do anything to embarrass your father or ruin his public image. I know what it's like to attend boring political functions when you'd rather be outside hanging with your friends or at home playing video games. I know how hard it is to create your own identity when everyone—including your family—expects you to follow in your father's footsteps, regardless of whether or not you're interested in politics."

Jefferson had grown very still. "I hate politics," he said sullenly.

Brant managed a dry chuckle. "So did I. I joined the FBI to get *away* from bureaucrats. Go figure."

Jefferson loosened his hold on Samille, but only a fraction. "Look, Agent Kincaid, I appreciate what you're trying to do. But you don't know my father. He demands perfection from everyone, especially me."

"That may be true," Brant agreed, "but he's your father, Jefferson. When all is said and done, he only wants the best for you. He loves you no matter what. I saw that with my own two eyes the night we questioned you. You want to make Ashton Spangler proud? Turn yourself in, and help us find the person who gave you these drugs. Will you do that, Jefferson?"

Jefferson hesitated, torn with indecision. Brant waited in silence, his muscles taut and primed for the teenager's next move. Detective Lopez and the others stood poised for action as well.

With a muffled cry Jefferson released Samille and tossed the semiautomatic to the ground. Parham and Grimes were instantly upon him, forcing his arms behind his back and handcuffing him. Lopez knelt on the ground and retrieved the discarded weapon. Using his fingertips, he slipped it inside a clear glassine bag.

Samille passed the detective the small bag of pills, then stepped forward and removed the black mask from Jefferson Spangler's face. Frightened blue eyes met hers before he ducked his head in shame. Tears rolled down his face. "I didn't mean to hurt you, Ms. Broussard," he sobbed. "I swear to God I didn't."

"Tell it to the judge, kid," Detective Grimes muttered. He proceeded to read Jefferson his rights as several police cruisers screeched to a halt at the alley's entrance.

Samille walked over to Brant as he returned his Glock to his shoulder holster. Onyx eyes glittered with emotion as he gazed down at her. "Brant—"

"Are you all right?" he demanded gruffly.

She nodded, chilled to the bone. She didn't want to think about how close she'd come to dying tonight. Later, when the shock wore off, she knew she'd have no choice. "Thank you, Brant," she said softly. "If you hadn't been here—"

"Put this on." He shrugged out of his blazer and draped it around her bare shoulders. It hung past her knees. He drew back and looked at her. "You did really well. I'm proud of you."

Her mouth twisted ruefully. "Even if I almost got myself killed." She watched as Detective Grimes and another police officer escorted Jefferson Spangler to the nearest squad car. "It's crazy. He sold drugs to his classmates and threatened my life, yet I can't help feeling sorry for him."

"He's a disturbed kid," Brant murmured.

Suddenly the club's back door swung open to reveal Jack. His blond hair was windblown, sweat dampened his flushed face. He strode quickly to Samille. "I heard what happened. Are you all right?"

Brant scowled at him. "Where have you been, Burdett?"

"Chasing down a suspect."

"*What?*" Brant and Samille exclaimed in unison.

Jack nodded grimly. "I was headed inside the club when I spotted a guy matching our description, black mask and all. He was standing right there at the corner—" Jack pointed to the end of the alley. "He saw me and took off running. I went after him."

"Why didn't you call for backup?" Brant demanded.

"No time. Besides, I didn't want to pull anyone off surveillance in case it wasn't our man."

"Well," Brant drawled sardonically, "did you catch him?"

Jack shook his head. "I lost him a few blocks from here. It's like he vanished into freakin' thin air." He bristled at the glint of suspicion in Brant's eyes. "What? You think I'm making this up, Kincaid?"

"He's not," Samille said quickly. "I think I saw him, too. He was standing on top of that brick wall, just watching us. Now that I think about it, it was a little strange. Creepy." A sudden tremor shook her. She burrowed into the warmth of Brant's blazer. "Jefferson grabbed me while I was distracted by the other guy. By the time I glanced back, he was gone."

Detective Lopez strolled over to them. "Grimes and I are taking Spangler down to the station for processing. You following us?"

Brant nodded, his shrewd gaze still fixed on Jack. "Care to join us, Burdett, or will you be chasing more masked phantoms this evening?"

Jack's jaw tightened with anger. "I'm coming."

"Parham can take you home in the van," Brant said to Samille, waving Michael over.

"That won't be necessary. I can drive myself."

"You're in no condition to be driving, not after what you've been through tonight." His tone hardened, leaving no room for argument. "Parham will drive you home, and I'll arrange to have your Jeep towed to my place."

Without another word he turned and started away with Lopez. Jack gave Samille's shoulder a comforting squeeze before following the others down the alley.

Grinning, Michael dangled a set of keys in front of Samille's face. "Pretend you're riding shotgun on one of our raids," he suggested.

Samille mustered a wan smile. "You really know the way to a girl's heart, Irish."

"In late-breaking news tonight, D.C. police are reporting the arrest of a suspect in the drug poisoning case that left ten local teenagers hospitalized just over a week ago. According to a police spokesperson, tonight's arrest outside a popular nightclub in northwest D.C. came as a result of an undercover sting operation assembled by D.C. police, the DEA, and the FBI. Although authorities will not confirm the identity of the suspect at this time, sources close to the investigation say that the individual arrested was already considered a 'person of interest.'

"In the meantime, I've talked to some people who were inside Club Zydeco when the arrest occurred." Leslie Cook, the blond-haired WJLA Channel Seven news reporter who always managed to break the big stories, turned to a group of young women beside her.

Seated on the leather sofa in Brant's living room, Samille grimaced when she recognized Zaria, Amber, and their friends from the club.

"We came here tonight to see Da Omen," Zaria announced excitedly, vying for the camera. "We never expected anything like this to happen!"

"Did any of you actually witness what happened?" Leslie Cook demanded.

"Not really," Zaria answered again, solidifying her position as the group leader. "We were sitting at our table when we heard that there was some sort of commotion outside the club. A few people tried to go find out what was happening, but no one was allowed to leave. There were guards posted at all of the doors, including the back door, and they told us they were acting under the direct orders of the FBI."

"Did people begin to panic when they weren't allowed to leave?"

"Most definitely! We started wondering if the club was being raided by the feds or if the building was under attack by terrorists. By the time we were allowed to leave, only a couple of police cars were still hanging around. And that's when we found out that someone had been arrested!"

"Thank you, ladies." Leslie Cook turned and gazed into the camera lens with a somber expression belied by the gleam of excitement in her green eyes. "We'll keep you posted on this situation as more details unfold. Reporting live from northwest D.C., I'm Leslie Cook."

Samille punched the television off with the remote control, grumbling under her breath about media vultures and their insatiable appetite for sensationalism. She knew it was only a matter of time before they learned about Jefferson Spangler's arrest, and then everything would *really* hit the fan. Senator Ashton Spangler's political rivals and critics would have a field day with the scandal of his son's illicit behavior. The story would be splashed across the front page of every local and national newspaper, and there would be hours of coverage and analysis on CNN and every talk radio station across the country. In an effort to do damage control, the senator's staunch Republican supporters would make their rounds on *Meet the Press* with Tim Russert and *Hardball* with Chris Matthews.

The fate of the nine teenage victims who remained comatose would become an afterthought.

Samille groaned and hunkered down into the afghan she'd found in the hallway closet. An hour after returning to Brant's town house, she still couldn't shake the chill that had permeated her flesh and settled into her blood, a chill that had nothing to do with the cold.

Images raced through her mind in fast forward. One minute she'd been on the dance floor pretending to have the time of her life, and the next minute she'd been fighting *for* her life. Jefferson Spangler had been scared and frighteningly unstable tonight. As he held her at gunpoint, Samille had smelled his fear and heard the sheer desperation in his voice as he shouted threats. She shuddered to imagine what might have happened if Brant hadn't been there. He'd contained the crisis by getting Jefferson to confide in him, trust him.

She owed Brant Kincaid her life.

She wrapped her hands around a warm mug of coffee she'd diluted with cream and sugar. She hadn't changed out of her leather outfit since Michael dropped her off. She'd toed off her boots and headed straight for the kitchen to make a cup of instant coffee, hoping to chase away the chill. Two cups later, and with the thermostat reading eighty-four degrees, her teeth were still chattering.

Samille got up and walked to the kitchen to nuke her coffee in the microwave. When she heard the garage door open, she hurried to meet Brant at the top of the stairs. Anticipation and an unnamed emotion clutched inside her chest as she watched him climb the stairs toward her, his dark, intent gaze never leaving hers.

When he reached the landing, she forgot to take a step backward. He towered over her. "I was waiting up for you," she blurted. "What happened with Jefferson? Did he talk?"

Brant nodded, his expression grim. "He confirmed what we already knew, that he sold the drugs to his classmates. Andrew Cason was his regular dealer. On the day Cason was murdered, Jefferson was intercepted by the person who gave him Utopia." He relayed Jefferson's account of the clandestine transaction.

Samille frowned. "And he doesn't know what the guy looked like?"

"He never got a good look at him. He said it was nighttime and the guy wore dark clothing. Including a black parka."

Their eyes held for a prolonged moment. "Lots of folks in D.C. wear black parkas," Brant said, responding to Samille's unspoken question.

"True," she agreed slowly. "Even slick attorneys like Salvatore Carrella."

"Doesn't matter. Without a solid physical description of Jefferson's dealer, we're essentially back to square one."

"So what happens now?"

Brant grimaced. "Spangler's a juvie, so we had to release him to the custody of his father. We filed an out-of-custody warrant, but once Child Protective Services takes over, there's no telling where this case could go. It'd take an act of Congress to have Jefferson booked into juvenile hall. And considering who his father is . . ."

"He could very well walk," Samille finished in disgust. Political privilege was an ugly reality in the world they lived in. "I'm surprised the senator consented to having his son questioned at all."

"I honestly didn't think we'd be able to squeeze anything out of Jefferson tonight. He was a total wreck by the time we reached the station. He was crying and shaking so bad he nearly went into convulsions."

"Dear God. Is he *that* terrified of disappointing his father?"

"I don't think it's the senator he's worried about. Something else is scaring that kid. Something or someone."

Another chill washed over Samille. "The man Jack was chasing. The man standing on top of the wall." She saw the skepticism in Brant's eyes and added insistently, "I *saw* him, Brant. He may be the one we're looking for. You have to consider—"

"I could have lost you tonight."

The rest of her admonition died on her lips at his hoarse whisper. She gazed up at him, her heart constricting at his tortured expression. She pressed trembling fingers to his lips, shaking her head. "But you didn't lose me," she said softly. "You saved me, Brant. I owe you my life."

His arms went around her and crushed her to him with sudden urgency. In that moment he didn't care about the investigation or phantom bogeymen in dark alleys. All that mattered was this woman in his arms, this woman he'd grown to love more than his next breath. He couldn't imagine his life without her, didn't *want* to imagine it without her. Even after Jefferson Spangler was taken into custody, Brant's pulse had not returned to normal. He couldn't stop thinking about how close he'd come to losing her. He couldn't stop visualizing how disastrous the outcome would have been if Jefferson had pulled the trigger. He shuddered and held Samille tighter.

She slid her arms around his waist and pressed her cheek to his chest, absorbing his strength and the rapid rhythm of his heartbeat. "It's all right," she murmured soothingly. "I'm safe. You made sure of that."

Brant lowered his head and crushed his mouth to hers. Need, hot and potent, swept through her, burning away any lingering remnants of cold. He bent her back over his arm, his mouth trailing heat down the side of her neck to her exposed cleavage. Her breath caught sharply, and she clung to him on a dizzying wave of pleasure. With a muffled groan Brant swept her into his arms and started for the stairwell leading to the third floor. His eyes never left hers. The expression he wore was fierce, determined, intense, as if he thought blinking or glancing away would cause her to disappear.

He reached the third floor in a matter of a few long strides and continued down the corridor to his bedroom. He turned on the bedside lamp, then deposited her gently in the middle of the enormous bed. Even as he stepped back to remove his boots, he never looked away. He tugged his shirt over his head and impatiently flung it aside.

Samille sat up on her knees and drank in the sight of him. With those broad shoulders and a wide chest planed with hard, sinewy muscle under deep mahogany skin, Brant had the body of a warrior. She gulped hard at the sheer magnificence of all that male flesh.

He came toward her slowly, holding her captive in the heat of his intoxicating gaze. Her heart pounded when he stopped before her and stared down at her through heavy-lidded eyes. Sinking his hands into her thick hair, he lowered his mouth to hers. His lips traced the outline of hers, memorizing the shape and texture. Samille wound her arms around his neck, holding him closer. His fingers skimmed the smooth curve of her jaw, brushed down to the delicate arch of her throat, and caressed her bare shoulder.

Samille trembled beneath his touch. He coaxed her lips apart with his tongue, plundering the silky heat of her mouth when she opened eagerly to him. Their tongues mated in an urgent, erotic dance that sent waves of indescribable need crashing through her. They kissed deeply and passionately, their hungry mouths parting and meshing as one. Samille kissed Brant's face, his neck, trailed a greedy path to his earlobe with her lips and tongue, and delighted in the shudder that convulsed him. When they at last drew apart, both were trembling.

"Samille." Her name emerged as a hoarse sound of need. "God, you are so beautiful. And this outfit . . ."

She gave him a naughty smile. "So you *do* like it."

He laughed, a rough, husky sound. "You'd better believe it. But I'd like it even better if you never wore it in public again."

Her eyes on his, Samille reached for the zipper of the leather bustier. Slowly, deliberately, she began to unzip the garment, knowing there was nothing underneath to separate her nudity from his hot, possessive gaze. "For your eyes only," she whispered seductively.

When the bustier fell open, Brant's sharp intake of breath was barely audible. But it was enough to fill her with pleasure and an incredible surge of feminine power. She trembled as his smoldering gaze roamed across her jutting breasts with a reverence that took her breath away.

"Samille," he uttered huskily. He stroked the underside of one plump breast, causing the dusky nipple to tighten in a rush. His fingertip brushed her nipple before his palm covered her breast completely, absorbing the weight in his hand.

"You are . . ." His words trailed off. With an awed shake of his head, he leaned down and took her nipple into his moist mouth.

A muffled cry escaped her. Her back arched to meet him more fully. He suckled the sensitive peak, his tongue tracing a pattern that was slow and maddeningly erotic. Liquid heat spread the length of her body and pooled between her legs.

Brant trailed a hand down her waist, tracing the graceful flare of her hip as his mouth moved to her other breast. He wanted to devour her, to bury himself deep inside her and make love to her until time stood still. He eased her down onto the bed and covered her body with his own, commanding himself to go slow, to cherish and not ravage her.

Samille reveled in the solid warmth of him against her, strength and hardness everywhere she touched. She wrapped her arms around his back, so broad her fingers couldn't meet in a circle. His hand skimmed along her flesh where her miniskirt had ridden up her thigh, snaking higher until he cupped her bottom through her silk underwear. She sucked in air sharply and clung to him, her senses careening out of control.

His skilled hands continued their foray, gliding along her body, easing the leather miniskirt down the length of her legs and tossing it to the floor. Heart thudding, Samille raised her hips so that he could remove her panties.

"So beautiful," he whispered against her mouth. Eyes locked on hers, he reached down and found the silken juncture of her thighs. He cupped her gently before slipping a finger inside her incredible wetness, and Samille let out a sharp gasp.

"*Brant,*" she whimpered, arching against him as her entire body threatened to spiral into oblivion. Her head rocked back and forth against the pillow as his finger caressed her innermost core, bringing her a pleasure that was almost excruciating in its intensity. He suckled her breast simultaneously, driving her toward the point of no return. She writhed against him before reaching down to tug impatiently at the zipper of his pants, wanting to be joined with him before she spontaneously combusted into flames.

Sensing her urgency he obliged her, raising himself above her so that she could finish undressing him. Her hands trembled as she pulled down his trousers and briefs. Her whole body trembled with the need to have him inside her. Her seeking hand found his smooth hardened length.

Brant closed his eyes and groaned as her fingers stroked him in a relentless, tantalizing rhythm. "Samille, you're driving me insane," he uttered thickly.

"Payback," she murmured, a seductress in all her glory with her wild mass of black hair spread across his pillow. His gaze devoured her—the dark gypsy eyes shimmering with passion, the swollen lips moist and slightly parted. And her glorious body, satin brown skin riding gentle curves, a flat stomach, and those long, incredible legs ready to cradle him and lead him straight to paradise.

Levering himself on one hand, Brant reached into the nightstand drawer for a condom and tore open the foil packet. Samille took the condom from his hand, and he moaned as she slowly covered him, her fingers warm and sure. He moved between her legs with an urgency he could no longer contain. Their eyes locked as he entered her with one long, deep stroke. He thought he would die on the spot from the exquisite agony of her silken tightness surrounding him.

Samille cried out wildly and flung back her head as waves of ecstasy rippled through her, rocking her to the very core of her being. Clutching his big shoulders, she drew her legs up and wrapped them tightly around his waist. He uttered a low moan as he stroked deeper, holding her face between his hands so that he could watch her expressions of rapture.

Her hips lifted to match his rhythm as she gasped his name, clenching around him in throbbing ecstasy. He plunged hard and fast, learning her, loving her, giving himself to her as completely as he took. Nothing else mattered. The world around them ceased to exist. There were only the two of them, only their desperate movements in the intimate glow of the room, the building liquid fire between them as they shared passionate kisses and whispered endearments to each other.

The end came for both of them in a shattering climax. Her cry became his own, both of them lost in each other, not knowing where one began and the other ended.

Samille buried her face in Brant's shoulder to absorb the violent shudder that swept through her. Even as the tremors continued through her body, she rocked her hips against him to prolong the delicious sensations. She stroked her hands across his damp back, feeling the taut muscles begin to relax as he lay against her, his hardness still buried inside her.

Samille's breath caught when he shifted his weight slightly so as not to crush her, still keeping their bodies joined. Her lingering arousal intensified, and this time her hips moved against his almost of their own volition.

Brant lifted his head to look at her. His expression was both hopeful and inquiring.

"*Yes*," she breathed, answering the unspoken question. To leave no doubt in his mind, she tightened her legs around him. He thrust deep into her, drawing a hoarse cry from her lips as tension built inside her body once again.

With a sense of incredulity, Brant felt his heart begin to pound faster. He should have known that once would not be enough when it came to loving Samille. Suddenly voracious, he thrust into her until he could go no deeper, then withdrew and plunged again and again.

Samille dug her nails hard into his back as she tried not to succumb to the exquisite pressure rising dangerously inside her. She wanted their lovemaking to last forever.

Brant pulled her legs higher up his body until they wrapped around his upper torso, giving him a deeper angle of penetration. When he drove into her again, she responded with a loud cry of ecstasy and arched against him. Bracing himself on both arms, he thrust harder and faster until Samille's entire body went taut beneath him and she cried out his name. The spasms that rocked her were his undoing. At the feel of her teeth on his shoulder, he dropped his head and sheathed himself as deeply inside her as he could, then moaned loudly as he came.

They lay clutching each other for several minutes, their ragged breathing the only sound in the room. Samille sighed contentedly as she felt the last of the sexual tension ebb from her body. Relaxation poured through her limbs.

Slowly Brant withdrew from her and rolled them both over carefully, facing each other. He stroked her slick back, felt her body relax under his lazy touch. He pulled the thick coverlet over them.

"Are you okay?" he asked huskily.

Samille's lush, pretty lips curved in a sultry smile. "Never been better."

Brant smiled wolfishly before reaching across the nightstand to switch off the lamp. He tucked her head beneath his chin and drew an arm protectively around her. He had never been more pleasantly exhausted in all his life, yet he wanted to make love to her again and again. Whether or not he had the stamina was inconsequential. His appetite for her was insatiable.

"Samille."

She had grown still. Her heart beat steadily in contralto with his own. He smiled, pleased by such a simple thing as Samille falling asleep in his arms.

"Sweet dreams," he whispered into the quiet darkness before a deep, languorous slumber overtook him.

CHAPTER 17

When Samille awakened in an unfamiliar room the next morning, she was a little disoriented. The bed was enormous with a carved mahogany post at each corner and covered with a thick cream coverlet. The bedroom was more of a suite, impossibly large and practically empty save for the huge bed and a matching dresser and nightstand.

Outside, the morning sky was overcast. Rain fell in huge pellets, lashing against the picture window and rooftop. A quiet grayness enveloped the room.

Drowsily Samille became aware of a masculine arm draped over her waist as she lay on her side. Although heavy, the weight was far from unpleasant. Nor did she mind the solid warmth of the male body spooned against hers. She smiled, flooded with vivid, erotic memories of the night before. She and Brant had made love, and the experience was unlike anything she'd ever imagined.

For several moments she simply basked in the rightness of waking up in his arms. She felt warm and secure, like nothing or no one could harm her as long as she remained where she was.

Brant's breathing was deep and even. Carefully Samille

lifted her head from the pillow and peeked over her shoulder. Her breath caught as she gazed upon Brant's sleeping face, hard angles and planes softened by thick black lashes that fanned out in perfect formation from his closed eyelids. She let her eyes roam over him, tracing the new growth that darkened his jaw, the sensuous curve of his lips, the broad expanse of his shoulders—and returning to linger on his sexy mouth. He was, quite simply, the most beautiful man she'd ever seen.

Struck with a sudden wicked thought, Samille raised one arm above her head and stretched languidly beneath the covers, feeling deliciously sore in places she'd never known existed. As she stretched, she deliberately rubbed her backside along the muscular length of Brant's body. He responded with a low groan, hardening immediately.

"Keep it up, woman," he warned in a husky growl that made her toes curl, "and I won't be responsible for my actions."

Samille chuckled. "Good morning. I was just testing a theory."

"And that would be?"

"Don't worry. You proved it with flying colors."

"Oh, is that right?" Brant tightened his arm around her waist and turned her over to face him. His piercing dark eyes glittered with warmth as he took in the sight of her in his bed.

"Hey, beautiful," he murmured affectionately. "Sleep well?"

"Most definitely. I can't remember the last time I slept so well, if ever."

"I was just thinking the same thing." His expression turned roguish. "We should do this more often."

Samille smiled sultrily. "I was just thinking the same thing."

Brant brushed his thumb across her soft lips. He searched her face for any sign of regret, but saw only relaxed contentment. He bent his head and kissed her gently, then pulled her into his arms.

Samille snuggled against him, fitting her head beneath his chin and draping her arm across his wide torso. Thunder rumbled and rolled across the gray sky as rain continued to pelt the window. "Mmm, this is *soo* cozy," she purred. "I wish we didn't have to go anywhere. I wish we could just stay here all day and listen to the rain."

"I'd like nothing better," Brant softly agreed.

Both fell silent with the unspoken reminder of what awaited them beyond their private world. A murder investigation. Nine comatose victims who were running out of time. A sadistic predator with a penchant for nursery rhymes. An unstable teenage suspect who seemed to fear his own shadow.

Samille's mouth twisted ruefully. "You know, I thought you were going to kill me last night when I suggested the ménage à trois to Damien Johnson."

"Don't remind me." Brant's tone was surly. "That was a risky stunt you pulled. If he had taken you up on it, I would've had to kill him."

Samille chuckled. "Nah, I knew he wouldn't go for it."

"And how's that?"

"Damien Johnson is an egomaniac. He built his reputation on being this suave lover boy. He wasn't about to risk being upstaged in the bedroom by a superior male specimen—don't laugh, it's true! He took one look at you, Brant, and realized he'd probably be outmatched in a threesome. He didn't want to take a chance on me spreading the word to all my girlfriends."

"And you figured all this out within minutes of meeting the man?" Brant's tone was dubious.

"Yep." Samille grinned. "I grew up with three men and

am surrounded by testosterone in the workplace. It doesn't take much to learn the different male archetypes and become an expert at what makes you guys tick."

A strong, deep laugh burst out of Brant. The sound reverberated against Samille's ear and filled her belly with liquid warmth. Brant angled his head to the side to get a better look at her face. "So you're telling me that you've got all men figured out? Is that it?"

"Not quite." Samille planted her chin on his chest and gazed into his eyes. "I'm still trying to figure you out, Brant Kincaid. And something tells me I never really will."

Brant reached out, trailing a finger lightly down the length of her spine from the top of her neck to the small of her back. Obsidian eyes drilled into hers. "Never say never," he said softly.

Samille shivered, unable to break the spell of his hypnotic gaze. Another rumble of thunder rattled the window. Brant's eyes never left hers. "Why don't you sleep well, Samille?"

She blinked as if emerging from a trance. "What?"

"You said you couldn't remember the last time you'd slept so well. Why?"

"Oh." She curled up on her side and rested her cheek against his chest. His heartbeat was strong and steady. "I guess for the same reason *you* don't sleep too well. Nightmares."

"About your parents."

Samille nodded slowly. "I have a recurring nightmare about the car accident that killed them. It started the very same night they died, and twenty years later it hasn't changed."

Brant gently stroked her hair. "Tell me about it."

She hesitated, biting her bottom lip. She'd never told anyone outside her family about the dream. Not even

Amanda knew. She'd met Brant Kincaid the week before, and she wanted him to know everything about her.

"My parents were killed the day after my ninth birthday. They were coming home from work when their car was struck by a drunk driver. They died almost instantly. In the dream, I'm nine years old and I appear at the crash scene." Quietly she told him about wearing the sunflower-colored dress and reaching inside twisted metal to join her parents' hands. She told him about the other car's miraculous transformation and the menacing silhouette behind the wheel as the vehicle charged toward her. She ended with an explanation of the therapist's interpretation of the dream.

"You have a couple of psychology degrees," she said to Brant with a faint smile. "Do you agree with the diagnosis, Doc?"

"What do *you* think?" he asked gently, turning the tables on her. "Do you think you were trying to preserve your parents' relationship in the afterlife?"

Samille nodded, her expression solemn. "Definitely. They meant the world to each other, Brant. In a way, it was almost a blessing that they died together. I don't think one could have survived without the other."

Brant nodded slowly. His heart melted at the image of Samille as a little girl, facing the terrible reality of a future without her parents. "And what about the other part? Are you still afraid that something's going to happen to you?"

"I don't know." She frowned thoughtfully. "I guess on some subconscious level I *do* fear dying at the hands of another person. Is that because of the way my parents died, or because we live in such a violent world?"

"I think it's a combination of both."

She nodded in agreement. "But that doesn't mean I've accepted death as an inevitability—by no means.

The entire time Jefferson Spangler held a gun to my head, all I could think about was finding a way to escape, to somehow reach my gun and defend myself. I could see in your eyes that you were pleading with me to stay calm, not to give up. And you know what? I didn't."

"I know you didn't." Brant pulled her against him and kissed the top of her head, her forehead, her mouth. Samille curved her arms around his neck and kissed him with equal fervor. She felt an intoxicating rush as his tongue dove into her mouth and took hot possession of hers. Need and a desperation she'd never known pounded through her. She moaned as his strong fingers swept down her back and grasped her buttocks, holding her tightly against his rigid erection. Her nipples hardened against his chest. Her thighs trembled.

"It's almost eight o'clock," she rasped against his mouth. "We should really be getting dressed and—"

"We've got time," came Brant's husky response. Without releasing her he reached into the nightstand for a condom and sheathed himself before lifting Samille over his body to straddle him. She cried out sharply as he penetrated her, filling her.

His smoldering gaze held hers as he gripped her waist and began to stroke inside her, slow and deep. "Now what were you saying?"

"We've got time," she breathed.

News of Jefferson Spangler's late-night arrest erupted across the airwaves that morning. By eight o'clock, every television station across the country was broadcasting its own version of the dramatic events leading up to the arrest. Reporters descended upon St. Anthony's Prep, hoping to get reactions from Jefferson's instructors and classmates about his involvement in the drug poisoning case. No one got past the main gate.

The political pundits wasted no time making their rounds on the morning talk shows to speculate on how the scandal would affect Ashton Spangler's political future. The senator's own supporters began damage control, urging the public not to rush to judgment and reminding everyone that Jefferson Spangler was innocent until proven guilty.

A heated debate was raging on WHUR 96.3 as Samille drove away from the DEA laboratory in Maryland. One caller was defending his belief that all politicians were corrupt and abused their positions to get out of trouble with the law. "Jefferson Spangler won't do any time," the caller staunchly vowed. "He's rich and privileged, and his father is friends with the FBI director. Wake up, folks! They're all in it together—the police, FBI, DEA—"

"Give me a break," Samille muttered impatiently as she switched off the radio. Even if there were a grain of truth to the caller's assertion, she wasn't in the mood to indulge conspiracy theorists.

Lab results had confirmed that the substance found in the teenage victims' bodies matched the drug she'd bought from Jefferson Spangler. Samples of the drug and the plastic vial had already been sent to the FBI for fingerprinting and DNA analysis, although no one was overly optimistic about the outcome. Whoever manufactured Utopia had been methodical, both in the creation of the drug and its targeted distribution. It seemed highly unlikely that the same individual would have been careless enough to leave fingerprints.

They'd held a press conference that morning to stem the media firestorm surrounding Jefferson Spangler's arrest. Chief Rucker assured the public that he and his law enforcement colleagues were committed to seeking justice for the hospitalized teens. Despite the limited information they released about the undercover operation that ensnared Jefferson Spangler, one resourceful *Washington Post* reporter managed to learn the names of the task force members. When Samille checked her voice mail messages, she was unnerved to find a message from the reporter requesting an exclusive interview. Samille promptly deleted it.

The next message raised the tiny hairs at the nape of her neck. Six eerie words were whispered into the phone: "One down . . . how many to go?"

Brant's sixth sense was on alert mode.

He'd been on edge since receiving a call from Hank Warner, the retired FBI agent he had enlisted to watch Samille. Warner reported that he'd picked up on an unmarked vehicle following her. Brant had instructed Warner not to let Samille out of his sight, then hung up and cursed a blue streak. The idea of their suspect pursuing Samille both enraged and terrified him. He was tempted to call her and insist that she remain at his town house until further notice, but he knew she'd never go for it. She was as determined as he was to solve the case—if not more so. It was all she'd talked about over breakfast that morning. She was the first woman he'd ever slept with who hadn't wanted to spend the morning after discussing their future.

Brant didn't know whether to be relieved or unsettled.

After spending the afternoon in briefing sessions, Brant hit the streets of northeast D.C. to look for Willie Brooks. He walked down a narrow side street and passed an abandoned office building covered with graffiti. Other than a homeless man huddled on the sidewalk, the area was deserted. It was nearing five o'clock, and the sky was overcast with the threat of more rain.

Brant knelt for a moment to tie his bootlaces. Then, with lightning-quick reflexes, he spun and grabbed the unsuspecting figure who'd been stalking him for the last three blocks. He jerked him into a nearby alley and shoved him against the wall, pressing his Glock into the man's solar plexus.

"Who are you and why are you following me?" Brant demanded, low and deadly.

Panicked green eyes met his beneath the hood of a gray sweatshirt. "Hey, man, don't shoot me!"

"Give me one good reason not to."

"Because the last I checked, federal agents aren't supposed to shoot unarmed people, Special Agent Kincaid."

Brant's eyes narrowed on the stranger's pale face. "How do you know my name?"

"I have a message for you."

"From who?"

"I can't tell you that. Let's just say it's a mutual friend. I have an address—"

"Don't move," Brant warned as the man reached for his pocket. Keeping the Glock firmly in place, he patted him down quickly. Satisfied that the man wasn't armed, Brant retrieved a slip of paper from the front pocket of the stranger's sweatshirt and gave it a cursory glance. "What is this?"

"He wants you to meet him there. Tomorrow afternoon at three."

"What for?"

"He has some answers for you. But you have to come alone. No cops, no feds—or he'll walk."

"How do I know this isn't a setup? Why should I trust you?"

"I wouldn't set you up, Kincaid." The man stared into

Brant's hard, suspicious eyes and gave a nervous laugh. "Something tells me I'd spend the rest of my life looking over my shoulder. Uh, could you ease up on the jugular vein? You know I'm not packing a piece."

Slowly Brant lowered his weapon and took a step back. "Get out of here."

Frowning, he watched as the man took off running in the opposite direction. He considered, then discarded the idea of following him to see who had sent him.

He'd find out soon enough.

Brant pocketed the piece of paper with the address written on it and headed for the nearest metro station.

CHAPTER 18

"You're glowing, you know."

Samille laughed and choked on a mouthful of rum and Coke. Setting her glass down on the countertop, she grabbed a napkin and wiped her mouth. "What on earth are you talking about, Winters?"

Amanda grinned at her. "You've been glowing all night. And your eyes lit up like a Christmas tree when *he* walked in."

Samille blushed and stole a glance across the room to where Brant, Jack, Michael Parham, Marc Lopez, and Rick Grimes were huddled around a pool table in a corner of the darkened bar. Smoke hung in the air, competing with the odor of fried crab cakes and barbecue ribs—the Friday night special. The small dance floor was sprinkled with couples swaying to Eric Clapton on the jukebox.

"See what I mean! You can't keep your eyes off him."

"That is *not* true." Samille jerked her gaze away from the sight of Brant leaning on his pool stick, sleeves rolled to his elbows, strong white teeth flashing in a grin as he awaited his turn. It was obvious from Lopez's disgruntled expression who was winning the game.

"Whatever you say, Broussard." Amanda took a sip of beer as she eyed the group of men. "Not a bad-looking bunch. We'll be the envy of every woman in here when we leave with them. Detective Lopez is kinda cute, isn't he?"

"Oh God. Please don't tell me you're interested in him."

"Why? He isn't married—I already checked out his ring finger."

Samille chuckled. "He's a playboy, Amanda. He'll break your heart. Speaking of which, don't look now, but it seems you have a not-so-secret admirer. Guy sitting alone at the end of the bar. Wait, don't look yet. . . . Okay, he's checking his Blackberry. Now you can look."

Amanda took in the stranger's pressed business suit and neatly trimmed dark hair, and wrinkled her pert nose. "He looks like a Hill staffer. Bor-ing. Anyway, don't try to change the subject. We were discussing your love life."

"*We* were not discussing anything. *You* were."

"Semantics." Amanda's hazel eyes twinkled with merriment. "It agrees with you, you know."

"What?"

"Sex. You should have it more often."

Heat suffused Samille's cheeks. "I never said anything about—"

Amanda laughed. "You didn't have to. It was written all over your face the minute Brant walked into the bar tonight. You had the look of a woman who'd been breathlessly awaiting her lover." She wrapped an arm around Samille's shoulder and hugged her. "I'm so happy for you, Samille! For as long as I've known you, you've been a workaholic and so repressed I often wondered if you weren't really an undercover nun. And now look at you! You wear skirts even when you're not due in court! Great outfit, by the way. Very stylish and sexy."

"Thanks," Samille said, glancing down at herself self-consciously. She wore a red top with a scooped neckline over a pleated steel-gray skirt. The short, flirty length of the skirt was accentuated by a pair of strappy four-inch heels she'd splurged on at Macy's. She felt soft and incredibly feminine, and for the first time ever, she liked it. Perhaps Amanda was right. Perhaps being in love *did* agree with her.

This time when she looked across the room, her eyes connected with Brant's. The heat of his onyx gaze beckoned to her, caressing her flesh and wrapping itself around her like a seductive embrace. She shivered and found herself unable to look away. Fully aware of his hold over her, Brant let his mouth curve in a slow grin that was so sexy, so *deliberately* sexy, that it made her toes curl.

Watching the charged exchange, Amanda grinned. "Why don't you go over there and ask him to dance?"

Samille finally forced her gaze away from Brant, and not a minute too soon. Those sinful eyes of his were turning her to molten lava on the bar stool. "Dance? Um, no, that's okay. He's playing pool with the fellas. I'd hate to interrupt."

Amanda snorted. "I'm sure Brant wouldn't mind the interruption—nor would the others, for that matter. It looks like he's beating the pants off them. They could probably use the reprieve."

"Well . . ."

"Come on, don't be shy. Go claim your man, girl, before that hussy in the skintight leather pants makes a move on him. She's been ogling him since he arrived."

Samille laughed. She, too, had noticed the woman watching Brant, but she'd been trying not to let it bother her. After all, Brant Kincaid was a very handsome and virile man. What kind of future could she expect to have with him if she became insanely jealous every time he turned a woman's head?

"Go on," Amanda urged, nudging Samille off the bar stool. "I'll go find something romantic on the jukebox."

As Samille approached the pool table, Brant and the others looked up and smiled at her.

"Excuse me, fellas," Samille murmured, sidling up to Brant and taking his hand. "I need to borrow Agent Kincaid for a few minutes."

Lopez, Grimes, and Parham chuckled and clapped Brant on the shoulder. "You lucky son of a gun," they congratulated him.

Jack scowled. "Come on, Sammy, we're in the middle of a game here."

"I'll bring him right back, I promise."

Samille led Brant onto the small dance floor. His hand was warm in hers, and their eyes met in silent passion as the first notes of Whitney Houston's "You Give Good Love" filled the room. Brant drew her into his arms, and she laid her head against his shoulder as they began to move together. She reveled in the warmth of his body against hers, the strength of his arms around her, the hardness of his chest and abdomen rubbing against her breasts and making them tingle. She wanted to cradle his face in her hands and press her mouth to his. When she lifted her head from his shoulder, the eyes that met hers were smoldering.

"You are so beautiful, Samille," he said in a low, velvety timbre that sent heat pouring through her veins. "I want to make love to you. How long do we have to stick around here?"

Samille's heart pounded with anticipation. "Tonight," she promised softly. "Tonight I'm all yours."

They danced, so absorbed in each other that they were oblivious of everyone else in the bar. They didn't even notice when other couples paused to smile and stare at them as they swayed to the sensuous ballad, their bodies moving as easily and gracefully as if they'd been created for each other.

Across the room, Amanda watched the couple with satisfaction. Samille's face was radiant as she stared up at Brant with a faint, secret smile meant just for him. His dark head was bent toward hers, so close that they were a heartbeat away from kissing. As he gazed down at her, his love was unmistakable. They were one, a fact that was obvious to everyone within a thousand-mile radius. Even their friends stopped playing pool long enough to watch them.

When Amanda's gaze landed on Jack, she cringed at the look of stark fury and betrayal on his face. Oh God, she hoped he didn't make a fool of himself.

When the song ended, Brant and Samille reluctantly drew apart. Brant touched her face, brushing the pad of his thumb across her slightly parted lips. "We'll leave soon," he said huskily. It wasn't a request.

Samille nodded, not trusting her voice. She walked back to the bar and reclaimed her seat next to Amanda. "I need another drink," she said, signaling the bartender.

Amanda laughed. "No wonder. Girl, you and Brant Kincaid are *hot, hot, hot!*"

The first thing Brant noticed as he returned to the pool table was Jack's infuriated expression. He braced himself for the inevitable confrontation.

Jack charged toward him. "You bastard," he said in a harsh whisper. "You knew how I felt about her, and you went after her anyway. Jesus, Kincaid, you're in love with her!"

"Don't make a scene, Jack," Brant said evenly.

"Why not? Afraid she'll see what a conniving bastard you are? I spilled my guts to you, man! How could you go behind my back and make a play for her?"

Lopez, Grimes, and Parham were watching the

exchange with wary expressions. Brant pushed his face into Jack's. "I'm not going to have this discussion with you, Burdett. Not here, not now."

"That's right, Kincaid, take the high road," Jack said, sneering. "You always like to play the hero, above reproach. You can do no wrong."

Brant's eyes turned flinty. "You've had one too many beers, Burdett," he said with menacing softness, "so I'll forgive you for the stupid things coming out of your mouth."

"Oh, really? And what if I tell you that I never bought the story about the reason your brother was killed? What if I tell you that I think he was killed over drugs?"

The fury that hardened Brant's eyes was as lethal as the slice of a well-honed sword. "*What* did you say?"

"You heard me. I think your precious twin was a pusher who made the wrong person mad, and that's why—"

Jack never knew what hit him. One minute he was on his feet, the next he was sprawled across the floor, warm blood gushing from his nose, his left eye swelling from the impact of Brant's fist.

Brant stood over his crumpled form, his dark eyes filled with controlled rage. "Get up," he said through gritted teeth. "Get up so we can finish this."

Samille hurried across the room, pushing through the throng of spectators to reach them. "What happened?" she cried, kneeling on the floor beside Jack. He moaned and cupped a hand to his nose. Blood seeped between his fingers.

"What happened?" Samille demanded again, lifting frantic eyes to Brant's face. He merely regarded her in stony silence. Lopez, Grimes, and Parham looked anywhere but at her.

She cradled Jack's head in her lap. "What did you do, Jack? Why did Brant hit you?"

"Ask *him*," Jack mumbled.

Samille looked askance at Brant. A shadow of cynicism curled his mouth as he met her gaze. He seemed to be awaiting a decision from her. When she didn't move, he turned on his heel and walked out. Lopez went after him.

Amanda materialized with a makeshift ice pack and towel. She handed both to Samille. "Courtesy of the bartender," she said dryly, "who says Brant and Jack are no longer welcome at his establishment."

Samille cleaned Jack's nose and the nasty cut above his eye. "I don't believe you two," she groused, "getting into a barroom brawl like a couple of gunslingers. You're supposed to be friends. What in the world were you thinking? And why didn't one of you guys step in and do something?"

Rick Grimes and Michael Parham recoiled from the accusing glare she sent them. "Hey, don't blame us! Everything went down so fast we didn't know what was happening!"

"I'll bet you had it coming," Amanda said, shaking her head at Jack. "Jesus, Jack, you always know how to ruin a good time, don't you?"

"Stay out of this, Amanda," Jack grumbled.

"Is there anything I can do to help?" The dark-haired stranger who'd been watching Amanda appeared. "Does he need an ambulance?"

Amanda shook her head. "Just a good shrink," she muttered in disgust.

Parham and Grimes helped Jack to his feet. His nose didn't appear to be broken, but he had a hellish night ahead of him.

"I'll give him a ride home," Samille volunteered. "He's in no condition to drive."

"That's all right, Sammy," Michael said. "I don't mind giving him a lift. We rode here together."

Samille shook her head firmly. "*I'll* drive him home, Irish. Besides, it'll give us a chance to talk. We have a lot to discuss, don't we, Jackie?"

Jack wasn't fooled by her dulcet tones. He knew he was in big trouble. He ducked his head and gave a feeble nod.

"You're going to have quite a shiner in the morning." There wasn't an ounce of sympathy in Samille's voice as she handed Jack a glass of water to take two aspirins with.

When he'd swallowed the tablets, she took the glass and set it down on the coffee table. Jack watched through one eye—the other was swollen shut—as Samille stood and began pacing the length of his living room. He wondered if she knew just how beautiful she was, how incredibly tempting she looked in her tight red shirt and pleated miniskirt. His eye roamed over her sleek calves, accentuated by those straight-up sexy heels.

She stopped suddenly in front of him, her hands thrust on her hips. "I want the truth, Jack. Why were you and Brant fighting?"

He groaned. "Aw, Sammy, do we really have to do this now? My head is killing me."

"Serves you right. No one told you to get into a fight with Brant."

"It wasn't much of a fight," Jack said ruefully. "In case you didn't notice, I'm the only one who had to be scraped off the floor and helped out of the bar."

Samille crossed her arms impatiently. "I'm waiting, Jack."

He sighed and pressed the ice pack to his throbbing eye. "It was my fault," he admitted, shamefaced. "I provoked him into hitting me. I told him the reason his brother was killed was that he dealt drugs." He winced at Samille's sharp intake of breath.

"*What*? Why would you say such a horrible thing?"

"Because I was mad, and people say stupid things when they're mad."

"That's no excuse for maligning an innocent person's character!"

"Well . . . during the trial there *was* some speculation that Bryan Kincaid's murder may have been drug-related." He paused, looking grim. "Of course, those rumors turned out to be completely false, a desperate ploy by the defense attorney to stir up controversy on his client's behalf."

Samille looked on the verge of strangling him. "So let me get this straight. You accused Brant's deceased brother of something that *you* knew for a fact wasn't true? How could you, Jack? I never thought you could sink so low. Why'd you do it? What did Brant do that was so terrible?"

Jack glanced away. "I don't want to talk about it, Sammy."

"Well, I do!"

"Do you really?" Jack challenged, coming off the sofa so suddenly that Samille jumped. He stood before her with a tortured expression. "Do you really want to talk about the fact that I've been madly in love with you for the past six years? That I've been trying to work up the nerve to tell you how I feel, knowing that you probably don't feel the same way?"

Stunned, Samille could only stare up at him. "Oh, Jack . . ."

"I don't want your sympathy, Samille." It was the first time in years he'd used her whole name. "I don't think you understand how difficult it's been to work alongside you every day, to pretend to have platonic feelings for you because I didn't want to risk losing our friendship. I've been going crazy, Samille. Slowly losing my mind every single day."

Samille's heart clutched painfully. "Oh, Jack, I'm so sorry. I know that's not what you want to hear, but I *am* sorry. If I've led you on in any way—"

Jack waved her off impatiently. "Don't be ridiculous. You haven't led me on. All you've ever done is be yourself—your sweet, stubborn, wonderful self. And that's the woman I fell in love with, almost from the day I met you." Bitterly he added, "I see it didn't take Kincaid too long, either."

"Jack—"

"You don't have to deny it. It was written all over your faces tonight. You're in love with each other. Christ, it happened right under my nose. I feel like such an idiot."

"I never meant to hurt you, Jack. Neither did Brant. He considers you a friend."

Jack snorted derisively. "Some friend. Let me tell you something about that. You have no idea how hard it is to be friends with someone like Brant Kincaid, to find yourself constantly playing second fiddle to him. He's smarter than me, a better marksman, more athletic. He probably even plays a musical instrument. God, Sammy, he's even a better pool player than me, and *I'm* considered a pool shark back home in Louisiana! Kincaid's like that childhood friend—you know the one. We all have at least one person like that in our lives. The friend who, no matter how hard you work and how much you accomplish, this person *always* outdoes you. It's worse when they're not even trying to compete with you!"

Jack sat down heavily on the sofa and dropped his head into his hands. "Score another point for Kincaid," he said resentfully. "Apparently he's better with the ladies, too."

Samille sat next to him and gently touched his shoulder. "I care about you, Jack. You know that. I'll always care about you. You've meant so much to me all these years."

"I know." He lifted his head and smiled weakly at her. "I guess I always hoped that somewhere along the way, you might fall as hard for me as I'd fallen for you. Some of the best lovers start out as the best of friends."

Samille smiled softly. "I know."

"Kiss me, Sammy."

"*Excuse* me?"

"Kiss me. Prove that you don't have any feelings for me."

"You *really* took a shot to the head, didn't you? Jack, I'm not going to kiss you. And for the record, I don't have to 'prove' anything to you." She rose from the sofa, glancing around the living room. "Where are my car keys?"

Jack held up the cluster of keys. "I'm not giving them to you unless you kiss me."

"*What?* Jack, this is crazy. I don't want to kiss you. We're friends, for God's sake!"

"Friends who may or may not really be soul mates." He stood and blocked her path to the front door—not that she was going anywhere without her keys. "If we kiss and you feel absolutely nothing, then we'll both know, once and for all, that it wasn't meant to be."

Samille arched a dubious eyebrow. "And what if *you* feel nothing?"

Jack chuckled. "Sammy, I get turned on whenever you just *look* at me. Trust me, I'll feel something." He put his hands on her shoulders and leaned close. "Just relax."

Samille rolled her eyes in exasperation. "This is so

juvenile. We're not in middle school, you know. And I really don't think—"

Jack covered her mouth gently with his own. Samille forced herself to remain perfectly still, even as a giggle bubbled up in her throat. It wasn't an entirely unpleasant kiss, as technique went. It was obvious that Jack Burdett was no stranger to kissing and pleasuring women. But the earth didn't tremble and she didn't see stars. Not even stardust.

Jack drew away slowly, reluctantly, and stared at her. "Well?"

Samille's look of patent regret said it all. "I'm sorry, Jackie. It just wasn't there for me."

He nodded forlornly. "I figured as much. I've never seen you look at any man the way you looked at Kincaid tonight, the lucky bastard. Here, take your keys. Better not keep him waiting any longer."

"Are you going to be all right, Jack?" she asked softly.

"I'll be fine. Just a little heartbroken, that's all. I'll get over it. I have no choice."

Samille curved a hand around his cheek. She tsk-tsked at his swollen left eye and battered nose. "Get some sleep. I'll call you in the morning to see how you're doing."

He grunted, flopping onto the sofa and grabbing the remote control off the coffee table. "One more thing, Sammy."

She paused at the door, one eyebrow lifted inquiringly.

Jack wore the oddest expression. "In the interest of full disclosure—since it appears you and Kincaid plan to have a serious relationship—ask him about Darrell McCants."

Samille frowned. "Who's Darrell McCants?"

"Ask Kincaid."

* * *

Samille let herself into the dark town house and climbed the stairs to the second level. She paused on the landing, listening for sounds from above. Met with silence, she decided Brant must have already gone to bed.

Shoving aside her disappointment, she went to the kitchen in search of baking soda. She moistened a paper towel, dipped it inside the baking soda, and began dabbing at the small bloodstain on her skirt. Grumpily she vowed to send Jack the cleaning bill.

"Finished tending to poor Jackie?"

Samille bolted around, heart in her throat. Brant stood in the entrance, his shoulder propped against the door frame as he watched her. He wore a pair of low-rider jeans, and his chest and feet were bare. She wondered how long he'd been standing there.

"You scared me! I thought you were sleeping."

"I didn't know whether you'd be coming back tonight."

"I drove Jack home. He told me what happened. Brant, I'm sorry for what he said to you. He deserved to get decked, and then some."

Brant lifted a sardonic eyebrow. "Well, that's a surprise."

"What?"

"For once you're not defending Burdett. I'm shocked."

Samille didn't miss the sarcastic undertones in his voice. "What Jack did tonight was indefensible. He had no right to say what he did. I'm sure he regretted the words the minute they left his mouth."

Brant's expression hardened. "There, that's what I expected."

Samille blinked, nonplussed. "What did you expect?"

"For you to make excuses for him. You just can't help yourself, can you?"

"What are you talking about? I'm not making excuses

for him! He was dead wrong for hurting you like that, and I told him so."

"I don't need you to fight my battles," Brant growled. "I'm a big boy. I can take care of myself."

"You certainly proved that tonight, didn't you?" She blew out a frustrated breath, the stain on her skirt all but forgotten. "What's going on here, Brant? Why are you mad at me? Did you expect me to walk out of there and leave Jack bleeding on the floor?"

His answer was an uncomfortably long silence during which his piercing gaze examined every feature on her face.

"What do you want from me, Brant? Do you want me to leave? Fine, I'll go." She dropped the paper towel in the trash and started from the kitchen.

Brant reached out and grabbed her arm, pulling her around to face him. Her breath caught at the burning intensity in his dark eyes. He raised a hand and touched her cheek, stroking his fingertips down her jaw. "Don't go," he uttered raggedly.

Samille trembled at the raw vulnerability in his voice. "No," she whispered as the fight drained out of her. She shut her eyes as if she could wish the whole disastrous night away. "I won't go. I'll stay as long as you want me to."

Brant kissed the side of her neck, her cheek, and whispered huskily, "Then you'll stay forever."

Blindly she turned her mouth into his, and he kissed her with the kind of passion that flared instantly out of control. She opened her mouth hungrily beneath his and felt an intoxicating rush as his tongue collided with hers. Heat bloomed just beneath her skin and pooled thick and liquid between her legs. She could taste his need—his and her own. She wanted to give in to it and obliterate everything else from her mind. She didn't want thought or reason or logic. She wanted Brant.

He lifted her into his arms and carried her to the counter. Her eyes widened momentarily, filling with surprise and heady anticipation. Her knees parted and he stepped between them, leaning down to reclaim her lips. Sinking his hands into her hair, he slanted his head over hers to work the kiss at a deeper angle. Samille hooked her feet behind his thighs, drawing him even closer.

Heat and need flared between them, fueling their passion as the kiss deepened, grew more urgent. Brant raised her shirt above her head and tossed it to the floor. His smoldering gaze upon hers, he lowered his head to brush his mouth over the mound of her breast through black lace. Her body went up in flames and her nipple hardened, straining for his touch. He obliged her, unclasping the front hook of her bra and cupping the weight of her breast in his large palm, his finger stroking the sensitive peak.

"God, you are so beautiful," he murmured, his voice filled with a reverent awe. "I can't get enough of you."

She gasped as he took her nipple between his lips and caressed it with his tongue. Desire, raw and unleashed, tore through her. It welled up inside her and came out in a sob against his mouth when he lifted his head to kiss her again. She ran her hands across the smooth, muscular expanse of his shoulders and chest as their tongues tangled in a wild, erotic dance.

Voracious now, Brant reached down and tugged at her panty hose, sliding the sheer nylon off her legs and sending her stiletto heels clattering to the floor. Her panties quickly followed. Samille unbuttoned the snap of his jeans and unzipped them with impatient fingers, and he covered himself with a condom. He was stiff and throbbing with hunger for her, which made his hands a little rough as he pushed her legs apart.

The urgency he felt made him thrust deep with a single

stroke, penetrating her as far as he could. Samille moaned with pleasure. Her legs were spread wide to accommodate him, her arms back on the counter to support herself as he withdrew, then thrust again and again, a pounding rhythm that rocked them both to the core.

She threw back her head. Her eyes were closed, but Brant couldn't stop looking at her exquisite face, at the ripeness of her breasts, at their urgent coupling. Samille was insatiable, licking her lips and gyrating her hips to take in more of him. The sensations were so wonderful, so completely erotic, that it felt like the first time for him.

He grasped her buttocks and lifted her off the counter, driving into her until she arched against him with a loud cry. He felt the rapid contractions of her climax as he kept thrusting, plunging into her until he could take no more. He shuddered and groaned, his entire body growing taut with the force of his release.

For a long while they remained locked in that position, Samille's legs wrapped around him, neither willing to end the embrace. Slowly he eased her back onto the counter and kissed her lips, then her closed eyelids. "You're incredible," he whispered.

She smiled dreamily without opening her eyes. "Mmm. You're not too bad yourself, Brant Kincaid."

Brant kissed her again, then picked her up and carried her upstairs to his bedroom.

"I take it Burdett told you everything. About his feelings for you?"

Samille nodded, nestled in the curve of Brant's arm as they snuggled beneath an afghan on the floor. He'd built a fire in his bedroom, and the logs made a soft crackling sound as they burned. Rain pelted the rooftop and windows in a soothing downpour.

"It was pretty uncomfortable," Samille admitted softly. "Jack and I have always been such good friends. It was hard to let him down like that." She decided not to tell Brant about the experimental kiss. There had been enough bloodshed that night.

She angled her head to look at him. "How long have you known about his feelings for me?"

"He told me last week." Brant gazed down at her. "The same day you and I kissed for the first time. By then I knew I was a goner. It was all I could do to keep from telling him to stay away from you. I was insanely jealous at the thought of you with him—or *any* man, for that matter."

Samille warmed with pleasure at this revelation. "I felt the same way when Angel Hart came on to you at the bakery. I wanted to scratch her eyes out. You may recall my little tirade in the car afterward?"

Brant chuckled. "I was afraid to hope that was the reason for your reaction."

"Fear no more. It *was* the reason." She grinned sheepishly. "Since we're in confession mode, I might as well tell you that I've had a little crush on you since the day I saw you at the academy six months ago. Amanda told me who you were, and when I got home I pulled up your dossier and read all about you. You probably thought I did all that research once I learned we'd be working together, but no, it was well before that." She sighed dramatically. "I guess that officially makes me a loser."

Brant grinned. "Then I must be a loser too, because I invited your training instructor to lunch in an effort to pump him for information about you. He wouldn't even give me your name; apparently he felt quite protective over his female students. I left Quantico that day and spent the next six months wondering about the sexy mystery woman in baggy shorts."

"You did not!"

"I did."

"You are so lame!" Samille laughed, propping herself on one elbow to punch him playfully on the arm. "Why'd you give up so easily? You could have approached me and introduced yourself."

"True. But I figured a beautiful woman like you had had more than enough of being approached by strange men. And I didn't think my ego could withstand a rejection from you."

"Oh, I don't know," Samille said with a demure smile. "I might have made an exception for you."

"Might, huh?" Brant's eyes danced with amusement as he reached over and tickled her in the ribs.

She squealed, scooting away to evade his marauding fingers. As their laughter subsided, they gazed at each other.

"It was kismet," Samille murmured. "Our paths were destined to cross again."

"I think you're right." He smiled crookedly. "Kismet. You sound like my sister Zora. She's into astrology and all that stuff. The two of you will get along great."

Samille's heart skipped several precious beats. Her eyes searched his face. "You want me to meet your family?"

"Yeah," Brant said huskily. "I want you to meet them while they're here for Thanksgiving. Will you?"

She smiled softly. "I'd love to, Brant."

"Good." He cupped her face gently in his hands and leaned down, kissing her tenderly on the lips. It wasn't a kiss meant to stir passion, yet her pulse skipped just the same.

He drew away and gathered her into his arms. They were silent, listening to the rumble of thunder outside.

After a while Samille broached the subject that had been nagging at her conscience since she'd left Jack's apartment. "Brant, I need to ask you a question."

"Go for it."

"Who's Darrell McCants?"

He stiffened, and immediately she knew she'd struck a raw nerve. She lifted her head to look at him. His expression was hard, shuttered.

"Brant?" she ventured cautiously.

"Who told you about him?" he asked in a low, icy voice.

"Jack." Samille hesitated, suddenly wishing she'd kept her curiosity at bay. "He told me to ask you about Darrell McCants. In the interest of full disclosure, he said."

"Oh, is that right?" The corner of Brant's mouth twisted scornfully. "Remind me to thank him the next time I see him."

"Brant, what's wrong? If you don't want to talk about it—"

"I don't, Samille. If I could go the rest of my life *not* talking about it, I would." He shoved aside the afghan and stood. Instantly Samille missed the warmth of his body. She sat up and watched as he crossed the room to stand before the picture window, turning his back on her.

When he finally spoke, his voice was low and brittle. "Darrell McCants is the thug who killed my brother."

She gasped. "Oh, Brant . . . I'm so sorry."

He stared out the window. "When I joined the FBI eleven years ago, McCants was serving his sentence at Rikers. I'd established some contacts in the prison system through my college internships, which enabled me to keep tabs on him. Not long after I'd been with the Bureau, McCants was paroled on a minor technicality involving one of the jurors from his trial. The woman had given false information about herself that wasn't discovered until years later, information that had no impact on the outcome of the verdict. McCants and his attorney held a press conference to publicly celebrate the victory.

McCants couldn't keep the gloating smile off his face."
His tone hardened. "For my family, it was like losing
Bryan all over again. We felt victimized, cheated by the
legal system."

"Understandably so," Samille murmured.

"It didn't take McCants very long to hook up with his
old running mates, who were members of one of the
most notorious money-laundering syndicates in New
York. The FBI had been monitoring the group for a
while, but the investigation wasn't going anywhere. I
went to my director and asked to go undercover to infil-
trate the group. Make no mistake about it: I knew the
risks involved. I knew there was a strong chance that Mc-
Cants would recognize me and blow my cover. But I
didn't care. I wanted to nail him so bad it was all I could
think about, day and night."

"But didn't your supervisor know about your personal
history with Darrell McCants?"

"He didn't make the connection—not until I was already on the inside. By then, he knew he couldn't risk
the operation by pulling me out. The setup worked to
our advantage anyway. The group had operations in the
Bronx, Brooklyn, and Queens. I got in quickly and made
myself indispensable to the boss, Chavez Trujillo. In no
time at all I'd been promoted from foot soldier to lieu-
tenant. He made me second in command of the Bronx
division since I already had 'ties' to the community."

Samille frowned. "But you're from . . . Oh, I get it. If
he put you in charge of the Brooklyn division, someone
from the community may have recognized you. So you
told him you were from the Bronx."

Brant nodded grimly. "McCants's territory was
Queens, so we never ran into each other. I was making
a lot of progress, giving the Bureau vital information
they needed to strengthen their case against Trujillo's

group while seemingly working my way to the top of the organization."

He paused and shook his head, and Samille wondered if he was reliving the things he'd been forced to do while undercover. She'd heard horror stories about undercover agents soliciting prostitutes, selling and becoming addicted to drugs, even murdering innocent people. She didn't want to imagine the atrocities Brant may have been forced to commit, things that would probably turn her blood cold.

And yet she had to know.

"Brant," she said quietly, "what happened? What did Jack want me to find out?"

Brant turned enough for her to view his hard profile. "Eventually McCants became curious about me— apparently he'd heard good things from Trujillo and other members of the organization. I think he wanted to find out what kind of competition he had. He was territorial that way," he added sardonically.

"That night he came to the apartment building where our 'offices' were located. I was there alone finishing up some transactions. I thought he was someone else I'd been expecting that evening. He walked into the apartment, took one look at me, and turned white as a ghost. Hell, he probably thought he was *seeing* a ghost. He pointed at me and said, 'I thought I killed you.'" Brant closed his eyes, remembering his own cold response: "Wrong brother."

Aloud he said, "I knew my cover was blown. And I knew if McCants talked to Trujillo, I'd be as good as dead. McCants went for his gun. I didn't have time to reach for mine, so I lunged at him. We struggled, and I managed to knock his gun away while we fought. But McCants kept reaching for it, and then we both had our hands on it. I finally wrestled it from him and . . ." He paused, his voice growing hard. "There was a split second when I looked into his eyes and saw fear, a plea for mercy. I could have subdued him and handcuffed him. But all I could see was Bryan's bullet-riddled chest, his lifeless eyes staring up at me. And then McCants went for the gun again—and I shot him."

Brant kept his face averted, not wanting to see the horror and revulsion on Samille's face. She hadn't said a word. At any moment he expected her to stand up, pack her belongings, and get as far away from him as possible. "Trujillo and key members of the organization were convicted and sent to prison," he continued. "When it was all said and done, my supervisor recommended my transfer to D.C. He figured I needed to get out of New York, get a fresh start somewhere else. Away from Bryan's ghost, he said."

Anger filled him and made him lash out suddenly, "Now you understand why Burdett wanted you to know about McCants. He wanted you to know that the man you'd become involved with was a cold-blooded murderer. You should thank him for looking out for you."

"Bull. We both know the only reason Jack told me about Darrell McCants was to come between us." She inhaled shakily. "You're not a cold-blooded murderer, Brant. You were acting in self-defense. Darrell McCants had every intention of killing you—"

"But he didn't, did he?" Brant bit out. "I had the opportunity to arrest him and take him into custody. But I didn't. I shot him, Samille. I wanted to kill him, and I did. The truth is, I asked for the assignment because I wanted to finally confront my brother's killer. I'd lived for that moment for six long, excruciating years. So, yeah, the official report was that I'd acted in self-defense, but deep down inside *I* knew the truth, even if no one else wanted to acknowledge it."

Samille's throat tightened. "Brant——"

"The funny thing is, I'd always thought avenging Bryan's death would help bring closure, but it didn't. It only made me miss him more. And killing Darrell McCants took me a step closer to the edge, to that fine line between who I'd once been and someone I hardly recognized." He looked at her then, and Samille's heart lurched at his ravaged, tormented expression.

In a chillingly soft voice he said, "You need to ask yourself if I'm the kind of man you want to be involved with. Because if I'm not, we need to stop wasting each other's time."

"No!" she exploded, lunging to her feet. "I won't let you do this. You've been looking for an excuse to push me away, to keep punishing yourself for the past. But I won't let you!"

"Samille——"

"Look, I can only imagine how difficult these past several years have been for you. Your emotions have probably vacillated between guilt over killing Darrell McCants and an overwhelming sense of relief and vindication. And there's nothing wrong with that, Brant. If I'd been older when my parents died, I might have felt the same way about the drunk driver who killed them. I would have wanted revenge, too!"

"But you didn't," Brant ground out. "And you weren't a federal agent sworn to uphold the law, not to take it into your own hands."

"You had no other choice. Darrell McCants was going to kill you if you didn't kill him, and that would have been unthinkable! Not only for your family, Brant, but for me as well. Because God help me, I can't imagine what my life would have been like without you in it!"

Brant's expression softened as he stared at her, incredulous. Quietly he said, "You can't mean that."

"I can, and I do." Holding his dark gaze, she closed the remaining distance between them. "Even if I wanted to walk away from you, I couldn't. I love you, Brant. It terrifies me to realize how hard and fast I fell for you." Reaching up, she laid a hand tenderly against his cheek. "I'll always be here for you, darling. But you have to learn to trust me. You have to stop pushing me away."

Brant's heart constricted with an emotion so intense it made him ache. He looked into her luminous eyes and saw his life spread out before him, saw what could be with Samille by his side. "Have I told you," he said huskily, "how absolutely incredible I think you are?"

Her eyes twinkled with mirth. "You may have mentioned it once or twice. But feel free to tell me again. I never tire of hearing it."

He caught her face between both hands and slanted his mouth hungrily over hers. Samille rose in his arms, pressing her body against the solid length of his. "You're incredible," he whispered between deep, lingering kisses. "I love you. Love you so much."

Samille's heart soared at his fervent declaration. "Oh, Brant—"

"I don't deserve you, but I'm not about to let you go."

"Good," she murmured, "because I'm not going anywhere."

CHAPTER 19

The clock struck two in the silence of Brant's study the next afternoon. He worked quietly at the computer, entering data and accessing files. In a corner of the room Samille sat curled up in a leather armchair, poring through a volume of drug case studies and scribbling notes.

Suddenly she froze.

"Oh my God," she whispered.

Brant glanced up from the computer. "What?"

Samille's eyes raced across the page she'd been reading. "In 1990 there was a drug poisoning case in Oaxaca, Mexico. Ten villagers became suddenly and mysteriously comatose after attending a festival in the *zócalo*—that's the main marketplace, like downtown in a major city. Doctors determined that the victims had been poisoned with a rare herbal substance that no one had ever heard of. Everyone was baffled, including the healers that were sent to revive the victims. People began to speculate that a curse had fallen upon the village. Six months later, a young man came forward to claim responsibility for the poisoning. At an early age he'd learned how to mix herbs from his grandfather, a medicine man. Villagers reported that the boy hadn't been the same since his grandfather's accidental death. So he concocted this lethal herbal mixture and gave it to those he held most responsible. After he confessed, he produced an antidote that counteracted the drug's toxins. All of the victims made full recoveries."

Samille raised widened eyes to Brant's face. His gaze was sharp on hers. "Are you thinking what I'm thinking?" she asked with rising excitement. "What if there's an antidote to Utopia?"

Brant looked dubious. "It's kind of a stretch, don't you think?"

"Maybe, but so what? We have nine teenagers lying in comas with little or no hope for recovery. If there *is* an antidote for this drug, we can save them. If not, well, we're back to square one. Nothing ventured, nothing gained." She crossed the room quickly and dropped the book onto Brant's desk. She stabbed a finger at it. "What if our suspect got the idea for Utopia from reading about this case in Mexico? You have to admit the similarities are pretty uncanny."

"They are," Brant admitted. "But would the average criminal go looking for ideas in"—he scanned the spine of the book—"*Toxicological and Pathological Drug Epidemiology: An International Case Study?*"

"There's only one way to find out. Doesn't the FBI have access to library records, to find out who's reading what and where?"

Brant's expression was neutral. "You need a search warrant to get your hands on library records."

"Come on, Brant, don't be such a G-man. We don't have time to wait around for some judge to grant us a search warrant!" She leaned across the desk intently. "Don't forget you're not the only one in law enforcement. You and I both know there are ways to get around pesky little loopholes like search warrants."

Brant regarded her in silence for a moment, dark eyes narrowed, the ghost of a smile playing around the corners of his mouth. He got up suddenly. "I have to go. I have an appointment at three."

"But what about—"

"I'll see what I can do. You may be on to something, Broussard." He strapped on his shoulder holster and picked up his Glock. In a black sweatshirt, black jeans, and black Timberland boots, he looked decidedly menacing.

"Where are you going?" Samille asked. "You've been so secretive about it."

"It's nothing for you—"

"To worry about. I know, I know. That's the standard line you feed me every time you're hiding something from me. If I didn't know better, Kincaid, I would think you were really a spy for the Bureau. I know for a fact that you have foreign counterintelligence training."

He winked at her. "If I told you I was a spy, then I'd have to kill you."

She grinned, hopping onto the corner of his desk. "Well, don't expect me to sit around waiting for you on a gorgeous fall Saturday."

"Where are you going?"

"I haven't decided. Aunt Noreen invited me to attend a poetry reading with her later this afternoon." She gave an ambivalent shrug. "But I don't feel like being cooped up indoors. It's a great afternoon for a walk around the Tidal Basin."

"No, not alone."

She frowned at the terse command. "Brant—"

"Wait for me to get back," he said in a softer tone. "I shouldn't be gone too long. We can take a walk together, and then we can go somewhere nice for dinner. How does that sound?"

Samille smiled. "I was just thinking how great it would be for us to go on a *real* date together."

"Great minds think alike." He smiled down at her. "I'll hurry back, I promise."

"You'd better. I won't take kindly to you being late for our first date."

Brant started for the door, then stopped. He walked back over to the desk and reached into the bottom drawer. Samille frowned as he pulled out the semiautomatic she'd used for target practice at Quantico.

He handed it to her. "Hold on to this."

She gave him a questioning look.

"You said it yourself: I'm not the only one in law enforcement. You're investigating a high-profile criminal case. I think you should be well armed. If you decide to go out for a while, take the gun with you." His gaze softened. "Do it for me, all right?"

She nodded slowly. "All right."

Leaning down, Brant gave her a hard, swift kiss on the mouth. "Don't think I forgot about that G-man remark, either."

She laughed as he headed out the door.

Samille's cell phone rang shortly after Brant left. She dug it out of her purse and answered, "Hello?"

"Is this Ms. Broussard?" came a low, tremulous voice.

"Yes." Samille frowned. "Who is this?

"Jillian Carrella. You told me to call you if I had information . . ." Jillian trailed off uncertainly.

"Yes, I did tell you to call me. What would you like to talk about, Jillian?"

"I'm scared, Ms. Broussard."

Cold unease slithered down Samille's spine. "What are you afraid of, Jillian?"

"M-my father. Not that he's going to hurt me or anything," the girl hastened to clarify. "I'm afraid he's already hurt someone else. A man named Andrew Cason. He used to hang around the school sometimes, waiting for Jefferson. But I haven't seen him in a while. . . . He's dead, isn't he? Andrew Cason?"

Samille answered with a question of her own. "Jillian, why do you think your father would hurt Andrew Cason?"

There was silence on the other end. And then Jillian's small, hesitant voice returned. "A few months ago I met Andrew Cason at the mall. He told me he was a talent scout searching for aspiring models and actresses. He said I had an unusual look, and he could probably find work for me at an agency. I wasn't even interested in modeling or acting, Ms. Broussard, but that day had been tough for me. A bunch of kids had given me a hard time at school, and I guess I was feeling a little down in the dumps. I went home and cried on Dad's shoulder. He told me not to worry about those stuck-up rich kids, that one day they'd all be working for *me*. And then he gave me a wad of cash to go shopping at the mall." She laughed a little. "That's always been his philosophy. If you feel bad, spend money until you feel better."

Samille thought it was a lousy message to teach a child, but she kept her opinion to herself. "What happened with Andrew Cason?" she asked gently.

"I met him at his studio. It wasn't really a studio though—it was a dump in a bad neighborhood."

"He took you to his apartment?"

"Yeah. He said he was just getting started in the business, so his money was still pretty tight. I'm so stupid, Ms. Broussard! I actually believed him. He had business cards, camera equipment, props. I figured a pervert wouldn't go to such lengths if he wasn't *really* a talent scout."

Samille was almost afraid to ask. "Did he hurt you, Jillian?"

"He didn't molest me, if that's what you mean. We started out with head shots, then Andrew gave me outfits to change into. After a while he convinced me to take my clothes off. He said modeling agencies preferred to see nude shots of prospects they were considering. He said girls who sent nude photos had a better chance of getting signed, because it demonstrated their willingness to take risks, and showed they were confident about their bodies. By this time I really wanted to be a model, Ms. Broussard. I'd never thought of myself as beautiful or graceful. I wanted to prove myself to all my stupid classmates. So I let Andrew take the nude photos. Little did I know—" Her voice hitched, and she burst out angrily, "Little did I know he was just using me to get back at my father!"

"Wait a minute. Andrew Cason was blackmailing your father?"

"Yes. He'd gone to my father for legal representation a few years ago. He was in a lot of trouble with the DEA and wanted Dad to be his attorney. Dad told Andrew he had too many priors on his record, and he didn't think he could help him. I guess Andrew really got mad. So the day he approached me in the mall wasn't a coincidence. He took the nude photos of me and sent them to my father. He threatened to put them on the Internet if Dad didn't give him money. But it wasn't a one-time deal. Andrew claimed to have rolls and rolls of film. Every time my father sent money, Andrew released more negatives and photos to him."

So the packages Willie Brooks delivered to Salvatore Carrella *had* contained damaging photographs.

"I'll never forget how angry my father was," Jillian continued brokenly. "I've never seen him like that. He was mad at me for being naïve, but he blamed it on Bradley Whitfield and his friends for making me feel so horrible that day. And he was furious with Andrew Cason. I thought he was going to kill him!"

Both fell silent for a moment. And then Samille said quietly, "Do you think he finally did kill Andrew?"

"I don't know, Ms. Broussard." Jillian's voice was a haunted whisper. "He's been acting so weird lately. He's never at work when he says he is. And he's so mean and impatient with me. I honestly don't know what to think."

"Where are you, Jillian?"

"At my mother's house in Virginia. She's out of the country on an assignment—I caught the bus here to hang out for a while. I'm scared, Ms. Broussard. What if my dad is in trouble?"

"Jillian, I think you should tell the police what you know about Andrew Cason. They've been investigating his murder and would be very interested in hearing what you have to say."

"I can't go to the police! Dad would freak. He'd kill me if he knew I was talking to you! He said he doesn't trust you or Special Agent Kincaid."

"Your father might be in trouble, Jillian. You can help him by coming forward with what you know." Samille paused. "I could go with you to the police station, if you'd like. That might make it a little easier for you."

"It might . . ." Jillian hedged.

Samille was already striding toward the front door. "I'll pick you up at your mother's house."

Jillian gave her the address and directions. "Please get here soon, Ms. Broussard."

* * *

At exactly three o'clock Brant entered a warehouse in a dilapidated section of southeast D.C. He was met at the entrance by the same pale man who'd followed him the day before.

"I'm supposed to frisk you," he told Brant in an apologetic voice. "You know, to check for weapons, listening devices, that sort of thing."

Brant said nothing as the man patted him down quickly, as if he were afraid he'd be shot if he took too long. His fear, or inexperience, caused him to miss the Sig Sauer strapped to the middle of Brant's back.

"Wait right here," he instructed before hurrying away to retrieve whoever had summoned Brant to the warehouse.

Brant stepped farther into the building and looked around. The place was almost in total darkness, save for the shafts of afternoon sunlight slanting through the dusty windows. It was enough for Brant to see that half of the room was filled with rows of long narrow tables and benches. He wondered what was on the other side of the curtained wall.

"I knew you'd come, Kincaid, and I knew you'd be punctual."

Brant turned toward the familiar voice. He frowned at the sight of Willie Brooks being pushed toward him in a wheelchair.

"What happened to you?" Brant demanded. "Why are you in a wheelchair?"

"Nothing unusual about a sixty-eight-year-old man in a wheelchair," Willie answered blithely. "Most of the fellas I knew in Nam are either dead or hooked up to respirators. I think I'm in pretty good shape, considering."

Brant wasn't buying it. "The day I met you at the bakery, you were as healthy as a horse. Five days later you're practically an invalid?"

Willie exchanged amused glances with his companion. "Didn't I tell you he's relentless, Conrad?"

The man named Conrad smiled, still eyeing Brant a bit warily.

"If you must know, Kincaid—and it seems that you must—someone tried to kill me on Wednesday night. Now, this shouldn't come as any surprise to you. You warned me that my life was in danger with Andrew's killer on the loose."

"And you didn't listen. What happened?"

Willie sighed heavily. "I was trying to get to the bakery to leave a message for you. It was night, and someone was hot on my heels. He caught up to me in the alley and shot me in the chest." Brant swore under his breath, and Willie grinned. "As luck would have it, I was wearing my trusty ol' Kevlar."

Brant's mouth twitched. "Luck, huh? You always walk around wearing a bulletproof vest?"

"Only when I know a homicidal maniac is after me." Willie's grin faltered. "This guy was cold-blooded, too. Methodical. His gun had a silencer, and let me tell you, if it wasn't for the half-drunk couple who stumbled into the alley at that precise moment, I think this guy would have put a bullet between my eyes just to make sure I was dead. He ran off, and I told the couple to call nine-one-one. Thank God for cell phones and half-drunk lovebirds who decide to take romantic moonlight strolls through dark alleys."

"Thank God," Brant said gruffly, surprised by how relieved he felt. He was even more fond of the old man than he'd thought. "Are you sure you're all right?"

"Other than a wounded ego and a fractured knee, I'm fine. Ten years ago that guy wouldn't have gotten anywhere near me. But I'm not as fast as I used to be, and these arthritic bones couldn't handle the impact of my fall when he shot me."

"Did you get a good look at the shooter?"

"Didn't matter. He was covered in black from head to toe." Willie paused, frowning. "But I have a pretty good idea who it was. That's what I called you here for, Kincaid."

"Hope I'm not interrupting," said an amused voice from the door.

Brant whirled around. His muscles tightened as Jack Burdett sauntered toward them. As he drew closer, Brant saw that Jack's left eye was swollen shut. The surrounding skin was bluish black.

Willie Brooks whistled softly. "What happened to *you*?"

Jack sent Brant a sardonic look. "I had a run-in with the law."

"Looks more like the *law* ran into *you*." Willie divided a nervous look between the two men. "I take it no introductions are necessary."

"What are you doing here, Burdett?" Brant asked in a low voice. His muscles were rigid, primed for the unpredictable.

"I followed you. I stopped by your place this morning to apologize for what happened last night. You were leaving as I arrived." He shrugged. "I was curious, so I decided to follow you."

Brant looked at Willie Brooks, then at Jack. "What's going on? How do you two know each other?"

Willie and Jack exchanged glances. "It's a long story," Jack answered.

"I've got time," Brant said tersely.

Jack sighed, a sound of frustration mingled with resignation. "I guess it was only a matter of time before you found out anyway. I know the kind of investigator you are, Kincaid. You're like a rabid pit bull—once you've got an idea in your head, you won't let it go until you've exhausted all angles. I know you've been digging into my background, trying to find a connection between me and Jefferson Spangler."

When Brant said nothing, Jack chuckled softly. "Of course you have. And by now you've probably figured out that Jefferson is my half brother. The great, venerated senator from Louisiana is the bastard who knocked up my mother thirty-five years ago and ordered her to have an abortion when she told him about me. Ashton Spangler had a political future that didn't include a plain Jane waitress from the wrong side of town as his wife. He told her he wanted nothing to do with either of us, and sent her packing. She raised me by herself without a single dime from him."

"So you came to D.C. in search of revenge," Brant stated flatly.

"I came to D.C. to find closure," Jack corrected. "I went to Spangler's house one day and formally introduced myself. I don't know what I was expecting from him. I didn't want money, and I definitely didn't expect him to open his arms and call me son—I probably would've decked him if he'd tried to touch me. I guess what I wanted was an acknowledgment. I wanted to hear him say he'd made a huge mistake, that he'd lived with regret all these years for rejecting us. When he opened his mouth to speak, I think I actually held my breath. And then he told me to get out of his house before he called the police." His mouth twisted contemptuously. "At least the bastard didn't deny being my father."

"When did you start blackmailing him, Jack?" Brant asked quietly.

"Not too long after that." Jack's blue eyes turned icy. "I remember looking at an ugly antique vase in their living room and thinking that it had probably cost more than the trailer my mother and I used to live in. That *one*

vase probably could have paid our medical bills, bought
my mother some nice dresses, and put me through college. I decided it was time for Spangler to share the
wealth. I told him I'd go straight to the media about his
'youthful indiscretion'—as he called it—if he didn't start
forking over some dough. He's a smart man. He knew
what the scandal would do to his reputation, so he
agreed to my terms. I'll spare you the details of our 'set-
tlement,' but suffice it to say that my mother will never
have to scrub another floor or take another order from
a rude customer again. She, of course, thinks I got a pro-
motion at work."

"How did Cason find out you were blackmailing
Spangler?"

"Jefferson told him. The kid came home early from
school one day and caught me at the house collecting
payment from his father. Spangler made up some lame
excuse about who I was and what I was doing there, but
I think Jefferson put two and two together. Apparently
he'd once overheard his parents arguing about a child
Daddy Dearest had fathered out of wedlock. Jefferson
told Cason that he took one look at me and just knew I
was his brother. Somehow Andrew pieced everything together, and the next thing I knew I was sending him a
cut to keep him quiet."

"Which is how you and I met," Willie Brooks chimed
in. "I delivered the payoff to Andrew myself. 'Course, I
had no idea what it was for. Andrew never told me you
were Ashton Spangler's son. He just said you were an old
friend who owed him some money."

"Apparently your employer took a lot of secrets to his
grave," Brant said dryly. "Which brings me to my next
question, Burdett: did you kill Andrew Cason?"

Jack didn't blink. "No, I didn't. Not because I didn't
want to, believe me. God knows he'd given me more than

enough reason to want him dead. But I didn't kill him. I figured someone else would eventually do the honors."

Brant's eyes narrowed on Jack's battered face. "You have to admit you make a pretty good suspect, Burdett. The way you followed me here today seems calculated, as if you wanted to stop Mr. Brooks from telling me what he knew about you. When you walked through the door, I half expected you to pull a gun on us."

"Made me a little nervous, too," Willie Brooks admitted. "I brought Kincaid here to tell him I remembered delivering a package for you. I didn't know you were DEA until I saw you on the news the other day, and then I put two and two together. Andrew once told me that some folks in the DEA were after him."

"I didn't kill Andrew Cason," Jack said through clenched teeth. "I won't pretend to feel sad about what happened to him. He was a lying, manipulative, conniving piece of garbage who deserved to die."

Willie took umbrage to the vitriolic remarks. "Now wait just a minute. If it weren't for Andrew Cason, I wouldn't have had the funds to open this shelter! And Conrad here might not be alive!"

Conrad nodded vigorously. "That's right. I was on the verge of starvation when Willie Brooks invited me to this warehouse for a hot meal and a safe place to sleep. There are a lot of less fortunate people out there who feel indebted to Willie Brooks for his kindness and compassion, and I'm one of them. I owe him my life."

It was the most the man had said all afternoon, and for a moment no one spoke. Willie gave Conrad a warm smile of gratitude before returning his attention to Brant and Jack. "Look, I'm not saying I condone Andrew's behavior or the horrible things he's done. Maybe the reason I never asked Andrew what the packages contained is that I didn't *want* to know. The money he paid me to run his errands enabled me to save money and rent out this warehouse. There's a full-service kitchen in the back, and I have friends who come and help prepare meals for my homeless guests.

"I've never been an idealist, gentlemen. I've seen too much human suffering and depravity to possess an idealistic bone in my body. But I like to think that out of every misdeed and cruel act, something positive can come. This shelter has done a lot of good for a lot of people, and I intend to keep it that way." He jabbed a stern finger at Brant and Jack. "I don't have a permit and no Department of Health inspector has ever stepped foot through those doors, but no one's ever complained about the accommodations or gotten food poisoning, so don't you fellas go blabbering about this place to the feds or city officials. I don't need no meddling bureaucrats breathing down my neck."

"We wouldn't dare," Brant said, a smile lifting one corner of his mouth.

"After what I've done, I'm in no position to be reporting anyone to the authorities. Least of all someone who's helping people." Jack met Brant's eyes. "Look, Kincaid, I know you have an obligation to—"

Brant's cell phone suddenly vibrated. Excusing himself, he stepped away to take the call. "Kincaid."

"Brant, this is Hank."

A chill shot down Brant's spine at the obvious strain in Hank Warner's voice. "What is it?"

"I lost her, Brant. Someone slashed my tires while I was inside a store using the bathroom. It could have been random, but somehow I don't think so. There were some kids loitering around—they all claim they didn't see or do anything."

The anxiety in Brant's gut wound tighter. "Where are you?"

"A few miles from your house. I'm waiting for a tow." Hank paused. "She left in a hurry, Brant. Peeled out of here like Lucifer himself was on her heels."

Brant swore violently. "Thanks, Warner." He disconnected and was surprised to see that he had a text message. It was from Samille. She'd called an hour ago. *Just wanted you to know that Jillian Carrella called me after you left,* she wrote. *She thinks her father might be our guy. I'm picking her up from her mother's house and driving her to the police station to give a statement. Will fill you in later.*

Once he read the brief note, he realized why Samille had sent him a text message instead of calling directly. She hadn't wanted him to talk her out of meeting with Jillian Carrella. She knew by the time he checked his messages, she and Jillian would already be at the police station.

If they made it to the police station.

"Hey, Kincaid, where are you going?" Jack called after him.

Brant didn't stop to answer. As he bolted from the warehouse, he prayed he would find Samille before it was too late.

CHAPTER 20

Samille parked in front of a three-story colonial town house in Alexandria, Virginia. As she climbed out of her Jeep, she glanced up and down the quiet, tree-lined street. Dusk was approaching. The small parking lot was virtually empty. She hoped Detective Lopez was on duty tonight. She'd call him once she and Jillian were en route to the police station.

Jillian answered the door on the second ring and invited Samille inside. "Glad you found the place okay. Want something to drink? Mom usually keeps the refrigerator well stocked when she's out of town. She knows I like to crash here on the weekends. Gives me a break from Dad."

Samille smiled. "I'm fine, thanks. Are you ready?"

"Sure. Let me put on my shoes and we can go."

While Jillian was gone, Samille glanced around the small living room. It was obvious that Sophia Carrella didn't spend much time at home. A sofa and small bookcase were the only pieces of furniture. No paintings or family portraits hung above the fireplace mantel or graced the pristine walls. No bedroom slippers or dog-eared paperbacks peeked from beneath the sofa. The place lacked a certain . . . warmth. Samille wondered if this was a reflection of Sophia Carrella.

She wandered over to the bookcase, curious about the woman's reading habits. She half expected to see books about travel and photography, and was surprised instead to find scientific medical journals. Rows of them. *Journal of the American Medical Association, Therapeutic Drug Monitoring, Hospital Pharmacy*—

She froze.

There, tucked into a corner on the bottom shelf, was *Toxicological and Pathological Drug Epidemiology: An International Case Study.*

Suddenly she felt a shadowy presence hovering nearby. She whirled and found herself staring down the nose of a service revolver held by Jillian Carrella. Hatred twisted the girl's features, making her eyes gleam in the dimness of the room.

Fear jammed at the base of Samille's throat. "What are you doing, Jillian?"

"What does it look like?" Jillian said, sneering. "Did you really think I was going down to the police station with you to rat out my own father? Why would I do that?"

"Because you want to help him," Samille said, managing to speak through lips almost too dry to form the words. "You're afraid he may have hurt innocent people."

"*Innocent* people? What innocent people? You mean that disgusting creep Andrew Cason? Or those horrible kids I go to school with?"

Comprehension slowly dawned. "You killed Andrew Cason and poisoned your classmates."

"That's right, Ms. Broussard. *Me*, not my father." Jillian flicked a dispassionate glance at the bookcase. "I guess you figured out where the idea for Utopia came from. You're smarter than I gave you credit for. Beauty and brains—aren't *you* lucky?"

"Not so lucky. I've got a gun pointed at my head for the second time in two days. What *is* it with you St. Anthony's students?"

Jillian smirked. "Very funny. I assure you I'm nothing like Jefferson Spangler."

"Oh, really? And how's that?"

Jillian took a step closer. "I'm not afraid to pull the trigger."

Samille swallowed and forced down nausea. The weight of her semiautomatic rested against her hip, a comforting reminder that she wasn't completely defenseless. "I guess I don't have to ask about your motives," she said, hoping to distract Jillian long enough to grab for her weapon. "How did you do it, Jillian? How could you just walk into Andrew Cason's apartment and shoot him in cold blood?"

"He *betrayed* me, Ms. Broussard." Jillian's voice vibrated with fury. "I don't think you understand how utterly humiliated I was when I found out he'd used me to blackmail my father. When I went to his apartment that morning, he was at the computer downloading the nude photographs of me. He didn't even bother to apologize or try to hide them. He was so sure of himself, so confident that I wouldn't do anything, that he actually turned his back on me. And I raised that gun and put a bullet through his brain."

"And then you panicked," Samille said quietly. "After you killed Andrew, you took the computer so that no one would ever see the photos."

"I didn't have time to hang around deleting files, and I didn't think the police would notice the missing computer."

"Special Agent Kincaid did."

Jillian gave a dismissive shrug. "Doesn't matter. The trail never would have led back to me, anyway. I knew once the police found Andrew's daily planner, Jefferson would become the focus of the investigation."

"Which *you* helped by volunteering information about him selling drugs to his friends."

Jillian smiled narrowly. "Just doing my civic duty."

Samille shook her head. "So you wanted to get back at Andrew for the way he'd treated you. Revenge is a classic motive. Predictable, too."

"You think I care? I'm not trying to go down in serial killer history! In fact, Ms. Broussard," Jillian said with cold satisfaction, "I don't plan to 'go down' at all. No one will ever know I was here with you."

"What do you mean?"

"You don't really think this is my mother's house, do you?" Jillian shook her head, mockingly sympathetic. "Poor Samille. You came over here with such noble intentions. So eager to do your job and make Agent Kincaid proud."

"Who lives here, Jillian?"

"Ah, Ms. Broussard. So glad you could join us."

Samille whirled toward the new voice. A tall, dark-haired man draped in black had appeared to her left. She immediately recognized him as the hooded stranger who'd waited outside her apartment to ask for directions. She remembered the prickle of unease she'd felt then. With good reason, apparently.

Jillian didn't look at all happy to see the newcomer. "What are you doing here, Chad?"

"I take it you weren't expecting me." The stranger shook his head in mild reproof. "What were you planning to do, Jillie? Kill her here and frame me for the murder? Or maybe you planned to go with her to the police station to tell them about me, to save Daddy Dearest from further investigation. Is that it?"

At Jillian's startled look, he laughed—a thin, menacing

sound that sent chills up and down Samille's spine. "My phone is bugged. I listened to your entire conversation with Ms. Broussard, and then I waited out back for her to arrive."

Samille divided a wary look between the two. "What's going on here? Who are you?"

"Chadwick Preston, senior congressional aide to Senator Ashton Spangler." Chad offered a congenial smile. "I overheard Jillian confess to killing Andrew, but I couldn't stand by and let her take credit for what happened to her classmates. Utopia is *my* invention, not hers. I believe we should always give credit where credit is due, something few people understand."

"*You* poisoned those teenagers? Why?"

"Why not?" Still smiling, he took a step forward. Although he hadn't drawn a weapon, Samille had no doubt he was armed. "You have no idea what it's like working for a man like Ashton Spangler. He's the most self-centered, egotistical, coldhearted bastard I've ever had the misfortune of knowing."

"Ever think about finding another job?" Samille muttered.

"Of course. But that would have been too easy, Ms. Broussard. Spangler merely would have found another lapdog to take my place. He has hundreds of people lined up and eager to work for him, as he's fond of telling me. He likes to remind me how fortunate I was to land the position of his senior congressional aide. Of all the qualified candidates he could have chosen, he chose me. Never mind that I graduated summa cum laude from Harvard, made law review, and interned with Supreme Court justices on my own merit. That egomaniac Spangler wanted me to believe he'd done *me* a favor by hiring me.

"So when my father got sick during campaign season,

the almighty senator wouldn't allow me to return home to visit him. His reelection bid was more important than my father's cancer! When Dad died six months later, do you know what Spangler said to me?" Chad's mouth twisted with bitter irony. "He told me that my father had been proud of my decision to remain in D.C. He said my father understood that my political future was more important than being there to watch my old man die. How's that for compassion?"

"I agree that Ashton Spangler behaved like a heartless bastard." Samille was amazed that she could sound so calm, so rational, when every cell in her body was screaming in alarm. "But you're an adult, Chad. You could have insisted on going home to visit your father. *You* made the decision not to go, no one else."

"You have no idea what kind of power the senator wields," Chad hissed furiously. "You should see the way people cater to his every whim. If he'd lost the election, he would have found a way to blame me for it. And he would have used his influence to completely ruin me!"

"So your decision not to go home was really about *you*, not your father." Samille shook her head. "I don't get it. If your beef was with Spangler, why bring innocent people into it? Why target those teenagers?"

"Why else? To set up Jefferson Spangler. You can't imagine how much I've enjoyed watching the senator fall apart at the seams over this whole scandal. Oh, his people are doing their spin jobs, but I think the senator knows it's over. And if this crisis doesn't ruin him, I have another ace in the hole that will. Once his loyal constituents learn that he has an illegitimate son he's been paying off to keep quiet, they'll demand his immediate resignation. I'm already drafting his resignation speech, as a matter of fact. Let's see," Chad drawled, glancing at his watch, "the anonymous letter and photos I sent should be arriving at the *Washington Post* any minute now. It'll be tomorrow's front page story."

Samille shook her head in disbelief. "How'd you do it, Chad? How did you sell drugs to Jefferson Spangler without him recognizing you?"

A smirk tugged at his thin lips. "With the use of a cleverly constructed prosthetic mask, color contact lenses, and a neat little trick called voice modulation. Poor Jefferson never suspected a thing. It was almost too easy."

"But you killed Bradley Whitfield. You went out of your way to sneak into his hospital room, inject him with cyanide, and leave a note. It seemed so calculated, so personal. Why?"

Chad appeared vaguely amused. "Ask Jillian. Killing Bradley was her idea. Once we decided his fate, we decided they all had to die. Like ten little Indians." He chuckled, low and sinister. "I thoroughly enjoyed slipping in and out of Whitfield's room like a ghost, then heading to the security unit to alter the surveillance tapes. Volunteering at the hospital had never worked more to my advantage. I knew every corridor like the back of my hand, knew the names and shifts of hospital staff, had unlimited access to meds—which came in rather handy for my little creation. Everyone trusted me implicitly—doctors, nurses, lab techs, even the security guys. It didn't take much to convince the night guard to let me hold down the fort while he took a ten-minute snack break. And, to his credit, he was smart enough to keep his mouth shut after Bradley died—after all, he wanted to keep his job."

Chad smiled, taking a moment to relish his own ingenuity. Samille eased a fraction closer to the bookcase. If she could just keep enough distance between them, perhaps get on the opposite side of the bookcase. At the same time, she couldn't risk drawing Jillian's eye.

Suddenly Chad's attention snapped back to the girl. "I'm curious, Jillie. Which one was it? Did you lure Ms. Broussard here to kill her, or to tell her about me in some warped attempt to strike a plea bargain?"

Jillian kept the gun trained on Samille. "Don't be stupid. I wasn't going to double-cross you!"

"Prove it," Chad said. "Shoot her."

"Don't do it, Jillian," Samille said, focusing on her anger instead of her fear. "Can't you see that he's using you? Just like Andrew did. You don't have to kill again, Jillian. It's not worth it."

"Shut up!" Jillian shouted. Her finger tightened on the trigger, but she didn't pull it. Tears filled her eyes as she struggled with indecision.

"That's what I thought." Before Samille could react, Chad drew a pistol from his cloak and fired at Jillian.

The impact of the bullet threw her backward. A scream tore from Samille's throat as the girl's body crumpled to the floor.

Calmly Chad turned the gun on Samille. "It's a shame you had to be brought into this, Ms. Broussard. But once you and Agent Kincaid paid a visit to the school and questioned Jillian, I knew you'd be a liability. No offense, but I decided eliminating you would be a tad easier than going after Kincaid."

"He knows I'm here," Samille said. "Before I arrived, I called and told him that I was meeting Jillian."

Chad smiled narrowly. "Jillian told you she was at her mother's house. By the time Kincaid shows up on Sophia Carrella's *real* doorstep, it'll be too late for you. No one will even know to look for you here."

The instinct for survival shot adrenaline through Samille, jolting her into action. She grabbed a tome from the bookshelf and hurled it at Chad. It connected with the side of his head and sent him staggering backward with a vicious string of oaths.

She ran into the foyer and lunged for the front door. It was locked.

From the living room, Chad chuckled. "It locks from the inside. Guess I was wrong about our Jillian—she *did* plan to kill you. Now I'll have to avenge her death."

Samille rushed for the stairs leading to the second floor, terror clogging her throat and choking the air from her lungs. On the second floor, she raced down the narrow corridor, passing the bathroom and a small bedroom, buying herself time before Chad reached her. She ducked into a room at the end of the shadowy hallway and flattened herself against the wall behind the door.

She heard him coming up the steps, slow and deliberate. "It was so easy to manipulate little Jillie," he said in a mild, conversational tone. As if they were playing a harmless game of Hide and Seek. "I first met her at a St. Anthony's function that I attended with the Spangler family. By then I'd already planned how I was going to set up Jefferson. His illegal drug activities made him such an easy target, but I knew I'd need an accomplice—preferably one of his classmates. The moment I saw Jillian Carrella, sitting all alone and waiting for her workaholic father to show up, I knew she'd be perfect. We hit it off right away. She responds quite well to the least bit of male attention. Poor thing—it makes her easy prey for scumbags like Andrew Cason."

Samille held her position, hidden by the partially open door. She could hear Chad stepping into the first bedroom, looking for her.

"I knew I'd have to eliminate Cason in order to get to Jefferson," he continued. "Oh, I'd have killed him myself in a heartbeat, but once Jillian told me what he'd done to her, I thought it was only fair that *she* have the pleasure of killing the bastard. I think it was therapeutic for her. After that, she decided the rest of her enemies had to die as well, starting with Bradley Whitfield. Caitlin Childress was next. Oh, I tried my best to get to pretty little Caitlin. I even came to the hospital disguised as a priest, but to no avail. The security measures you'd implemented presented more of a challenge than I'd anticipated. You can imagine how terribly disappointed Jillian was. She'd become quite merciless in her quest for revenge. She even asked me to get rid of Cason's homeless sidekick—a little old man, mind you. Guilt by association, she said."

The sound of his laughter drifted through the shadowy darkness to mock Samille, wrapping icy fingers of horror around her heart.

"Both she and Jefferson proved to be extremely apt pupils, quite deserving of their academic status at St. Anthony's. It was so easy to convince Jefferson that he needed Utopia instead of marijuana. And I knew he'd come back for more. He couldn't resist the opportunity to make history with this case. He suffered from the same God complex that afflicted his father, only Jefferson lacked the backbone to carry out anything. I was downright amused by how terrified of me he was. I think he'd half convinced himself that I was a wraith, the Grim Reaper come to steal his soul." More eerie laughter skated along Samille's nerve endings. "I knew he'd eventually get caught if he went to the club to sell Utopia, which is why I suggested it.

"I had to be there to see the arrest for myself. I regret that you were distracted by my appearance in the alley, Ms. Broussard. For what it's worth, I never believed for one moment that Jefferson would have shot you. He's a spineless coward. But maybe it would have been better for you if he *had* shot you, because he probably would've missed."

His footsteps came nearer. Samille held her breath, sweat beading her forehead and dripping into her eyes. She scarcely allowed herself to blink.

"I assure you, Ms. Broussard," Chad said, low and menacing, "you won't be so lucky this time. I have no intention of missing."

Finally he came to a stop in the open doorway.

Samille was already waiting for him, legs planted apart, the semiautomatic raised to shoulder-level as Brant had taught her. She aimed straight at Chad's chest and fired. With an expression of outraged disbelief, he pitched backward against the opposite wall and slid to the floor.

He'd assumed Samille wasn't armed when she tried to escape from him. Just as she'd calculated.

Breathing hard through her nostrils and keeping her gun trained on his motionless form, Samille hurried over to check his pulse. There was none.

Taking no chances, she grabbed his pistol and bolted downstairs to where Jillian lay in a pool of blood. Hastily Samille yanked off her own sweater and knelt on the floor. "Jillian!" she cried, using the sweater to apply pressure to the gaping wound in the girl's abdomen. "Jillian, can you hear me?"

Jillian's eyelids fluttered, and Samille nearly swooned with relief. "M-Ms. Broussard . . . I'm sorry . . . P-please help me."

"Hold on, Jillian! Help is on the way. I hear sirens— the neighbors must have heard the gunshots and called the police. You're going to be okay. Just hang on."

Jillian nodded. "There's . . . a . . . cure. H-he made it . . . J-just like in the book."

"Where, Jillian? Where's the antidote?"

"Upstairs. S-second bedroom. Everything's there . . . I'm sorry. P-please tell my dad—"

"Shh, save your energy. You can tell him yourself." Flashing red and blue lights lit up the living room like fireworks.

As Jillian closed her eyes, Samille murmured, "Hold on a little longer, Jillian."

CHAPTER 21

New York City
Three weeks later

Samille smiled at the dark-haired twin boys who'd been vying for her attention since she joined them in line at the Rockefeller Center skating rink. The holiday season was officially under way in New York City. The giant spruce tree located at the head of Rockefeller Plaza glowed brilliantly against the backdrop of moonlit skyscrapers. Skaters, young and old, glided around the ice rink, waving to family and friends who awaited their turn to show off. A dizzying procession of shoppers bustled to and from stores in search of the perfect gift. Christmas carols wafted from speakers to serenade the skaters, completing the air of festivity.

One of the little boys, obviously the boldest of the pair, blew Samille a kiss. She threw back her head and laughed. Seeing the exchange, the twins' mother offered a sheepish smile. "Miguel can be quite a flirt. He takes after his father."

"It's all right," Samille said. "I'm flattered, actually. They're adorable."

The young woman's smile widened. Vague recognition filled her eyes as she studied Samille. "You look familiar. Have we met somewhere before?"

Samille feigned mild bewilderment. "I don't think so."

She knew why the woman recognized her. Her photo had been splashed across television screens and newspapers for the last three weeks. Reporters had camped out at her apartment and the Broussard home in Maryland in order to interview her about her role in the successful apprehension of Chadwick Preston, the criminal mastermind behind the poisoning of ten Washington, D.C. teenagers. The case of the "Georgetown Ten"—as the media had dubbed the victims—had captured national headlines and fueled talk of a TV miniseries. Samille, Brant, and other members of the task force had already been contacted about book deals. All had declined.

Samille's involvement in the case had raised public awareness about the role of DEA diversion investigators. Just that morning, she and her colleagues had received a memo announcing Congress's intention to pass legislation that would give diversion investigators law enforcement capabilities.

Thanks to information provided by Jillian Carrella at the crime scene, the remaining nine victims had received an antidote to counter the effects of Utopia. All were expected to make full recoveries.

Jillian had not been as fortunate. She'd died at the hospital shortly upon arrival. Salvatore Carrella was inconsolable. He blamed himself for not being a better father, for missing the warning signs that his daughter was in trouble. All he'd ever wanted was to protect her, he tearfully confided to Samille at the hospital. From Andrew Cason, from the cruelty of her classmates, from the police. He'd even tried to shelter Jillian from the knowledge that he was dating someone. Instead he'd snuck around behind her back, snapping at her whenever she questioned his whereabouts.

Despite Jillian's own confession and the incriminating evidence that was discovered in her bedroom afterward—Andrew Cason's missing computer and a diary detailing the chilling murder plot—Samille simply couldn't accept that Jillian Carrella had been a cold-blooded murderer. Like the worst of predators, Chad Preston had discerned the girl's weaknesses and ruthlessly exploited them to serve his own sadistic purposes. *He'd* turned Jillian into the monster she became.

Samille glanced up at the electronic monitor that provided an unremitting feed of headline news. *Bowing to political pressure, Senator Ashton Spangler expected to announce resignation as early as tomorrow morning. Spangler's staunchest supporters agree that resignation is the best decision. Jefferson Spangler expected to plead guilty on possession and distribution charges in exchange for a reduced sentence.*

"Hey, beautiful," Brant said softly in Samille's ear. Despite the brisk December night, heat flooded her veins.

She turned to him with a smile. "There you are. I was beginning to wonder if you'd deserted me. Well, technically, I suppose *I* did the deserting. The skating rink was calling to me, and I couldn't wait to get in line. I hope your friends weren't offended that I wandered off without saying good-bye?"

Brant chuckled. "Not at all. I told them about your love affair with the ice rink. Even a couple of hardened NYPD cops can appreciate the magic of skating at Rockefeller Center during Christmastime."

Samille's expression gentled. "I can't tell you enough how much I appreciate you bringing me here, Brant. It means a lot to me."

"*You* mean a lot to me," he said softly.

They gazed at each other, both remembering how per-

ilously close they'd come to losing each other again.
Brant had been half crazed with worry by the time he arrived at Chad Preston's town house on the heels of
county police and EMS. He'd taken one look at Samille
in her stained halter top, hands and arms smeared with
Jillian Carrella's blood, dark eyes glistening with unshed
tears—and he'd felt the bottom drop out of him. He'd
swept her into his arms and taken her straight home,
and hadn't let her out of his sight since.

"I spoke to Jack today," Samille said. "He seems to be
holding up okay. His attorney is working out a deal that
might enable him to get probation."

Brant nodded slowly. "Good for him."

"I think he's gradually accepting the fact that he'll
never get his job back. He knows his freedom is the most
important thing at this point." She paused, her tone soft-
ening. "He said you spoke to the U.S. Attorney on his
behalf, which seemed to help a great deal. He was very
grateful, Brant. Thank you."

"Don't mention it." Something in his subdued tone
told Samille he didn't want or need her gratitude.

He glanced beyond her shoulder and grinned. "Looks
like you have secret admirers. Should I be worried?"

Samille turned her head and gave the young twin brothers a conspiratorial wink. They giggled and clamped
mitten-covered hands over their mouths.

"They remind me of Bryan and myself at that age,"
Brant said quietly. There was no pain in his voice. Only
poignant reflection.

Samille cradled a hand against his cheek. "I love you,"
she said simply.

Brant caught her hand and brought it to his mouth.
He gazed into her eyes as he kissed her open palm, then
each fingertip one at a time. Samille tingled from head

to toe. He drew close and murmured against her lips, "They're playing our song. Shall we?"

He led her onto the ice rink as, to her immense pleasure, Whitney Houston's "You Give Good Love" began to play. Holding hands, they skated slowly to the center of the rink. It took Samille several moments to realize that no one else had joined them.

She glanced around, equally curious about the sudden hush that had descended upon the gathered crowd. All eyes seemed to be focused on her and Brant.

Samille turned back to him. "I wonder what—"

The rest of the query died on her lips. Brant had dropped to one knee in front of her, and was gazing at her with such love and adoration that her heart swelled.

He took both of her hands in his. "Coming here with your parents once brought you happiness, laughter, and memories to cherish for a lifetime," he began in a voice made even deeper with emotion. "In the spirit of new beginnings, it seemed only fitting that I bring you to this special place to ask you one very important question: Samille Cara Broussard, will you do me the incredible honor of becoming my wife?"

Samille clapped a trembling hand to her mouth as tears rushed to her eyes. "Oh my God," she whispered. "Brant . . . oh, baby . . ."

Brant smiled. "Is that a yes or no?"

Sheer elation swept through her. She laughed and blinked rapidly through the mist of tears. "Are you kidding? Yes! Yes, Brant, I'll marry you!"

She threw her arms around his neck as he stood and lifted her into his arms, swinging her around. A collective sigh of approval went through the crowd, followed by cheers and applause as the couple kissed.

Setting Samille back down, Brant reached inside his coat pocket and withdrew a tiny velvet box. Samille gasped as he slid onto her finger an exquisite princess diamond ring encircled in white gold.

"Do you like it?"

"Oh, Brant, I love it," she breathed. "It's beautiful."

"Not nearly as beautiful as its new owner." Lovingly he stroked a fingertip down her cheek. "Come on, let's get out of here."

He took her hand and led her from the ice rink. They sat on a nearby bench to replace their ice skates with their own shoes. As they got up and moved through the throng of spectators, people congratulated them and called well-wishes. Several men, demonstrating the irrepressible spirit of New Yorkers, pounded Brant on the back and gave him sly grins. Brant grinned so hard his cheeks hurt.

They walked to the corner of Forty-eighth Street and Fifth Avenue and hailed a cab. When Brant instructed the driver to take them to the luxurious Plaza Hotel in Manhattan, Samille gave him a surprised look. "I thought we were having dinner with your family in Brooklyn tonight?"

"Tomorrow night. Your family arrives tomorrow afternoon."

"My aunt and uncle are coming to New York?"

Brant nodded, a smile tugging at the corners of his mouth. "Nate and Jared, too. We couldn't very well have an engagement dinner without your favorite cousins present."

"An engagement dinner?" Samille felt like a broken record, repeating everything he said. "When did you plan all of this?"

"I didn't, actually. Your aunt and my mother took it upon themselves once they found out I was shopping for engagement rings." He shook his head with a mild grimace. "Remind me never again to ask my sister for advice about jewelry. She must have called my mother as soon as

we got off the phone. Mom has already commissioned one
of her best artists to paint our wedding portrait and is getting the cottage in Venice ready in case we decide to honeymoon there. She and your aunt are planning several
events leading up to the wedding, including but not limited to a series of bridal showers for you and a formal
dinner reception at the art gallery. Your aunt thinks her
landscaped garden would be perfect for a wedding—Mom
took a tour during her visit and completely agrees. And if
I'm not mistaken, your aunt has contacted all of your
Louisiana relatives to put them on standby until a date is
announced. Mind you, all of this activity was based solely
on Zora's hunch that I was about to propose to you."

Samille laughed, remembering the beautiful, impul-
sive woman she'd met on Thanksgiving. She and Zora
Kincaid had bonded almost immediately and now spoke
frequently on the phone.

Samille had enjoyed meeting all of the Kincaid women.
They were a strong-willed, feisty lot who loved without re-
serve and were fiercely protective of their own—especially
Brant. Their devotion to him was evident within moments
of encountering the three women and watching their in-
teractions with him. Samille felt privileged, quite frankly,
to have been welcomed into the fold with open arms.

She hadn't known what to expect when Grandma Kincaid, the matriarch of the family, had pulled her aside
after Thanksgiving dinner at the Broussard home.

"The moment I saw you and Brant together," confided
Evelyn Kincaid, "I knew you were perfect for each other.
I've never seen my grandson look so relaxed and happy.
And peaceful. He finally looks at peace." She paused,
her expression thoughtful as she regarded Brant across
the room, deep in conversation with Gabriel Broussard.
"I believe you've healed my angel's broken wings,
Samille."

Samille had smiled quietly. "I think we've healed each other."

"Don't be mad at Zora," she said now, making an exaggerated show of admiring the fourteen-carat diamond ring on her finger. "The woman has excellent taste in jewelry."

Brant pretended to look wounded. "Don't I get credit for picking it out all by myself?"

"Of course, darling." Samille sent him a knowing smile, seductive and alluring. "And tonight I'll show you just how *much* credit you get."

He groaned, pulling her into his lap and curving his arms around her waist. "Don't tease me, woman, or I won't be able to resist taking you right here in the backseat of this cab." As it was, he'd already have to make a concerted effort to take things slow once they arrived. He wanted Samille to enjoy the entire seduction experience he'd arranged—the champagne on ice, the trail of rose petals leading from the door of the suite to the satin-covered bed, the plump strawberries dipped in imported chocolate, the seductive wail of John Coltrane's sax in the background.

Samille wore an amused expression. "I wonder what your mother and Aunt Noreen would have done if they'd had to cancel the engagement dinner."

Brant shook his head. "I had no intention of taking no for an answer, Samille."

"Is that right?"

"That's right." His mouth curved into a slow grin. "And I figured you wouldn't be heartless enough to turn me down in front of all those people."

She laughed. "A safe calculation." She draped her arms around his neck and leaned close to capture his bottom lip between hers. Alternately nibbling and suckling, she murmured, "I'm thinking May is a good month for a wedding."

"March."

She arched an eyebrow. "That soon?"

"Sweetheart, if we could turn this cab around and elope to Vegas without sending Noreen Broussard and Audre Kincaid into cardiac arrest, I'd do it."

"So would I. In a heartbeat." She grinned. "No pun intended."

Brant smiled, tucking an errant strand of her hair behind one ear. "March it is, then. And it gives those women less time to plan so many events."

Samille chuckled. "I've never been into planning weddings. As a little girl I didn't dream about what kind of gown I'd wear or what my Prince Charming would look like. I was too busy roughhousing with Nate and Jared to be bothered with such girlish frivolities. And then in college I became a feminist and decided that if I ever *did* consent to getting married, I'd hire a wedding consultant or make my fiancé handle the details."

Brant's eyes danced with amusement. "Still feel the same?"

She shook her head shyly. "I'm looking forward to planning our wedding. As you were rattling off the list of things your mother and Aunt Noreen were planning for us, I actually found myself getting excited. That's not to say I don't find their zeal a bit, uh, alarming—"

"That's putting it mildly," Brant grumbled.

Samille laughed. "They'll definitely have to be reined in a little. But I liked some of their ideas. As long as the weather cooperates, I think a garden wedding sounds incredibly romantic. And I'd love to spend our honeymoon in Venice. Going for long romantic walks and moonlight canal rides, touring ancient cathedrals." She sighed. "Now that's what I call a honeymoon."

"Making uninterrupted love to you night and day," Brant said in a deep, velvety voice that made her pulse race, "*that's* what I call a honeymoon. Everything else is just the icing on the cake."

Samille rolled her eyes, feigning exasperation as she muttered, "Men and their libidos."

He grinned. "We'll let Mom know that we want to use the cottage in Venice. She'll be thrilled. Speaking of which, are you sure you don't mind selling your condo to move into my place?"

"Not really. Besides, I haven't seen much of the condo lately anyway—thanks to a certain FBI agent who won't let me out of his sight. You know, Brant, it really isn't necessary for you to continue paying Hank Warner to keep tabs on me."

"When six months have passed without any incidents," Brant said darkly, "I'll revisit the issue."

Samille sighed, knowing it was an argument she couldn't win. "Another advantage of living in Arlington instead of D.C. is that it will give me a shorter commute to work." She had been offered a position as a forensic chemist at the FBI Laboratory in Quantico, Virginia. She'd also applied to a doctorate program in forensic science. Classes started in the fall.

"I'm so proud of you," Brant said softly. "Not only for the courage you displayed against Chad Preston, or the compassion you showed to Jillian Carrella despite what she'd done. Everything you represent makes me proud to stand by your side, Samille. I'm proud to have you as my partner."

Samille swallowed a hard lump in her throat. She was touched beyond measure by his earnest words. "That means so much to me, Brant. Thank you."

He grinned at her. "Hey, Broussard," he teased, "don't go getting all choked up on me."

She laughed, dabbing at the corner of her eye. "You're ruining my tough-girl image, Kincaid."

He chuckled. "Maybe one day I'll end up as a profiler in the Behavioral Sciences Unit at Quantico. We could commute to work and have lunch together. How does that sound?"

"I think it sounds absolutely wonderful." Samille remembered Amanda's prediction about their future as a crime-solving husband and wife duo that coauthored best-selling books on criminal psychology. "Brant?"

"Hmm?"

"If we ever have a son, I'd like to name him Bryan."

Brant's face gentled as he stared at her. "Thank you," he said with aching tenderness. "I'd like that very much."

She smiled. "Good."

"You know what Willie Brooks told me a few weeks ago? He said he believed that out of every misdeed and cruel act, something positive could come. I haven't always subscribed to that notion; in fact, it's safe to say I *never* have. Until now." He curved a hand around her nape, his eyes roaming across her face as if he couldn't believe she was there. "Never in my wildest dreams could I have imagined that something as incredible as our relationship could come as a result of something as tragic as the case that brought us together. We've been through so much together in such a short span of time."

"We have," Samille said softly. "And I know this might sound a little corny, Brant, but I feel like everything I've ever done or experienced in my life was leading me to this moment. Leading me to you."

"I feel the same way." He brushed his lips across her cheek before finding her mouth, coaxing her into a stirring openmouthed kiss that left them both a little breathless. As the cab approached the Plaza Hotel, they drew apart and gazed at each other. Their eyes silently communicated what their bodies would soon share together.

"Come on," Brant whispered huskily, "let's go inside and get started on Bryan Samuel."

"Bryan Samuel. Oh, I like that very much." Samille's smile turned naughty. "Mmm, something tells me I'll be saying *that* a lot tonight."

Brant threw back his head and laughed. "Sweetheart," he drawled, "if I have it my way, you'll be saying it every night for the rest of our lives."

Dear Readers:

I hope you have enjoyed following Brant and Samille on their journey to solving a chilling mystery—and falling in love. As a romantic suspense writer, I love exploring the dynamics between two people who find themselves battling an unseen enemy, as well as their feelings for each other.

If you read my previous novel, *With Every Breath*, you already know how much I love my smart, sinfully handsome FBI agents—hence Brant Kincaid was created. As for Samille, I first learned about DEA diversion investigators after meeting one at the hair salon. (You just never know who may be sitting under the dryer next to you!) After listening to a description of a diversion investigator's duties, I was intrigued. By the time I left the hair salon that evening, Samille Broussard was born.

If you're interested in learning more about DEA diversion investigators, please visit the Web site at www.dea.gov.

I love to hear from readers! Please e-mail me at author@maureen-smith.com, and visit my Web site at www.maureen-smith.com for news and updates on my upcoming releases.

Take care and happy reading,

Maureen Smith

ABOUT THE AUTHOR

Maureen Smith is a public information officer at Northwest Vista College in San Antonio, Texas. As a former freelance writer, her feature articles appeared in various newspapers, magazines, and online publications. Her romantic suspense novel *With Every Breath* was released in November 2004 and was nominated for a Romantic Times Reviewers' Choice Award. Maureen was also nominated for an Emma Award in the categories of Favorite Hero, Favorite Romantic Suspense, Author of the Year, and Book of the Year.

Maureen lives in San Antonio with her husband, two children, and an adorable black and white cat named Ace.

BOOK YOUR PLACE ON OUR WEBSITE AND MAKE THE ARABESQUE ROMANCE CONNECTION!

We've created a customized website just for our very special Arabesque readers, where you can get the inside scoop on everything that's going on with Arabesque romance novels.

When you come online, you'll have the exciting opportunity to:

- View covers of upcoming books

- Learn about our future publishing schedule (listed by publication month and author)

- Find out when your favorite authors will be visiting a city near you

- Search for and order backlist books

- Check out author bios and background information

- Send e-mail to your favorite authors

- Join us in weekly chats with authors, readers and other guests

- Get writing guidelines

- AND MUCH MORE!

Visit our website at
http://www.arabesquebooks.com